THE YUGOSLAVIAN

In Search of Mara Jovanović

THE YUGOSLAVIAN

In Search of Mara Jovanović

by

THE BLACK ROSE

Andrich Publishing
New York

Cover photograph by The Black Rose
Text layout & cover design by The Black Rose

Paperback ISBN: 978-0-9663329-0-2
Electronic Book-MOBI ISBN: 978-0-9663329-4-0
Electronic Book-EPUB ISBN: 978-0-9663329-1-9

Library of Congress Control Number: 2016946703

Scripture quotations are from The ESV® Bible (The Holy Bible, English Standard Version®), copyright © 2001 by Crossway, a publishing ministry of Good News Publishers. Used by permission. All rights reserved.

~ To My Readers ~

I am The Black Rose: author, photographer, and filmmaker. I was born in Chicago, and I currently resides in New York with the love my life, my Hokkaido Dog, Kuma. I am a fiction author, and my genres are suspense, thrillers, crime, romance, and espionage. My writing is deeply rooted in interpersonal relationships: people's feelings, thoughts, emotions, and the intimacies between two people that truly love each other despite the circumstances surrounding them.

I write about love, honor, and doing the right thing, even when it seems disadvantageous, even when it's not the popular path to take. My writing is a gift from God. As my stories develop, I appreciate and learn from them. My desire is to tell stories that make you think and make you feel. If I accomplish that, I've achieved my goal.

Thank you for reading The Yugoslavian. I hope you enjoy the story!

Sincerely,

The Black Rose

"I came in like a lion, but I left like a lamb."

The Black Rebel, 1995

The Word Became Flesh

"In the beginning was the Word, and the Word was with God, and the Word was God. He was in the beginning with God. All things were made through him, and without him was not any thing made that was made. In him was life, and the life was the light of men. The light shines in the darkness, and the darkness has not overcome it."

John 1:1-5

CHAPTER ONE

It was autumn, yet it felt like winter, as a frigid wind spun dry leaves around the Black Rebel where he waited in the darkness at the edge of the forest. Clouds covering the waning moon made his movement indiscernible as he left his hiding place and approached the loosely guarded entrance to another detention camp. This camp, strategically positioned in the densely forested mountains northeast of Sarajevo, was nothing more than an abandoned mine redesigned by xenophobic extremists. Regardless that this camp was run by Serbian loyalists, he was not partial; he equally targeted Croatian and Bosniak loyalists.

He stood idle in the shadows at the entrance to this makeshift prison. With his dark camouflaged face and form, his presence was undetectable in the murky light coming from inside the camp. He listened to the sounds from inside as he backed against a section of wood and brick wall installed specially for this containment facility. Then, from around the corner, careless footsteps shattered the forest's silence. Without making a sound, he pushed his night vision goggles up from his face, unsheathed his knife, and waited. He knew it was not one of his men. They were waiting in position, waiting for his signal.

Standing still, he bowed his head as he heard his prayer inside his mind: *The LORD is my shepherd; I shall not want. He makes me lie down in green pastures. He leads me beside still waters. He restores my soul. He leads me in paths of righteousness for his name's sake. Even though I walk through the valley of the shadow of death, I will fear no evil, for you are with me; your rod and your staff, they comfort me.*

"Please Lord." He paused reverently. "For those who cannot help themselves. I *know* you are listening." Again, he paused. "Please, forgive me," he murmured in a barely audible tone.

Taking a deep breath, all else became extinct. He closed his eyes, and the footsteps grew louder, as his concentration locked to the sound of the approaching soldier. In his mind, he saw the soldier's feet treading the crusted, hard ground. He briefly wondered if the soldier suspected anything—he thought not. Then his thoughts turned to what his premeditated action would be. He momentarily reconsidered what he was thinking and sheathed his knife. But he had long vanquished his humanity and, in its place, he had released the uncontrollable beast of vengeance from the muddled shadows of his soul.

"No time for reason," he thought. Just then, part of the poem *The Charge of the Light Brigade* by Lord Alfred Tennyson came to his thoughts, *"...Theirs not to make reply, Theirs not to reason why, Theirs but to do and die: Into the valley of Death Rode the six hundred..."*

When he opened his eyes, the soldier stepped into view. Faster than the eye could see, his left hand emerged from the darkness. He cupped the soldier's forehead and pulled him back toward him. His right arm immediately put the soldier into a chokehold until he fell limp in his grasp. With little effort, he pulled the unconscious soldier further into the darkness. The only sound to be heard was the soft thud his body made when it touched the ground. There it lay, silent and helpless, as were the cries from the victims of this war. For a moment, he looked at the soldier, noticing that he did not have night vision goggles, and he imagined the soldiers inside were without them as well. All the better, for he and his men would have the advantage.

He released a deep, soundless breath, then signaled the others. At once, twenty men armed with automatic rifles, various pistols of their choice, and night vision goggles exited the darkened forest. In silence, they pursued their predestined routes toward the camp. Another man emerged from the trees nearest to the camp and approached the wood and brick wall. This was Sergej, the first commanding officer of this renegade militia. He approached the Black Rebel, as he was now best known, however, to his most trusted friends, he was Ivan.

Sergej looked around cautiously. He then stooped and removed the unconscious soldier's rifle and ammunition, then tied his hands behind his back, and bound his feet. In a single movement, he lifted the soldier over his shoulder, carried him into the forest, and laid him down behind a row of wild plum bushes. He then returned to Ivan.

Ivan watched his men moving through the obscured bush-lined road to take their positions. With little effort, his men crept through the darkness as, one-by-one, they rapidly disappeared into the shadows where they waited for Ivan's next signal.

Looking at Sergej, Ivan whispered, "Spare as many soldiers as you can." He then looked to his waiting men and motioned them into action.

Without hesitation, their grappling hooks locked over the top of the wood and brick wall. Like agile spiders, the men scaled the wall and quickly disappeared on the other side, their movement was unnoticeable this eerie night. With a second signal from Ivan, they cut all power to the camp. They had already jammed the local radio and cell frequencies where available so that any attempts to call for help would be in vain.

Without a doubt, Ivan knew his men would do as ordered. They would fight for whatever prisoners were still alive there. And though Ivan's orders were to save as many of the opposition's soldiers as possible, he knew most of them would die. He also knew that within the minutes to follow little justice would be present.

Ivan took a deep breath and waited at the entrance. Then within seconds, he heard the skirmish begin as the first grenade exploded two hundred feet to the right. The main gate opened, and one of his men signaled for him. He entered with his rifle poised as he walked swiftly behind his men and toward the center of the facility. The sound of discharging rifles was deafening as the opposition's soldiers returned fire upon their attackers.

The Rebel force spread through the camp like an uncontrollable fire, darting in every direction, while six specially selected men continued to clear Ivan's path toward the headquarters of the camp. Ivan's goal was to find the commanding officer and take control of the camp. But the opposition's soldiers kept firing at them, and without any choice, they fired back.

These soldiers were not seasoned military men. They were not the real army. They were only men that were willing to debase their countrymen. Still, it was no different from the Croatian and Bosniak sides in this war. No matter to what extent, they all tortured, raped, pillaged, and killed, leaving no innocence behind. They all slaughtered lifetime friends for their beliefs, whether newly-adopted or deeply and secretly hidden for decades, for that was the way of war.

Though Ivan had taken no side in this war, and only helped the helpless where others looked away, he wondered how he differed from them. He knew that there was no compassion in this war. And from his part in it, he felt there was little compassion left in him.

As if standing outside of himself, Ivan saw his bullets enter the opposition. He watched with bittersweet emotion as the men he shot, shuddered and crumpled in pain, as blood and tissue burst from them: some deaths were instantaneous, some were enduring. With every injury the enemy sustained, a diminutive part of Ivan died. The vileness of war forced Ivan to utilize defensive tactics as he attempted to protect those who could not protect themselves. Because of this sense of duty, he had to get the prisoners. He had to save them if it were at all possible. He had to save them, so he could return them to their homes once this situation was over, and for a moment he wondered, "Would it ever be over?"

Just then it was as if Hell had opened its doors, and all its demons surrounded Ivan and his men, as soldiers attacked them from all sides. Where did they come from? There were so many that he wondered if they multiplied before his eyes, or if it was just a horrific illusion. However, from the point of entry, there was no return. As equally, there was no going back to the way things were before the war for the Black Rebel.

His soldiers rapidly made their way through the camp striking down men, young and old. Without question, or remorse, they cut down anyone who aimed at them. And though they began the raid by loudly requesting the soldiers inside to surrender, none had complied. Then as quickly as the raid began, it ended, and the dead littered the frost-covered ground inside the compound.

It was over, and, breathing rapidly, Ivan stopped where he stood in the center of it all. The salty tang of fresh blood filled the frozen air, and the land was crimson under his feet. In silence, he walked among the dead as his men searched the remaining grounds of the compound. Looking off to the left, he saw several of his men standing around a small group of Serbian soldiers that they had forced to kneel on the ground as they bound their hands behind their backs. Then they blindfolded the soldiers so they would have limited information to pass on to anyone after they had gone.

"So few saved," he thought, then with apprehension, he approached the entrance to the prisoners' barracks. The entry's simple disguise was barely discernible by aircraft because the entrance was the opening to the old mine. The entrance doors were thick wood held to the stone surround with iron hinges. Each door had a single small window, with no glass, only iron bars across the opening.

From where he stood, Ivan could hear the sounds of the men who waited inside and wondered what had happened outside. As he stood before this opening to Hell, as he saw it, he knew the men inside questioned their own fate. Perfectly still, he observed the effort put forth for one brother to degrade another. His eyes passed over the threshold of a nightmare, which it appeared that he could not awaken from. For countless times, so it seemed, he was to witness the suffering of his compatriots—a sight for which he could by no means prepare.

Breaking his silent meditation, Sergej approached him and said, "All the remaining prisoners are inside. They were clearing this camp. UN forces are coming within the month. They transported all able-bodied prisoners a few days ago. The soldiers don't know where to, probably out of the region, but most likely they're dead in a pit somewhere." He shook his head. "It makes no sense to leave these prisoners. As for their soldiers?" He sighed. "The camp is clear. Twenty-two dead, twelve wounded, but alive. Some escaped into the woods. Should we go after them?"

"No. Tend to the soldiers' wounds. Then we need to hurry and clear out before other forces come to help," Ivan said, and paused as he looked at the opening to the mine. "And the men?" he then asked, curious if there were any fatalities among the Rebels.

"Few injuries, nothing serious." Sergej took a breath, then expelled in quickly. "They didn't expect us."

Ivan returned his attention to the purpose of this raid, and that was the prisoners. What waited behind the open wooden doors? This dark threshold demanded his entrance. With reverence to the visions of his past and similar encounters, he closed his eyes to gather his strength. In momentary silence, he needed to call on his courage to look upon the survivors inside. Judge and jury were his responsibilities—ones he did not want, but nonetheless had.

Opening his eyes, he walked forward. As he entered the mine, he slipped centuries back in time, despite his knowledge of the modern era. In one overwhelming punch, the exceedingly familiar stench of decaying flesh, mixed with the rusty essence of blood, stung his senses. Accompanying this was the underlying, but no less putrid odor of vomit, urine, and excrement. But none of these could overpower the intangible pungency of fear. For that, there were no words to describe what only the senses could detect.

Unnoticed by his men, a shiver coursed the length of his body. He deeply inhaled the prisoners' fear as if that single act could pull their suffering into him and relieve them of it, even if only temporarily. His men walked before him with torches to light his way. He slowly moved through the half-lit entrance and noticed a mound of rotting body parts to the right of where he stopped and stood. He imagined that the masters of this camp had cut up the dead and possibly live prisoners' bodies with the remaining prisoners forced to watch as warning to them. From first glance, he imagined that mound of rotting flesh to be the prisoner's food supply; forced cannibalism, another rumor come true of war.

Continuing on, he saw what any compassionate person could not even consider existing in modern times; remnants of events only to be read about in medieval accounts of the conquerors and the conquered. He now witnessed archaic atrocities reminiscent of when the Ottomans fought hard to occupy his country.

Stunned by disgust, he wondered, "Were these methods really archaic, or are they current?"

From all he had witnessed during this war, the world had not changed except for the worse: history repeated on purpose, history repeated for a worthless cause. These sins momentarily threw him back in time as he beheld the tangibility of hate. Too many times had he seen this type of cruelty during this war, and every time his soul shook.

He saw one group of naked men and one group of half-dressed men whose clothing was rotting from their bodies. Some looked as though they had not eaten in weeks. Their bodies were so dilapidated that only their true belief in some Higher Power had sustained them to this point. "How did they survive this?" he wondered.

He then saw men without fingers and one man missing a hand, but whether that had happened at this camp or elsewhere, he could not tell in the dim light. He saw two dead men that hung from nooses about their stretched, bruised, and broken necks; however, if they had hung themselves to escape their fate, he could not tell. And if torture was not enough for these men to endure, several of the corpses had been castrated. Whether that had happened before or after they had passed, again, he could not tell. Shaking his head, he did not look further for it was only a repeat of the camps that had come before this one.

As if he could have expected a difference, what he witnessed was a facility of complete dehumanization. This made him wonder where these prisoners' mothers, sisters, wives, and daughters were. What fate had they suffered? How many had been raped, tortured, and mercilessly killed? But worse, how many were left alive to live with their scarred memories? How many were left alive to wonder what fate befell their loved ones?

"Who will care for all the orphans this war has left behind? What will be their futures?" he thought.

In all of this, his anger grew as he saw nothing of life, only of death; only beaten, broken, and tortured men whose singular sin was not being on the right side—whatever side that was. But there was no right side, not really. If he had any remorse for the massacre that he had just ordered, what he now witnessed vanquished all sorrow. A sickening joy filled him for the soldiers that lay dead outside. In his heart, he knew he was Vengeance for the crimes committed against the prisoners of this camp. And because of this, his soul quaked at the thought of his purpose, for before this war, his purpose was different, his purpose was peaceful, but this war had changed that.

Sergej walked up to Ivan and reported, "This doesn't make any sense. The prisoners are Bosniak, Croat, and Serb." He shook his head. "Twenty-nine in all."

Ivan turned and looked at him. "What?" he asked, uncertain that he had heard right.

Sergej nodded. "Yes. All three sides are represented here, but the soldiers were Serbian." He paused. "This must be a dumping ground."

Ivan stood still for a moment as he thought. He looked at the prisoners. His men were examining their wounds, giving them water, and talking with them.

"It doesn't matter. Get me the status on their injuries," Ivan said, then he walked a few feet away as Sergej started taking a tally of who would survive. Letting go a controlled breath, he whispered, "Please let them be in salvageable condition…Please, Lord."

Ivan stared blankly while the prisoners looked at him as if he were their savior. Though his soul twisted in agony for their suffering, his eyes comforted them as his men continued their examinations.

Then, breaking the solemn atmosphere, one man started to scream as he begged to be killed. Angry at this man's outburst, Ivan turned around and walked to him. Pointing at the man, his temper flared. "No! You will not die here and not by my hand! You will survive because I'm sick of death!"

The man was then silent. He looked up at Ivan, who stared down at him briefly. Disgusted, Ivan looked away; he could not look at his men either. They stood strong, healthy, and proud as their hearts cried silently for these tortured victims. Ivan's men were fortunate compared with the many tragedies they had encountered, but their safety was the reward of their risk. Those that did not risk were sure to perish, just as those that ran away from this war were sure to lose everything they once knew, everything they once claimed to love.

Ivan then looked back to Lukáš, who was tending to the man who begged to die. "Get him up and get him in a truck. Get them all in the trucks. I want out of here!" Ivan ordered, then he turned around, and walked out of the mine.

Sergej followed him and stood by his side. "With care they should all make it," he said, then he was silent, waiting for Ivan's next orders.

"Make them comfortable and warm for the ride to the camp. They are our prisoners now. See if any of them knows where the others were taken," Ivan said in a gentler tone, as he shook his head and swallowed hard. He fought his tears, although Sergej could see his sorrow. Following Ivan's command, Sergej walked away and issued Ivan's orders to the men, and at once, they started moving the prisoners from the mine.

As Ivan stood alone, he looked up at the night sky. Where was God? Did He not have eyes? Could He not see the mess men had made of His world? After all this, Ivan doubted the existence of anything except war, hatred, and death; the evils of Hell had been loosed upon this land. Then, for a moment, his mind slipped away from the camp as he recalled the countless children of this country, whose small and blameless bodies he had personally buried—without a chance for life, their lives so violently torn from them. He remembered the helpless postures of their bodies as he carried them to individual unmarked graves; he refused to bury any of his country's dead in mass graves as his men had recommended. But had these children not died, the crumpled lives of parentless, distorted childhoods would have been their fate. Regardless of the outcome, war destroyed all: those who died, and those who remained to mourn the dead.

Returning from the private images in his mind, Ivan wanted to speak God's name for relief from his persecution, though his lips failed to protest the betrayal he felt from God. His eyes had seen much suffering from this war. But this was not war, this was butchery and mutilation. To tear the dignity from a man because he was not of your heritage, or did not agree with everything that had happened, was an unforgivable sin. Were not all men created equally? Was there no Divine Right to correct all the atrocities that cursed the world? Because of all Ivan had seen in his life, without question or regret, he felt hate was much stronger than love. That made Ivan wonder if God hated His creations this much to allow all of this carnage and suffering?

Standing alone, Ivan closed his eyes. In a memory from his childhood, he heard the words of a priest who spoke of God as love. That made Ivan curious. In his heart, he could not imagine any love greater than the hatred he had witnessed; however, he would soon learn that he was wrong. Love would always prevail despite suffering. Out of all the emotions granted to man, love was certainly the strongest. But the line between love and hate was nearly fictional. Then he briefly remembered that priest's words, "It is the misused purpose of love that creates hate." Ivan wondered if that was so. Could all that he had witnessed during this war be rearranged to prove a purpose of love? Pulled away from his thoughts, he stood still as he heard his men helping the prisoners.

"War," he whispered, and secretly hoped God heard, but when he opened his eyes, he saw little hope. The warmth of his tears reminded him of his mortality, but his people did not see him as mortal—to them, he was immortal. Like the phoenix that rises from the ashes, the Black Rebel would persevere and continue to fulfill their expectations. He felt some Higher and Holy Power had chosen him for the task of aiding his people. Because of that, he did not question his part in this war, only complied with what he considered the will of this Higher and Holy Power.

In his mind, he could not fathom the primitiveness of those who strove to conquer this land. But they were his people not so long ago before envy divided them, making enemy from brother—Cain and Abel revisited as he witnessed the devastation that consumed this land. Yugoslavia, the country of his youth, was now a country divided: divided by greed, divided by hate, and divided by the Peacekeeper nations who had waited for the slightest error to subjugate his country. To bring order was their excuse for interceding. And their presence, though somewhat good, only kindled this primeval, burning fire of resentment. Their presence seized his country and used it as a tool to gain power.

Even so, the problem started within the country. For greed and hatred to

9

force the fellowship of a nation into a reversion to barbaric means for solving disputes, was beyond his comprehension. The systematic destruction of this country's goodwill had led to the disintegration of men's souls. Souls lost to the recurring traumas that plagued the hearts of all men, with man-made law overruling that of Divine Law. The theme was, do to others what you would never allow done to you, and do it all to get what you want.

"Greed," he whispered, but he was talking to himself as he shook his head and sighed.

This setting of civil war placed man against man, and for what? Land and resources? Or was it about religion again? No, the participants of this war were not concerned as much with religion as they were with power. Independence from a forced society was what the newly-seceded countries wanted, while those believing in Yugoslavia were determined to hold the country together. And to the outside world, Bosnia was a pawn in the game now played; like children tugging at the same toy until it tears to pieces. Who knew which region would be next?

For what does it profit a man to gain the whole world and forfeit his soul? Ivan remembered hearing quoted. And again, flashes of that priest he once knew surfaced in his memory, but this war had killed him too. Shaking his head, Ivan looked at the night sky with reverence. Had his belief in God disintegrated? Although he still prayed, he hoped that he did not pray in vain. To him, the only chance to keep freedom for those he helped was to take risks.

Pondering these issues, he heard these words inside his head: To you, O LORD, I lift up my soul. O my God, in you I trust; let me not be put to shame; let not my enemies exult over me. Indeed, none who wait for you shall be put to shame; they shall be ashamed who are wantonly treacherous. Make me to know your ways, O LORD; teach me your paths. Lead me in your truth and teach me, for you are the God of my salvation; for you I wait all the day long.

Ivan's prayer renewed his strength. His tears had now vanished from his momentary lapse of being just a man and nothing more. With a forsaken sigh, he lowered his head and walked back toward the mine to where he saw Sergej standing.

"The mine is clear. All the prisoners are loaded in the trucks," Sergej said.

"Get them on the road and get the other vehicles up to the entrance, then get the horses up here," he said.

"Ivan, load the horses in the last truck and drive back with us," Sergej recommended.

Ivan shook his head. "No, it's not safe. We cannot travel together and there is only one road back to camp. You lead the convoy back. Rurik, Dragan, and Miloš will ride back with me."

"Alright," Sergej said, then he left to ready their departure.

Ivan walked inside the mine and looked around. The prisoners were removed, and all that remained were those that were already dead when he and his Rebels had arrived. Turning around, he exited the mine. He walked past his remaining men who were assembled and stood shoulder-to-shoulder in silence. Their eyes followed Ivan's every move as they awaited his command and, as they waited, they witnessed his despair.

Without glancing their way, Ivan walked past them as he wondered what could possess a man to demoralize and punish another with such vehemence as he encountered. Thinking, as he walked on, he shook his head as though he carried on a private conversation with that Higher Power.

Catching up to Ivan, Sergej called to him. "Hey? What about the bodies?"

Ivan slowly stopped walking. Pointing the barrel of his rifle toward the ground, he looked over his shoulder toward Sergej. "Have the men burn the compound. Burn everything inside the walls, but first, make sure all the dead are dead."

"And those left alive," Sergej said, referring to the soldiers they had captured.

"Secure all of them off to the side of the main road, including the soldier in the woods. Their fellow soldiers will find them soon enough."

"I don't think that's wise," Sergej said.

"Why waste? As evil as it was, they were only doing what they were told."

"They enjoyed what they did," Sergej stated.

"I'm sure they did, but they will have to answer to God for their sins," Ivan said, not wanting to talk about it just then.

"They will say something," Sergej commented.

"What will they say? They don't know anything to say anything," Ivan said, concluding the debate, then he walked on.

Sergej returned to the row of waiting men. They listened to their orders and, when dismissed, they immediately prepared to burn what remained. Sergej then told Rurik, Dragan, and Miloš to bring Ivan's and their horses to the entrance and wait for further orders.

Ivan stood waiting at the entrance to the compound as his men completed their task. Within five minutes, they had moved all the Serbian soldiers into a safe position outside of the compound. They then prepared the compound to burn with a single trail of fuel ending at Ivan's feet. With his men safely outside the walls, Ivan tossed a flaming torch to the ground and lit the fateful stream of fuel. His eyes followed its consuming blaze as visions of the countless men he saw die from the foolishness of this war flashed before him.

The fire rushed along the branching trails of fluid as the entire compound began to ignite. From behind, Ivan heard his horse snort and spook as the flames reached toward the sky. As his men stepped the horses back and away, Ivan stood in place and continued to watch the flames enter the mine where the corpses of the dead prisoners lay. Now the only redeeming factor was that there was silence from inside. The souls of those who had died there had now left this earth and found peace elsewhere, or so Ivan hoped.

The sound of the trucks behind Ivan pulled his attention from the blaze. He looked toward the sound and saw the helpless faces of the prisoners watching the compound burn. He saw a warped satisfaction radiating from their eyes, and he was happy that they were still here to witness this place of damnation destroyed. Ivan then looked at his horse as the sound of the burning compound reached out toward him. He heard the vehicles with the prisoners drive on, then stop at the edge of the forest. He returned his attention to the consuming flames as Sergej waited patiently outside the first truck of the convoy.

"I hope this is what you wanted, Lord," Ivan whispered as he looked up to the sky one last time before he turned and walked away.

Taking his horse's reins from Rurik, he looked at Sergej, who nodded, then climbed into the truck. Mounting his horse, Ivan paused. He wanted to look back at the compound again, but only shook his head and tapped his horse's sides with his heels. At once, his horse moved, stepping sideways as Ivan turned slightly to see that his men were ready. With a nod of his head, the convoy headed back toward the main road, while Ivan and his three men turned their horses toward the forest. With another tap of Ivan's heels, his horse headed toward the mountain pass that led back to the Rebel camp now positioned in the mountains south of Sarajevo. Without need of any order, Rurik, Dragan, and Miloš followed him.

"It will be snowing soon," Ivan thought as he rode on before his men. In less than one month, a blanket of white would cover all that had happened at this old mine with only occasional memories protruding from its pure façade. The memories of those who had passed on here would survive only in the minds, and hearts, of Ivan and his men—the dead's eternal memorial.

CHAPTER TWO

It was early morning when they finally reached the Rebel camp. Ivan dismounted his horse near his tent and gave him the other half of an apple he had eaten on the way back to the camp. He then handed him over to Rurik. "Rub him down well," he said, patting his horse on the shoulder.

Rurik then led his horse into a cave where they hid their animals, vehicles, food, and ammunition. Ivan walked alone to his tent and, once inside, he closed the tent's flap to block the chilled winds and his men from entering.

Heaving a distressed sigh, he lay on his makeshift bed and stared blankly toward the top of the tent's grayish, muddied roof. He tried to remember what it was like before the war began and he could not remember. It seemed that there was always fighting, always war. Frowning at this thought, it was as though the war always existed and, in a peculiar way, it did.

From the start of this war, its innocent citizens were treated as if they were nothing more than animals to be disposed of at the will of whoever was in control. This reminded Ivan of childhood memories of Nationalist hate that still lingered in him; however, that was the past, and this was a new memory, but with the same type of aggressors. At lightning speed, memories from his life passed through his mind, exhausting him as he wondered, "What next?"

The newest rumor from one of his informants was that a woman, traveling for the Serbians, trafficked their strategic information. Because of this, both Croatian and Muslim/Bosniak forces were searching for her, as well as the Serbians. This vague rumor depicted that she was tall, slender, spoke English, and was attractive, but it was a fact that she was not from the Balkans. The persuasiveness of this rumor convinced Ivan that his next step was to find this woman. Find and capture her to prepare for the next attack on Sarajevo, its surroundings, or whatever region would be next.

"A woman," he whispered, then thought, "What I wouldn't give to be with a beautiful woman now instead of alone in the middle of this war."

His mind wandered away from that thought as he rubbed his tired eyes. A winter-like rain softly began to fall, rain like tears from heaven. But were they the tears of angel's falling to cleanse the earth of its human iniquity, or was it only a reminder of the loneliness to which mortal man was subjected?

Shaking off those thoughts, he knew that not only Serbian forces searched for him, but Croatian and Bosniak forces searched as well. He also knew they searched for Mara Jovanović, the little sister of his deceased friend, Petar. Though it was Ivan's initiative, Ivan, Sergej, and Petar began this wanted militia labeled the Black Rebels. He knew this war was coming; it was inevitable from the beginning. Ivan was their leader, his mind differed from other men, as he always knew what to do and when to do it. His strategic abilities often pulled his men from potential disaster, as did his selfless acts of courage. He was not afraid to risk for what he believed in and, because of this, his people saw him as the heavenly answer to their prayers. In opposition to his people's view, in the depths of his heart, he saw himself as a devil.

Pushing all this aside, the thought of Mara made him smile as he remembered the many times he played with her. How quick she was to learn. He had managed successfully to get the manuscript she had written to America—almost seventy-five handwritten pages of her opinion of the war. Seven years old and she already was a politician, a thought that made him smile. His smile grew larger as he remembered the day she came home from school with the idea to write about the war.

Out of breath, she stormed through the kitchen door at the Jovanović home, which now was long gone. Petar had gone to school to walk her home, but when she heard that Ivan, Idy as she called him, had returned from Belgrade, she ran all the way to the house. Once through the door, she ran straight into Ivan's arms as he bent down to hug her. Settling herself comfortably on his lap, she pulled out a piece of paper from her pocket. On it was information about a writing competition for an educational grant. Reading the notification, Ivan noticed the name of the organization: *The Children's Writing Foundation.*

Examining Mara's determined expression, Ivan knew she wanted to enter the competition and she wanted to win. But she did not want to send one of the many stories she had already written. Instead, she wanted to

15

write a new story; this one would be about the war, or at least as much as she had experienced in her lifetime.

As if Ivan had any choice, he approved her idea. Smiling at him, she slid from his lap. Taking him by the hand, she pulled him to her bedroom and, once inside, she commanded his undivided attention. Regardless that he had urgent business to discuss with Petar, her relentless gaze forced him to sit beside her at her little desk, while she spoke aloud and began to write.

He listened to her honest words as she described the war through her child's eyes and strangely, the more he listened, the more she sounded like him. In some surreal way, she belonged more to him than to anyone else. Out of everyone she knew, she loved Ivan most of all. In his heart, he felt that she was his little gift of joy; one of the few people who completely understood him, no matter what he did. Even though, at times, his actions made her cry.

Thinking back, he remembered the day he brought her to Saint Michael's Church in Dovlići. Remaining in Sarajevo was not safe for her after her family was killed. Not having anyone he could trust to watch her outside of the country, Ivan brought her to the same person who took him in after his parents were killed. He left her with the Mother Superior at Saint Michael's church where he knew she would be safe for a little while. Mara understood when Ivan warned her not to tell anyone who she was. He also instructed her not to speak English, or tell anyone she was from Sarajevo, and he knew she would obey.

The day he left her there, it was a parting of tremendous sorrow. She cried in his arms, and clung to him when the Mother Superior took her from his embrace, for he could hardly let her go. All he could remember was her calling to him. Her tiny outstretched hands groping toward him in desperation as the Mother Superior carried her in the opposite direction. Though he always treated Mara as she demanded, as if she were an adult, he suddenly saw her as the delicate child she actually was, and her cries tore his heart in two. He was leaving her and breaking his promise to always be with her.

As he walked away, down the stone corridor, he could feel her tiny hands reaching out toward him and he heard her calling through her sobs. "Idy, come back...Don't leave me...Idy, I love you. Please take me with you, please." The further he walked, the fainter her voice became. He could not turn around because he did not want her to see him cry. She always saw him as strong, and he did not want to disappoint her as he had disappointed himself so often.

Expelling a deep breath, he felt his heart stop for a split second as his thoughts briefly returned to the present. Then with a thud, it continued beating. Fading back into his daze-like remembrance, he recalled when things were somewhat normal. It was the last time he returned from Belgrade before he hid her. They sat at the kitchen table after dinner as Mara's mother washed dishes in the sink. Mara was sitting on his lap as they reviewed the final sections of her story for the competition.

Mara suddenly wrapped her arms backward around Ivan's neck and spoke to her mother as though Ivan was not there. But with complete love for him, those actions identified his presence. "Mama, when I grow up, I want to marry Idy."

Her mother looked over her shoulder and smiled at Ivan. Then Mara giggled as Ivan tickled her and gave her a kiss on the cheek, then answered in a soft tone, "When you grow up, I will be an old man and you will need a young man."

"I don't care, I will marry you anyway," she insisted.

"Why?" he asked, then laughed at her determination. Yet, her answer was anything but simple. Her answer brought reality back into his life, a reality that he tried desperately to push aside when he was with her.

"Because then you will always be with me," she answered. Turning around on his lap, she held him tightly about his neck. It was as though she felt danger looming, and she was correct. Three days later, a sniper searching for the Black Rebel killed her brother. Shortly after his death, an explosion demolished the Jovanović's home. Her parents were killed while Mara was at school: all in search of the Black Rebel, all in search of Ivan.

Exiting his memories, Ivan's smile vanished as he remembered the war's impact on his life. He shook his head and released a short sigh. His mind returned to the description from the informant as he thought, "What if it isn't a woman? What if a man is passing the information? What if there is no one passing anything? A woman would be an ingenious choice, but she would have to be insane."

Ivan was no longer certain what the correct answers were. He only knew he would do what was necessary to continue defending people. To continue helping those choosing to stay in Sarajevo, and the surrounding towns, holding strongly to what belonged to them. He would continue to do what everyone expected, regardless that only few knew him. However, what did they expect of the Black Rebel? A miracle?

CHAPTER THREE

At the Children's Writing Foundation's headquarters in Manhattan, Tess walked quickly through the reception area, then into her private office where Willis waited for her. The last group of entries had arrived for the grant competition she sponsored. Tess and her reading team had already read around five hundred submissions and had chosen the winners for the national side, but the international entries consumed more time, frequently due to translating the documents before reading.

Willis stood when she entered the room. He shook his head before kissing her on the cheek. "You know, when I agreed to be the Secretary of your Foundation, I thought it would be easy, but this is ridiculous. Look at this!" he said, pointing to her desk.

She looked at the stacks of envelopes that covered her desk, then looked at him. Placing her hands on his shoulders, she turned him to face the door. Then giving him a slight shove, she spoke sternly, but affectionately, as she said, "Willis, go to lunch and make it a nice long one."

He laughed and turned back around. "Okay, okay! I won't complain. Friends don't complain, *supposedly.*"

She smiled at him and sat behind her desk. He sat on the opposite side and began dividing the stacks, taking the thinnest entries for himself, then passing the thickest ones onto her. Then he started sorting another stack as she sat reading one entry from France.

"This is quite good. Did you read this one? It's all about a little girl and a wild bird, Peugeot. She named her bird after the family's car. She writes that the bird hung onto the car's antenna from one end of Paris to the other. When they got home, the bird flew to her shoulder and decided to live with them," she said, then laughed, but thought the story was original.

"Oh, God, what's this? Tess, look at the size of this," he said as he lifted the last envelope on the desk.

She glanced up at the envelope he held. "What is it? The children's version of War and Peace?" she asked, and smiled, but was in shock at the size of the entry.

"What language is this?" he mumbled under his breath as he pulled out the envelope's contents.

"Let me see the envelope," she said. She put down the papers in her hand and reached across the desk as he handed the envelope to her. She read the return address. "This came from Belgrade. How did it get out of the country? We had complaints that none of the children from Yugoslavia's war zones could get their stories out. I wonder how this one got out," she said, thinking about how many other applicants' entries did not arrive because of the war.

"Here's the foreign language manuscript and what looks like the English translation. What is their language?" he asked as he handed her the manuscripts.

She shook her head and laughed at him. "Willis, you went to Harvard. The language is Serbo-Croatian. Well, actually I think they are now considered two separate languages: Serbian and Croatian. But they're all based on a Štokavian dialect, then they break off into sub dialects like Kajkavian and Čakavian. I remember reading that Serbian, Croatian, Hungarian, Romanian and, I think, what they speak in Kosovo, are all based on that original Indo-European language," she said, then opened the cover to the entry.

Willis raised his eyebrows and stared at her. He did not know if what she just said was correct, but he was amazed that she knew it. "You're the only person that knows these things, or is even talking about these things," he commented.

"That's silly, Willis." Without a second thought, she returned her attention to the manuscript in her hand.

Reaching across the desk, he handed her a sealed envelope. "Here, this has your name on it. It says 'Foundation Chairman.'"

Pulled away from the manuscript, Tess took the envelope from him. Looking at it for a moment, she then opened it and pulled out a letter. Glancing at Willis, she then read it to herself.

Dear Foundation Chairman,

I am writing to you on behalf of a little girl who hopes to win the writing competition you sponsor. She speaks English, but does not write it yet, so I will translate her message for you. She is a good child, who loves God, and loves her country, what is left of it. She is Croatian, and her story is true as seen through the eyes of a child caught between evil and evil. She has lost her brother in this war, but she is a strong child and many love her. If you met her, you would love her, too. But meeting her is impossible, and I know that understanding what is happening here is difficult.

She first heard about this competition at the beginning of the school year and, since then, she has written her story with the desperate hope of your judging in her favor. The following is what she wishes for me to tell you:

My name is Mara Jovanović. I am seven. I live in Sarajevo. I love to write. I want to write books when I grow up, and I hope to win this competition. I do not want the money for myself. I only want to win to get my family out of the war, away from the fighting, and safe from death. I do not want all the award money, only enough to leave Sarajevo. Please give the rest of the money to someone else, and please think of me when you choose the winner. Please, do not forget me.

Thank you & God bless you, Mara Jovanović/translation by Idy

Looking around, Tess knew this book was more than a simple child's story. Someone had written the first part of this letter on the child's behalf and, in this letter, this child begged for help.

Seeing Tess' peculiar expression, Willis leaned forward and reached for the letter. "What does the letter say? Let me read it," he said.

"*No!*" she said, pulling the letter close to her chest and staring at him.

"What do you mean, *No?* I'm supposed to see everything that comes across your desk, so let me see it!" he said.

She only looked at him.

Analyzing her expression, he plopped back against his chair. Then squinting at her, he tried to decipher her disposition. Unable to, he shook his head. "Tess, when are you going to stop trying to do everything on your own? When are you going to accept help? That's what I'm here for. Now let me see it!" he said impatiently as he held out his hand.

"No, Willis! You can read whatever else you want, but you cannot read this letter or anything involved with it. This was written to me, the Foundation Chairman, not the Foundation, which really wouldn't make any difference because I am the Foundation," she said, then she stood up and placed her briefcase on the desk. Opening it, she set the original and translated manuscripts inside it with the envelopes and the letter, then closed and locked the case.

"Where are you going? Are you leaving me with all this?" he asked as he stood.

"I'm going home, and I'm going to read this there. I don't want any interruptions. Call me if you need me, but only if it's a matter of life or death."

"Okay. You go home and read this *private* manuscript. I'll call you later. We'll go out to dinner, and you can tell me all about it then. Deal?"

"You and me? Or you and me, and some of your single male friends?" she asked. As she walked around her desk, he stopped her. She shook her head at him, but he only looked guiltily at her when she smiled at his concern. "Willis, when are you going to quit trying to fix me up with your society pals? I'm not interested, so please stop it."

"Tess, you can't be alone the rest of your life. You're always alone. It's not right."

She took a deep breath. Then exhaling slowly, she said, "I already took my shot at not being alone. It didn't work then, and I don't have the time or the inclination now. So, please, Willis, stop trying so hard."

He could only stand there as she walked to the door, but before she stepped into the hallway, she turned around and said, "Get the reading team to go over the rest of the manuscripts and, Willis, take the rest of the week off. I'll take care of everything. I'll see you later." Then without another word, she vanished from the doorway.

Willis knew that once she had made a decision, there was no changing it. Collecting the remaining manuscripts, he carried them to a room at the end of the hall where the foundation's reading team was busy evaluating the final entries from the international division, or so they thought. They were not happy to see him enter with a high stack of envelopes, but they agreed to finish the remainder by the next morning.

CHAPTER FOUR

Once back at her apartment, Tess switched on the usual lights and lit the fireplaces in her bedroom and living room. Walking into her office, she sat behind the desk, removed the manuscript from her briefcase, and stared at the cover. She then opened the letter and read it again. Although she had not read the entry, she felt that what she was about to read would be devastating. With that thought, she placed the letter aside and opened the cover to the little girl's story.

For three hours, she sat at her desk and read. The child, Mara Jovanović, had written almost seventy-five pages, but one of the first stunning sequences was Mara's detached description of her older brother's murder. This sequence gave Tess her first up close chill from the conflict in Sarajevo.

They call it war, but I see death. A man killed Pety with a gun. I saw this and remember I was walking with Idy. He picked me up and carried me when it began to rain. Idy always carries me home from school when it rains. He says he does not want me to get wet because I will get sick, but Idy wants to carry me because I splash in the puddles and make him wet.

That day, I saw Pety walking across the street. Idy saw him too. Idy looked up when he heard a noise. Pety started to cross the street and Idy yells to him to get back, to hide. Idy pulls me inside a shop. I hear a gun: pop, pop, pop, pop, and Pety falls in the street. I heard Idy whisper his name. I try to get down. I want to go to Pety, but men in uniforms go to Pety. Idy says to be quiet, not to speak. Pety does not move. Idy does not let me look. He takes me home.

The men in uniforms come to the house. Mama cries. Papa cries. I cry. Idy cries. Idy holds me and says not to worry. Idy says that Pety is in heaven. I ask why. Idy says it is what God wants for Pety. He says that I have Mama and Papa. I have Idy too. I always have Idy. But death chases me and soon it will catch me. Idy protects me from death, but Idy says I must play hide and seek with death. I do as Idy says. Idy loves me and I love Idy.

As Tess continued reading, she learned that Mara had seen many people killed during the war. Even school friends shot by civilians firing at random from passing cars. It was difficult to comprehend that a seven-year-old child wrote what she held in her hands. The manuscript contained such political undertones, and informal discussions of strategies and ideas, that any normal child would not desire to consider. Then, just when Tess thought the newness of the story was through, Mara described a new character: The Black Rebel.

Bad people want the land. They want to take it from us. The Black Rebel will not let them take the land. The Black Rebel will save the people and the land. The world forgets us, forgets Sarajevo, and forgets the war. They all forget. If they do not think about us, we are not real. But we are real. We cry. Who hears us cry? No one, but the Black Rebel. He dries the tears of the people.

Idy says, to kill is how bad people win. The people of the land do not die, they fight. Sarajevo is the home of the good people not the bad people. The Black Rebel hears the people, his people, he says. He loves his people. His people love him. He is strong—his life for the land and for the people. Idy says the Black Rebel will fight for what is right in God's eyes. God is on the side of the good people of Sarajevo. Idy prays with me at night. He prays for the people. I pray, God Bless the Black Rebel.

"God Bless the Black Rebel," Tess echoed as her gaze wandered to the telephone on her desk. "Who is the Black Rebel? Black Rebel," she said aloud.

Recalling part of the history of Yugoslavia, she remembered a book she once saw about Josip Broz Tito titled *Red Rebel,* but this Black Rebel intrigued her to learn more about him.

She looked at her watch. It was three-thirty in the afternoon. Reaching for the telephone, she dialed a friend who currently held a desk at the New York Times. Perhaps he would know who the Black Rebel was.

"Hello? Yes, George Preston, please," she said.

After several minutes, the phone clicked and a man said, "Preston here."

"Hi George, it's Tess. How are you?"

"Hey, Tess. I'm doing well. How are you? What's up?"

"Do you have a minute? I need your help with something."

"Sure, what is it?"

"Today I read something on the war in Yugoslavia and it mentioned a character called the Black Rebel. Ever hear of him?"

"Not that I recall, but there are many rebel forces over there. It could be any of them. I know of the Croatian Black Legion, an elite military force.

They were considered similar to Hitler's SS in Croatia during World War II. You know, Ustaše. They're still active, but Black Rebel doesn't come to mind. So, you want to know who he is, or who they are."

"Yes. I want to know who he is, that is, if he's real."

On the other end of the line, George jotted notes, then said, "I'll research it for you. I'll call you back when I find something, maybe later today, but definitely by tomorrow," he said.

"You're great, George. I really appreciate it."

"What are friends for? You've certainly been there for me more times than I have fingers and toes," he said, then he was momentarily quiet. "Tess, tell me, why do you need to know who this Black Rebel is?"

She was silent. She was not sure why, she only knew that she had to know as much about him as possible. "I just need to know," she said.

"Tess, for a woman, sometimes you really walk the edge. First farmers, now what sounds like a Nationalist rebel? You—"

"*No!* Non-Nationalist. He's definitely on the side of the citizens of Sarajevo, not any political cause," she said, having interrupted him.

"Okay, non-Nationalist, perhaps freedom fighter. So, are you going to tell me where you heard this name?" he asked.

"Does it matter?" she asked, stroking the top of Mara's manuscript.

"I guess not, as long as it doesn't get the American government upset with you. Is it part of a new novel? If it is, and it's based on truth, especially truth over there, I'd think twice, Tess."

"No one pays that much attention to what I write about. I don't kid myself. People read my novels because they like stories about romance, sex, and love, and, of course, the bad guys getting their comeuppance."

"I can think of one of your novels where the bad guys didn't get their comeuppance. Instead, they got angry with you for what you wrote," George commented.

"I can't worry about that now. Look, I'll wait for your call. I really appreciate your help. Thanks, George."

She disconnected the call before he could scold her further, then she sat in complete silence. She knew he was right. She could not write about the Black Rebel, especially if he was real. If she made public any part of Mara's book, it would cause problems since there were passages within it that were not exactly flattering to the Super Power government's involvement in the war. She smiled at the thought of a seven-year-old child's book causing problems for any government.

After all, the Super Powers did not agree with what was happening in Sarajevo, and they publicized any and every bad deed committed by the Serbians during the war as an excuse for their involvement in the war. But she knew that the Press said nothing of the atrocities caused by the Croatian and Bosniak forces. That vexed her because the lack of equal public reporting convicted Serbians worldwide, not just those involved in this war.

"But were as many of them guilty as the press declared?" she asked herself. Reflecting on her own experiences with people from different cultures, she was not able to answer herself. Shaking off her thoughts, she began to flip back through the manuscript. In her mind, this child had won the competition, but she would wait for the reading team's final review and comments on the remaining entries. Only then would she let the committee know her decision.

CHAPTER FIVE

Later that evening, Tess was sitting at her computer, working on her latest novel, but stopped to answer the telephone when it rang. "Hello?"

"Tess, it's George. Are you ready to hear what I found? You won't believe it, I guarantee you."

"Does he really exist? Do you have any photographs or names? Is it a man?" she asked curiously.

"It's a man. No one knows who he is because no one's ever seen him."

"So then, how is anyone certain of gender?"

"All leads conclude that the Black Rebel is a man. And you're right in that he's definitely non-Nationalist. He's most likely of mixed heritage, maybe Croatian mixed with Serbian, but definitely not a Muslim. He could be German, Russian, or anything else as well, a real mystery man."

"I bet he's tall and handsome," she said, smiling to herself.

"Tess," he said in a scolding tone.

"Yes, George," she answered sarcastically.

"What are you planning? Are you going to write about him?"

She laughed to herself. "Maybe I will. Maybe I'll immortalize him in a love story, or something."

"Tess, you always write about men. Why is that?"

"I find men fascinating. Well, many of them are and, from the sounds of it, the Black Rebel definitely is."

"You say that because you're a woman, not a man, which is a good thing," he answered. "Now, down to business. First, the good side: it's rumored that this man provides food and supplies to some of the residents of the city of Sarajevo along with the surrounding towns, shelters, and such, and he's been doing this long before any outside assistance. He campaigns against local and regional Nationalist aggressors, mostly traditional Serbian, Croatian, and Bosniak extremists."

"Is there a difference between aggressors? Aggression is aggression."

"Maybe at first there was a difference, but now they all blend. Now the new governments are just trying to get their piece of the pie. He's aided some civilians in Croatia during their sieges, and now he's doing the same thing in Bosnia."

"So he was involved in Croatia's independence?"

"Toward the end, but he disappeared, then reappeared in Sarajevo. It seems he has a history of showing up where governments don't want him. Though in the beginning, he didn't interfere much with traditional Serbian, Croatian, or Bosniak armed forces, only targeted extremists, but the worse the war got in Sarajevo, the tougher he got. He doesn't like detainee camps either. Overall, he isn't partial; he'll go after all of them. Off the record, I suspect he's a big time Croat, but not a Nationalist, or a Fascist," he said.

"What makes you say that?" she asked, curious as to how he arrived at that conclusion.

"Remember when I mentioned the Croatian Black Legion?"

"Yes. Is he one of them?"

"I don't think so because he's been accused of using force against Ustaše wannabes."

"But the key word here is *wannabes*. So, they wouldn't be the traditional Ustaše, right?"

"True, so he could be Croatian."

"What about the Bosniak Mujahideen forces?"

"Like I said, he'll go after them if they run detainee camps, which they do. All sides have detainee camps. He doesn't like extremists, and his reputation shows that waste makes him angry. Now is where his reputation starts a rapid decline. It appears, from reports of mysterious nighttime aggression, that he attacks those who have made the last advance. He also goes after troops in a weakened state, but that are doing something dishonorable to the civilian population."

"So he defends everyone?"

"Yes and no."

"Okay. So is he fighting to keep Yugoslavia dismembered?"

"Well, it seems this new separation of state is to his liking and maybe he wants to keep it that way. So that, again, leads me to believe that he's a Croat. But maybe in reality he doesn't care who is in control and just wants the war over with."

"Does that make sense?"

"There's no sense to be made without the whole story."

"So he does this all by himself? He's a one-man army?"

"No. He has his own army or, for now at least, we'll call it that. It's unknown how many men he has in it, but they're strong, real strong, but not overly aggressive. However, it sounds like he could be just as violent as those he tries to stop. One rumor says he has Vatican backing and, if so, that's one deep pocket helping him forge ahead. With that backing, he and his group would most likely be Roman Catholic, not Serbian Orthodox. And if so, he's Croatian."

"Perhaps they use religious vindication as their battering ram."

"Perhaps, because they don't attack like the others to control land and kill mercilessly. They attack to defend, and when they do, they do tremendous damage. Remember that attack at that abandoned mine northeast of Sarajevo last month? That place was supposed to be one of those Serbian detainee camps. Remember that incident?"

"I remember reading about it in an independent news journal."

"The event was picked up on US reconnaissance satellites. He did that. Everything was burned to the ground."

"The article said that no prisoners were found and that the soldiers found there, were dead prior to their bodies being burned. So he really doesn't like suffering."

"It doesn't matter. To walk into a Serbian detainee camp and cut soldiers down like that...That's guts, Tess. This guy kills people. He doesn't have to think twice about it. He's an executioner, a 'tyrant' as he's called by the press and international governments. He's worse than SS, or the Black Legion. From the sounds of it, nighttime is his forte, like a wolf at night, strong senses: darkness, black, cunning, retaliating Black Rebel, and those are only a few of the ways he's been described. He's one man you wouldn't want to meet in a dark alley."

"I don't know about that. He sounds intriguing. I'd meet him in a dark alley."

"Please, Tess, don't even consider that," he said in warning.

"Did you find anything else?" she asked, changing the subject while she secretly pondered the idea about meeting the Black Rebel.

"Just that he's a wanted man. It's all very low key, but NATO forces want him, the Serbs want him, the Muslims want him, and the Croats want him. Everyone wants him, and they don't care if he's dead or alive.

They actually prefer him dead, but they have no idea who he is, where he is, or how to get him. Regardless, they just want him stopped. He interferes with the big boys' war games. Every time the warring sides stop for negotiations, he pushes his side to further and better advantage."

"Wait. What *is* his side?" she asked, doubting George's conclusion that the Black Rebel was only Croatian.

"I still say Croat. His side, or better, his purpose, is helping keep local Roman Catholics alive."

"But you said he fights against everyone. So wouldn't he help all civilians as well?"

"No proof that he helps all."

"Hmm, he's very interesting, a very complex man."

"What he is, is a force beyond other rebel forces, and no one likes that. Since he took up defense in this Bosnian siege, it's presumed that he has ties there."

"So maybe he's from Bosnia? Maybe from Sarajevo?"

"Where he's from doesn't matter. It's what he does that upsets the apple cart. The big boys like to talk and negotiate, make their deals, set their embargoes, and make their millions. But not this guy; he's all action. This war has gone on so long that it's no longer a matter of winning. It's now down to, how much will you pay me to stop killing those I see as my enemies? Now the victims in this war have seen that the rest of the world has been making money off their suffering and they want compensation; however, I doubt that any government will make the Serbs dole out remuneration. But all three sides, Croat, Muslim, and Serb, now see that no one is winning, and they'll start negotiating their way out of the corner they're all in."

"Wait. Croatia and Serbia were in negotiations amongst themselves as to how they were going to split up Bosnia, weren't they? Maybe that's what upsets him?"

"I doubt that matters to him. He plays the real war game. He plays by *his* rules, he plays to win, and he takes orders from no one. No one knows exactly what he wants, but it's obvious that he wants the bad guys gone, and by 'bad guys' I presume that means extremists. It seems that he'll keep going after them as long as they're a threat to the civilian population. And, well, other than that, there's not much else to tell. He is what he's known as…a phantom, and as quickly as he appeared, when it's over, he'll disappear as if he never existed, except in the minds of those he helped."

Thinking about the Black Rebel and Mara, Tess was silent, and her silence concerned him.

"Tess? Don't make the Black Rebel a new character in your next novel. Don't even mention his name to anyone else. You'll end up dead and, most likely, from the man himself. His reach is long. Don't fool yourself into thinking he can't get to you here. He wants to remain anonymous, so let him remain anonymous. His image tells that much about him. It's obvious that he has resources from the international community, so he doesn't need your help."

She was still quiet, and that spooked him further.

"Tess, do you hear me? I don't want to be writing your obituary."

"George, I wouldn't do anything to risk anyone's life, let alone a man as brave as he is. Truly, I was just curious as to who he was."

"Just think about it before you do anything. Please, Tess," George insisted.

She smiled and looked back at the manuscript. "I will, and thanks, George. Can I get a hard copy of all this?"

"I'll send it by your office tomorrow."

"I won't be there. Send it by my apartment if you will."

"Alright, tomorrow. Good night, Tess."

"Good night, George, and thank you so much."

She hung up. Picking up the manuscript and letter, she then left her office and walked to the bedroom. Lying on the bed, she eventually fell asleep and dreamt of what the Black Rebel was like.

For the next two days, Tess remained at home. On the morning of the third day, she received the evaluations from the reading team. Her decision was correct in her assumption that Mara's work was the most outstanding. The committee agreed when they read carefully selected sections of Mara's manuscript. She only allowed them to read the parts that did not contain political, Idy, or Black Rebel information.

In her mind, she felt that keeping incriminating details from them was best. It was enough that the person who translated the manuscript read the information. Most likely, Idy translated it since he had translated Mara's letter. That thought eased her mind somewhat, but why she did not know; however, the task now was to find this child. And so, the search for the young authoress began.

CHAPTER SIX

Almost two weeks had passed, and Mara was still not found. This challenged Tess' resolve to find Mara, Idy, and possibly the Black Rebel, and Tess now had decisions to make, because her search had become an old frustration.

At home, sitting behind her desk, she daydreamed as the autumn rain fell heavily on her balcony. The deafening sounds of thunder echoed from the sky, promising the usual overpowering crack of lightning that would fill the air with menace. Lightning was different on the sixteenth floor, more realistic for some reason. As if being elevated, it could pass through you on its journey to the ground below.

Lost in thought, she sat mesmerized, as in her mind she envisioned the tragedies detailed in Mara's manuscript. This little girl's words had won her heart with compelling descriptions of the war in Bosnia; Mara's life had been heart wrenching and tragic. Tess thought about Mara who, at seven, had lost her only brother to the fighting that endured past the lives and dreams of the people the war was intended to help. But then, when did war actually help anyone?

From Tess' unconfirmed, but quick investigation, she also found out that both of Mara's parents were dead; although, obviously, they were alive when she wrote her manuscript and letter. Their deaths happened when Mara was at school. A bomb exploded in the yard of her house. Tess surmised that Nationalists, no doubt, killed her parents, but for what reason she did not know. She briefly thought about the tragedy of Mara's family and wondered what effect that had on Mara.

After repeated calls to the Bosnian Embassy in Washington, DC, they finally confirmed Mara's parents' deaths; however, they had no evidence on Mara being alive or dead. The Embassy's only comment was that government officials took all orphaned children to churches or other facilities in the surrounding areas until kith or kin could claim them. When Tess asked at which facility the child could be, they did not know, and, more likely, she felt they did not care. This lax attitude vexed her, and beyond these facts, as a whole, the Embassy was of little assistance.

"Who is Idy? What sort of man is he?" she wondered as she sat reviewing the life story of one child caught between "evil and evil" as Idy, Mara's translator, had stated in his letter. From the words Mara wrote, it appeared that there was little good in her life. But ever present were fears and lost causes, and the only person who remained that loved her was Idy.

"Death chases me and soon it will catch me," Mara wrote. Truth, with painful descriptions of suffering, that no adult should have to endure, let alone a child. Still, adults had caused this civil war, and children were one of the many long-suffering victims of it.

Then, suddenly, that anticipated and deafening crack of lightning sounded. Tess gasped and looked around the room. In her imaginings, it sounded more like the explosions she envisioned from Mara's descriptions than a natural phenomenon.

Picking up the manuscript, she knew Mara was the only child who could have won her competition. Besides writing much more than any other entrant, Mara wrote with complete conviction for what she felt. It was not a child's story, but an adult's story trapped inside a helpless little girl. What Mara had seen in her short life, Tess could only wonder about. She imagined that those who surrounded Mara must continually discuss the war in order for her to have such precise views. To Tess, this meant that Idy would have the same precise views.

She sighed, and said aloud, "Tess Fordel, philanthropist and promoter of the fine art of writing, gives an award to a child of civil war in Bosnia." She laughed at herself. "I wonder if that's what George would write? If he ever found out the truth." She sighed, then thought, "What a soft life I've had compared to this child. She needs much more than this award."

Shaking her head at her thoughts, her attention strolled into the recesses of her mind. The impact of Mara's story affected her with great force. And now, after submitting her story with the explanation that she only wanted the money to help her family leave the war zone, Mara had vanished. Tess did not know what to do. She felt responsible for Mara, who wrote to her with the sincere hope of winning. She was counting on the money to help her family, and now Tess felt strangely responsible for her family's fate. Why, she did not exactly know; nevertheless, somewhere in this little girl's story, Tess found something of herself. It was not something she could put her finger on, though all the same it was there. It was something tragic that made her stop and evaluate her own life.

As she sat staring into space, the telephone rang. Again, startled back to the present, she answered the call. "Hello?"

"Tess, it's Willis. We haven't found the girl. It seems she's actually disappeared. Most likely, she's dead. But even with the cease-fire, there's so much fighting going on over there. Are you sure you still want to try to find her?" he asked.

Before responding, she looked at Mara's manuscript. "I have to. This child dared to tell her story. She reached out to me, and I have to get this money to her. If the authorities can't find her, it doesn't mean she's disappeared, it means they're too preoccupied to look."

"When she sent her manuscript to you it became public domain. I say publish it and let her come to you," Willis recommended.

"No. That wouldn't be right. That would be dangerous. I have to go and find her, and I have to go alone," Tess answered.

"Talk about dangerous. It's not safe for a woman to travel alone to those types of countries. You really should let me go with you. Come on, reconsider," he suggested.

"You've got to be joking. We live in New York City. Not that I believe it, but it's ranked pretty high on the nastiest, most crime infested cities in the world list, and you worry about me going to Bosnia," she said.

"Damn it, Tess! There's a war going on there! Countless women are raped and brutally murdered daily over there!"

"What do you call what's happening here? One Mafia boss is killing another. Street punks slit each other's throats. Daily, in this country, women and children are raped and brutally murdered by their husbands, boyfriends, brothers, and fathers! People steal your cars, your jewelry, and the clothes right off your back, if you let them; and let's not even talk about Ponzi schemes, and you speak of war. What sheltered Americans we are. You set Americans aside as if we're some special breed. We're all people; we're just in different situations."

Knowing she would get off her soapbox quickly, he said nothing.

Laughing quietly to herself, she rationalized her thoughts. "Seriously, I must find her. The bylaws of the Foundation state—"

"Oh, forget the bylaws! Who follows those anyway?" he said, upset that she worried about that at this moment.

"My Foundation's bylaws state that all awards are to be issued within three months of judgment. That only leaves me until the end of January. I'm not cheating such a talented child out of her award. Too much time has already passed while her government sits around not keeping track of its children. She risked a lot in sending me her story and, no matter what it takes, I won't let her down." She paused, waiting for his comment, although he felt outnumbered. When he said nothing, she continued. "Don't worry, Willis. I'll be fine. George has given me the name of a friend of his, a journalist in Sarajevo. I'll be staying with him."

"Huh, a journalist! I can only imagine. He doesn't even know exactly why you're going there. If he knew, he'd never let you go. Still, I don't know why you don't let me tell anyone you're going."

"No one should know where I'm going besides you and George. There is a war going on there, and American's aren't allowed to travel there now. And besides, you know what people think of Eastern European countries: Communism, Socialism, and all that. What they don't understand, they fear. They think everyone else is a barbarian. What they need to do is take a good look in the mirror before they put labels on someone else," she said, then laughed to herself. "People are deeply stupid, but people are just people regardless of where they live. So, no more discussing it, I leave tonight."

"How long are you going to be there? You may never find her, and what if you get into trouble? Who's going to help an American? Just remember, you may have an objective view of them, but I don't think they'll have such a positive opinion of you. Things are very tense over there with Americans. To them, you're nothing more than a Capitalist. You represent the enemy," he said, trying to change her mind.

"I know that, but, for Mara's sake, I have to risk something. I won't let her down. If I did, it would be against everything I stand for, everything the Foundation stands for. The money is for underprivileged children to further their education. And what's more underprivileged than a child in the middle of a war? If she doesn't get the money, because I don't try to find her, what's the point?" She released a heavy sigh. "Don't you understand?"

"Yeah, I understand. I understand you're as stubborn as a rock."

"I never knew rocks were stubborn, just hard." She chuckled. "Like my head, I guess."

"No," he said with quiet admiration, and he did admire her. He did not have the courage to do what she was going to do. She was walking into a war zone to award a child fifteen thousand dollars. Knowing Tess, she would do everything she could for the child as well. He was happy when she refused his offer to join her. The thought of this trip frightened Willis, but many things frightened him.

Willis was a good person, but he was of gentle character, raised in a quiet world. Wealthy from the start, he assumed his father's place, taking an exalted position at one of the country's largest financial institutions. The notion of struggle was foreign to Willis, but not to Tess. From a young age, her life had given her different experiences. She always strove to do what was right for others. The easy way was not usually the right way. She had her dreams and her goals, and her Foundation was one of them. It was always her desire to help others whenever possible. And now, regardless of what it took, her goal was to find Mara. She could only hope that she was not too late, and that tragedy had claimed the life of little Mara Jovanović.

Tess packed after concluding her conversation with Willis. Waiting for the limousine that would take her to the airport, she read a recent article about the cease-fire in Bosnia and the proposed peace accord between Serbia, Croatia, and Bosnia. Despite the cease-fire, Tess was going right in the middle of it, she was going to Sarajevo.

Since the beginning of the Yugoslav war, most US airlines would not book flights from the US to any cities in any of the current or former Yugoslav provinces. So Tess used a European airline that stopped in London. From there, she would depart for Budapešt, and then, via a Red Cross aid plane, she would fly into Belgrade. From Belgrade, she would take the train to Priboj, a town south of Belgrade and east of Sarajevo, near the Serbian-Bosnian border. Once in Priboj, she would take the reporters' transit bus to Sarajevo.

Herbert Strassburg, the journalist she was to contact upon her arrival in Belgrade, would meet her at the bus in Priboj and escort her the rest of the way. Strassburg agreed to help her when he found out who she was; however, there was little security in that thought considering the volatile nature of this war. Strassburg truly thought she was there to report information back to George, considering the Times would not let George travel to Sarajevo. Regardless, so much was uncertain, and she did not know what she would find when she arrived in Sarajevo.

Once at John F. Kennedy airport, she hurried to her gate. When she walked into the boarding area for her flight, she felt the same feeling that she had only experienced one other time in her life. That time, she felt a Higher Power had sent her to a more remote part of America to help a man about to lose his farm, and almost all else he had in his life along with it. Remembering that time, she now had the same overwhelming emotion. She had to go, though she did not know exactly why. For certain, this trip would only complicate her life. For so long she had fought to rid her life of complications, but despite the consequences, she could not turn back now.

As the flight attendant took her ticket, Tess paused at the gate and looked back into the waiting area. She felt it would be a long time before she would see it again. Perhaps she would not see New York again. This trip would change her life. That much she knew as she stood there frozen in place.

"Is everything alright, Miss Fordel?" the attendant asked.

Tess' attention immediately emerged from her private thoughts as she looked at the attendant and answered, "Yes, everything is as it should be."

Whatever her fate, she smiled. Then, placing her life in God's hands, she turned back around and walked down the jetway to the plane. From that point on, she would not question this decision again.

CHAPTER SEVEN

London was complicated. Military police scrutinized all passengers traveling to countries surrounding Yugoslavia, or its former provinces, stating that their inspection was a required terrorist check. They had delayed Tess' outgoing flight four hours so far, and there was no indication that they would release it for departure any time soon. Patiently biding her time, Tess sat inside Heathrow Airport while her luggage sat in a holding area. Yet, she was not alone in her wait, other passengers waited alongside her. She looked at them, and most of them were asleep.

Due to this delay, she worried that she would miss the Red Cross flight departing Budapešt for Belgrade. Wanting to arrive in Budapešt on time, she changed airlines and obtained a seat on another flight, which had already been delayed half a day, but was finally cleared to depart in a half hour. She was immediately issued a ticket because she told them her final destination was Budapešt to divert their thoughts of her traveling beyond that point. The airline located her luggage and promptly arranged for it to be loaded on the new flight. "A much better situation," she thought, after a four-hour layover. Now everything was set, or so it appeared.

Once she arrived in Budapešt, she had to rush to a military installation at the airport and go through security. Not to her surprise, this flight was also delayed, although only an hour and because of weather. She was the only American on the flight to Belgrade, which made her wonder where the other passengers were from. When she looked down the long row of filled seats in the passengers' waiting area, several men smiled at her as their female companions were busy with other things.

"Men from Belgrade," she said under her breath, then she shook her head, and laughed to herself.

The plane eventually boarded and she sat alone in a row of three seats, although several men attempted to join her during the flight. Being polite, she allowed them to sit with her, but ignored them as she worked on her laptop. In time, they went away; however, when she walked to the back of the plane, the same men would follow her and attempt to speak with her again.

"They just don't give up," she whispered. "Men from Belgrade, men from Belgrade, men from Belgrade," repeated in her mind like a broken record, but she did not even know if these men were actually from Belgrade, or if they were from elsewhere. When she boarded the flight, she was told that the passengers were all reporters and medical personnel, but no one mentioned where they were from.

Finally, after what felt like hours, the captain announced their final approach into the Airport. All she could think about was catching the next train south from Belgrade. She would contact Strassburg before she boarded the train and, once she met with him, they would travel together to Sarajevo where she would stay in a facility provided by the London Post. And now, because of the delay, she would not have much time to contact him. The trains going south were sporadic, and she did not know what to expect as far as departure times.

Once through airport customs, a man named Bora Oddelek met Tess. He recognized her immediately due to a photograph the Belgrade travel agency provided. Approaching her, he introduced himself and showed his credentials as proof of his identity along with a letter of welcome from his agency. He collected her luggage and continued to a car he had parked nearby. From there, he took her to the train station to inquire about the trains scheduled to depart that afternoon.

Tess was waiting outside on the train's platform while Oddelek spoke with the station master regarding the train's late arrival. Several people passed her on their way walking along the platform, but she hardly noticed any of them. She was tired and not prepared for the situation.

When Oddelek returned to her, he explained that the train would not arrive for two more days and, if she liked, she could exchange her ticket for later departure. With an annoyed smile, he then asked, "What would you like to do, Miss Fordel?"

Sighing and smiling briefly, she looked at him. "I don't really have a choice, do I?"

"Yes, you do. You can go back to your country, or you can go to a hotel and wait. What will it be?"

His ill-mannered gestures annoyed her. Without saying a word, she looked at him, thinking, "Now this is a perfect example of male chauvinism." Then Willis' words regarding foreign opinions of Americans came to her, and her expression changed. Through sarcastic thoughts, she smiled and said, "Mr. Oddelek, thank you for pointing out my options. It is my decision to wait. I understand there are several five star, first class hotels in Belgrade. Once you exchange my ticket for the next available departure, whether it is in two days or two years, you can take me to a hotel. That is, if assisting me further isn't inconvenient for you. I know you were only to take me to the train station, and I would not want to detain you any further than necessary," she said, still smiling, as she witnessed his embarrassment.

"Please, Miss Fordel, I will be most happy to arrange your ticket and take you to the best hotel in Belgrade. I will do that now, if you'll wait here for me," he said, then he left her and returned to the ticket window.

Tired, she sat helplessly on her luggage and waited. "Men from Belgrade," she said again to herself as her mind wandered to the Black Rebel.

Ivan stood on the opposite platform and watched Tess. He pretended he was waiting for another train, but, in fact, he was extremely interested in her. He found her attractive, and his mind slipped away from his real reason for being there; he was looking for someone, a female spy working for the Serbian government.

Thinking back, he remembered the vague description of the spy. Now looking at Tess, she and that description came together in Ivan's mind. Continuing to watch Tess, Ivan scrutinized her as he leaned against a post, pretending to read that day's paper.

The woman he sought was tall and slender, just as Tess was. He had also found out that the woman was dark-haired and light-eyed. Tess had dark brown hair, though dark sunglasses hid her eyes from his view.

More than likely, the woman was not from the Balkans. She would speak fluent English with no obvious accent, but it was not known if she were English or American. And though Ivan was too far away from Tess to hear her conversation with Oddelek, he distinctly heard her speaking English. The last rumors about the woman he sought were that she would travel alone and was noticeably beautiful.

The left side of Ivan's lips rose in a seductive smile as he reveled in the similarities between the spy's description and Tess. "Noticeably beautiful," he whispered.

Still, the deciding factor would be if she were looking for Mara. Everyone was looking for the Black Rebel: Croats, Serbs, and Bosniaks. It was still unknown who was responsible for the explosion that claimed the life of her parents, or the murder of her brother that day he was walking on Sniper's Alley. That was the new name for the main boulevard—*Ulica Zmaja od Bosne*—meaning Dragon of Bosnia Street, which it was given due to the number of deaths there by snipers.

Since Mara's brother knew the Black Rebel, those searching for the Black Rebel felt that Mara would know him also. Therefore, they felt it would be advantageous to use a woman to find her, and once they found her, they would eventually find the Black Rebel.

It was also rumored that this spy was a point of contact for Serbian officials outside of the country. She would depart London for Budapešt, and make contact with Serbian officials along the way, then go to Belgrade. Because of this rumor, the Croats and Bosniaks needed her stopped, as equally, the Serbians needed to find her in order to obtain the information she carried. As Ivan looked at Tess, he found she fitted the spy's description, especially in her outward attractiveness.

When Oddelek returned, and asked Tess additional questions, Ivan watched them. She placed her hand to her forehead and spoke softly to Oddelek. Even though Ivan had moved closer, he was still too far away to hear whether she had an accent, but again, he was sure that they spoke English because Oddelek was speaking it. He noticed her smile briefly, then Oddelek walked back to the ticket window.

So far, Ivan found nothing suspicious in her behavior: no looking over her shoulder to see if anyone watched her, no jitteriness or jumpiness, as could be expected. Still waiting for Oddelek, she stayed seated on her luggage and rested her elbows on her knees. Then she removed her sunglasses. Looking up to the cloudy sky, she wondered if it would snow.

Ivan continued to watch her and, though she did not notice him, he noticed her eyes of pale moss green as he thought, "Light eyes."

She was too exhausted to notice anything and, though it was morning, all she wanted to do was take a shower and go to bed. She placed her chin in her hands and closed her eyes.

Oddelek returned to her and tapped her on the shoulder. Startled, she sat straight and looked at him, then standing up, she slid her sunglasses onto her face. Oddelek lifted her luggage from the platform, then they walked through station with Ivan cautiously following them. Oddelek left her at the curb with her luggage, then went to get the car. As she stood patiently waiting, she thought about Mara. Now that she was in Serbia, she began to better understand the girl's story, things there were difficult, and this was not even the war zone.

Ivan looked around. He noticed men stopping and staring at Tess, and making somewhat lewd remarks. Hearing this, and seeing their stares, Ivan became defensive. Without reason, he felt oddly protective of Tess as if she were his.

Standing inside the depot, Ivan watched from a window. Oddelek quickly pulled the car to the curb, placed her luggage in the trunk, helped her inside, then he entered the car and drove away. Ivan walked from the depot to an available taxi. Once inside, he ordered the driver to follow Oddelek's car.

After a moderate drive, Oddelek pulled the car up in front of one of the most exclusive hotels in Belgrade. Oddelek helped Tess out, then handed her luggage over to a bellman. They then continued into the hotel where he acquired the best room available for her.

Ivan warily waited in a taxi down the street until Tess and Oddelek had left the car. After seeing them enter the hotel, he then requested the driver pull up to the entrance. He stepped out of the taxi and waited outside until he saw Tess and Oddelek walking toward the elevators. Only then did he enter.

He looked around the lobby, then walked to the front desk. Smiling at the clerk, he requested a room near the woman who had just checked in. As Ivan slipped a tip across the desk, the clerk grinned back at him. With a raised eyebrow, he laughed knowingly, then quickly checked Ivan into the room directly across the hall from Tess. Ivan inquired as to the woman's name and her purpose for being in Belgrade. The clerk told him that her name was Tess Fordel, but all the clerk knew was that she was from New York City and was waiting for the train south.

Taking his key, Ivan walked to the elevators and rode up to his floor. Getting out on the eighth floor, he walked slowly toward his room. On his way, he passed Oddelek, who was now leaving. Oddelek stepped into the open elevator and, when the elevator doors closed, Ivan went to his room. Once inside, he immediately placed a telephone call to an apartment across the city.

The phone rang in Sergej's apartment and he answered it, saying, "What now?"

"Your wife doesn't love you anymore. That's not my fault," Ivan said, then he was silent, waiting for Sergej to answer.

"Well, it has to rain sometime," Sergej said, then waited.

All was clear. "I think I've found her. She's at the M at 805. I'm across the way." Ivan paused and shook his head, thinking about her. "She fits the description. Actually, not exactly, she's more attractive. You should see all the men she passes; they stare like hungry wolves. They aren't smart to send such a woman. She's too noticeable."

"Perhaps that's their plan. They want her to be noticeable. The more men she meets, the more she can make available to them," Sergej suggested.

"She'll have a big job keeping those wolves at bay. They won't be that easy to pass off like men from home," Ivan said protectively.

"How do you know?" Sergej said and laughed because he heard anger in Ivan's tone. But was it anger at having to fight a war, or was it because Ivan did not want any men around this new pawn.

"I'll make contact and let you know. So far, things fit. She's on her way down, but I'll keep her here for at least one day, depending. I'm not sure if I'll allow her to go, but if so, it won't be alone," Ivan said.

Although his message was choppy, in the event anyone listened in on the line, Sergej knew what Ivan meant. Tess was at the Metropol in room 805, and Ivan was across the hall in 806. Tess would be traveling down, which meant south, but there was no need to say she was taking a train. Regardless of how she would get to Sarajevo, if she were the woman they were searching for, Ivan would accompany her.

"She has to be the one. She's not one of them, or us. Why would they choose someone from so far away? She tops the list," Ivan said.

This told Sergej she was Tess Fordel, the first name they received from outside sources. Sergej also knew that Ivan meant that she was American when he said from so far away.

"*They* have bad reputations. They think *they* are liars and cheats, selfish also. I can only imagine they pay her very well. I don't know. Even with the proposed deal, this won't end well, or quickly."

There was silence on the line as Ivan thought. His mind sped through recent events as his visions of the future made him shake his head. He secretly wondered why a woman like Tess would get involved in this war. Not having an answer, he said, "When I know something, I'll be in touch."

"Good," Sergej said, then he ended the call.

Walking back to the door, Ivan looked out the peephole. Thinking about the situation with this new player, Tess Fordel, he walked back to the telephone and called the clerk at the front desk. He requested the front desk call his room when the woman in 805 left. The clerk agreed, knowing there would be another tip in it for him.

After that, Ivan left the hotel and returned to his apartment to gather his things for his upcoming trip to Sarajevo. Once he was finished, he returned to the hotel in anticipation of a call from the front desk clerk.

CHAPTER EIGHT

Exhaustion consumed Tess. Once in her room, she lay down immediately and fell asleep. At half past five that evening, she awoke. The room was dark except for the reflection of the streetlights that showed through a small slit where she had left the drapes open slightly. Reaching for the lamp switch, she turned it on and sat up. It took a moment for her to realize where she was. She sighed deeply and looked around the room. Standing up from the bed, she walked to the dresser as she said, "I'm coming, Mara. I'm coming."

Opening her luggage, she gathered her toiletries and walked into the bathroom. Turning on the shower, she removed her clothing and stepped inside. "At least the shower works," she thought as she stood under the soft stream of hot water. Already she missed home. She missed the comforts of her apartment. Was it that, or was it that she was simply tired of being alone all the time? Trips such as this would be more pleasant having someone significant to share them with.

When she was finished, she stepped from the shower, reached for a towel, and thought, "Life's an adventure! Don't be such a spoiled American." Drying herself quickly, she wrapped her wet hair in a towel, then slipped into her robe. After drying her hair and dressing, she telephoned the front desk and asked about the hotel's restaurant. The clerk told her it was open and asked if she wished for him to reserve her a table and if she would be dining alone. She told him that she would be having dinner in the hotel and that no one was joining her, and so he agreed to reserve a table for her. Taking her briefcase, she left the room and walked down the hallway to the elevators.

Before Tess had left her room, the telephone rang in 806. The shrill sound broke Ivan's peaceful meditation where he lay on the bed with his eyes closed. Taking a deep breath, he reached for the receiver and answered, "Hello?"

"Good evening, sir. Miss Fordel is on her way to the dining room."

"Alone?"

"Yes, sir. So she said."

"Thank you," Ivan answered, then hung up. He rose from the bed, walked to the door, and carefully opened it. He looked out into the hall and saw Tess push the elevator call button. She looked different now that she had rested. She stood straighter after sleeping, and that gave her the appearance of confidence. She stood there patiently waiting, wearing an ankle-length dress of wine-toned soft wool, but no coat; obviously, she did not plan to leave the hotel. Ivan noticed she carried her briefcase, and he was curious to know what was in it.

She turned slightly, and he viewed her from the front where he noticed a slit from the hem of her dress, moving up the front and stopping above the knee. The front of the dress buttoned down to the waist. She left the two top buttons open, revealing an acceptable amount of cleavage, but perhaps she should not have left it that way because she was not in America.

Although she had already passed, her perfume lingered in the air. As he closed the door, it wafted its way inside his room. He smiled. Brushing his hair smooth with his hands, he reached for his suit jacket and put it on. He then left his room and headed downstairs to the dining room.

Exiting the elevator, she then walked through the lobby. She stopped at the front desk and asked where the dining room was. The clerk pointed in the direction she needed to go, and she smiled, thanked him, then walked on. The other elevator doors opened and Ivan exited. Making a brief stop at the front desk, he slid payment for the call to the front desk clerk, who raised his eyebrows and gave a cunning smile. Then Ivan went straight to the dining room, for he frequented the Metropol and knew exactly where the dining room was.

Once at the restaurant's entrance, Ivan paused before he entered; he waited for the maître d' to seat Tess before seating him. Watching her from the entrance, he noticed that when she walked through the dining room, every man there turned and smiled at her.

"Men from Belgrade," she thought. Smiling, but looking past them all, she walked by them as they turned and watched her from the back. Laughing quietly, she sat at a table near the windows. After a few moments, the men turned back to their conversations, although periodically they turned to look at her.

Having watched as she made her way through the dining room, Ivan noticed the reactions of the other men. He imagined they fantasized about the possibility of being with her as some men will do. He, too, smiled, and enjoyed her walk as much as they had. When the waiter approached, he requested a table directly in her view, but two tables away.

She did not notice him as he sat, although his eyes never left her. She was busy looking through her briefcase for the papers about Mara. Finding them, she pulled them out. She closed the case, and set it on the floor next to her chair, as the waiter handed her a menu written in Cyrillic, then he walked away.

"I wish I were at a diner with pictures on the menu," she thought, then laughed to herself.

The waiter heard her laughing and returned to the table. Smiling at her, he looked back and forth from her eyes to her breasts. As she helplessly looked up at him, he immediately understood the problem and went on to describe the items on the menu in English. She smiled and was grateful that he understood, even if he were looking straight down her dress.

She never thought about bringing a phrase book with her, though she would buy one before she left Belgrade. Her only concern was finding Mara, and with that thought, her expression became serious as she listened to the waiter. Not being that hungry, she heard him mention an appetizing salad. She ordered it, requested a cup of tea, then the waiter left.

She picked up the dossier on Mara and studied the information. Engrossed in her notes, she still did not notice Ivan, although he watched her. He also watched the men in the room as they periodically looked at her. Without realizing it, his expression was stern toward them. They noticed his obvious attraction to her and, considering he was the only man alone in the room, they smiled, knowing he would get her.

Unaware of their macho games, Tess continued reading. But when the waiter brought her tea, he winked at her and motioned in Ivan's direction. She frowned slightly at him as he turned and walked back into the service hall that led to the kitchen. Watching him walk away, she had no idea what he meant by his motion. Curious to figure it out, she then looked around for what he had motioned to. She slowly observed everything and everyone as her eyes panned the room, but she stopped searching when her gaze found Ivan. He smiled slightly at her when he saw her take a small gasp. That must have been what the waiter meant by his gesture.

She turned to look out the window. "He is the most handsome man in the room," she thought. No. He was definitely the most handsome man she had ever seen. "This is not what I need right now," she thought.

Looking back at him, this time he smiled seductively at her. He expected her to look back at him and to notice him. Lowering her gaze to her papers, she recorded a mental photograph of him. She would definitely include him in the book she would write about her trip to Yugoslavia.

She tried to concentrate on the papers in her hand, but still strained to listen to him as he spoke quietly to the same waiter. She peeked at them over the tops of her papers, and saw the waiter approaching, as she thought, "Oh, here it comes, the dinner proposition, and then, of course, the love making proposition."

Playing dumb, she smiled as the waiter leaned down toward her. Pointing discreetly toward the handsome man two tables away, he whispered in her ear, "The gentleman at that table would be honored if he could join you for dinner. That is, if you are not meeting anyone."

She looked directly at Ivan as the waiter had relayed his message. Ivan smiled politely while waiting for her answer. She displayed no emotion as she thought of what to say. This man was too handsome for her to be anxious about. "He would be so easy to fall in love with," she thought, because she felt that was what had just happened. Then ignoring what she felt, she thought, "Honored? Aha."

Smiling at the waiter, she answered, "You may tell the gentleman that I am not meeting anyone and, if he desires, he may join me."

Feeling as if he were the supreme matchmaker, the waiter puffed out his chest and returned to Ivan, who patiently waited for acceptance or rejection of his offer. Smiling triumphantly at Ivan, the waiter whispered Tess' response as if it were his personal victory; all the while Ivan smiled seductively at Tess as his gaze never left her.

"Let's see how this Yugoslavian man attempts to seduce a woman," she thought as she motioned to the free seat across from her.

As Ivan stood and began his approach, she examined him. He was impeccably dressed in what she surmised to be an Italian tailored suit of fine black wool, a small collared, silk-knit, polo-styled sweater in deep blood red, and Italian loafers in black leather. His chestnut-toned hair was smoothly brushed back away from his face. As he walked, she noticed subtle hints of golden highlights woven amongst the waves of darker strands. This made her imagine that he spent much time outside.

Despite her observation detecting a slightly dangerous aura of mystery about him, past his distinct and refined facial features, there was something of extreme kindness about him. And though she should have been frightened of him, fear was the last emotion he roused in her. Without having yet met him, something about him made her feel secure, but why, she did not know.

As he neared, she noticed his sensuous lips that continued smiling during his approach. He was tall, about six-feet-four she guessed, and with every step nearer, the more handsome he became. Though she noticed all of this in a single glance, it was his eyes that held her captive. His hazel gaze did not waver from hers. It was obvious that he pondered questions about her that showed in his eyes of green and compassionate brown with their soft, sable-hued lashes.

Smiling as he reached the table, she looked at the chair across from her, then back at him.

He did not sit. Instead, he stood next to her, looking at her as he extended his hand in greeting. Not knowing if she spoke the native language, he introduced himself in Serbian. He then, suggestively, insinuated how they would spend the rest of their evening, which he insisted would last into following afternoon. And all the while he spoke, he gazed seductively into her eyes while he scrutinized her to gauge her response.

Slightly embarrassed, she smiled as he withdrew his hand. "Oh my, what did I expect?" she whispered, and stifled a laughed, wondering what he had said. "I'm sorry. I'm not laughing at you, only at myself. I don't understand a word you said, but perhaps you have no idea what I'm saying either. So, this should be a very interesting dinner."

Ivan smiled at her because he did not know if she understood what he had said, or if she were embarrassed by it, or worse, insulted. Hearing her admit that she did not know Serbian, he was happy that she did not understand his forward introduction. Up close, there was something special about her, and he would never have wanted to embarrass or insult her. Then with a slight, but beautiful, Eastern European accent, he translated his words into English, but changed them from their original forwardness.

"Forgive me for presuming that you speak the native language. I said, 'Thank you for allowing me to join you. I was dining alone and could not help noticing you, as did every other man in the room. But I am the fortunate one, for I am privileged to share your company.'" He paused and extended his hand to her again.

She had stopped laughing and smiled as she gave him her hand. She heard more sincerity in his voice than she had expected.

"Allow me to introduce myself. I am Ivan Đurić," he said, then he bent over, and kissed her hand.

The touch of his soft, warm lips forced her to smile as she looked away to the empty chair across from her. "So you are Serbian?" she asked as she looked back at him.

He straightened up quickly, and his expression questioned her comment. "And what makes you think that, because of where we are?"

"Just a bad guess," she answered, sensing that she had offended him.

He smiled and let her hand go, then he sat across the table from her. Shaking his head slightly, he ignored her question regarding his nationality, but instead he asked, "What is the name of my beautiful dinner companion?"

"Tess Fordel."

"What is Miss Tess Fordel doing in Belgrade? It is *Miss*, isn't it?" he asked.

"Yes. It is Miss. And what am I doing in Belgrade?" She shrugged. "Well, I don't know exactly. I should be in Sarajevo this evening."

He was silent. She presented three supporting facts to link her to the Serbs: her appearance, her native language, and her destination. He frowned, then asked, "And what would you be doing in Sarajevo? Do you have business there? In case you don't know, there is a war going on in Bosnia."

Nodding, she thought of the two-day delay she now faced. She glanced down to the papers in front of her, then back at him. "Yes, I know, and yes, I do have business there."

"This doesn't frighten you?"

"Yes, it does, but there's something I need to take care of there. If it weren't for the train being delayed for two days, I would already be there, but something always has to happen," she said, glancing at her papers again.

Looking at the papers, then back at her, he asked, "Is this delay causing many problems?"

"Not really, I guess. I don't know what I'll find when I get there. I don't even know if the person I'm looking for is there," she said, then looked at him. Although her answers superficially implicated her, her attitude was wrong. Still, it could be an act to mislead any opposition.

"Why do you keep looking at those papers? Have they something to do with your upset over the train?" he asked.

"Yes, they do," she said, and to his shock, she handed him the papers. "Do you see the person's name at the top of the page? I'm searching for that child and I haven't any idea what she looks like. I only know where she once lived. I don't even know if she's in Sarajevo anymore. Possibly—"

She stopped, almost unable to continue. He studied her disposition and he noticed the change in her voice when she continued.

"Possibly, she's dead." Her eyes misted as she turned away to look out the window. It had started to snow and, smiling slightly, she said, "It's snowing. How pretty."

Seeing Mara's name, Ivan frowned. This was the final fact that linked her to the rumor. He immediately looked around the room. His eyes searched for anyone new that had entered or had observed them. All he saw were the same faces. It was as though he were invisible. Feeling temporarily safe, he quickly read the papers as she continued watching the falling snow. He found nothing in their contents that linked her to the war, except her search for Mara, but what was in her briefcase? Perhaps other information was inside it.

"Why do you search for this little girl? Are you a relative?" he asked, setting the papers down in front of her.

"No," she answered.

"What do you want with her?"

"You wouldn't believe me if I told you."

She roused his interest. He needed to know the truth, so he continued prompting her for answers as he said with a smile, "Maybe I would."

"Do you work for the government?" she asked.

"No, but perhaps I could help you find her."

She hesitated, looked at him carefully, then asked, "Do you know her or her family?"

He paused before answering. Her directness was unexpected and this threw him momentarily. She had caught him off guard, though he masked his uneasiness with a shrug, and said, "No. I don't know this child. Certainly the name Jovanović is common in this country, and probably there is more than one Mara Jovanović." He paused. "Why do you seek this child?

If she is not a relative, why search for her?"

"You wouldn't believe me." She shook her head. "I barely believe myself sometimes."

He found her comment strange, and he could only surmise that if she were the spy, she appeared to dislike what she was doing. Perhaps she was disgusted and reconsidered what she did? If so, then perhaps she would be willing to change sides, or perhaps this was all an act for his behalf.

Leaning closer to her, he smiled and said, "Perhaps I would understand. We'll never know if you don't tell me, and it certainly can't hurt, can it?"

She sat back, glanced at the papers, then at him. His curiosity intrigued her. "I guess not. I am the sponsor of an educational grant program called The Children's Writing Foundation and—" She stopped, not knowing exactly how to explain what she was doing there.

Hearing this, he stared in shock. He knew that foundation name. If she were who she said she was, then she was the person he had written to for Mara. This he had not expected. Sergej only obtained her name a few hours prior to her arrival in Belgrade. They did not have time to get any information on her, so he had no idea who she was before now.

"Please continue," he said as he noticed her somewhat helpless gaze.

"Well, it's a foundation that sponsors college educations for underprivileged children. Although it's called The Children's Writing Foundation, they don't have to pursue writing careers. They can study whatever they want. I named the foundation this because the children write an original story and the most creative story wins. The little girl I'm searching for entered the competition and has won an award for the story she wrote and, well, I'm here to see that she gets it," she said as she looked straight at him and witnessed his disbelief.

He could not get a grasp on her. This made no sense to him. His entire body questioned her statement. Out of the many entries the Foundation must have received, it was quite uncanny that Mara's was the one to win. Even though he allowed Mara to write her story and letter the way she chose, she did not need money to get out of Sarajevo. Ivan could have moved her and her family at any time from the war zone, although Mara was unaware of this. Mara's family, like many others, chose to stay put and stay in control of their homesteads. But after Mara's brother was killed, Mara wanted everyone she loved to be safe and away from the fighting.

"What?" he asked.

"See? I told you that you wouldn't believe me."

He quickly corrected his impulsive comment. "No. I believe you, but I don't understand what you mean by award. Is it a certificate, or is it a trophy? What is this award and why are you bringing it to her? What is it you do that you come here from America to bring an award? Sponsors of foundations don't usually go to so much trouble. They pay people to do these things for them, don't they?"

Although she had leaned closer to him when she was speaking, she now sat back and stared at him. His intuition shocked her. "How do you know I'm from America?" she asked.

"I travel to America frequently. Besides, you have no obvious accent that links you to any Eastern or Western European country, or Australia, or any other British speaking country. Therefore, you must be American. Or perhaps I'm wrong. You could be from Canada, but I doubt it."

Now she was the one to pause before answering. She looked deeply into his eyes as they questioned her, and now many questions formed in her mind about him.

"You know, not too long ago I read a paragraph in a travel book on Yugoslavia, about Belgrade to be exact. This book said for women to beware of men from Belgrade. It warned not to walk down the street alone. It read, and I quote, 'Men from Belgrade can be persistent, rude, and somewhat dangerous.' And now I cannot help feeling that you want something from me. Is there something specific you seek by asking me to join you for dinner, Mr. Đurić?"

Her blank expression patiently waited for his imminent response. He was shocked at her perceptiveness and, as he sat there looking back at her, he debated how to answer her question. Giving forth a guilty smile, he sighed.

When he did not answer immediately, she felt there was something he wanted from her. Perhaps he was a government official investigating Americans. That was something she did not need. Perhaps he was just a man who made love to as many women as he could sway to his will. From his blatant handsomeness, getting any woman he wanted did not appear difficult for him.

Wondering what she was thinking, Ivan still did not respond, he only waited to see what she would do. Opening her briefcase, she placed the papers inside, shut the lid, then snapped the locks closed. Folding her napkin, she placed it on the table and stood up.

Seeing her standing with her briefcase in hand, he panicked. In a most seductive tone, and with alluring eloquence, he attempted to apologize, as he said, "Forgive me if I offended you. Please, don't leave. I won't ask any more questions. I'll sit here quietly and admire you."

"I guess it's true that it's an international flaw in men to flatter their way out of holes they've dug for themselves. I'll tell you something, Mr. Đurić, compliments don't work on all women. So, you can put your seductive glances away, because they don't work either!"

Immediately, Ivan's smile dissolved. As she stepped away from the table, he again attempted to persuade her, as he said, "Please stay. What about dinner? You agreed that I could join for dinner, didn't you?"

"Don't forget, I'm American. And most Europeans believe that Americans never say what they mean. Enjoy dinner by yourself, or maybe you can go in the bar and pick up a pleasing Serbian girl. Perhaps they won't mind your interrogation, and will fall for your typical seduction attempts," she said, then smiled, turned, and walked toward the dining room's entrance.

Ivan stood up, attempting to show respect for her, but all he could do was watch her walk away. As she exited the room, every man watched her. Once she was out of sight, they turned their attention to Ivan, who stood staring at the entrance to the dining room as if there was a chance that she would return. Then letting go a deep breath, and shaking his head, he sat back down.

Signaling for the waiter, he asked him for her bill. The waiter informed him that she had just signed for it at the front desk on her way back to her room, as she asked to have her dinner brought there instead. Then the waiter leaned closer to him and said in a private tone, "Don't worry, my friend. Tomorrow is another day," he then walked away.

Slightly discouraged, Ivan stood. Reaching into his pocket, he slipped money on the table as a tip. Then slowly walking from the dining room, he stopped at the front desk and asked about Tess. The clerk told him that she had indeed returned to her room. He reminded the clerk to inform him the next time she left, or requested anything.

The clerk nodded when Ivan slid more money across the desk to him. "The next time I see Miss Fordel, or she calls, I will ring your room, Mr. Đurić," the clerk answered, donning a large smile as he stuffed the money into his trouser pocket.

Ivan walked to the elevators and went upstairs. Pausing outside Tess' door, he felt his persistent questions truly offended her. Even if she were a spy, she was still a woman, and he knew that he had used the wrong approach. He liked her style. She was strong and precise about her intentions. She differed from other women he knew. She was strong, but not pushy about what she wanted. Once provoked, she walked away to avoid further confrontation. This made him wonder if possibly she was exactly who she said she was. And even though he longed to believe it, he could not imagine any American going to this much trouble to find a child in a faraway land.

With a final glance toward her door, Ivan unlocked his own and walked inside. Not turning on the lights, he hung his jacket in the closet. He then lay on the bed and thought about her. If she were not the spy, she was definitely the type of woman he would want to spend time with, serious and private time. That thought pleased him as he remembered her sweet smiles before he angered her and caused her departure. As he lay there, he thought about her until his eyes eventually closed.

Now there was a new twist to the game. What if she really *was* the same person from the Foundation? What if she really *was* there to give Mara the award money? If so, she was in danger. He could not allow her to get involved in this war; it would not be fair. Conversely, her presence there gave credence to the rumor of the spy. The fact that his informant knew she was arriving in Belgrade proved that too many people knew she was there, and that was extremely dangerous for them both.

In the back of his mind, he hoped Tess was there to find Mara on behalf of her foundation and not to ultimately identify him. Ivan knew eventually he would discover the truth and, with that thought, he finally slept.

CHAPTER NINE

The telephone rang loudly, waking Ivan abruptly from what was a beautiful dream about Tess. With his eyes still closed, he reached for the receiver. His voice strained as he cleared his throat and answered the call. "Hello."

It was the front desk clerk. "I am sorry to wake you, Mr. Đurić."

"Yes," Ivan answered.

"Miss Fordel has ordered room service. Her breakfast should be delivered within thirty minutes. Shall I have the waiter knock on your door first? Perhaps you would like to deliver it?" the clerk suggested.

Running his hand through his hair, Ivan then reached for his watch on the bed stand. Looking at the time, he thought for a moment. "Yes. That is good. Have her cart brought to my room, but not before thirty minutes," he said, then he hung up the telephone.

He quickly showered, shaved, and dressed. Somehow, he would apologize and convince her to spend the day with him. He did not know how he would achieve this; he only knew that he would, no matter what it took. This time he would be a less suspicious and more convincing liar, if lying were required.

While waiting for room service, he made several telephone calls. The first of which was to Sergej, whom he instructed to be at the hotel within twenty minutes and be ready to search Tess' room should he be successful in convincing her to spend the day with him. During the last call, he heard a knock at his door. Concluding his conversation, he walked to the door and opened it to see a waiter standing outside Tess' room with a room service cart.

"Just a moment," he said.

Stepping back into his room, he slid into his suit jacket, then his coat. Walking out into the hall, he closed his room door, then handed the waiter a tip. After the waiter entered the elevator, Ivan lifted the dome to her breakfast. She had ordered soft boiled eggs, toast, and fresh fruit. Off to the side was a pot of coffee and a small pitcher of cream. Placing the dome back down, he gently knocked on Tess' door.

"Yes?" He heard her say through the door.

"It is room service, Miss," he answered, then looked through the peep-hole. Although they were designed for viewing to the outside, from the right angle, the curve of the glass allowed an outsider to see blurred movement from within. He thought he saw a nude figure walk past the door. The image was not focused, but what he imagined he saw was enough to make him take a deep breath.

"Just a minute, please," she answered as she slipped into her robe.

Nervous as to the outcome of this encounter, he did not know what to expect as he waited for her to open the door. What would her reaction be when she saw him with her breakfast? He heard the door unlock, then it opened. As he glanced down, waiting for the door to promptly slam in his face, he did not realize it, but he was holding his breath. After a few seconds, he noticed that she did not even look at him. Pulling the door open, she was already walking back into the room. He started to breathe again and broke a gentle smile as he watched her.

She wore a long black cashmere robe and her hair was loosely pinned back and away from her face. Her perfume, powders, and lotions lightly scented the air. These attributes changed the appearance of the room, telling all who entered that a woman was there. These were all the delicate details lacking in his room and in his life. And, for a moment, he fantasized about her turning around and being happy to see him.

"Please leave the cart inside the door, if you will," she said as she walked to retrieve her purse from the small table near the window. As requested, he pushed the cart inside and went to close the door. Walking back toward him, she looked inside her purse as she asked, "Do you prefer dinars or dollars?"

He did not answer; he only admired her as he stood watching her from the entrance. As she neared him, she noticed his polished boots and, just then, she realized he was not a waiter. Her gaze slowly moved up his handsomely clad body until their eyes met. Giving a weakened sigh, her wallet dropped back into her purse, and the entire mood in the room changed. Not knowing what to say, Ivan only looked at her.

She shook her head at him. "I get it. You work here. Did you come up here for the tip?" She pulled her wallet back out from her purse. "Here, take it all, then please leave," she said, tossing it at him.

He caught the wallet, but when it hit his chest, the change compartment opened. Coins scattered in all directions, clanking as they hit the wall and each other on their journey to the floor. Tossing her purse on the bed, she turned, walked to the window, and waited for him to leave.

His romantic vision was instantly spoiled. His smile straightened as he stood there looking at her. But what could he realistically expect? The way they parted the previous evening was not exactly cordial, and though he should have considered her gesture selfish, arrogant, and typically American, somehow he understood, and knew he was to blame. He had not known what to expect, but felt he got what he deserved. He somehow knew she did not do it to be selfish, arrogant, or typically anything. Her reaction was just feminine, which he told himself was justified. Just then, he felt that perhaps he frightened her, but that was not his intention.

Without saying a word, Ivan bent down and picked up the coins. Placing them back into the wallet's change compartment, he straightened up and walked to her. Standing at her side, he held the wallet out to her.

She did not look at him, nor did she take the wallet from him. She only verbalized part of the warning from the previous evening as she whispered, "Persistent, the book was right."

"At least she's not calling me rude and dangerous as well," he thought. Then in a yielding and rejected tone he said, "I'm sorry about last night, and I'm sorry that I came here now."

She did not acknowledge his apology. So, he attempted to capture her attention by holding her wallet closer to her as he said, "I only wanted to—" He stopped. Seeing her now, he did not know what to say. When she did not look at him, what could he say that would be appropriate?

"Only wanted to what? To question me more? Is that it, Mr. Đurić." She paused briefly. "If that is your name," she said as she walked back toward the door.

This was the only time he used his real name with a stranger since the war began and she questioned its validity. When he used aliases, people questioned their validity also. How stupid was life. It did not pay to be honest, nor did it pay to be dishonest. Small facts like these made life annoying. Ignoring this thought, Ivan placed the wallet on the bed next to her purse and walked after her.

Having stopped at the cart, she lifted the dome to see her breakfast. Making a faint, displeased vocal gesture, she lowered the dome. She was not hungry after seeing him, but was it because of his persistence, or was it because she was attracted to him? She knew the answer; his persistence was not the reason, because she found it hard to think of anything except him since they had met.

"I did not come here to question you. I only wanted to see you again before I left. It's not every day I meet an intelligent and beautiful woman such—"

"Please stop with the compliments. They won't get you anywhere. I thought I made that clear last night," she said, interrupting him as she shook her head, then added in a whisper to herself, "The book was right."

He was a tolerant man, but his patience was wearing thin. Regardless that he wished he could turn back the clock, and start over from when he first approached her table the previous evening, he knew that was impossible. He now knew that she could provoke him, a fact he rather enjoyed. He always enjoyed lively women and this, though somewhat irritating, was nonetheless stimulating. It was much more enjoyable than being with men all the time and much more pleasing on the eyes, even if not on the temperament. She was a puzzle to him, and he was determined to figure her out.

Looking down at her, he attempted to use his resolve to provoke her as she had provoked him. Perhaps through provocation, there would be a neutral point where they could actually smile and break through their suspicions. This thought made his present fierce determination turn into a more passionate resolve.

"The book was not right. Not all men from Belgrade are rude, persistent, or dangerous. And, possibly, if you allow me a second chance, I can show you the truth about men from Belgrade." He paused, stepped closer to her, and added, "At least about one man from Belgrade." With an expectant smile, he continued looking at her.

Turning toward him, she was less angry, but still worried, and he could see it in her expression. "Not persistent? What do you call how you are now? Please tell me, Mr. Đurić," she said, and looked into his eyes as she waited for his answer.

He was suddenly angered by her cool tone. He briefly questioned that perhaps she did not like men. Fervently dismissing that idea, his demeanor changed, and, suddenly, he was like a little boy not getting his way. "If a man doesn't pursue a woman, how does he get to spend time with her?

How do American men get to spend time with the women they like if they don't pursue them? Please tell me! I'm not American! Please enlighten me, because you appear to have all the answers."

With his hands on his hips, Ivan turned away from her. He looked around the room and his intolerance of the situation showed. He could not understand it. He never had so much trouble with a woman before. But then, as he turned back and looked at her, there was something different about her, something he could not identify—a certain determination surrounded her as if for protection. Though this attitude made him suspicious, it also provoked in him a protective feeling for her.

Looking up at him, Tess could see he was seriously upset; she imagined that this was beyond his normal game. Looking at him now, she saw an unusual, but gentle, strength in his eyes. Despite that he had taken the time to see her again, he appeared preoccupied with situations beyond his control. She quickly rethought the situation: persistent, suspicious, or determined? Or was he only lonely, as lonely as she was? She could not decide. Regardless of the previous evening, or his presence in her room just then, there was no reason to be cruel.

"Why don't you tell me what you want? Perhaps that's a better way to start," she said in a softer tone, attempting to lift his angst. She smiled at him, though smiling at him was not difficult; his attractiveness made it hard not to.

Taking a deep breath, Ivan ran his right hand through his hair. This made her smile more as she recognized this was a sign of his frustration in not knowing how to handle her. That simple gesture briefly melted her suspicions. He then noticed her smiling at him and saw that the neutral point was now. From her comment, she allowed him the second chance he had requested. That meant she possibly liked him. It also meant he had to listen carefully to everything she said. Whether she knew it or not, she told the truth when she spoke. It was only a matter of analyzing her words and her tone.

"I wanted to ask you if I could show you Belgrade," he said as he looked at her and smiled.

"I thought you said you were leaving," she said as her smile turned innocent and confused.

"I have business in Budapešt, but I don't have to be there today. I was going to leave today if you refused me the privilege of your company. You said you had two days until your train leaves, so I postponed my departure hoping that you would say yes. I thought you might like to see some of what there is to see in Belgrade." He paused briefly. "From an insider's point of view. You know," he paused longer for emphasis, then added, "from a man from Belgrade's point of view. But if you would rather not, I'll leave. It is obvious that you are already involved with another man back in America and my persistence, as you called it, makes you uncomfortable. It was foolish for me to think that a woman as—"

He hesitated, wanting to choose a word that would not be too flattering. In the back of his mind, he knew he had to get her out of that room. Two of his men, Sergej and Alek, waited to search her room for information. Yet, in truth, he wanted to spend the day with her. He wanted to know her because she intrigued him. Because of that, he knew he would enjoy finding the answers to the many questions about her that flew around in his head.

"Well, a woman as *nice* as you would be waiting for a man to come along," he concluded.

"I see. I've gone from intelligent and beautiful to nice. Thank you!"

Again, she provoked him. He felt that no matter what he said, or how he said it, she would say the opposite. And again, his frustration showed. "Are all American women so difficult? I can't win with you, can I?" he asked.

"Win? Women around the world are all alike. If you wish to take them out, it is customary that you ask them, not insinuate your desire to do so," she said. Then she walked past him to the closet and retrieved a dress. Without looking at him, she walked into the bathroom and closed the door, leaving him alone to think about what she had said.

She was correct. He had not asked, he only said that he wanted to ask. By not asking, he surmised her answer to be no and, with that, he had made the decision for her. Again, she spoke the truth, but this time she led him to what she wanted, and that was to spend the day with him. Realizing this, Ivan smiled. She had seduced the great seducer. He laughed silently and shook his head. She was no less sly than he.

At this point, he would normally want to tease her by opening, then slamming the door to pretend that he had left. He was curious to see if she would come after him. But he imagined that her well-mannered character would disallow her from pursuing him. Remembering that she said her purpose was finding Mara to give her the winning award, he knew if that purpose was real, she would let him leave. Then she would head out to Sarajevo on her own, but he knew she would never make it alive, that was. That thought frightened him. Was it bravery or stupidity? He could not figure it out, and he did not have time for games with her.

Determined to get his way, he stepped to the bathroom door, knocked lightly, and asked, "Miss Fordel, may I please show you Belgrade? I promise to show you the very best Belgrade has to offer. Would you honor me with your company? Please, say yes."

"Under one condition," she said from inside the bathroom.

"And that is?" he asked as he leaned closer to the door. With her statement, she agreed, but he could not imagine what that one condition could be.

"That you stop calling me, Miss Fordel," she answered, then she was silent.

Hearing her turning the door handle, he quickly stepped back. Then the door opened and, seeing her dressed, he was again taken aback by her beauty, and he stared at her.

"Please, call me Tess and, if you permit me, I will call you Ivan, not Mr. Đurić."

He smiled as he examined her standing there in her black dress of soft wool that hugged her form with precision. His eyes followed the front slit from its top to its hem and back up again as his gaze moved over her body, eventually returning to look in her eyes.

Her hair hung behind her shoulders in soft cascading waves. Taking a deep breath, he could smell her perfume: spiced and delicate, like the scent of sandalwood and flowers in the breeze after a cooling spring rain, just as the sun would begin to warm their petals.

"Will that work, Ivan? Or is it, Mr. Đurić?"

"It is Ivan, Tess," he answered in a slight whisper, then donned a large conspirator's smile.

"Good. Shall we go?"

"What about your breakfast?" he asked as he stepped aside and looked at the cart.

"I'd rather spend time with you than eat cold food."

He smiled at her comment. She had gotten him to do exactly what she wanted, and he was as happy as a schoolboy with his first crush. He walked to the door, opened it, and pushed the cart into the hall. Stepping back inside, he removed a long black shearling coat from the closet. Holding it out for her, she turned and slid her arms backward into it as he pulled it up onto her shoulders. She walked to the bed and put her wallet back into her purse. He walked to the dresser, retrieved her gloves and scarf, and handed them to her. Extending his arm to her, she gladly accepted it, then he walked her to the door.

She suddenly stopped. "Hold on. I forgot something," she said as she slipped her arm from his. Walking back into the room, she opened her briefcase and pulled out her laptop computer.

He watched her from the doorway as she removed a disc from it and placed it in her purse. She then folded the papers on Mara from the previous night and placed them inside her purse next to the disc. Closing and locking her briefcase, she placed it inside a drawer, closed the drawer, then returned to his side.

"What is that you took out of your laptop?" he asked.

"It's a disc. On it are several novels I'm working on and information about the child I showed you last night. I have no safe place to keep it. If any of this information was lost, I don't know what I'd do," she answered.

"Novels? You're an author? How intelligent," he said, wanting to compliment her in an unobvious way, a way her suspicions would allow. Smiling at her, he gently folded her arm through his as it was before.

"Yes. I'm an author," she answered, and smiled back at him.

They then left the room. He closed the door behind them and walked her to the elevators, where he pressed the elevator call button, and they waited.

In a moment of absolute quiet, Ivan leaned slightly down toward her. As his lips neared her ear, he whispered, "And you are beautiful also." Then he stood straight and looked ahead as though he had not uttered a word. Even though she smiled, in the back of his mind, he wanted to know exactly what information about Mara was on the disc she had placed in her purse.

The elevator doors opened and they stepped inside. Riding down to the lobby, he was silent, and she was the first to speak. Her words told him that she knew exactly what he was up to, but she did not appear to mind.

"So, Ivan, are you always this quiet when you get your way?" she asked.

Turning to her, he grinned. The tender look in her eyes stifled his first response. Yet, to further confuse the situation, when he looked into her eyes, he saw no menace, only complete attention to him. That look made him think that if he were actually getting his way, she would be in his arms. He would be kissing her, not just looking at her, but he shook that thought from his mind.

"I was thinking of where to take you first. I don't know about you, but I'm hungry. Let's go to breakfast. Somewhere out of the hotel. Would you like that?" he asked.

She smiled and nodded.

The elevator doors opened, and he placed his arm around her shoulder as he escorted her through the lobby. Several of the same men from the dining room smiled at Ivan when they saw them together; they envied him. Despite the scene they played the previous evening, these men surmised Ivan must have been with her that past evening, and from his expression, it must have been pleasurable.

Ivan ignored all the guests in the lobby except for Sergej and Alek. He glanced sideways at them and nodded. They pretended not to see, though he knew they saw him. They were waiting to see him leave with a woman. If Ivan left alone, they knew it was not safe for them to go to Tess' room. If Ivan left with a woman, it would be Tess, so they knew all was clear.

Sergej watched Ivan walk past with his arm around Tess' shoulders as he smiled brightly and spoke to her. Sergej thought Ivan had exaggerated when he had said how much more attractive she was than their informant's vague description. When Sergej looked at Ivan, he saw Ivan was not pretending to be happy. Ivan enjoyed himself as he walked with Tess. Though Sergej had not met her, he doubted that she was the spy, if there was a spy to begin with. Something about Tess did not fit the profile. Regardless that he could not pinpoint what that something was, he wondered if Ivan felt the same thing, or if Ivan would persist in his investigation.

Alek watched Ivan and Tess walk by. He smirked and commented, "Rough job he's got!" Sergej grinned, then they walked to the elevators.

Once Ivan and Tess were outside, the cold morning air surrounded them as he quickly placed her inside a taxi. It was an especially frosty morning. During the night, the snow had turned to freezing rain, and before sunrise, it turned back to snow, which caused a damp chill in the air. After giving the driver directions, Ivan then sat back and returned his arm to rest around her shoulder.

"It's a cold morning in Belgrade, but it will warm up as the day goes on," he said, and smiled at her.

She did not appear to mind the cold weather, but she came prepared with a warm coat. New York was cold in the winter, so this was nothing for her; however, her coat would have to stay in Belgrade if Ivan decided to take her to Sarajevo. All he needed was for someone to see her in something expensive, even as simple as it was. That would identify her as an outsider, and that would definitely get them killed. No. He would have to get her something else to wear should they go, but that could wait until later.

He then felt her give a small shiver and automatically, he moved his hand up and down her arm attempting to keep her warm. "We're going to a restaurant in Skadarlija, which is Old Belgrade. I hope you will like it. The area is like Montmartre in Paris and the food is very good. They don't serve breakfast at this restaurant, but the owner and I are good friends. When I'm in Belgrade, and I'm alone," he said, then gave a laugh, "which is always, I go there."

Pausing, he noticed her smiling at him, and her smile reflected complete trust in him. He enjoyed that and realized that he had not been granted any female companion's complete trust in the past. For a moment, he hoped she would always look at him that way.

"But today is special," he said.

"Why?" she asked.

"Because you are the first woman I will share my secret hideaway with." Smiling, he lifted her gloved hand to his lips, kissed it, then set it back down on his lap where he held it.

Though Tess did not know why, she felt strangely comfortable with Ivan, and that could only make the day more pleasurable.

CHAPTER TEN

After a short drive, they arrived at a quaint restaurant and, as promised, the area was like Montmartre. Quickly exiting the taxi, they hurried up a walkway and entered the front door of their destination.

The restaurant was empty, which proved to Tess that Ivan appreciated his privacy. Looking into the main dining room, the clerestory windows, the beamed ceiling, the highly polished wood floors, the fire burning in the fireplace, and the tables covered with crisply starched white cloths made guests feel welcome. This warm atmosphere was a wonderful invitation from the cold outside.

Ivan smiled and spoke with Jacek, the owner, as he approached them. From the hospitable tone of their conversation, it was obvious that Ivan did frequent this restaurant, and was well liked by the owner.

Jacek briskly shook Ivan's hand as he looked at Tess with an approving eye. "A new girlfriend? Very beautiful. An import?" he said in Serbian.

Ivan smiled, then answered in Serbian, "Yes, yes, and yes!"

Turning around, Jacek spoke loudly to two other men standing near the kitchen, then he turned back around. Ivan smiled at Tess, placed his arm around her, and introduced her to Jacek. "This is Tess," he said, then he turned to her. "Tess, this is Jacek, my friend, and the owner of this restaurant."

"It is my great pleasure to meet you, Tess," Jacek said, then extended his hand to her. She gave him her hand, then he kissed it, but when hearing Jacek's name, her smile straightened slightly.

Ivan noticed this change in her expression. As Jacek turned and spoke with several men on his staff, Ivan leaned toward her and quietly asked, "Are you alright?"

"I'm fine," she answered.

"Ivan is back!" Jacek said to two waiters, who stared at Tess as they greeted Ivan from the bar. Jacek returned his attention to Ivan and his new girlfriend. He gave a laugh. *"Vuk!"* he said in Serbian, which meant *wolf.*

66

Ivan laughed, but noticed Tess looking around the restaurant, as she obviously thought about something else. Then Jacek motioned for them to follow him. Ivan smiled at Tess, took her hand in his, then they walked silently behind Jacek. As they passed through the front of the dining room, Ivan noticed the reactions of the other employees. They turned to see Ivan's companion and they smiled at her as she walked by; they were shocked to see him with anyone for breakfast. Ivan looked proudly at them, but when he looked at Tess, he saw that she ignored everyone except for him, and he liked that.

Having noticed Tess looking out the windows, Jacek showed them to an intimate table with a view of the courtyard, not Ivan's usual table nestled in the corner near the fireplace. Ivan helped her with her coat, then pulled her chair from the table allowing her to sit. Removing his coat, he placed it next to hers and sat adjacent to her, but near to the corner so to be close to her.

The snow fell softly on the courtyard landscape, and Ivan noticed Tess watching a pair of birds pecking at the ground where the kitchen staff had thrown out yesterday's bread for them. He looked away when the waiter approached, then spoke with him in Serbian in a friendly tone; it was obvious they too were acquainted. The waiter took their order, then they talked for a few minutes more. Once the waiter left, Ivan turned his full attention to Tess.

"You didn't tell me where you live in America. I guess there wasn't enough time yesterday for the conversation to progress," he said, as his smile was somewhat embarrassed.

"I'm sorry about last night. I was tired, and I didn't mean to be defensive," she said.

"Yesterday is gone. We're starting over this morning, and this time, I'll try not to ask so many questions." Since he felt offensive the previous evening, he thought it was fitting that he began the conversation, and so he answered his question first, by saying, "I live in Belgrade. I was born here, but traveled around the country with my family as a child. So, I have seen much of what once was Yugoslavia."

"Is Belgrade your permanent home?" she asked.

"I have an apartment here, and other places."

"I live in Manhattan," she said.

"Manhattan, New York?" he asked.

"Is there really any other?" she answered, then smiled.

"Did you always live there? I ask because you don't have that typical New York accent, but there is a trace of an accent in your voice."

"I was born in Chicago," she answered.

"Ah, yes, that is what I hear, so you lived there when you were young."

"I lived outside the city the majority of my life. I moved into the city of Chicago about six years ago, then two years ago I moved to Manhattan."

"Then this weather is nothing for you. Chicago is like Siberia; all that wind." He shook just thinking about it.

"Have you been there?" she asked.

"Where? Chicago, New York, or did you mean Siberia?" he asked, smiling at her.

"Any of them."

"Siberia? Never. Yet, many times to Chicago and New York. But New York is a rough city, don't you think?"

"Yes and no. No one bothers me. There are so many people around there: fifteen million, billion, trillion, or something like that," she said, and laughed. And when she laughed, he laughed with her. "So what do you do for a living, Ivan?"

"I am an architect. Well, actually, an architectural engineer: design, structural, all of that," he answered.

The waiter approached their table. He set down two cups of coffee with sides of fresh cream and sugar. Then he winked at Ivan, who shook his head slightly at him.

Ivan turned to Tess, and asked, "Is coffee alright?"

"Perfect, thank you. So, does that include mechanical as well?"

"Yes. I travel a lot. And lately, I've been working on disaster recovery support, structural recovery, and demolition. Then after that, I get onto the rebuilding phase. People don't understand that you need to know how to raze a damaged building before you can safely determine how to rebuild it."

"It sounds very complicated and devastating."

"It can be, but even when it's devastating, it's exhilarating to see areas renewed."

"That's amazing," she said, and smiled to herself as if she would laugh.

"What's so funny?"

"Here I sit, almost halfway around the world, with a structural scientist, drinking coffee, and waiting for breakfast. Life is unpredictable," she said, then changed the subject. "You seem to be very good friends with the owner."

"The restaurant suffered from a fire about eight years ago, and I redesigned it to reflect what it originally looked like before Jacek owned it. I also modernized it, sort of a mix of old world and new, clean lines. Since Jacek and I were friends long before the fire, I took care of everything for him. I acted as his general contractor, and oversaw the entire project, while he ran his business from a nearby location."

"It's amazingly beautiful," she said, looking around the main dining room, then back at him.

"It did turn out well. Maybe that's why I feel so at home here," he commented.

"When I was young, I thought about becoming an architect. I didn't do it though. But what I really wanted to do was sing opera. I didn't do that either."

"Why not become an architect?" he asked as his attention focused on her.

"My mother told me that being an architect was a man's job, so I chose a softer profession. Regardless, something tells me that I wouldn't have made a very good one. As architects, I think, sometimes, not always, men are less emotional and much more practical."

"And singing?" he asked.

She shrugged. "I was quiet as a child and never told anyone about that. So now, I'm an author and I'm happy. I truly can't imagine doing anything else, but when it comes down to it, singing wasn't God's will for my life."

He smiled at her reverent logic. "Writing is a beautiful profession for a woman. I think it gives a woman control of her life in a very feminine way. That is, if that is her wish. We all have second thoughts. There are times I wish I did something other than what I do now," he said, momentarily thinking about his part in the war. Not wanting to show his true feelings, so not to worry her, he quickly dismissed those thoughts, and said, "But even when every job isn't what you expect, all in all, there is purpose behind what I do. There is great satisfaction in designing structures and in helping people recover and rebuild their lives."

"I would imagine so," she said.

"But in a way, you *are* an architect. You design stories. To me that is very complicated, because you deal with something intangible. You deal with words. Whereas, with a building, I deal with tangible items that science proves will work when put together. But to hold a novel together, well, *that* is tricky."

She smiled at his compliment, then asked, "Do you work for a company in Belgrade?"

"I work for myself and I am based in Belgrade. I do some work here, but mostly I work internationally. In the past five years and before the war, I finished several projects in both Chicago and Manhattan," he said. And though he was more than happy to talk about himself and his profession all day, he had many questions for her, so he changed the subject back to her. Smiling, he leaned closer to her and asked, "Tell me what you write about. Novels are fiction, right?"

"Yes, fiction. I think people would say my stories are mostly love stories, or better labeled romantic suspense."

"Love stories from personal experience?" he asked.

She laughed. "Well, that may not be the best way to describe what I write about. That might make them tragedies."

"Then where do your ideas come from?" he asked.

"I have a conversation with someone about something, and it creates a story in my head, or something happens, and I start writing about it. But there's always some love plot involved." She paused. "Well, almost always."

"Love is a major component of life," he said.

"I guess it is," she commented.

"Tell me the title of one of your novels," he said.

She paused and looked off into space. Then turning back to look at him, she answered, *"Sergo Romanoff and the Russian Circus."*

"Russians?" he asked, frowning, then smiling.

"Not only Russians, but KGB agents in a Russian circus."

"You're joking? Right?" he asked as he pulled back from her, astonished that she actually knew KGB agents infiltrated and traveled in circuses, and had for years. Moment by moment, she became more interesting.

"No joke," she answered.

"How do you know about this circus-KGB-agent business?"

"I have my ways of getting information," she said as her left eyebrow lifted slightly.

Her seductive posture stung him and, if he did not know better, he should have been suspicious. But before he jumped to conclusions, he questioned her further, saying, "And now you're going to tell me you've written a *spy* or *war* novel about men killing each other. I would have to see this to believe it!"

"Well, it's mostly about a Ukrainian man that falls in love with an American woman."

Now, Ivan's left eyebrow lifted. An eastern European man with an American woman, an idea he enjoyed. He released a short sigh and, momentarily, tried to imagine him and her as a couple. What would their life be like?

"Love." His left eyebrow jolted up briefly. "That's a most difficult subject. War is much easier to deal with than love," he said.

"I guess it can be, but I do discuss the push for the continued spread of Communism. So, it's not all passionate kisses in the moonlight."

He found her attitude shocking in how she tossed love and war about as if they were synonymous. But, considering the circumstances, he preferred to concentrate on aspects of her writing other than war, as he asked, "Really? But there must be *some* passionate kisses in the moonlight."

"Well, to quote a very wise man I know, '*Love is a major component of life,*'" she said, paying homage to his previous statement, then she smiled at him.

"An American woman writing about Communism. And what's so interesting about Communism?" he asked.

She shrugged. "To some it's a concept, just as to some love is a concept," she answered, then she was strangely silent.

"Love," he whispered again.

"I think that's the problem with Capitalists," she said.

"What? Love is their problem?" he asked.

"The fact that they don't consider it and don't strive for it is the problem. At its deepest core, love is what the world consists of. True love is the only prize worth pursuing. It's the only thing worth fighting for, the only thing worth dying for," she said.

He smiled at her ideas. She was more romantic than he had imagined, but he changed the subject, as he asked, "Will you write about this trip?"

"Yes, I do plan to write about this trip and my search for Mara, but this book won't be fiction. I'll write about what I see here as truthfully and unbiased as possible."

"Other than the citizens involved, who truly cares about what's happening here?" he asked in a slightly arrogant tone.

"I don't know about anyone else, but I'm here because I care. This trip isn't a joke, and it certainly isn't a vacation. My purpose for being here is serious. I was asked to come here by someone very important," she said.

Thinking for a moment, he could not understand why she phrased her answer that way. Who was so important to make her come from America? However, he lost that train of thought when she continued speaking.

"Ivan, possibly because people here are so close to the fighting, they've started to give up, and from that, they think that no one else cares. With all the confusion, maybe they don't even recognize what side they're on. I would imagine everyone feels quite persecuted," she said as she glanced out the window, then back at him.

"What are you talking about?" he asked, because it was when she made those types of comments that he could believe she was a spy.

"I mean no disrespect, but everyone involved has an opinion about the disintegration of this country. I may be completely misinformed, but from an outsider's perspective and, beyond personal opinions, what is forgotten is that every harsh word and violent act leads to another. You speak of others not caring, but what about the people of this country. Don't they care about the country's future generations? War usually comes from people only caring about their own beliefs and forgetting about everyone else's."

Tess' opinion offended Ivan and it showed in his accusatory gaze. He felt she insulted him, and he briefly resented her being American.

Formulating his response, he looked her up and down, then said, "What do uninformed, spoiled, Americans know of the problems here? Your majorities sit in their safe homes with full refrigerators and full closets, believing everything the government sponsored media tells them. There's no fighting in your country, not like this civil war. Then your government points a finger at us for fighting for our beliefs. We don't have much now in this war torn country, but what we do have is dignity because of who we are, despite what region we're from. There has always been a degree of separation among Croatians, Serbians, Bosniaks, and all the rest, and there always will be. There will always be Nationalism. Individual states in America have different flags, different governors, and different laws, but they fit together because they grew together for one common cause. They don't have a history as countries at odds for hundreds of years."

Ivan paused for emphasis, while she sat patiently and listened. He was trying to curb his anger, but the harder he tried, the more intolerant of the situation he became. Yet, his intolerance was not because of her, but because of the war; however, without thinking, he directed his anger toward her.

"Let me ask you something. What do you think we were before Socialists? A joining of different regions created this land of the south Slavs, and it was ruled by outside kingdoms. Then, after those collapsed, the region was forced into a Socialist federation. It was only a matter of time before the federation split, and now the citizens of the different regions only wish to have peace. Despite who is right or who is wrong, the countries that have broken away from Yugoslavia only wish to have their independence— no more killing, just to get on with their lives. And now, suddenly, so many countries are trying to force negotiations for their own gain. But bogus treaties don't work, and sometimes they give away what people have fought for centuries to keep. No one understands, because no one has seen how men, that were once brothers, turn to nationalism without a second thought. The senseless killing of people that were once their neighbors, just because they have no defense, is unforgivable. That is something you, along with your countrymen, would not appreciate."

Ivan looked at Tess and wondered if she understood. Or did he intimidate her. She sat straight and stared back at him. He could tell his words hurt her and, though that was not his purpose, he did not apologize, but continued along the same vein.

"Tell me, Miss America, the United States of America is known as a free nation of Capitalists. What would happen if radical nationalist leaders emerged in America? What if they imposed their laws and broke up the status quo of your country because of their obsession with their personal heritage? What if they proceeded to cleanse the land of citizens not of their heritage, and slowly expanded their borders taking land away from the rightful owners? Would the American government allow them to do this? Or would they fight for the citizens of America? Fight for what they believed in and what rightfully belonged to them? Fight for what America stands for? You cannot take someone's farm because you want to expand your borders, or you don't like the owner's heritage. That farm, most likely, has been in someone's family for hundreds of years."

Indignantly imagining he had cornered her, he stared at her and waited for her response. He was sure that, being an American, she could not possibly care to know the truth of the situation in his country. The opinion of Americans there was one of overt monetary entwinement. Ivan found this especially true of the American sympathizers that contributed to the Black Rebel Cause because they once owned businesses in the former Yugoslavia. They aided the Rebels in hopes that they would one day reclaim those lost businesses. But that was the way of the world, not a concept created in America.

Tess looked straight into Ivan's eyes, and her answer surprised him and his ideas. Her tone was serious and unruffled, and from her demeanor, he knew she curbed her temper.

"It appears that you have already decided what side I'm on, as if I need to take sides, and without allowing me the courtesy of having a belief, you have formed one for me. And now, you persecute me for what may not necessarily be *my* belief, only *your* misconception. Sound familiar? So, like last night, maybe I should leave you to have breakfast with your opinion of me, instead of me."

Without another word, Tess looked out the window and rested her left cheek in her left hand as tears formed in her eyes. From this, Ivan knew he had truly offended her, which was not his conscious intention. Her response made him analyze his harsh statements about her country. When he thought about what she had said, again, she was right. She had not actually said anyone was right or wrong. She only recognized the confusion of the circumstance.

Further analyzing her words, she simply stated that future generations, meaning the children, were suffering and would continue to do so. An insight he and his colleagues knew well as they strove to help those citizens that chose not to surrender or to leave their homes. Then he wondered if the killing would finally end if the war stopped. It had not truly ended for hundreds of years, and he felt that now would be no different.

Exhaling deeply, he reached for her right hand. When he touched it, she pulled it away and placed it across her lap. He could see a tear moving down her right cheek as she looked out the window. Trying to compose herself, she was still distant from him, which upset him immensely.

Moving his chair even closer to her, he wiped the tear from her skin. Looking at his moist fingers, he could feel her kindness. "Do your words have anything to do with this missing child?" he asked.

She pulled further away from him, then shook her head. "I don't think you'd understand, Mr. Đurić."

She was calling him *Mr. Đurić* again, which made him realize the depths his words had reached. It also made him feel that, perhaps, she had now changed her mind about spending the day with him. He knew by her reaction that she listened carefully to the things he said. She took his words seriously, especially when he was upset. He did not respond immediately. Instead, he allowed himself time to figure out what his next words should be, and not just react.

"I thought we had an agreement. You were not going to call me, Mr. Đurić. Have you changed your mind? Would you prefer I take you back to the hotel? I will if that's what you want," he suggested.

When she did not answer, he attempted to explain his attitude. But again, his tone became firm as he neared the end of his statement. "I don't want to insult you, but the opinion of Americans isn't one of love in this region. It's difficult to explain. You would have to live this life to understand its meaning. And possibly, you couldn't begin to understand because you have America to escape to. So, tell me what you want to do, because I won't apologize for my beliefs." He heard her soft sigh and knew she would answer, but what she would say, he did not expect.

She slowly turned to look at him, and relayed what she felt about Mara. "You can call America a Capitalist country, which it is, and you can call me Miss America if it makes you feel justified. Perhaps I am a Capitalist. I do have a full closet, and enough food in my refrigerator, when I'm home. But am I less human because I have more than others do? God gave me many things, but I think it's what I do with what I have that counts. Hoarding things for oneself, when those around you are in need, makes one less human, and the world overflows with those types. I'm not here to criticize you or your countrymen, nor am I expecting answers regarding reactions, or solutions to situations as my government may. I'm here for one reason, and that is to find a little girl who asked me to help her and her family. Right now, she's the most important person in this world to me."

She paused and shook her head. Looking at the table, she was silent, and he waited to see what else she would say. But when she looked back at him, he saw her sorrow, and before she spoke further, he already understood, because he had written Mara's letter.

"That's the reason I'm here. She begged me to come with her story, and I came to help her and her family. My only fear is that I'm too late, because I waited for the authorities of your country, former country." She took a breath. "Whatever you want to call it. Filled with your people, divided or not, to find her. I counted on people like you, with opinions like yours, to help me find one child, and they simply refused," she said.

Again, she looked away. She did not want to see excuses in his beautiful hazel eyes. At that moment, she could not bear it. But her affection for Mara, whom she had not met, moved Ivan. He gently turned her face toward him. He wanted her to look into his eyes. He needed her to see his apology, see his sincerity, not just hear it.

"I had no idea that her asking you for help was your reason for being here. Perhaps you are the only person, from here or elsewhere, who truly cares. You don't know the danger you place yourself in, as you came all this way to dry the tears of one child. When the natives of this country are seizing any opportunity to leave here, you walk into the middle of a civil war to answer the call of one little human being." He smiled doubtfully, and shrugged. "How can that be? You're right. I don't understand. Are you that blind to the danger? Or are you that compassionate toward human life?" he asked.

Looking directly into his eyes, she saw something very different from what she thought she had turned away from. In his eyes, she saw compassion and understanding, not excuses or defenses. She thought for a moment, as her eyes locked to his unwavering stare. She then broke a smile; however, when she answered, her choice of words placed distance between them, which he detested.

"I don't know, Mr. Đurić."

When she looked down, he sensed she felt deeply for the cause of Mara. He did not want her leaving, and his gentility displayed that he did not want to be without her, as he asked, "I will take you back to the hotel if it will make you happy, but do you truly want to leave me?"

Shaking her head, she forced a brighter smile to hide her upset. She knew that as he argued with her, he also respected her. "I think I just had my first real debate with a man and about something that mattered more than where I put his shoes," she said.

Her comment made him smile. He wanted to hold her hand, and because of her genteel understanding, he wanted to hold her, but he refrained. In the back of his mind, her feelings for a child did not mean she was not the spy. If she were, perhaps she thought her part in this war was correct. But as he looked at her forgiving expression, he found it hard to believe that she was any side's liaison. Because of what he saw in her, he began to rationalize the situation.

Breaking the tension, the waiter rolled their breakfast cart up to the table and placed their silverware in front of them.

Picking up the knife to her right, she laughed at its sharpness and size. "It's a good thing this wasn't here five minutes ago. I might have poked you with it for calling me, Miss America," she said.

Her comment took him by surprise. Smiling at her, he pushed it aside when he looked into her eyes. "Well, it would have been none less than I deserved," he said.

"What are we having for breakfast? It's not pig's feet or brains or anything like that, is it?" she asked, smiling mischievously at him.

Laughing quietly at her ideas, he shook his head, thinking how innocent she could be. He then moved his chair closer to the table and said, "No. Nothing like that, unless you want that. I'm sure Jacek could find a little jar of pig's feet in the back somewhere for you."

"Oh, no thank you," she said, smiling and laughing slightly.

You're having a Serbian breakfast this morning. On your plate is what is called kačamak, which is a type of polenta. There are rovito jaje, which are soft-boiled eggs, and a variety of meats. In the center plate, there is a variety of breads, some sweet and some plain, some filled with meat, some filled with cheese. And then there is kajmak, which is a thick cream, made fresh daily. Try it, you'll like it," he said.

"I've heard that before from other men."

"And have you taken the advice of these other men?"

"Not in a very long time, but I will now. This is a trip for firsts, and this will be the first time I completely trust a man when he tells me that I'll like something," she said. Then she did something that he would have never imagined she would do. It told him that she was a Catholic, something he did not expect. Making the sign of the cross on herself, she folded her hands, bowed her head, and prayed silently over her food. Then crossing herself again, she smiled at him, lifted her fork, and began to eat.

He watched her carefully as his expression was frozen in a gentle smile from her reverent gesture. This was something he learned as a boy, but had forgotten as a man, although she had not forgotten. She appeared to have a different set of standards by which she lived. Perhaps that was why God had chosen to bless her more than He did others. And so it appeared, by her need to find Mara, she did not hesitate to give those blessings away.

Ivan smiled and waited for her decision on his choice for breakfast. Tess noticed him watching her. "If you don't hurry up, I'll eat yours too!" she said. He took this to mean that she enjoyed his choices, and with that acknowledgment, he began to eat.

During breakfast, they discussed other topics and avoided any mention of the hostilities that waited in the next region. One topic they discussed was about getting a book published, the good and bad points of the process, and how she started her writing career. Though as she spoke, he knew she thought about her mission as her eyes drifted off to the courtyard outside. Although, was her mission as she said, to find Mara Jovanović to give the award to, or was she the woman he sought to stop from bringing information to one of the aggressors of this war? Was she the woman who searched for the Black Rebel?

CHAPTER ELEVEN

As Ivan and Tess dined and enjoyed their conversation, Sergej and Alek searched her hotel room for any leads as to the purpose of her trip. Opening her briefcase, they found travel documents, information on her foundation, including a letter of congratulations to Mara, book outlines, itineraries, telephone numbers with scattered addresses, and Tess' laptop.

Turning the laptop on, Sergej found a password was required, but within a few tries, he had access to her entire hard drive. Opening the few files listed, he saw they were books. Searching further on the drive, he saw nothing other than system and software files, so he turned it off and copied the model and serial numbers from the bottom.

When Sergej went to place her laptop back into her briefcase, he noticed something in the front pocket of the lid. Pulling it out, he saw it was a black leather bound Bible with a Celtic cross embossed on the cover. He opened it. On the inside was a dedication page where Tess had signed her name as the giver and the receiver. Fanning quickly through the pages, he saw she had highlighted passages discussing faith and compassion. Seeing this, Sergej smiled.

Alek noticed him reading and approached to see what held Sergej's attention. Seeing Tess' Bible, he said, "You don't see that in a person's briefcase very often."

Sergej shook his head. "No. You don't," he said. Then he reverently closed the Bible, slid it back into the pocket of the lid, then closed and locked the lid.

Searching through her luggage, they only found clothing including her delicate undergarments in soft silk and satin. "Ivan," Sergej whispered as he shook his head.

The two men smiled at each other and closed the suitcase. If she were involved with the opposition, they found nothing in her room to prove it. From her used boarding pass, which Sergei found under her laptop, the address on her letterhead, and the serial number from her laptop, they would check the validity of her identity, then check into her past. But it would be up to Ivan to get her to reveal her true purpose for being there. If anyone could get a woman wrapped around his finger, Ivan was certainly the one to do it.

Quickly tidying the room to appear just as she had left it, no trace remained of their presence. They then left the hotel for Sergej's apartment on the opposite side of town.

CHAPTER TWELVE

Once Ivan and Tess finished their meal, Ivan reopened the subject of Tess' trip to Sarajevo. He hoped to be able to learn more about her purpose without being overly inquisitive.

"Tell me something? Where do you plan to stay once you get to Sarajevo? Do you know anyone there?"

Before she answered, she thought about the journalist she was supposed to contact when she arrived in Belgrade. At first, she was hesitant to answer his question, but she then felt his knowing would do no harm.

"I don't know anyone in Sarajevo. A friend in New York arranged for me to stay with a journalist named Herbert Strassburg at a London Post facility. I'm supposed to call him before I leave Belgrade to let him know I'm coming, but since the train is delayed two days, I haven't contacted him yet."

Ivan's expression strained. He knew Herbert Strassburg. He also knew that an explosion near the southeastern Bosnian border of Serbia had claimed Strassburg's life two days past. Against the cease-fire, an anti-Super Power campaign made him a target, and his death was a warning for the international community to stay out of the fight in Bosnia.

To Ivan, this was another confusing fact. Strassburg was undeniably anti-Nationalist and continually risked his life to portray the strife of civilians in the hot beds of the war. He wondered why she associated with someone like him *if* she were a spy. Now that he thought about it, he could not tell her the truth about Strassburg because he did not want her leaving him and going home.

Shaking his head, he snapped from his private debate. "I know him. We met once here in Belgrade, and I saw him several times in Sarajevo. He's no longer in Sarajevo. He was transferred out last week," he said, disliking lying to her, but finding it necessary.

"Just my luck. I guess I'll have to call George and see if he knows anyone else I can stay with."

He frowned at her apparent lack of concern. From her tone it appeared she did not care where or with whom she stayed, as long as she got to Sarajevo.

"You don't care who you stay with? That's very dangerous," he scolded, as he was concerned for her safety.

"I wouldn't stay with just anyone. I know George would put me with someone safe. I trust him," she answered.

"George? George who? George Washington?" he asked. He was curious who George was, and suddenly, he felt slightly jealous.

She laughed at his attempt to make her smile, and when she smiled, so did he. "No, not the late, great president, George Preston. He's an independent photojournalist currently working for the New York Times."

Ivan sat back and looked at her. How many rabbits could she pull from her hat? "The same George Preston who covered the recent disruption in China?" he asked.

"Yes. The same George Preston."

"The same man who covered Somalia and Apartheid in South Africa?" he asked.

She nodded her head as she smiled. She was proud of her friend's accomplishments and, actually, she was happy when anyone accomplished their goals.

"Now that's an interesting man. How did you meet him?" he asked.

"I met him at my first book signing about four and a half years ago. He said he wanted to meet the author who made him cry with words. I figured it was because my book was so poorly written, though he scolded me when I suggested that. We've been friends since then," she said.

"Friends, or, *friends?*" he asked, as his male curiosity was piqued, and again he felt slightly jealous that another man would possibly have had the privilege of intimacy with her.

"Just friends," she answered, and laughed slightly at what she imagined him to be thinking.

"I see. Does he know anything about your search? Does he know anything about this little girl, Mara? Where she could be?" he asked.

"No. He's not really sure why I'm here. Willis Beechum, the Secretary of the Foundation, knows about Mara. He knows that I'm here because she won the writing competition; however, he doesn't know all that she wrote about," she said as her expression changed.

"What do you really know about this little girl? Do you know anything about her besides what she wrote in her story? How many people have read what she wrote?" he asked.

"I'm the only one that read the entire story since it arrived at my office. As a matter of fact, it was so compelling, I read it several times. Her book came in with a copy translated into English, so the person who translated it read it. She doesn't write English yet, so he, I'm presuming it's a man, whom she says also protects her, wrote to me on her behalf. Of course, the Foundation had segments checked to make sure they matched the original transcript, which they did. I showed only selected portions to the Foundation committee. I felt, well, I felt some parts were sensitive. All I really know about Mara is where she used to live. Her house is gone, and no one seems to know where she is. And her parents—"

Pausing, she frowned. As she looked down, tears welled in her eyes. He allowed her a moment to compose herself because he could tell Mara's story affected her deeply.

"I found out from the authorities that her parents are dead. They were killed in an explosion that destroyed her house while she was at school. To make it all worse, she wrote that she saw a sniper gun down her brother before her eyes. What trauma for a child, but it's the way she writes that isn't like a child. She writes like an adult; her views are so simple, but so psychological. I can only imagine she's surrounded by, or was surrounded by, people who discussed this war in great depth."

"Did you bring the copies of the book with you? Perhaps I could read them and find clues for you?" he asked, curious as to where the copies of Mara's book were.

"No. I left them in New York."

"You said you felt parts were sensitive, so did you leave them in your office, available for others to read?"

"No. Both copies are locked in my safe deposit box."

"The contents must be very sensitive," he said because he was happy she felt so protective of them, but wondered how he would get them out of her safe deposit box should the need arise.

Pulled from these thoughts, he noticed her shaking her head as she looked out the window. He could tell that she still thought about the child's plea for help. Then she looked back at Ivan as if he had answers to her questions.

"I don't know what to do, and I don't know how to find her. All I have is a list of different shelters in towns surrounding Sarajevo where she may possibly be. The only link I have to her is a man she loves, this protector. She talks about him throughout the book. She calls him…well…the letters are I, then the letter d with a slash going through the stem, and then the letter y. I don't know how it's pronounced," she said.

Hearing Mara's pet name for him, Ivan's expression turned serious. Tess' remembrance of his name proved that she carefully read Mara's letter and story. But, was it because she was moved by Mara's plea for help, or was it because she needed to find Mara for whoever paid the highest price, expecting that finding Mara would locate him. He had the same unanswered questions in his head, but he shrugged off the importance of her knowing the name Iđy.

"What a strange name. It certainly isn't Croatian," he said, then added, "It would be pronounced with a soft g like the word germ. Igy is how you would say it in Croatian."

She looked at him when he referenced Croatian. Was he giving her a clue to his true side in the war? She recalled that he said he was born in Belgrade, but that did not make any difference. He could still be of Croatian descent. She brushed it off as nothing serious, considering that the letter said Mara was Croatian, and she had mentioned it to him previously.

"I didn't think so. I imagine it's a term of endearment for this man. Or perhaps it's a mispronunciation of a more difficult name," she commented.

"Does this book say where to find this man with this strange name? Does it give any leads to his identity?" he asked, playing dumb.

"No. It only says how he protects her and her family. That was when her family was alive. It tells of how much she loves him. He must be very kind and very brave for a child to love him so much. She admires him with such intensity. If I could find him, then perhaps I could find her," she answered, then added, "But I don't have the slightest idea were to begin looking for him either."

"You said you have a list of shelters. Could I see it?" he asked.

"Yes," she said. Sorting through the papers from her purse, she pulled it out and handed it to him.

Taking it, he looked it over. He was curious to see if Dovlići was listed, and it was. "There are many shelters here, but I don't know if all are still in operation, and several are in dangerous locations. Dovlići is in an especially dangerous location. You should not go there," he said, then handed the list back to her.

"That's what I thought may be the situation. But the shelter in Dovlići was one of the shelters taking in children when Mara's parents were killed. So, at some point, I have to go there," she said as she slid the list back into the pile of papers, then back into her purse.

"And what will you do if you find her?" he asked as he secretly wondered how he would keep her away from Dovlići.

"I will give her the award she's won," she answered, imagining that would be obvious.

"Award? What is this award she's won?" he asked, again playing dumb, but knowing it was the grant.

"Fifteen thousand US dollars," she answered.

He was silent and wondered if she carried that sort of cash on her in the middle of a war. He did not think the Foundation would hand the money to Mara. He imagined the foundation would reserve and invest the funds in her name for her college education, not give a cash award. In his mind, he could not imagine any person giving cash to a child. What an enticement for someone who knew where Mara was. He was now more suspicious of her than ever, although he was not angry.

"Who gives that much money to a child, especially a child in the middle of a civil war? That's like signing her death warrant. What person does this? How can—"

"I am the person!" she said, interrupting him hastily. Suddenly she felt he had more arrogance than anyone she knew. Standing up, she grabbed her coat and purse, then turned to look at him. "Thank you for breakfast, Mr. Đurić," she said. She then slid from behind the table and left the restaurant.

Not only did she leave the restaurant, she left Ivan alone with his attitude. He shook his head and stood up. Reaching into his pocket, he set money on the table for the bill and tip, grabbed his coat, then hurried after her. He gave a waved to Jacek, who called to him as he passed through the entrance, then to the cold outside.

Looking down the street, he saw her walking away. Keeping his eye on her, he put on his coat and called out as he chased after her. "Tess? Come back here!" Catching up to her, he pulled her back by the arm to stop her from walking away.

She tried to go around him, though he continually blocked her path. Yanking her arm from his grasp, she turned and started to walk in the other direction.

Again, he stepped in front of her, stopping her by holding both her arms. "Wait! Stop running away!" he said, slightly impatient with her.

She refused to look at him. All he had done since they had met was to criticize her intentions; however, when she thought about it, he was right. What person in their right mind would walk into a war-torn country and hand a child fifteen thousand dollars? They would have to be stupid, though she did not know what else to do. But she did not have the cash with her. She had a secured account in Switzerland ready to transfer the funds at a moment's notice.

"You didn't let me finish," he said.

He felt her distress, and wanted to regain her interest, but she paid no notice to him. She only looked around for a way to get back to the hotel, and, unintentionally, she ignored him as he stood in front of her, needing her attention.

"Please, don't ignore me when I talk to you. Look at me." He gently pulled her closer to him as he commanded her attention. "Please, Tess, look at me. I don't ignore you when you talk to me, do I?"

Obeying his request, she looked at him. From behind her sunglasses, he saw her helpless expression, an expression that made him want her. As he was lost in her desperation with her, he moved to kiss her, although she closed her eyes and turned her head. This caused him to back away. He was put off by her denial of what he was beginning to feel, and that was his growing affection for her.

"I'm sorry. I didn't mean—" he said, fumbling with his apology. "These people who give this money, do they approve where it goes?"

She opened her eyes and looked back at him. "These people consist of me. I earn this money, and I started the foundation that gives it to the children. I answer to no one about what I do with my money, Mr. Đurić," she said in a kind tone.

By her addressing him formally, he knew she was genuinely upset with him. But he needed her to forgive him. He did not want her to be hurt by his thoughts and ideas.

"Well then, you are the kindest of women; one who truly cares enough to give of herself and to risk her own life for a single child," he said.

Slipping his arm around her shoulders, he tried to walk her back to the restaurant, but she did not move with him. She stood there, staring down at the walkway as she thought about how impossible it was to find Mara.

"Come with me. Let me take you inside before you get cold," he said as he stepped in front of her again.

She shook her head slightly, and whispered. "No. I have to go. I have to find her. I have to help her."

Her confusion was contagious to him. He carefully examined her anguished disposition and, in her expression, he saw her determination. She appeared consumed with the task of finding this child and, for that instant, he believed she was telling the truth. Feeling her need, in his moment of weakness, his heart reached out to her.

"I will help you find her. I promise you, I will. If you permit me, I will take you to Sarajevo. We will look for her together. Just give me today and tomorrow to show you Belgrade. For that was my first promise, and if I cannot keep my first promise, how might I keep my second?" he asked.

He touched her pale cheek as her moist eyes looked up at him and questioned him. She sighed as she debated his offer. He felt she was considering refusing him because of his past comments, and he needed her to say yes to him now.

"We will go to Sarajevo together, and I will protect you while you are there. I give you my word. Tess." He paused. "Please, allow me to keep my promises."

She smiled, and Ivan took that to mean she agreed to his offer. He leaned toward her, kissed her cheek, then stepped to her side. Putting his arm around her shoulders, he walked her to the street. They stepped into a taxi, and he requested the driver take them to the Kalemegdan Fortress. He thought she might like seeing this. It was a beautiful place where, due to the cold weather, they could walk virtually undisturbed. This was a place where they could be somewhat alone.

Despite the cold, they walked about the grounds of the fortress until they stopped near the Messenger of Victory—a statue placed atop a massive column overlooking the junction of the Rivers Sava and Danube.

Looking up at it, Tess felt extremely small in her efforts. Ivan could tell she tried to be pleasant, but finding Mara constantly pulled at her psyche. He could tell she thought about Mara's story and its tragic message. Unbeknownst to her, Ivan had translated Mara's story into English. And now, he was spending time with the woman who sponsored the competition Mara so desperately wanted to win.

"Very peculiar odds," he thought, because he did not expect anyone to pay attention. He did not expect the words of a seven-year-old child to affect anyone, and certainly not this woman, whom he suspected of intervening with his Cause.

With a sigh, she turned away from the statue and walked to the railing. Standing there by herself, her eyes locked on the convergence of the two rivers, while her mind slipped into private thoughts as she questioned Ivan's offer to take her to Sarajevo. "Why would he offer to walk into a war zone?" she wondered.

Pushing his suspicions aside, Ivan walked up behind her. His intention was not to trap her, but to comfort her, as he slid his arms on each side of her then grasped the railing to shelter her from the cold.

Seeing his hands on the railing, she smiled, and she felt his warmth behind her. Through all their disputes, it was obvious that she more than liked him. As stubborn and self-righteous as he appeared on the outside, when she looked into his eyes, those beautiful and welcoming hazel eyes, she could only see goodness and strength within him that she greatly admired.

Ivan moved his lips close to her ear, and she could feel his breath on her skin; it was warm and soft as it moved her hair. She briefly closed her eyes, momentarily enjoying the sensation, as he asked, "Am I boring you with the history of my country?" He hoped she would turn to face him. With her lips so near his, again, he would attempt to kiss her.

"No, Ivan, not at all. It's all fascinating," she answered, but did not turn toward him.

"If I do bore you, will you tell me?" he asked. In his growing affection for her, he moved his hands over hers and closed his fingers around them.

"Don't be silly," she said, then unexpectedly pressed back against him and rested her head against the side of his face. Closing her eyes, she gave forth a contented sigh.

Welcoming this, he smiled and felt she trusted him. And from this, he knew he should trust her, but, in his mind, visions of war were always present and that made him trust no one. Yet, he wanted to enjoy being with her. He did not want to think about fighting for his Cause, at least not for a little while.

In a romantic gesture, Ivan moved Tess' hands up from the frozen railing. Bending her arms across her chest, he did not let go of her hands, but held her. Kissing her hair tenderly, they stood there in silence as they continued to watch the rivers flowing into one another. In his mind, he felt his wish to be with a beautiful and gentle woman was finally granted. Despite who she was, or her purpose, he appreciated her presence. In his heart, Ivan knew he would remember these precious moments for the rest of his life, moments he longed for since he first laid eyes on Tess.

CHAPTER THIRTEEN

The rest of the day, Ivan showed Tess the highlights of Belgrade. From the tourist attractions to the locals' favorite places, she saw everything he wanted to show her. When they passed his apartment, he was tempted to stop and take her up to it. He was curious to see how she would feel being there alone with him. He was also curious to see how he would feel having her there with him, although he knew it would make him happy. However, he decided then was not the time for those questions to be answered. When the sun set, he noticed she was tired, and so they headed back to the hotel.

When they arrived, they made their way to the dining room. Sitting at the same table as the evening before, the conversation slowed once dinner was over. The entire day, he carefully observed her, and the more he listened to her, the more he felt she was just who she said she was, the chairperson of the writing foundation.

Seeing Tess' obvious concern for her purpose for being in his country, Ivan reopened the subject of Mara as he asked, "Why do you give money to children? I know they write stories and send them to you, but why *you?* Why do *you* do this for children?"

She was silent as she looked at him. Trying to think of an answer not driven by impulse, she gave the only answer she could. "If you can write, you can read. And if you can read, you can better understand the world and its different societies. Knowledge is the key to destroying prejudice and individual hate, which always culminates in violence against the innocent." She paused. "That's why I give money to children."

Ivan smiled. He understood her intention, but his disbelieving gaze appeared to question her motive. She noticed this, and she needed to make him understand what she was trying to accomplish.

"Am I that confusing? I guess I haven't explained it properly. I don't just walk up to the winner of the competition and hand them the award money. This money goes toward furthering their education. It's invested for them through the foundation and, when the time comes, it's used by the individual winners to assist in paying for their college education. But first, they must successfully complete their education up to that point. Then the money is available for their use. Depending on the age of the child that wins, and the economy, by the time the money is dispersed, it could be much more than the original award. And all of it goes to the children," she said. Looking at him now, she saw he completely understood her motives.

"People need kindness more than anything. It's just my way of trying to help. What else can I do? I just want to share what good I have in my life. In order to be seen as good, you must be good by God's standards—which should be every human's life goal. Good people are kind in their actions toward others, and kindness is proof of God's love for mankind."

"But the money, where does it come from?" he asked.

"From my writing. I earn the money, and I fund the Foundation myself. No one gives me donations. I don't care for donations because people can seldom detach themselves from what they give. People want to control everything. If I accept donations, the donors would want to control my actions and the Foundation's actions. But most of all, they would want to control the futures of the children who receive the awards. That wouldn't be fair."

He understood, but his curiosity surpassed these thoughts, and so he asked, "What will you do when you find this child?"

"I don't know. Her situation is completely different. I'll give her the money now, and still help her in the future with her education. She only wants it to escape from this war and take with her those she cares about. She doesn't even want the entire award, just enough for her, and whomever, to get safely away. Now with her parents and her brother gone, and possibly Idy too, what else can I do?" She shook her head. "I must help her. You can't look the other way when someone, especially a child, asks for your help as she did. How could I ignore that?"

She looked at Ivan and sighed softly at the thought of Mara being lost and alone. Ivan had smiled slightly at the mention of Mara's pet name for him. Tess did not even know he was Idy, but she worried about him as well. What would Tess do when she found out who he was? If he truly planned on being with her as a man, and not merely a friend, at some time, he would have to tell her. He briefly wondered how he would do that.

"And what if her entire family is dead? You aren't planning to take her back to America, are you?"

"Why not? If she has no one, except Iđy, perhaps I'll take both of them back with me, at least until the war is over and the region is safe. That is, if that's what they want."

Regardless that Tess had no authority to take Mara, the thought of his never seeing Mara again pulled at his heart. Out of anger and thinking that Tess wanted to control a child's life, just as he felt a Capitalist would, he snapped. "Regardless of the situation, it's not right to take a child from her home to a strange Capitalist country like America! It's not the right thing to do! This is where she belongs. Here in *her* country with *her* people, who share *her* values, who understand *her,* and who love *her.*"

His stare was demeaning. From his comment, Tess surmised that he saw her as a woman without compassion or love. However, his comment made her slightly defensive in that he would prevent an orphan from reaching safety, even if only temporarily, until the war was over, so she asked, "What's better, Mr. Đurić, a strange Capitalist country or civil war?"

Without really knowing why, he had lost his temper. He leaned toward her and squinted at her in an attempt at intimidation as he sarcastically said, "Capitalism is war, Miss America!"

Ivan's attempt at intimidation was as futile as the previous evening's attempt at seduction. He soon understood this from her response, and even before she spoke, he could see defiance in her eyes.

"Ha! You're insufferable!" she said.

Standing up, she threw her napkin at him. It hit his chest, though he did not flinch. He sat there proudly, and completely submerged in his superior, manly attitude, which momentarily displayed his enjoyment of her frustration with him.

"Please enjoy the rest of the evening, Mr. Đurić!" she said as she grabbed her coat and purse, walked out of the dining room, and left him sitting alone at the table.

Pondering the situation, Ivan remained frozen in his now less proud and further shocked posture, as he thought, "What just happened?" He could not figure it out. Every time they ate, they argued. Every time they argued, she walked away from him. Every time she walked away, he wanted to go after her, take her in his arms, and kiss her. The more he thought about it, the more sense Tess made and that made him care all the more for her. She provoked him: not only his anger, but also his desire. If he were going to be master over this woman, he needed to pay attention and try harder not to incite these types of reactions from her. Shaking his head slightly, he laughed as his mind deliberated that potential sequence of events.

Paying the bill, he stood up, grabbed his coat, and went after her. He was certain she would be in her room, but when he passed the front desk, the clerk signaled to him. "Mr. Đurić, Miss Fordel didn't go to her room. She left the hotel," the clerk said.

"Did she get into a taxi?" Ivan asked.

"No. She walked down the street in that direction," the clerk said, motioning to the left.

Ivan smiled and put on his coat. Walking out the lobby's entrance, he had to find her. Her travel book was right. The men in Belgrade were persistent, and during this current conflict, they could be rude and, some of them, dangerous. He did not want to think of her walking around at night alone because of his arrogance. Despite her upset with him, or any gentlemanly obligation, he *wanted* to be with her, so he went to find her.

After about twenty-five minutes of searching and inquiring about her in clubs and shops open late, he had not found her, and he decided to go back to the hotel. Perhaps she had only walked around the block, then returned to her room.

Ivan slowly made his way into Tašmajdan Park. As he rounded the front of St. Mark's Church, he saw a familiar shape sitting on the top step near the entrance. At once, he issued a sigh of relief, then the edges of his lips curled up into a soft smile. Beyond all doubt, he recognized the shape to be Tess. She sat with her chin in her hands, and her elbows resting on her thighs as she looked directly down the avenue in front of her.

Admiring her, he momentarily stood in the dark shadows about twenty feet away from her. Without making a sound, he walked up the side steps and approached her. "So I see you've successfully escaped the rude men of Belgrade," he said, stopping next to her.

"The book was wrong. It's not men, it's man; the persistent man of Belgrade," she said, omitting his reference to 'rude' from her statement. "It was nice of them not to mention your name, leaving innocent women unaware of your identity." She then sat straight and began to laugh, but not at him, just at herself.

He sat next to her and put his arm around her. His attitude now was humble as he leaned toward her, and asked, "Am I that bad?"

She shook her head and looked into his eyes. "No, I am. I was rude to you again, and after all your concern and taking such good care of me to-day. I'm sorry, Ivan. I didn't mean it. I'm angry with myself and my inability to accomplish what I came here to accomplish. Because of that, I was cruel to the kindest person."

He stroked her cheek and smiled at her. Few women he knew would admit their mistakes. Most women he had known would compensate by passing blame onto someone else, but not Tess. When she was wrong, she knew it and she was sorry.

"Please forgive my ignorant opinions. I have no right to think the way I do, or talk to you as I have," she said and added, "You're right about everything."

Looking at her in the muted light, he felt uncannily drawn to her. He saw her as a compassionate soul, fighting a hidden battle with no one to help. The gentle words of her apology made him want to protect her from the evils of the world. Her gentle words made him smile at her.

"I'm hardly right about everything. Besides, it takes two to have," he paused, thinking of the right word, "well, let's just call it a debate. So there's nothing to forgive." He smiled. "Let's go back to the hotel," he said, and began to stand.

"Ivan," she whispered.

The tenderness in her voice pulled him back to her side. In silence, he smiled and waited for her next words.

"Thank you," she whispered, then she leaned toward him, and kissed him at the side of his mouth.

He only watched as she pulled back, stood, and waited for him. He could have easily taken her in his arms and kissed her. He knew he could just as easily take her back to the hotel and make love to her. He wanted to, but not then. The Cause weighed heavily on his mind as did the question of whether she was involved in some way. Perhaps she deceived him. Perhaps she knew exactly who he was and sought to mislead him. Until he was certain that she was not against him, he planned to enjoy her company as much as he could, but he would continue to pay close attention to all she said and did.

With his arm around her shoulder, they walked back to the hotel. Escorting her to her room, he stopped at her door. Gently taking the key from her hand, he opened the door with it. Returning it to her, he then stood there smiling at her. However, it was an awkward moment when either she should invite him inside, or tell him good night. Studying her demeanor, she appeared unable to do either.

He smiled and placed his hands on her shoulders. "You haven't forgotten that we're going to Sarajevo together. I always keep my promises," he said.

"I don't hold you to that promise. I understand you made it in a hasty moment. I don't expect—"

His frown was first to interrupt her. Once she stopped speaking, he addressed her ideas as he said, "I made no promise in a hasty moment. I decided to offer to take you to Sarajevo last night. I just didn't have time enough to tell you. If you remember, you left me to have dinner with myself."

"I did do that, didn't I? Still, I don't expect you—"

He moved his right hand from her shoulder to her cheek, stopping her words, as he looked at her affectionately. He felt she was struggling to convince him that he was not obligated to fulfill his promise, but he knew that.

"Perhaps you would rather not be with me?" he asked.

"Ivan, I enjoy your company more than anyone else's. But this search is my problem, not yours. If you change your mind when it comes time to leave, I'll understand," she answered.

"Then it's settled. We'll go together, and what we find is what we find, but we'll find it together. So, don't call your friend George. You will have a place to stay, a safe place."

He stroked her cheek again. Seeing she was tired, he concluded their evening. An evening he would have preferred turn out differently, but now he knew there were more evenings to come.

"Can we spend tomorrow together? There is more of Belgrade that I would enjoy showing you. That is, if you permit me," he said.

"I'd love to. Will you call me in the morning, or do you wish me to be ready at a certain time?"

"I'll call you in the morning, but until then, if you need me, I'm right across the hall."

Bending to look around him, she glanced at the door to his room. Pointing to the door, she played with him. "You're right over there, in that room? You're not going home?"

"No. Last night, after dinner, I went back to my apartment and packed a bag. I came back here so I could see you again before you left. I thought if I stayed at home last night, and came back this afternoon, I would have missed you," he said, not thinking she would have asked.

"I see. So, if I need help, I can just start screaming and you'll come to my rescue," she said.

As she looked up at him, again, he felt powerfully drawn to her. Pushing his feelings aside, he smiled serenely at her, as he said, "Naturally, unless you prefer I let you scream, which I wouldn't allow, regardless of your preference."

"I promise not to bother you while you sleep. I'll wait for your call," she said as she looked toward her room.

"Until tomorrow," he said, then he kissed her cheek. "Good night, Tess." Looking into her eyes, he let go a small, sad breath. He did not want to say good night. He wanted to stay with her. He would have preferred to take her back to his apartment to be alone with her; however, he could not do that just then, but soon, he hoped.

"Good night, Ivan," she said, smiling as she stroked his arm. Then she turned, entered her room, and closed the door.

He stood there briefly. Her affection was genuine and, despite his suspicions, he hoped that she would share more of it in the days to come. Smiling to himself, he turned and walked to his room.

Opening the door, he stepped inside. Again, he did not turn on the lights. The room was bright enough from the reflection of the city that shone through the windows. He sat on the bed, picked up the telephone, and dialed Sergej to discuss the arrival of the train.

On the first ring, Sergej answered. "Zdravo."

"Bring it early tomorrow. We're going in the morning," Ivan said, purposely not referring to what was being brought in early, or to where they would be going.

"Do you think that's wise? If she is the one, anyone could piece it all together," Sergej said, referring to any man with Tess potentially being identified as the Black Rebel. Then he asked, "Is she the one?"

"Perhaps."

"I don't think she's involved. I think you're wrong. We found nothing that connects her to anything. All that was on the laptop were a few files containing books and software. There's a letter there for you know who from her group."

"What does it say?"

"Congratulations and instructions." Sergej paused. "Did you know she has a Bible in her briefcase?"

For a moment, Ivan thought about it. "What kind?"

"A standard English version, not Orthodox," Sergej answered, then added, "She's not the one."

"Perhaps. But if she is, she has what we need on a disc she keeps with her. I'll get her to show me tomorrow. I won't go all the way, you will, I'll leave as usual. Have me picked up there. After things are taken care of, we'll meet you at home."

"If she's not the one, what is she doing here?" Sergej asked.

"Just like the letter says, congratulations. Quite a coincidence. I didn't think anyone would pay attention to the entry, but she's looking, along with others." He hesitated and sighed. "I'll let her search awhile. She'll leave when she sees the truth. She can't handle this, she'll run home like a frightened child."

Ivan was momentarily quiet as he thought about the situation. He felt uneasy for even thinking about taking Tess to Sarajevo. Regardless of the cease-fire, there was an ever present and significant element of danger there, but just then, he had no other choice.

"I want you to stay with her after I leave. Watch her. I don't want any harm to come to her. If she is the one, we need her. And if she is, perhaps I can convince her otherwise. We'll see what happens."

"And if she's not?" Sergej asked.

"We'll still see what happens."

"This isn't good. It's not right."

"Just watch her. Don't let anything happen to her and don't waste time. Do you understand?" he said, though he knew Sergej was right.

"Yes," Sergej answered, knowing Ivan meant to get her out of sight once she was off the train.

If she were the Serbians' spy, and was found out to be there, her presence in Sergej's house would pinpoint the location of the Black Rebel for the Serbians, as well as, the Croatians and the Bosniaks. If she were, Ivan would take care of her in time, but how, he did not know.

On the other hand, if she were not the spy, her life would be in danger. If she were not, Ivan would give her a couple of weeks in Sarajevo, then he would take her back to his apartment in Belgrade. In the back of his mind, he would do anything to spend time with her. Despite any consequences, he promised to protect her, and he would keep his word, even if he had to protect her from herself.

"I want you to bring her home. She will have my room. Put the small bed inside the room. Unless I'm with her, I can't take care of her," Ivan ordered.

"Anything else?"

"Have Mama make the room pretty for her. Can you do that for me?"

Sergej heard a strange gentility in Ivan's voice. He felt Ivan was bringing Tess for reasons other than discovering her purpose for going to Sarajevo. From Ivan's brief descriptions, Sergej was anxious to meet her. He was anxious to learn what type of woman had finally pulled Ivan's interest away from the war.

"I'll take care of it. Everything will be ready when you arrive." Sergei paused as he smiled briefly to himself. "Tomorrow then."

The line went dead, and Ivan hung up and lay back against the pillows. Closing his eyes, he inhaled a deep breath, then exhaled it slowly as he contemplated the situation. He did not want her to be a spy. He needed her to be telling him the truth. He needed her to be just who she said she was, but also, he needed her to be the answer to his prayer. Contemplating issues until the morning, he planned how he would get the truth from her, and, as a result, he did not sleep that night.

CHAPTER FOURTEEN

At half past six the next morning, Ivan rang Tess' room. She had been awake late, writing her first impressions of war torn Yugoslavia. She had not even put her laptop away; just fell asleep on top of the covers.

Hearing the telephone ring, and with her eyes closed, her hand groped for the receiver on the nightstand. "Hello?" she answered.

"Good morning, Tess. Did I wake you?" Ivan greeted.

"Ivan? What time is it? Is it late?" she said as she rolled onto her side and reached for her watch. Squinting, she tried to focus to see the time. She set her watch back on the bed stand. Then sitting up, she moved the hair behind her shoulders and looked around the room. Looking to the entrance, she smiled thinking how Ivan was just across the hall from her.

"I did wake you. I'm sorry. Go back to sleep. I'll call you later."

"It's alright. I'm up and, I kept my promise, I didn't scream all night."

"How unfortunate for me, but I have good news for you. The train has arrived this morning. We will leave after breakfast. So, if you're up, get dressed, get packed, and, Tess, wear something that you can move about easily in. And if you have low-heeled boots, wear them."

"Okay."

"I will be outside your door in one hour."

"Are you sure?"

"Sure about what?"

"Sure you want to waste your time with me? You don't have to, you know. I can go on my own. I'm sure you have better things to do," she said, then asked, "Don't you need to be in Budapešt?"

"No, I cancelled that trip."

"But—"

"One hour! Or I'll get a key, come into your room, and dress you myself. Do you understand?"

"I'll be ready. I'll see you in an hour."

"Until then," he said, then he hung up.

She got out of bed, showered, and dressed. Once packed, she locked her luggage. She then walked from her room and knocked on Ivan's door.

From the delicate tapping he heard from outside, he knew who it was before he opened it. "Hold on, Tess," he said loudly. Folding the morning's paper, he rose from his chair near the window and walked to the door. Opening it, he saw her standing there and smiling at him. She was dressed and ready to go. She even wore her coat.

"Good morning, but how were you so positive it was me?" she asked.

He smiled at the sight of her. Reaching for her hand, he kissed her once on each cheek, then gently pulled her inside the room, but left the door open. "Good morning. What else but a woman has such a light touch? Besides, it's too early for the maid, and no other women know I'm here."

"I doubt that. Women not know you're around? I don't think that's possible." She laughed to herself because he was too attractive for women not to notice him. She noticed him, but that was what he wanted.

He smiled at her comment, then asked, "Are you ready for breakfast?"

She nodded.

Walking to the phone, he called the front desk and requested a porter bring their luggage downstairs. Returning to her, he shook his head as he looked down at her. "We have one problem. You can't wear this coat in Sarajevo," he said.

"Why can't I wear this?" she asked, looking down at her coat, then back at him.

"As soon as you step off the train, someone will see your coat and know you're a foreigner. Not that you will be walking in the streets, but you need something ordinary, something simple."

He paused. He did not know how to explain exactly what she would find in Sarajevo. How could anyone explain destruction and desperation caused by war?

"Before we go to the train station, I'll get you something appropriate, something less noticeable. Here it's not a problem, but in Sarajevo, you want to look insignificant. You don't want to draw attention to yourself. You want to look like you belong there and, at this time, this coat doesn't belong there."

He looked at her as she stared toward the bed. She obviously did not know what lay ahead in Sarajevo. He wondered what she thought this war was about, and he tried to imagine what she thought she would find once she was there.

"I don't think you know what you're getting yourself into by searching for this child. The other day you said that you didn't know what you'd find when you got there. I can tell you what you'll find," he said, then taking her by the hand, he sat her on the bed and looked at her as she waited for him to explain. Seeing her expectant expression, he did not know where to start.

"What will I find when I get there? Please tell me, Ivan," she said, then took his hand, and pulled him to sit next to her.

He gently stroked her fingers as he looked at them. How innocent she was, even in her dealings with him, how trustworthy. He hesitated momentarily, and she heard him release a small, helpless sigh. Then he started to explain the desolate atmosphere of Sarajevo.

"You wake in the morning, look outside, and think it's mist you're trying to see through, but it's not. It's smoke from the bombing from the night before; it lingers just above the city." He paused, seeing this vision inside his mind. "The stillness of the night holds it there. In the morning, when the city begins to breathe, the smoke clears, and it's then that you see the carnage and ruin. Such a waste." He paused briefly. "In war, even when there is no sound, there is sound. The sound of war, even when silent, has its own deafening ring." He shook his head as he relived this scene in his mind. "You will see mostly death and destruction. Bombs have exploded everywhere. Shootings happen constantly. You trust no one when you're there, not unless I tell you they're safe. Do you understand?"

She nodded as she looked up at him. From his words and expression, she knew that he had seen this first hand. That made her wonder why he would go back.

"You don't walk the streets without me, or someone I send with you. You don't stand by any windows; you become a target by doing that. Again, unless I tell you someone is safe, you speak to no one. You look at no one. You tell no one who you are, or what you're doing in Sarajevo."

Tess was completely absorbed in what Ivan was saying. He could tell that she was searching her mind for some similar situation she may have experienced; however, in her eyes, he could see that she found none.

"Tess, you're walking into the middle of a war. You must always pay attention to what's going on because even with the cease-fire, it's still war. Are you positive that you want to do this? Does this child mean that much for you to risk your life? I ask because I don't want a crying woman on my hands. There's no time for tears or hysteria once we're there. Do you understand?" he asked.

She nodded, but he saw the slight fear in her gaze as she tried to pull her hand from his. But his grip clamped down on her wrist, and his tone became strict. "Decide now if you can handle this. No one will blame you if you change your mind. After all, you're a woman and not meant for war."

Feeling his grip loosen, she pulled her hand from his and stood up. Looking down at him, she shook her head, almost dismissing his comments. Then walking to the door, she turned and looked back at him. And though her stance displayed determination, her voice was fragile. "Please, stop trying to frighten me," she said, then she turned and left the room.

As he stood up, he heard her room door open, then close. He did not want to discourage her from going, but he wanted her to have some concept of what she would find when she arrived. Still, nothing he could say would lessen the shock of a city torn apart by civil unrest.

Taking his jacket from the closet, he put it on, then he put on his coat. Walking to her room, he knocked softly on the door. The door opened half way, and for a moment, she stood looking down, but then, she looked up at him. He pushed the door open and walked past her and into the room. She turned around and saw him where he stood, staring out the window. Examining the weather, he heard her walk toward her luggage.

The bellman arrived, knocked on the open door, and spoke to Tess in Serbian. Ivan answered the bellman in Serbian, telling him to take her luggage, and his in the room across the hall, down to the lobby. The bellman removed her luggage, left the room, and closed the door. She stood with her hands clasped behind her back as she stared at the floor, not knowing what to do next.

He turned around to look at her. Without her coat, his eyes carefully examined her. She was dressed as he had requested, wearing a pair of form fitting black trousers, a black v-neck sweater with another black sweater underneath, and a pair of black, low-heeled sheepskin boots. He tried not to be obvious in looking at her, though his eyes moved slowly up and down her body. He smiled; with the way she was dressed, he thought she resembled a cat burglar.

In the back of his mind, he had no idea how he was going to keep her out of sight once she arrived in Sarajevo. All he needed was for them to have an argument and her to walk out in the open without his protection. Though there was a supposed cease-fire in the region, tempers were volatile. People did things to others despite agreements, and in this war, so many did what they wanted without regard for others.

For a split second, he considered himself insane for taking her into the war zone. But the longer he looked at her, the more he understood he needed to spend time with her. He also needed to get to Sarajevo, and that was where she needed to go. If he allowed her to go alone, tragedy would find her, scarring her emotionally and physically, but with him, she would be safe.

Giving forth a deep sigh, he walked toward her, placed his hands on her arm, and asked, "Are you going to be upset with me the entire time?"

When she did not respond, he presumed his suggestion of her being upset was correct, but he was wrong. She was not upset, only apprehensive. As he lifted her head by the chin, her gaze moved toward his, though she said nothing, so he asked again, "Are you?"

"I'm not upset, but does this mean you're taking me? Are you willing to risk *your* life to go with me?" she asked, then looked away from him.

Wanting her to look into his eyes, where he felt she would see the truth, he stroked her cheek. Then he bent toward her and brought his lips close to her ear. "I am back and forth from there all the time. This trip is easy for me. So you should know that I do this because I want to. My fear is not for me, but for you," he whispered.

The gentility in his voice, and his choice of words, forced her to look at him. She understood what he was trying to convey, and she smiled to ease his frustration.

"Where's your coat?" he asked as he looked around the room.

"It's in my luggage. You said I couldn't wear it, and I didn't know what else to do with it. I never stopped to think about it being pretentious, and I never considered it obvious. I should have thought things through more carefully...I'm sorry, Ivan."

How he loved when she said his name. As its sound resonated in his head, a moment of silence passed between them. He wanted to tell her that she was not pretentious, but, before he could speak, she pulled away from him.

"I'll just get my things," she said.

He stopped her and retrieved her things for her. Handing her scarf and gloves to her, she put them on. He handed her purse to her, but he carried her briefcase. Taking her hand, he paused briefly as he looked down at her, donning a noble smile. She automatically smiled back at him. Regardless that she found comfort in his gaze, his words of warning swirled about in her head. Noticing her apprehension, he gave her hand an affectionate squeeze. He then led her from the room and closed the door behind them.

They went downstairs and had breakfast in the hotel's restaurant. She was quiet, so quiet that eventually he stopped talking until they had finished. Once he paid the bill, he stood and pulled her chair out for her. He then took his coat from the chair next to him and placed it around her as she stood, and his immediate reward for his concern was her smile.

"A little big, but thank you, Ivan."

"For now it will do," he said as he placed his arm around her shoulder.

He carried her briefcase as they walked to the lobby. He instructed the bellman to place their luggage into a taxi, then they stopped at the front desk. Ivan advised the front desk to hold Tess' room for her return. He was not certain when that would be, but he told the clerk to put the entire charge on his bill. The front desk clerk agreed that he would hold her room until she checked out, whenever that would be, then they left the hotel.

On the way to the train station, they stopped at a small shop where he bought her a new coat. A simple design of double lined, soft black wool with a large notched collar, and two buttons to close the front. It was a plain garment, though she thought it was lovely. Before they left the shop, she purchased a translation book, although now, she felt there was really no need for it with Ivan as her guide.

As they walked out of the shop, she grasped his arm, but it was the look in her eyes that stopped him in place. Moving up to his face, she gently kissed his cheek and said, "Thank you, Ivan, it's beautiful. The most beautiful coat I have. I'll think of you every time I wear it, which will be often."

Ivan looked at her, slightly shocked by her words and gesture. To him it was only a coat, nothing more than a necessity. Yet, to her it was a memory, something that would always remind her of him. That pleased him. He knew more strongly now that there was something different about her, and he was happy that he had the pleasure of sharing time with her.

Then, hauntingly, his suspicions spoiled his momentary happiness as he thought, "Is she the answer to my prayers, or a nightmare in disguise? Could she be what I've wanted my entire life, or is someone playing a terrible joke on me? Did someone find her for me, sending her to me, just to take her away at another time?" His eyebrows crinkled as he frowned at the thoughts passing through his head.

"Is something wrong? Did I do something to upset you?" she asked as she touched his forehead and tried to stroke the frown from his brow.

"No," he answered, not realizing his fear was visible.

Then returning to the taxi, they continued to the train station.

CHAPTER FIFTEEN

Once at the station, they walked together through the depot as Ivan looked around casually to see if anyone noticed them. There were few people there and it appeared that not many were going south that day.

Ivan stopped at the opening to the car where their compartment was located. Placing his hand on her arm, he turned her to face him. "Tess, are you sure about this? Are you sure you don't want to change your mind?" he asked.

She paused and looked at the steps of the train. He tried to imagine what she was thinking, though fear of what she would find was the only thought that came to his mind. From her expression, he felt she lacked the words to describe exactly what she felt. But he knew that fear of what she would find was only half of what she thought about.

"I'm trying to imagine the worst possible scenario. I know that my wildest dreams couldn't compare to the devastation of Sarajevo. But for Mara, I have to put my fear aside. I have to help her. Concentrating on my fear will make me fail to do what I know is right, what I must do, what I came here to do. She had faith enough to send me her story. Probably she never thought anything would come of it, but something did. And because of her courage, I have to call on my courage to answer her plea for help."

Saying nothing, he only watched her look away and heard her released a small, despondent sigh.

So many frightening scenarios flew about in her head, but she ignored them because of the strength she saw in his gaze when she looked back at him. "I know that once I step onto this train, I'm on my own. I will do what I feel I must do, and I won't cry or become hysterical," she said, addressing what she felt was his subliminal concern.

Ivan knew she was frightened of what she could not begin to imagine. But she was determined to find Mara and counted on her courage not to fail. Then she moved up the steps and slipped slowly away from his grasp.

He immediately placed his hand back on her arm and, turning around, she saw him smiling at her.

"You're not alone. I am with you. I will keep you safe, so don't be frightened," he said, trying to reassure her.

His comforting words forced Tess to smile. Through all his explicit opinions, she found him to be remarkably caring. It was as though he somehow knew the situation of the child she needed to find.

"Thank you," she whispered, then, still looking at him, she pulled away again.

Briefly forgetting his surroundings, he wanted to pull her back down and into his arms. He did not want to let her get on the train. He did not want her entering the danger that lurked in Sarajevo. Keeping her in the luxury of his apartment in Belgrade would be better. She need not be in Sarajevo for him to learn the truth of her purpose. She did not have to expose herself to the peril of this senseless war. But in her gaze, he felt her determination and knew he would not be able to keep her from doing what she said was the right thing to do, what she must do, what she came here to do.

Breaking their mesmerized stare, the station master announced the final boarding call over the loud speaker. He motioned her to continue up and into the train car as he followed. Taking her hand, he led her to their compartment. Once inside, he closed and locked the door, then pulled down the shades on the windows to the outer walkway. After placing their luggage in the overhead racks, he looked at her. Like an anxious child, she sat at the window, looking out as the train pulled away from the station.

Sitting next to her, he watched her. He had placed her briefcase on the seat across from them. Reaching for it, he lifted it, set it on his lap, then touched her arm. "Tess, show me your laptop, please. While you enjoy the scenery, let me read one of your stories."

She turned to look at him. He fully expected she would reject his request, but when she smiled at him, again, he doubted that she was a spy.

"Alright," she said.

He placed the briefcase on her lap, stood, and pulled a small table up from the wall under the window. Securing the table, he placed the briefcase on it to make it easier for her.

"This is the combination: zero, two, zero on the left, and zero, one, zero on the right," she said as she began to turn dials on the combination lock.

Sliding the buttons away from the center, the locks sprang open.

He was shocked. He could not imagine why she told him how to open her briefcase. But even stranger than her honesty was the fact that those numbers made up his birth date, October twentieth. How could she possibly know that? Could it be a lucky guess? This fact shook him deeply.

"Where did you get those numbers? What an odd sequence."

"Numbers?"

"Yes. The combination to the lock."

"Oh, they were part of an old phone number. It's easy to remember, so I use it for everything, even my computer at home." She thought for a moment, then asked, "Why is it odd?"

He deliberated quickly. What harm would it be to tell her his birthday? At that thought, he smiled, and said, "That's my birthday."

Her eyes widened and her eyebrows lifted. "Twenty ten?" She thought for a moment. "Oh, you mean, ten twenty? The twentieth of October? You're joking."

He shook his head. His eyes moved shyly from her, to her briefcase, then back to her face.

"Well, happy belated birthday!" she said and affectionately stroked his hand.

He looked at her as if he was awaiting a response. His expression made her frown slightly. "What?" she asked.

"And your birthday?"

"November eighth."

"Happy belated birthday to you also," he said in a softer tone.

"Ivan, if anything happens to me while I'm there," she said, but paused, and it seemed she did not know how to conclude her sentence.

"Nothing will happen, Tess," he said as he now saw the same fear that he saw earlier in her eyes.

"Well, if anything does, just call the number on the Foundation's letterhead. You'll find it in my briefcase. Ask for Willis. He'll take care of everything, any tragedies."

Her words caused him a pang of sadness. "Please, Tess, don't think that way. Nothing will happen, I promise you," he insisted as he placed his hand on her arm and tried to encourage her.

She smiled and lifted her laptop from the briefcase. As she did, he noticed her Bible as Sergej had mentioned. Reaching for it he asked, "May I?"

"Of course," she answered, allowing him to take it.

He opened it and saw notations regarding faith and compassion. Sergej was right; it was not an Orthodox Bible. He smiled and, again, he imagined that she was Catholic as he was.

While he read her Bible, she turned on her laptop, slipped the disc into the drive, and opened a file containing one of the novels she was working on. Then she sat patiently waiting for him to be ready.

After a few moments, he noticed she was still and he closed the Bible. "Thank you," he said and placed it back into her briefcase. He then reached for the laptop and, once it was situated on his lap, he began to read.

This novel was a love story, or so he surmised from skipping pages. The further he read, the more tragic the story became. The heroine was a woman with similar characteristics to Tess. The scene he read was of the heroine dying in the arms of the man she loved, a man who bore an uncanny resemblance to Ivan. He was tall with chestnut colored hair and hazel eyes.

For a moment, Ivan thought about the male character she described. It appeared that she enjoyed men with his characteristics. This made him happy. For a moment, he looked at her as she read through some of her papers. He wondered if she noticed the similarities between this character and him. Then he returned his attention to her novel. He continued to read the scene where the heroine sacrifices her life by stepping in front of a bullet meant for the hero during a duel. And all the hero could do was hold her and watch her life slip through his fingers. It was too late for proof of his love, only words of love, and that would have to suffice.

Ivan frowned slightly and looked at the seats across from them. In silence, he thought about the situation she had devised. He could not imagine what could cause such emotionalism to make her write with this amount of extreme sorrow. If he were the hero, he would not have allowed Tess to be shot.

As he continued reading, the heroine died, and Ivan felt his heart thump inside his chest. It was too heart wrenching and painful a story, so he closed the lid to the laptop and heaved a distressed sigh. Then handing the laptop back to her, he said, "Here, take this."

"I'm sorry, Ivan. Perhaps I chose the wrong story for you to read as a sample of my work," she said, when she noticed that he was upset.

"Could his love for her not bring her back to life?" he asked because he worried as if he were the man and she were the dying woman who loved him.

"Does a love that strong exist?" she asked, looking away from him.

"I think so. If you're with the right person, the person you were created to be with."

"It's all symbolic. Though the heroine had just stepped in front of a bullet meant for the hero, she was really dying of a broken heart. She had seen him long before he ever noticed her. She loved him silently for years, though never said anything, and never imposed her love on him. Then one selfless act of courage, as proof of what she felt for him, saved his life."

"Why didn't he know? Couldn't he see it in her eyes?"

"They weren't acquainted long enough. He was preoccupied with many other things in his life. He didn't have time for love."

He refused to accept her explanation and shook his head at her reasoning. His brow crumpled as he made an aggravated ticking sound with his tongue against the roof of his mouth.

"Make it a fairy tale. Make his love bring her back to life. Make them live happily ever after," he said as his frustration showed his true character.

She did not say anything, only admired him for the romantic he appeared to be at that moment in time. In the back of her mind, she knew exactly how romantic men could be when they believed in something as tender as love. They believed it, because, when with the right woman, they felt it.

"What would make you write this?" he asked.

"Life isn't always happy; it's more tragic than happy. I can't always write happy endings. It wouldn't be realistic."

He knew her words were true. Thinking of the tragedy in Sarajevo, he shook his head. How he wished he could write a happy ending for the conflict there; however, the damage was done and there was no going back.

"You're right. Life isn't happy all the time," he said, then paused, but then smiled slightly because he had the solution. "Change it. Make him see her love for him before the pistol is loaded. Maybe then he won't get himself into a position where a duel is necessary."

"I'll see what I can do," she said with a smile. Then trying to change the subject, she opened the laptop and proceeded to show him other novels she had written. Opening the file menu, she allowed him to look through the list.

As the files scrolled up on the screen, several caught his attention.

"What are these files?" he asked.

"Those are the main operating start-up files. The last one, I think, has to do with the modem. I send work to my publisher electronically."

The smile fell from his face. This was something he had not thought of. Perhaps she did not have the information yet. Maybe she was going to Sarajevo and would wait to receive the information, then pass it onto her connection. That would protect the receiver of the information and protect her on her way there; however, telephone lines were down in Sarajevo. "She must know that," he thought.

His eyes searched the air around him as he contemplated his foolishness in not realizing that the opposition would utilize such a simple tactic. How appropriate and unsuspecting she was. How honest she appeared. But the harder he tried to find flaws in her explanations, the more her story sounded true. "What a good choice they made in an author," he thought, then he looked at his watch. The train would be arriving at his destination in forty-five minutes.

"Tess, I need to tell you that I'm getting off the train in Požega. I have business there," he said, then he noticed her disappointment as her smile slipped away.

She sighed, accepting the situation. "Well, thank you for escorting me this far. I do appreciate it, Mr. Đurić," she said, then she closed the lid to her laptop and placed it back into her briefcase.

Seeing her upset over his having to leave, he abruptly felt guilty. "Did I say you wouldn't see me again? And you're calling me, Mr. Đurić. Why? Does my leaving make you angry, or sad perhaps?" he asked.

Through his suspicions, he was still a man and, though unsure of her motives, he enjoyed her company. He wanted her to tell him that his departure made her sad. He wanted her to feel the same insanity that was taking possession of his heart; however, much to his dismay, "I understand," was all she said. She closed her briefcase and snapped the locks shut. Then she sat back against the seat and gazed out the window at the passing landscape as she thought about the situation.

Leaning toward her, he took her left hand in his. His voice was smooth and full of concern, as he asked, "Are you sad because I'm leaving?"

"You owe me no explanation. I can't expect you to give up your time just to waste it with me."

Without saying the words he preferred to hear, she spoke the truth of what she felt. In her words, he heard her say it was sadness that she felt, not anger. This thought made him less stern.

"If I could take you with me now, I would. It's not safe for you to come with me. I will leave you with a friend; his name is Sergej. His house is where we will stay in Sarajevo. He is a fine man and a very good friend. He will guard you with his life. You *will* be safe with him."

"Will I really see you again? Or are you only saying it to make your departure easier? Because if so, it isn't necessary."

Lifting her hand to his lips, he kissed it. He wanted to answer her questions, but felt the less said the better. "You will see me tonight at Sergej's house. I'll arrive before dinner."

He did not want her to be frightened, but he saw fear lingering in her expression. Just then, he debated leaving her with anyone, even though he trusted Sergej with his own life.

"Why don't you rest awhile? We have a way to go yet," he said.

"I'm not tired."

"The ride from Užice to Sarajevo is long."

"Užice? Don't I get off at Priboj? I thought that was the closest stop to the border."

"It is, but that area is not safe, so you will get off at Užice. Do you think I'd actually let you go anywhere unsafe?" he asked, and his stern stare was a bit unforgiving of her ignorance of the situation. Then he noticed her fear had increased and he wished he had not said anything. "It will be alright. The point is to keep you hidden. No one must know you're in Sarajevo, let alone in this country."

"Why? I'm not doing anything wrong."

"In a way, yes, you are. To Nationalists, everything about you is wrong. And your country does not allow its citizens to travel in these regions unauthorized. Your being here has most likely broken several, if not every, law derived from the sanctions against Serbia."

"I had to do something."

"I understand that, but how did you get to fly from New York into Belgrade anyway?"

"I had a ticket to London, which then went to Budapešt, then from there, I would go on to Belgrade. But once I arrived in London, the flight to Budapešt was delayed. I thought it might have been because of sanctions, so I went to another airline and didn't tell them I was going from

Budapešt to Belgrade. If I missed the flight into Belgrade, I was going to have to take the bus, and that would have taken much longer."

"What happened in Budapešt?"

"Nothing. I boarded the plane to Belgrade and that was it."

"They didn't ask you why, as an American, you were going to Serbia?"

"Yes. I was questioned at the base," she said.

"Base? Military base? What airline did you fly in on?" he asked.

"I flew in on a Red Cross aid plane. I told them that I was going to join my colleagues with the London Post. So, I was able to get on their only flight this week."

"And they let you through on that line?"

She reached into her purse and pulled out a small envelope. Pulling out a passport sized booklet, she handed it to him. It was a press pass and a certified visa from the London Post. Accompanying this was a letter of introduction permitting her to cross the border into both Serbia and Bosnia via her employer, again, the London Post.

"Official paperwork usually speaks for you. I flew into Belgrade on a non-sanctioned plane, so I needed to be in Budapešt in time to make the Red Cross' flight."

"How did you get this?"

"I told you, I was to contact Herbert Strassburg, who works for the London Post and was stationed in Sarajevo and in Belgrade. It was all arranged between him and George Preston."

"That's very interesting," he said, wondering who else knew she was here other than her good friends George and Willis, and the late Herbert Strassburg.

"What was I supposed to do? Fly into Zagreb, then try to get to Sarajevo? It's twice the distance. Besides, the Croatian government had no idea where to begin looking for Mara."

Ivan stopped himself from what he was originally going to say. He had thought of something else that mattered more. "You contacted the Croatian government? Who? Where?"

"I first contacted the Croatian Consulate in New York, but they only referred me to the US Embassy in Zagreb. They sent me on to some temporary office of Civil Liberties in Zagreb, but I have no idea what they do, or how they were supposed to help."

"You're right. None of those offices would know how to find a child in

Sarajevo, nor would they care. Did you contact anyone else?" he asked.

"Several agencies in New York and one in Chicago, including the Red Cross. They both had lists of casualties from Bosnia, but none of them had information regarding children if they weren't confirmed fatalities."

"Did you contact NATO?"

"No. I didn't think they would be able to help."

"Did you contact the Serbian government, or any Serbian agencies in the United States, or here?"

"No. Why would I report a missing Croatian child to the Serbians? That would sign her death warrant."

Ivan smiled at her intuitiveness. From her expression, he saw she was slightly offended that he would consider her so foolish and he immediately apologized. "I'm sorry. I didn't mean to insult you."

"It's okay. I've been quite desperate to find her, so it was a logical conclusion."

"How can you be certain Mara is Croatian?" he asked, knowing he wrote that in his letter to the foundation on Mara's behalf.

"Iđy, Mara's protector, said that she is. If she's Croatian, do you think she's also Catholic?"

"Most likely. Why?"

"I didn't think of checking with any Catholic organizations. They may have been able to help."

"If they had, would you still have come here?" he asked, hoping her answer would be yes.

"Yes. She's alone out there, or so I imagine, because she did not mention any family other than her parents and brother. There's Iđy, who could be a relative, but I have no way of knowing." She paused briefly. "The world is scary enough, but to be so young and alone in the middle of a war." She shook her head. "I can't imagine it. She must be petrified."

He reached for her hands. Touching them, he felt her stress over her inability to find Mara and he wanted to relieve her of it. "Don't worry. You're doing much more than many others would," he said.

She smiled at him. "Thank you for your help, Ivan."

Just then, the look in her eyes, and the way she spoke his name, made him want her. His hand moved up on her arm as he moved closer to her to kiss her. Again, she looked down to her lap, then said, "I think I will try to rest awhile."

He let go of her arm as she leaned away from him and toward the side of her seat. Resting her head against the seat back, she closed her eyes. He smiled at her and sat back in his seat as his mind melted into private thoughts of how he was going to keep her hidden from the terrors of this war.

CHAPTER SIXTEEN

Some time had passed, and Ivan eventually emerged from his thoughts. He had been staring out the window and thinking. Looking at Tess, he then looked at his watch. They would soon arrive at Požega. Leaning toward her, he stroked her hand and softly said, "Tess, wake up."

Hearing him say her name, she took a deep breath and opened her eyes to see him smiling at her. For a moment, as in her hotel room in Belgrade, she had forgotten where she was. After a quick glance around the car, she remembered, then asked, "What time is it?"

"Time to wake up," he said as he stood up, reached to the overhead bins, and pulled their luggage down. Then he set them by the door in preparation to leave.

"Why are you taking the luggage?" she asked.

He turned around and noticed her uncertainty. Walking back to her, he sat next to her and held her hand. "It will be easier if I do."

"Why?"

"Tess, you want to get off the train as fast as possible. You don't want to linger in the station. If I take your luggage now, you will be able to get off the train and be out of sight quickly. Also, without luggage, you will look like a local, not a foreigner. Don't forget, there's a war going on here, and you need to look like you belong here."

As the train began to slow, she looked away from him. They were at the Požega depot. With several soft stopping movements, the train then stood motionless.

He still held her hand and moved toward her. He tried to enter her line of vision as he leaned over to look at her. "Tess, would you rather go back to Belgrade? The train will return tonight."

She shook her head and looked at him. He smiled at her and stood. Giving her a kiss on the cheek, her hand slipped from his as he stepped toward the door.

"I'm going to find Sergej. I'll be right back. Stay in here. Don't go walking around, please," he said. Then he slid the door open and placed their luggage outside the compartment. Turning around to see her, again he smiled, then he stepped into the walkway and closed the door.

Through the window, she saw him walk away from the train and into the depot. Following him were two men carrying their luggage, and she wondered where they came from. After a moment, Ivan came back outside, and a group of men approached him at the entrance. The men looked toward the window where she sat, then Ivan turned and smiled at her. Turning back around, he continued his conversation. The men appeared upset as they spoke with him, though within moments he appeared to calm them, after which he returned to the train.

Within seconds, Ivan slid the door open and entered the compartment with a man standing behind him. "Tess, this is my good friend, Sergej," he said, then he turned to Sergej and said, "Sergej, this is Miss Fordel."

"Miss Fordel, it is my pleasure to escort you to Sarajevo," Sergej said as he reached to shake her hand.

"Thank you. It's a pleasure to meet you, but please call me Tess," she requested while shaking his hand.

Sergej smiled, acknowledging her request, then Ivan began to speak to him in Serbian. As they talked, she examined them both. Looking at Sergej, he appeared about the same age as Ivan and was the same height with blackish brown hair, very short and neatly combed. He had warm brown eyes that displayed a compassionate expression. He was very clean, but oddly attired in plain, dark clothing. He wore two dark brown-green sweaters under a khaki colored coat of thick canvas. His black pants resembled military fatigues, with their many pockets, and they also were made of a heavy canvas. His boots were no different: high over the ankles with sturdy rope laces, thick soles, and tops in worn, dark brown leather.

Smiling to herself, she thought he resembled a soldier. She observed the way Sergej stood, and noticed that he listened carefully as Ivan spoke. It was as though he were taking orders from Ivan. Then Ivan suddenly turned and smiled at her as he had noticed her watching them. She smiled back at him, then turned to look out the window to search for the other men.

Ivan asked Sergej to leave them alone and, at once, Sergej stepped outside, then closed the door. Sitting next to Tess, Ivan saw doubt in her eyes when she turned and looked at him.

"Sergej is a very good man. He will watch out for you. If you need anything, tell him, no matter what it is."

She looked at him as a vague smile bent her lips. She did not know whether to believe him when he said he would see her later that evening.

Stooping in front of her, he took her hands in his and tried to reassure her that he was sincere. "Do you still think I'm leaving you?"

Her doubts lingered, and his words were their cause. Yet, words were all he had until the moment of truth arrived.

"I know when I say 'trust me' that you don't know me. I could be a madman. But I have promised you that you will be safe, and you will be, Tess."

He did not know why she trusted him. Either it was a fantastic setup, or she was so desperate to do what she set out to do that she would place her life in the hands of an unfamiliar man. And not only an unfamiliar man, but "a man from Belgrade," he thought, remembering her words. However, he failed to imagine that she liked him, or even cared for him, and that was why she trusted him. He failed to imagine that his true inner goodness shone through all of his opinions, and that being with him was the safest she had ever felt in her life.

"It's okay," she whispered.

"I *will* be there. I promise, and I do not break my promises, especially those I make to *you,*" he said.

Then the train's pre-departure bell sounded; a sound that suddenly caused Ivan tremendous angst, because the train would soon be leaving the station, and that meant they would be separated for a little while.

"Then I'll see you tonight. You'd better go before you have to jump from the train," she said.

He stood up, bent toward her to kiss her cheek, then he stood straight. Her hands slipped from his after he gave them one final affectionate squeeze. Then he smiled at her, and said, "Do what Sergej tells you. You can trust him as you would trust me. Remember, this is war."

She looked up at him and smiled mischievously. Though it was strangely inappropriate, somehow it was strangely appropriate.

"What's that smile for?" he asked.

"Who says I trust you, Mr. Đurić?" she said, playing with him.

He abruptly stopped smiling; her comment took him off guard, and he did not know what to make of it. Was she trying to tell him not to trust her? Or was she teasing him, playing with him, for leaving her in the safekeeping of his friend?

Seeing his expression, she felt he did not take her comment as the tease she meant it to be. Without answering her question, Ivan walked to the door and slid it open. Not looking back at her, he stepped from the compartment, then slid the door closed. He did not say good-bye, and all she could do was watch him leave. Now she felt that she might not see him ever again, and she panicked.

He stood just outside the compartment's door. From where she sat, she heard him speak briefly to Sergej in English so that any passenger who cared to listen may not readily understand. But he also spoke in English so that she would hear him.

"Take care of her," he ordered, then he turned around and walked away.

Sergej noticed the change in Ivan's disposition, and he wondered if it was because he was missing her already. As Ivan walked to the end of the train car, Sergej called after him. "What's wrong? What happened?"

"Protect her with your life," Ivan said over his shoulder, then he disappeared out the train door and headed to the depot.

The door to the compartment opened and Sergej entered. She looked at him as he stepped inside, and from her expression, he knew something upsetting had just happened between them. Closing and locking the door, he smiled, then he sat in the middle seat across from her. Opening his newspaper, he began to read.

She moved her briefcase and folded the table back down to the wall. She opened the window, leaned out of it, and looked for Ivan. Sergej smiled as he watched her. It appeared that she cared as much for Ivan as Ivan cared for her.

Ivan was standing with the same men, only this time, his back was to her. For a moment, she looked at him. He appeared angry, and she knew she was the cause. Then the train jerked forward once but did not advance. She motioned to Ivan and called to him as loud as she could over the train's engine. "Ivan! Ivan?"

Hearing the faint sound of what Ivan thought was her voice, he ignored it and continued with his conversation. But one of the men standing with Ivan motioned to Tess, and automatically Ivan turned around to see her. She was speaking to him, but he could not hear over the noise of the train. Though her words had offended him, the fear in her lost appearance compelled him as she was desperately trying to tell him something.

Before the train began to move, he walked back to the window of her compartment. Standing proudly with his hands on his hips, he looked up at her as one eyebrow rose, giving the impression of his intolerance of her. As the train slowly began to move down the track, he began to walk in time with it.

Her tortured stare made him listen more carefully to her words as her hands reached down to him; she desperately needed to touch him. Leaning over the edge of the high window, she was despondent, as she said, "I'm sorry. I didn't mean what I said. I do trust you, honestly I do. Please, forgive me, Ivan."

In an instant, his expression changed from stern to overwhelming joy. Grasping her outstretched hands, he kissed them and smiled. He wanted to pull her out of that window and keep her with him. He wanted to protect her, not leave her safety to anyone else. With him alone, she would be safe. But the train moved faster and he hurried to keep up with it so not to let go of her hands.

"Please be careful and come to the house soon," she said.

The increasing speed of the train forced their hands apart as it tore her away from him. And though he walked slower than it moved, he kept walking, as he said, "I'll see you tonight. I'll be there soon, I promise."

At the end of the platform, he stopped and watched the train leave with her leaning out the window and waving to him. The train moved around a turn, then she was out of sight, and that was his last glimpse of her. For a moment, he closed his eyes, embedding that last vision of her in his mind.

"Either she's the cleverest spy, and I'm the biggest fool in the world, or she's the most unusual woman ever," he thought as he rationalized the situation inside his head. Then Ivan recalled his wish after the attack on the last Nationalist detainee camp where he said, "What I wouldn't give to be with a beautiful and gentle woman."

Opening his eyes, he heard his men calling him, and so he walked back to them. Then they exited the depot, and getting into their cars, they left to take care of business.

CHAPTER SEVENTEEN

The train moved smoothly along its tracks. Sergej sat across from her reading the paper, though he periodically looked at her, and seeing her obvious affection for Ivan made him smile.

For several moments, Tess was silent as she looked out the closed window and thought about Ivan; she still saw his face as he waved good-bye. Then the silence became awkward to her, so she broke it as she said, "Sergej?"

He lowered his paper and looked at her.

Ivan's words passed through her mind when he had told her to trust Sergej as she would trust him. She smiled. "Ivan told me that I'm to stay at your house. I wanted to thank you for your generosity. It's very kind of you to open your home to a stranger."

Folding his paper, Sergej held it in his hands. He smiled at her, and when he answered, she noticed that his accent was heavier than Ivan's was. "You are not to think of yourself as a stranger. You are Ivan's friend, so you are my friend."

"Thank you," she answered.

"The house you will stay in has been in my family for a very long time. My brother, Stefan, and my mother, both whom you will meet, are actually living two houses away."

"I see. I look forward to meeting them," she said and smiled.

"Ivan told me you are from America, from New York City," Sergej said.

"Yes, I am, did he tell you why I'm here?"

Looking down at his paper, he said, "He did. He said you're searching for a child."

"Actually, two people. A little girl named Mara Jovanović and someone named Iđy."

Hearing Mara's pet name for Ivan, Sergej's gaze froze as he looked at her. He did not know what Ivan had written in Mara's letter that accompanied her manuscript, but he surmised that he had signed the letter as Iđy. Attempting to cover his shock, he laughed, then said, "That's a funny name."

"I feel like it's impossible to find her. It's as if someone's watching me search for her and laughing at me. I'm not going to hurt her." She looked out the window and sighed. Her shoulders slumped slightly at the thought of not finding Mara. And now that Ivan was gone, being there made her feel strange and awkward.

Seeing her uneasiness, Sergej slid to the seat directly across from her. "Why do you want to find this child? Why do you walk into the middle of a war to find her? Is she a relative?" he asked, attempting to feign ignorance of the situation.

"I thought for sure Ivan would have told you," she said, looking at him and waiting for his response. She was curious about how much Ivan had told Sergej. Did he already know the complete story behind her trip to Sarajevo?

"Why don't you tell me? Ivan is very private, and though he has mentioned some things, I would rather hear about it from you."

She began her story about her search for Mara. Sergej listened while she explained who she was and about Mara's book winning the competition. She then told him that she needed to find Mara before the deadline for awarding the money had passed.

Sitting there silently, Sergej observed her overall gestures as she relayed her desperate story. Though he did not know her, he felt her search was genuine. Her need to find Mara was real, not a façade for her to strategically align herself with the Black Rebel. Tess finding the Black Rebel was as impossible as Tess finding Mara. The fact remained that if Ivan did not want Tess to find Mara, she would not find her.

"Ivan said he would help me look for her, but I hate to pull him away from what he needs to do. He's a very kind man to take the time to show me around. Why he has, I don't think I will ever understand."

Sergej smiled. Hearing her talk about Mara, he understood Ivan's confusion over her real purpose for going to Sarajevo. As Ivan had mentioned, he thought that either she was the cleverest of spies or she was exactly who she said she was, the chairperson of the foundation who had come to give Mara her award. Regardless, as Ivan had said, time would tell the truth of Tess' purpose.

"Ivan keeps his word. If he said he would help you, he will help you. Many people depend on Ivan's help. And you are correct when you say he is very kind, that he is."

"Please finish reading your paper, Sergej. I didn't mean to interrupt you," she said. Then reaching for her briefcase, she unlocked it, and removed her laptop from inside. Closing the case, she set it on the floor next to her feet. Sergej was curious and so he watched her. Opening the lid, she turned it on with the intention to continue writing about her experiences since she arrived. Waiting for the files to load, she looked up and noticed him watching her.

"Do you want to see? Come, sit next to me," she said, motioning for him to sit beside her.

He played ignorant and moved to the seat next to her. She handed him the laptop and started a game for him to play, which he enjoyed.

As she reorganized her briefcase, Sergej periodically glanced at her and noticed that she reviewed the dossier on Mara. Suddenly, the laptop began to beep. Knowing the battery was low, he looked at her, but acted as if he had no idea what had happened. Reaching to the left side of the keyboard, she pressed a small button and the screen went black. He closed the lid and handed it to her.

"I'm sorry, but the battery needs to be recharged. I didn't plug it in last night. I worked the entire night until half past four this morning. I'll have to wait to recharge it," she said.

"Tess, I don't know if Ivan told you, but there is no electricity in Sarajevo. And, well, there is no running water either."

She laughed at herself. Shaking her head, she placed her laptop back into her briefcase, then closed and locked the lid, as she said, "Well, I asked for it and I got it."

"What do you mean, you got it?"

"I always find myself in strange situations, that's all. It's alright. I've been camping before."

"Camping?"

She looked at him. She could not imagine anyone not knowing what camping was. But Sergej related camping to the Rebel's camp in the hills south of Sarajevo. He also related camping to the fighting involving the Rebels.

"You know, you drive out into the country, usually the woods, sleep on the ground, try to fish, or hunt for your meals, but end up eating cold canned food, taking baths in cold lakes, and most of the time you are running away from bugs and snakes and things like that. Eventually you go home, extremely happy to sleep in your own bed. Then you wonder why you went in the first place and swear you'll never do it again," she said, laughing at herself.

"I see," he commented, and smiled briefly at her portrayal of camping.

"It's a horrible experience. You should consider yourself lucky if you've never had the pleasure of camping, at least like that," she said, then she noticed his serious expression. Yet, when Sergej stood and sat back across from her, she felt she had said something wrong.

He lamented as he looked at the empty seat next to her. "It sounds like living in war. Except for here, there is no fishing, or hunting, and most of the time, there isn't a lake to bathe in or even clean water to drink. And for so many, there is no going home because there is no home left to go to."

She was anguished from her ridiculous depiction of what Americans consider as an occasional frolic. Leaning forward, she tried to smooth over her last statement. "Sergej, I'm sorry. I didn't mean to joke about the situation here, only point out the luxuries that some people take for granted. Please, please, forgive me. I'd never intentionally mock the sorrows of your country."

Hearing her words, he looked up at her. The look in her eyes told him that she was truly sorry for the suffering his people endured. When she had leaned toward him, her necklace fell forward from her coat. It was an elegant diamond cross, set in white gold on a delicate chain. The cross was one inch long and from the light passing through the window, the diamonds cast spectrums that caught his eye. Staring at it, he motioned to it. "You are Christian?"

"Yes. Roman Catholic," she answered, looking at the cross.

"Some of the people you will meet in Sarajevo are also," he commented.

"But that's not really what this war is about, is it? It's not a religious war this time. War today is always political, I guess about politics and power. Someone always knows better than the next person, and one person is always greedier than the next," she said.

"In some ways it is about religious arguments, but mostly, it's about land. It's about what was Yugoslavia. It may not make sense to an American, with no offense."

"But it does make perfect sense. America faced this type of situation throughout its entire history. Whether it's been the current Americans, or

Native Americans, or the Spanish, the French, the English, all those who sought refuge in America had to fight to keep it from invaders and eventually from each other. We had a civil war, so Americans understand that. Trust me; quite a few American southerners still hold grudges against American northerners for abolishing slavery. What some people forget, sometimes, is how to respect the rights of others. Yet, once their rights vanish, suddenly personal rights are very important. That relates more to this war than anything does, but our wars today are of a different kind, mostly monetary, unfortunately. Ivan said that Capitalism is war. I didn't agree when he said it, but he was right. He's right quite often. He is a fascinating man," she said, smiling at her own last comments.

"True. But it is difficult to think of another country's war when you are in the middle of your own, Capitalistic or not."

"You're right, Sergej," she said. Then something about his name aroused her curiosity. "Sergej. That's a Russian name, isn't it?"

"Yes, it is."

"Are you Russian?"

He looked at her, not really knowing if he should answer. What difference would it make if she knew he was Serbian? So, he surmised the truth to be the best answer. "Well, before the war I would have answered Yugoslavian. However, now I answer Serbian, but that depends on whom I'm standing with. You must be very careful now with what you say and what you reveal to others. Sergej is an old family name from my great, great grandfather on my father's side."

"I see," she said.

From her tone, Sergej felt obliged to explain further. "A few of the people you will meet in Sarajevo have bloodlines from the different areas that once made up Yugoslavia: some Serbian, some Croatian, some Bosnian, and so on. Most have lived in Sarajevo, or the surrounding area, their entire life. Their families have been there for hundreds of years. But however history brought them there, when the war began, they were trapped there."

"Trapped?" she asked.

"If war started in your country and you left your home, the opposition would win by default. Would they not?"

"True. So, you're saying that by staying put, and living with war versus fleeing, they're holding on to their heritage and their land. But at the same time, they're trapped in the middle of a war."

"Yes. But this multinational situation makes this war difficult. Here you are under attack by segregated extremists."

"What do you mean? Nationalists?" she said, and as she examined his expression, she could sense his apprehension.

"Well, I don't know what you know about this country, or what Ivan has told you, or even what he would want me to tell you, but I will tell you what the world knows. There is much Nationalism in the former and current Yugoslav regions. In this present conflict, there are extremists on all sides: Serbian, Croatian, and Bosniak."

"You mean like Chetnik and Ustaše? Didn't both groups start around or before World War II?"

"Yes, but not all Nationalists from Croatia and Serbia are either of those two groups. And not all Serbians or Croatians are Nationalists," he said, then added, "But you know your history."

"A little, though, right now, I wish I knew more. So, you're saying that ordinary citizens would choose Nationalist sides because of their heritage and turn against those not of their heritage."

"Yes. Families of mixed origins have taken sides against each other. In other cases, your neighbor, who isn't of your ethnic origin, will take up arms against you because they are swayed to their ethnic Nationalism. And these are people that you had coffee with daily, helped in times of trouble, celebrated marriages and births with, then suddenly, they are pointing a gun at you." He shook his head. "All of this combined makes this a complicated war. It should be difficult to walk away from lifetime friends, but for many it is not. Ivan has refused to turn against his friends because they are of a different origin. To Ivan, a friend is a friend until that friend proves otherwise."

"What about Ivan?"

He looked at her. "What does she mean?" he wondered, but imagined that she asked about Ivan's ethnicity.

"His heritage? Is he Serbian like you? Or is he something else, or of mixed heritage?" she asked.

Sergej paused and she knew he deliberated his answer, which made her feel suddenly wrong for having asked. "I'm sorry, don't answer that, I shouldn't have asked," she said.

"I think Ivan can best answer that. Only Ivan has the right to say where he is from and who he is."

"You're a very good friend, Sergej."

"Everyone must decide for themselves. It is sad, but now people have to choose sides that, before the war, most people did not think about. When choosing, some people take the easy way out. They do bad things, and that accomplishes nothing, except failure," he said.

She looked out the window, and as she spoke, Sergej listened attentively. "That reminds me of a man I once knew in America. He wasn't American, not that it mattered. He appeared successful, and went along with whoever could give him what he wanted, but behind the scenes, he did bad things. When people began to see the truth of what type of man he was, he used the fact that he wasn't American as an excuse. Yet, all the while, he flipped back and forth between wanting to be American and not wanting to, which never made much sense to me."

"Was he a friend?" Sergej asked.

"He was never a friend. Friends help you when you're down. He had every opportunity an American had, I saw to that. He only took and never gave, unless it fit into the greater scheme of things he had already planned for himself. But that's not really giving, is it? He was what I call an 'I' man. Everything was 'I' with him. Not we, or us, not you, except to lay blame. No one else mattered." She stopped, thought briefly, then shook her head. "No. He was never my friend, though I was his greatest friend, and he threw me away."

Taking a moment to digest her words, Sergej surmised the man she spoke of was someone she once loved. He carefully tried not to belabor the issue, only prove he understood, as he said, "Some people have no determination. If this man wasn't there for you when you needed him, then he wasn't really a man, he was a boy." He hoped his statement was not too forward, for he did not wish to offend her.

From his statement, she found great affection in his words, and that made her smile. "We meet many people in our lives and all for different reasons. Even though I have my reason for coming here, my being here may help others in ways I don't yet know. So, I can't completely regret spending time with anyone I once knew. Every experience leads us to the next and to where we are today. All bad experiences help us recognize the good people we encounter in our lives. It makes us appreciate them more," she said.

"True. I will tell you again about Ivan. When others turned against their neighbors, Ivan did not do that. To Ivan, a friend before the war is a friend during the war, and after as well, unless the friend betrays him. Ivan does not conform to common rules like so many others. His friendship means much to many people. You can always count on Ivan."

"It appears you are the same," she said.

"We grew up together, and we have been through much together before and during this war. And I hope we will be together as friends long after the war."

"You know, if someone had told me that I would be placing my life in the hands of two such mysterious men as you and Ivan, I would have laughed. But here I am trusting two people I'm just getting to know, in a country where, without Ivan's and your help, I'd be lost, and I don't have the slightest fear of either of you." Shaking her head, she glanced away from him. Then she turned back to see him smiling. "See what I mean? Obviously that man from my past taught me the lesson of recognizing goodness."

Sergej knew Tess' words were true; she had placed her life in their hands. From her words and kind disposition, he knew that she was not a spy for any opposition. It would take a different type of woman to believe in the evils of any aggressor, and she was not that type.

Sergej now understood the affection he heard in Ivan's voice from the previous evening when Ivan requested that Mrs. Tomić make his room pretty for Tess. This was a significant proclamation on Ivan's part. It was not within Ivan's character to bring a woman home to stay at Mrs. Tomić's house. Ivan's honor would disallow this type of behavior if he were not prepared to spend his life with Tess. Regardless of his own needs as a man, Ivan would never insult Mrs. Tomić in that way.

Sergej now understood why Ivan allowed Tess to go to Sarajevo. Whether Ivan would admit it, his suspicions were only an excuse to be with Tess because he had deeper than basic feelings for her. Because of this, Sergej knew that Ivan had serious plans for himself and Tess.

They sat quietly for a moment while the train moved swiftly along the tracks toward Užice, the train's next stop. Sergej told Tess that they would get off the train and leave the depot immediately. "It is safer this way. We'll be there soon," he said, and looked at his watch. Then he looked back at her and his expression turned serious. "When you get off the train, you speak to no one, you look at no one, just follow me and get into the car.

Don't linger in the open. Your safety is very important to Ivan, and to me. Ivan does not take people into Sarajevo, he helps people leave. But for you, he has broken his own rules. So just follow me when we get off the train. Do you understand?" he said as he felt a change in the train's pace; it was slowing down.

Tess nodded and understood what she must do. She recognized the danger from his solemn expression, but his words about Ivan helping people leave Sarajevo troubled her. She could only wonder exactly what Ivan did in Sarajevo.

"Let's go now," Sergej said, then he stood, grabbed her briefcase, and walked to the door. Unlocking it, he slid it open and looked both ways. Turning toward her, he motioned to her to follow him, then he walked to the end of the train car. She followed him in silence and waited behind him.

The train was not near the town of Užice yet; it was at least another ten minutes away. Now seeing where they were, he wondered why it had started to slow down so far out.

He stood on the lowest step near to the exit. Sliding the window down on the door, he looked out. Spotting a familiar car near the woods, which paralleled the tracks to the north, he waved his hand quickly. Watching him, she saw him signaling to someone, but he suddenly pulled back inside the window. He did not look at her; he simply stood with his back to the side wall of the exit.

The train was moving at its slowest pace now, and she imagined since he brought her to the door that they were to get off soon. However, she had no idea they were still several miles from the town. "Are we getting off now?" she whispered as though she could feel danger ahead.

He held his hand up and toward her for silence. "No. There's a car coming up too fast along the side of the train. I can't see who is inside, so we can't get off yet. We'll wait until—" He did not finish his statement. He turned around and looked cautiously out the window to see an older mid-sized Mercedes sedan driving alongside the train, and in it he saw Ivan driving.

"Get off the train now!" Ivan yelled.

Ivan saw Tess standing behind Sergej with a shocked, but happy, look on her face. She was unaware of the danger that waited a couple of miles up the track; local military police waited for the train and they were searching for an American woman.

When Ivan left her in Požega, his men took him to meet with one of their Serbian informants. Strangely enough, this was the same informant that told them the rumor about the Serbians using a female spy. And now, the Serbians knew an American woman left Belgrade heading south. So there was a good chance that they knew why she went there, but how they could know, Ivan was not certain. Though they were not aware of when she left, they had been searching all trains and busses in the surrounding area for two days.

As the train continued slowly, Ivan drove further ahead. Stopping the car, he got out and stood at the side of the tracks as he watched their train compartment approaching. After seeing Ivan, the vehicles that were waiting by the woods, headed for the train.

"You must get off now. Ivan's waiting ahead for you," Sergej said, then he opened the door, and held out his hand to her.

She moved down the steps and looked out the door. From where she stood, she could see Ivan waiting for her at the side of the tracks. He was dressed differently now. He was dressed like Sergej, and now, he too, looked like a soldier. Then looking at her feet, she saw the ground moving past the last step of the train. Feeling slightly dizzy, she grasped the side rails for balance.

"Tess, get off now!" Sergej insisted.

"Just step off. I'll catch you," Ivan yelled as their train car approached.

Looking again at her feet, she closed her eyes, but when she did, her purse dropped from her grasp. Then looking forward, she leaned out the door. Without thinking, she closed her eyes again and stepped from the bottom level when she was about to pass Ivan. As her boots touched the snow covered ground, she felt Ivan's strong grasp keeping her from falling.

"That wasn't so hard, was it?" he asked.

She tried to steady herself. He smiled at her and pulled her toward the car. Slipping from his grasp, she turned, and hurried away from him.

"What are you doing? We have to get out of here!" he said, frowning, as he moved after her and grasped her by the arm.

"I dropped my purse," she answered.

He looked at her and saw she did not have it, nor had he noticed that she had dropped it. He looked at Sergej, who had leapt from the train and approached them; he did not have it either. Escaping Ivan's grasp for a second time, she hurried away from him to search for it, and so he followed her. Finding it embedded in a mound of snow near the tracks, she bent down to pick it up. When she stood straight, Ivan picked her up and carried her back to the car. He said nothing. He only looked at her and laughed under his breath. She smiled and thought how odd she must seem to him.

Reaching the car, he put her inside. As the other vehicles approached, he leaned toward her and said, "Give me your passport. Give me all your identification, including the London Post documents, and the information on Mara."

"My passport? My documents? Why?"

"Just give them to me, Tess," he insisted as he reached for her purse.

She quickly opened her purse and handed him all that he had asked for, along with her wallet. Inside the wallet were her driver's license and two credit cards, US dollars, and local currency.

"Don't worry, you're safe. Nothing will harm you," he said softly. Then he gave her a quick kiss on the forehead, smiled, closed the door on her side, and walked to the nearest car.

Sergej approached and put her briefcase next to their luggage in the trunk of the car where Ivan was standing. He then walked to Ivan who handed him Tess' identification and said, "Take these and keep them safe. Use them to check her out. I want a full dossier. I want to know everything there is to know about her."

Sergej nodded. "Okay."

"Go back to the house. We'll be there later," Ivan said, then he walked back to the car Tess waited in, and entered the driver's side. Shifting gears, he turned the car around and drove rapidly away. The other cars joined them: one car moved in front and two followed behind them.

Staring out the front window, Tess sat motionless, wondering what was going on. Ivan noticed her estranged disposition and said, "I told you you'd see me again."

"I'm happy to see you, but," she shrugged slightly, "what's going on? I thought you had things to do?" she said as she noticed his serious expression.

He did not know what to tell her, so he decided to tell her the truth, or at least partial truth. He glanced quickly at her, then back to the road. He hoped his words would frighten her. If she were the woman he searched for, he hoped she would know he cared about her; cared enough to risk his life to take her from the dangerous situation that had waited ahead for her.

Though she may be on the Serbian's side, he wondered, "What would they do once they found her? Or worse, if the Croats or Bosniaks found her first, what would *they* do?" As he saw it, being an American would leave the door open for any possibility.

"In Požega, I was told that Serbian military police are searching the trains going south. They are looking for an American woman. Do you know why they'd look for you? What would they want with you, Tess?"

"I," she stuttered, "I don't know. What makes you think I'm the one they're searching for? I can't possibly be the only American woman in the area."

Not answering her, he looked at her, and his expression displayed the ridiculousness of her statement. What other American woman would be right there, right then?

When he did not respond, she asked, "What would they want with me? Do you know?"

He did not answer, but looked at her again, then back to the road ahead.

She could not figure him out, nor could she imagine anyone wanting to find her there. Other than Willis and George, no one of any significance knew she was there, and now his silence made her suspicious.

"Ivan, do you still want something from me? Something you're not telling me?" she asked. She began to think that he suspected her of something. Perhaps that was the reason he insisted on taking her to Sarajevo and why he insisted on helping her search for Mara.

Ivan remained quiet. He did not know how to answer. He looked in the rearview mirror at the car with his men that followed them. Then one of the cars from behind drove away from the procession and headed south down a narrow road.

"Why did you want my identification and paperwork? Can you at least tell me that? What is it you want to know? If there is something, just ask. I know you don't know who I am. I could be anyone."

Surprised by her honest curiosity, he looked at her again. Slowing the car, he turned to another road heading north off the main road. The car that had been in front of them continued straight on. The car behind them followed the first car, and now Ivan and Tess were alone.

"Ivan, am I in trouble? In trouble with you?" she asked in a surrendering and low tone.

Hearing her words, he grasped her arm and pulled her toward the edge of her seat, so she would be nearer to him. Then he reached for her hand and held it; he did not want her to be frightened.

"I don't know why those men are looking for you. I was hoping you knew, but what I do know is that they would have taken you from me if you were on that train. I promised to protect you, and I will." He paused, wishing she would look at him, but she only looked down at his hand holding hers. "I gave your documents to Sergej. He will return them when we get to his house. If anyone stops us, I will tell them that you are my wife. Without any documentation, you have nothing to prove otherwise. This way you'll be safe."

She did not comment, but from her silence, he knew that she trusted him. Again, he doubted her ability to be the rumored spy. Though his story was half true, it was definitely possible that someone would stop them. However, he hoped from her passport and other documentation that he would learn about her past. Yet, until he did, he would remain guarded. Trusting the wrong person could lead to his death, and his death would leave Mara and his people without help, without a leader, without the Black Rebel.

CHAPTER EIGHTEEN

Ivan was quiet as he drove. Mulling over what he knew about Tess, he felt once she was in Sarajevo, the condition of the city would force her to leave. He had not planned to take her to any children's shelters so soon; however, when she reached for him from the train window, he decided to start that day. He had promised that he would help her, and though he knew Mara's exact location, he would let Tess search everywhere, except where Mara was.

In the back of Ivan's mind, his feelings were changing concerning Tess' intentions. If she truly searched for Mara, to give her the foundation's award, Ivan knew disappointment would consume her when she did not find Mara. If she were in Sarajevo for other reasons, the search would be of secondary importance, if not completely forgotten. Once in Sarajevo, she would most likely sway him from his promise to help her find Mara. From her appearance, he surmised her method would be sexual. And though that thought was a nuisance, it also made him smile, and he felt that now was as good a time as any to find out.

Turning from the main route, he drove onto a narrow road that led to a tunnel formed from the branches of the trees that grew near the pavement's edge. Leaning forward, she looked through the front window, smiling at the graceful formation and perfection of nature's architecture. The stormy winter sky was visible through their naked limbs, and she imagined what this passage would be like in late spring. How beautiful it would look with the trees covered with leaves swaying in the soft breeze blowing downward from the surrounding mountains.

Ivan drove slowly, allowing her to enjoy this natural phenomenon—one of the few remaining untouched wonders of the area. Then his eyes moved from her to something ahead in the road. Looking toward the end of the tunnel, he saw two men holding rifles and walking toward them.

"Sit back," he said, pulling her against the seat.

She looked ahead and saw the two men. Without realizing it, she leaned closer to Ivan as she tried to back away from them. Suddenly, his taking her identification and giving it to Sergej made perfect sense, and she was happy that he had done that.

"Whatever you do, leave your sunglasses on, don't look at them, and don't talk," he said and placed his arm around her shoulder.

She looked at him, though he did not smile as he slowed the car when they neared the men. He observed them: one was taller and older, and the second was fairly younger and shorter. Both men looked dirty, as though they had been in the wilderness for a long time. With their rifles aimed at the front seat, Ivan lowered the window and waited for them to speak.

Ivan listened past the two men and the sound of the car's engine. He needed to know if others accompanied them or if they were alone. As he listened, he only heard the sound of the soft autumn wind through the trees as it whistled and hummed through their barren, frozen limbs.

"What are they?" he thought. He needed to know whether they were Croats, Serbs, or something else. Knowing the area, he surmised they were not Bosniaks since most Bosniaks had been cleared from the area by either Serbian Military or UN Troops. He suspected defectors from the Serbian army, or the upstart of a small militia hiding outside Sarajevo as did his Black Rebels.

Before a word was spoken, Ivan felt no presence other than these two men. However, he was prepared; his loaded pistol was carefully placed under his seat. Also in preparation of any encounters, he carried two identifications: the first one said he was Daveed Milenković, a member of the Serbian Liberties party. The second claimed he was Ivo Zajć, a Croatian citizen, but more importantly, an executive member of the Croatian Delegate's Union, notoriously known as a front for Ustaše political and military loyalists.

The tall man on Ivan's side began to speak in a Serbian dialect. Ivan listened carefully as the man requested he step out of the car. Ivan turned to Tess and leaned close to her. "Don't get out," he whispered, then he kissed her cheek and slipped his arm from around her shoulder. Opening the door, he stepped out to speak with them.

Ivan and the man began conversing. Tess saw Ivan reaching inside his coat and handing the tall man a set of papers. He handed the man his identification and jurisdiction papers identifying him as Daveed Milenković.

The man holding his documentation bent down and looked at Tess, who looked the other way as he smiled at her. He then stood straight and looked at Ivan. "Who is the woman?" he asked.

"My wife," Ivan answered.

The man bent down again to see her. He said hello to her in Serbian. She smiled shyly at the man, then looked away again.

"She's very pretty," the man commented as he looked at Ivan.

The young man bent down to see her. With an enticing grin and a chuckle, he agreed with the taller man. However, Ivan glared over his shoulder at him, and immediately, the young man stood straight and stopped smiling due to Ivan's possessive gaze.

"My wife is shy," Ivan said protectively, as he stepped in front of the open window to block any other attempts by the tall man to look at her.

"What is your purpose in this area?" he asked.

"We are going to the church in Rogatica. My wife's sister is there. She is ill."

The man was briefly silent. Looking back at Ivan's papers, then into Ivan's eyes, he asked, "What does your wife's sister do at the church?"

"She is part of the remaining church staff."

Hearing this, the man gave a small smile and lowered his rifle, considering there was only one church left there and it was Serbian Orthodox; however, that was not their destination. The man motioned his young comrade to retreat back through the trees and immediately he did.

"You may pass, but you should not go there. It's not the same as it once was," the man said as he handed Ivan his documents.

Ivan understood the man's meaning. Rogatica was a site of mass murders, and he knew that the man wondered how anyone had survived there. Ivan nodded, placed his documents in his pocket, opened the car door, then got back into the car.

The man bent down when Ivan closed the door. Placing his hand on the car, he smiled and looked at Tess, as he said in Serbian, "I hope your sister is feeling better soon."

Tess had no idea what he said, but since Ivan was back in the car, she smiled. Then the man stepped back and away from the car. "Safe journey to you and your wife. Good health to your wife's sister. Be careful, there are many snipers about. God be with you," he said, then he waved them onward.

Ivan nodded, then drove away, leaving the man standing in the middle of the road. The man watched them for a few moments as they drove on, then he disappeared into the trees where the younger man had gone only moments before.

Ivan was quiet as he thought about this encounter. When they exited the tunnel of trees, the road split in two directions. He turned to the left and continued down a wider road. After another five minutes of driving, she saw the steeple of a church in the distance. She looked at him, but still he was lost in thought. His eyes did not move from the road before them except to look in the rearview mirror.

When they reached the church, he pulled to the back entrance to be out of sight, then he parked the car. Getting out, he closed the door. She watched him walk around the car and open the door for her. He held out his hand to her to help her to exit. Sliding from the seat, she accepted his assistance and stepped out into the cold. He closed the door behind her and held her hand as he led her to the entrance of the church.

Once inside, her reflexes made her look to the sides of the doors for holy water, but there was none. He stood at the doorway watching her. She crossed herself and genuflected toward a crucifix-less altar at the far end of the church. Comparing her to other citizens from America, he saw her as unexpectedly reverent. Just as when she prayed over her food, she did what she knew was right for the moment.

She walked to the last row of destructed pews, knelt on the stone floor, folded her hands, and stared down. Her posture resembled that of the statues of angels he once saw when visiting a cemetery in Milan: grief and serenity embellished in stone, and with the right light, they appeared life-like in their sorrowful prayers.

Observing Tess, Ivan knew she asked for help in finding Mara. And suddenly he wanted to go to her and tell her where Mara was, but he stood still, thinking about the consequences a single mistake would create. And though something deep inside his heart told him to trust her, in his mind, he could not completely. He feared not for his own life, but for the lives of those that depended on his efforts; however, mostly, he feared for Mara.

Then Tess stood up. She turned and faced him, and her expression was alert and expectant. He walked to her, took her by the hand, and as he led her to the left of where they stood, he said, "We start our search now. There are children here and perhaps someone here will know of Mara."

She smiled at him as they walked out the side door and entered a small annex building. Once inside, he conversed with an older woman who did not recognize Mara's name when he mentioned it, but she took them to see the children.

Ivan stood near the doorway while Tess walked through a small makeshift classroom. She looked at the children and smiled at them as they stared at her from their seats. She did not know what to look for, and all she saw were lost and frightened children.

Stopping toward the back of the room, she stooped down by one child as the others began to talk and go back to their work. The child, a little boy, showed her a drawing he was working on. He had sketched a picture of a house.

Seeing Tess had stopped there, Ivan walked to them to see what interested her about this child. The boy was speaking to her as she looked up at Ivan. Then the boy looked up at Ivan and continued to talk. Ivan stooped down to them while translating the boy's words for her. "He said this is where he used to live, before the bombs and the fighting began. This is where he wants to go."

"What is your name?" she asked the boy.

Ivan translated her question and, in a small, sweet voice, the boy answered, "Josip," then he smiled at her.

"Josip, your house is very beautiful. You draw very well," she said.

Ivan quickly translated her words. The boy smiled back at Tess, handed her the drawing, then spoke again. She looked at Ivan for the meaning of the boy's words.

"He says that he wishes for you to have his drawing because you are very pretty."

"Thank you, Josip," she said, then she took the drawing from him and kissed his cheek.

Just then, someone walking the halls clapped loudly for the children. Class was over and it was time for the children to eat. Ivan stood and held his hand out to Tess. Taking it, she stood up and watched the boy run down the aisle of desks, then out the door.

"Children are all the same, aren't they? No matter where they are, all they need is love and attention," she commented as she looked at the drawing the boy had given her.

"Possibly, but here they need protection more than anything else," Ivan answered.

She glanced at Ivan, then back at the drawing. Slipping her hand from his, she gathered the boy's crayons and placed them neatly inside a shoebox on the desk.

"A nurturing gesture, a gesture that appears to be second nature to her," he thought as her gesture made him wonder what her life was like back in America.

Looking at him, she smiled briefly. Then looking around the room, her expression saddened as she realized that the children in this place were more than likely parentless. Seeing her sadness, Ivan took her hand, then led her from the classroom and back out to the car.

From there they headed toward Sarajevo. Passing through the tunnel of trees, there was no sign of the two men who had stopped them earlier. Emptiness filled the passage. He knew the men were long gone, and, more than likely, back at their camp for the night.

Silent in contemplation, she sat close to the door. In her thoughts, she appeared too far away from him. Stopping the car, Ivan turned to her. He tried to bring her from her solitude, as he said, "Why do you sit so far from me? Come closer to me and tell me what you're thinking about."

At once, she looked at him, and the corners of her mouth attempted to form a smile, though it did not last. Reaching for her, he pulled her nearer as he stared into her eyes. And in her eyes, he saw her lost and alone, and he knew what she thought.

"They will all be like this; every child in every location. They will all be without their parents. Perhaps their parents are still alive, but there will be nothing of true happiness when you look into *their* eyes." He paused when she looked down. Then he lifted her face so he could look in *her* eyes. "Are you certain you want to look for Mara? Can you handle what you will find? Are you prepared for the fact that you may not find her?"

"I have no choice. I must search for her. I will endure whatever I must to try to find her, regardless of whether I do find her. She deserves my truest effort. Don't you think?" she said.

Her eyes gazed deeply into his, and he saw her questioning him. Then she looked away. He was confused. What he expected to see was sarcastic determination in finding Mara, but instead, he saw her devotion to Mara. He felt her need to find Mara as strongly as his need was to protect Mara from anyone searching for her.

Just then, he felt a strange oneness with Tess. Such mixed emotions coursed through him. He wanted to ask her what her real purpose was for going to Sarajevo. Alone and out in the middle of nowhere, there was no way she could defend herself. Feeling so deserted, she would possibly tell him the truth, if there was any other truth to tell.

Gathering his gumption, he looked at her. "Tess—" he started to say, but stopped himself as she turned to look at him. Seeing the same look in her eyes, he could not continue. He could not accuse her without better cause than his suspicion.

"Yes?" she answered.

"Nothing," he said as he shook his head. Again, he wanted nothing more than to hold her and tell her all he was beginning to feel for her, but he only took her hand in his, smiled, then resumed driving. In his mind, the security of Mara, his men, and his people was his immediate concern. Yet, in his heart, his vast and unexplored affection for Tess pulled him away from that.

On their way to Sergej's house, they stopped at a second shelter in Sokolac and the result was the same. The woman in charge had no children by the name of Mara Jovanović. There were several children the same age as Mara, but none appeared to have the intensity required to write such a compelling story.

Tess walked through the room as the children looked up at her and tugged at her coat as she passed. "Little games," she whispered as she looked over her shoulder and smiled at them.

Then one little boy, pulled her coat up instead of down. Turning around quickly she looked at him, and said, "Aren't you a smart little one."

The boy stared fearfully at her. She stroked his cheek and smiled. Then he laughed, and when she turned to walk away, he did it again. She looked at Ivan, who watched half-frowning and ready to intercede on her behalf. "This one must be from Belgrade!" she said, and smiled.

Ivan laughed and shook his head as he remembered her comment about men from Belgrade. In the back of his mind, he wondered if she really saw him as the book described: persistent, rude, and somewhat dangerous. If she did, would that eventually frighten her away?

That thought faded from his mind when she walked back to him. She shook her head over not finding Mara, or any child even close. With one final contemplative look back, she gave Ivan a sorrowful smile, then she looked away again.

Observing the forlorn expression in her eyes, he was sorry that he insisted she not cry. He could see her fighting her tears when she turned away from him. With a single step, he closed the distance between them. As he moved his arm around her to walk her out, she stepped to the side, walked from the room, and left him standing alone in the doorway.

When he exited the building, he saw her standing by the car waiting for him. Without a word, he walked to her, opened the door, and allowed her inside. He stooped next to her, then looked up at her. "Are you alright?"

Glancing sideways at him, she nodded, smiled, then looked out through the windshield.

He stood up and closed the door. Entering the driver's side, he started the car and drove from the building. Without asking her why she sat so far away, he reached for her hand and held it as they made their way home to Sarajevo.

CHAPTER NINETEEN

They arrived in Sarajevo at half past seven. In the darkness, she could not tell the total effect the war had on the city, but its aura was that of mortality. When you entered the city limits, it surrounded you with its eerie silence and frightening chill that passed through every citizen without discrimination. Yet, even in the darkness, she could tell what once was the delicate essence of this beautiful and cosmopolitan city was now long gone. The constant infusion of hostilities, compounded by the lost hope of a nation divided, had obliterated it.

Sergej's house was roughly two miles east and slightly north of the city. It was located on the lowest foothills of the mountain, and off a dirt road that extended from one of the main roads leading from the city. Other houses of similar structure surrounded Sergej's: older houses with dilapidated exteriors and barren foliage from the continuous assaults of the war.

Ivan parked the car in front of the house. Tess saw the drape at one of the second story windows move ever so slightly. Then the front door opened and Sergej walked out onto the porch and quickly closed the door behind him. From the rear of the house, two men walked toward the car as Ivan opened his door and stepped out. A quick conversation transpired between him and the two men while Tess remained inside the car.

When they finished talking, Ivan walked around to her side and opened the door. Reaching both hands toward her, he helped her out. The snow was ankle deep on the dirt road, and he placed his arm around her waist to steady her as she stepped to his side. As they walked up the stairs to greet Sergej, the two men got into the car and drove the car around the back of the house.

Sergej extended his hand to Tess and said, "I welcome you to my home. It isn't much right now, but you will be safe here."

Tess grasped his hand. "Thank you, Sergej. Your generosity is deeply appreciated."

Ivan stood back and noticed a strange unity between Sergej, who was his best and oldest friend, and Tess, who was his newest friend. He could not imagine what had happened on the train that made Sergej so responsive to her. His only hope was that his men would keep their minds on the war and not succumb to her obvious charm. At least not in the same way Ivan had already fallen prey to it. Tess was one thing Ivan did not plan to share with anyone, regardless of her allegiance.

Releasing her hand, Sergej stepped to the door, ready to open it for her to enter. Just when Ivan thought Tess had completely forgotten him, she turned around and walked to him. His expression was slightly fearful as he looked at her. Standing close to him, she looked into his eyes as she reached for his hand and said, "Ivan, please take me inside."

Smiling at her, he knew she did not want to enter without him. Her expression told him that she needed his guidance and protection and, just possibly, his affection. He was happy that she wanted to be with him and no one else. Because of this, he felt her growing trust in him. A trust he did not have in anyone except in the most faithful of his men.

"Don't be afraid. I'm here with you. I won't leave you," he said to reassure her. Feeling her fear in her trembling hand, he moved up the stairs to her side, placed his other arm around her shoulder, and embraced her in his protective care. He then walked her into the house.

The moment they entered, the men in the living room immediately became silent. They were not prepared for what Ivan brought with him from Belgrade. When Sergej said a woman was going to stay with them, they imagined someone ordinary, someone older perhaps, but not Tess. At once, the men stood and looked at her, though they said nothing. Sergej entered behind them, then closed and bolted the door. Looking at Ivan, everyone noticed an unusual pride in his expression as he smiled.

"I would like to introduce you to Miss Tess Fordel. Miss Fordel is from America." Turning to Tess, Ivan smiled at her affectionately. Moving his lips to her ear, he asked, "What do you want to be called? Miss Fordel or Tess?"

"Tess, please," she answered.

"You may call her, Tess," he said. Then he began to introduce her to each man, and as they shook her hand they flashed their most masculine smiles. As he spoke each name, he paused, giving her time to remember them. "Tess, I would like to introduce you to Rurik, Miloš, Nikola, Zoran, Željko, Tomo, Lukáš, Alek, Mihajlo, Dragan, Stefan, and Miša. Lukáš and Miša are brothers, and Stefan is Sergej's younger brother."

She smiled at them as they welcomed her. For being in war, these were some of the cleanest men she had ever seen and all quite handsome. Ivan looked at her with a smile that matched his men's. As he stepped forward, his arm slipped from her shoulder. Removing his coat, he tossed it on the sofa, then spoke to them in a Serbian dialect because Serbian blood outweighed Croatian blood among his men.

Turning her attention to the men, she noticed they periodically looked from Ivan to her. Suddenly, the situation became comical as she thought about what Willis would say if he knew she would be staying alone with so many men in one house. What would he say if he met Ivan? Willis was a dear friend, but such a timid man, so unlike Ivan.

Scrutinizing them, a Slavic folk song called "Hussars" came to her mind. Hussars were cavalry soldiers, and they were also considered highway robbers. But she presumed that soldiers had to be a little bit of both during a war like this one. Recalling the words of the song, she smiled, not realizing how accurate her comparison was.

Yet, when she looked at Ivan, her writer's imagination saw a very different image, one extremely romantic in nature. He was more like a hero from a historic tale, handed down from generation to generation, of a brave warrior saving villages from evil beasts. Why she saw him this way, she did not know. It was an overpowering impression as if it was meant to be. Wandering in her imaginings of Ivan, everything started to become surreal to her, and she realized the dreaminess of Ivan's presence continually forced her to trust him without question.

Then as her thoughts came back to reality, she heard Ivan still speaking to the men as he said in Serbian, "Tess is here with me. She is a guest of this house. You tell no one she is here. You are to protect her with your lives. Do you understand?"

Still standing behind Ivan, Tess removed her coat and handed it to Sergej when he asked for it. The men's attention left Ivan when they noticed her watching him. Regardless that she did not understand what Ivan said, she enjoyed the sound of his voice, the sound of his language. For a moment she thought how she would enjoy hearing him whispering his language in her ear, but when he stopped speaking, a peculiar silence filled the room.

"Do you understand?" Ivan repeated, trying to regain their attention.

Looking down the row of men, who stood like soldiers in front of him,

Ivan noticed they were looking at her. Turning around, he saw her smiling and stifling a laugh. He looked at Sergej for an explanation, although Sergej shrugged, unaware of what amused her, so Ivan asked, "What's so funny, Tess?"

"It's like having my own harem, so many men in one house," she said.

Ivan frowned, but Sergej laughed briefly and motioned for her to follow him to the dining room. As she followed Sergej, she looked back at Ivan, and her expression turned serious, confirming that her statement was a front to disguise her fear.

Again, Ivan saw that lost and helpless appearance in her gaze that called him to her. He looked at the men and saw their reactions to her enticing nature as they carefully watched her walk away. They then turned and looked at Ivan, all of them smirking slightly. Now Ivan wondered if bringing her to the house, with so many men, was the right thing to do. But what choice did he have? He could not let her out of his reach. Regardless, he had promised to protect her and having her with him was the only way he could keep that promise because his men were his army.

"Protect her with your lives. Do you understand me?" he repeated loudly, which commanded the return of their attention. They nodded and grinned at him, as he parted them to get to Tess.

Seated in the dining room, she watched him as he approached and sat at the head of the table to her right. The men sat down in the living room and continued their conversations. Sergej walked from the kitchen carrying a tray of food for them. He placed several plates of various prepared meats, bread, potatoes, and cheese on the table. He then handed them plates and silverware.

"Sergej, please don't wait on me. Tell me where things are and I'll get them," she said.

Sergej only smiled at her thoughtfulness, then he left them alone. Once Sergej had left, Ivan began to prepare a plate for Tess as she sat looking around the room.

The house reflected the atrocities of the war, of which not one corner was left untouched. She could tell that the walls had been covered with dainty patterned wallpaper in soft tones of transparent green and sky blue against a creamy background, but the constant penetrating fog from gunfire and explosions had dulled it. There was no electricity, and though they had generators, because of the noise they produced, they used candles and kerosene lamps to light the house, both of which left soot on the walls and ceiling.

The table they sat at was large and long, simple in style, and made of dark wood. The chairs that surrounded it were odd pieces, probably from different homes whose possessions bombs and thieves had ravaged. Thick tarp-like material, fashioned as drapes, covered the windows to block the interior light from exiting and the cold from entering. The living room was stark and a little frigid, but they had only just lit the fire when Ivan and Tess arrived. In there were two sofas and miscellaneous chairs, all of semi-dilapidated condition. The floors were wood, but no carpets were available to cover them. Like many of their possessions, they had been stolen when Sergej's family was temporarily forced out during an ethnic cleansing raid.

The theme of the house was aged and quaint, and showed much of the character of the area. She surmised that it was in Sergej's family for many generations, as Sergej had previously mentioned it was old. Nevertheless, as a whole, its entirety encompassed privacy and escapism from the war that raged outside its thick walls. Despite its ruined appearance, a feeling of complete camaraderie existed within this diminished domicile. From the moment Tess entered, she felt welcome, but simultaneously awkward as the men in this house questioned her presence with their expressions.

Ignoring their inquisitive stares, she looked back at Ivan. Since they first met, she had watched him, and she saw an indescribable heroism exuding from him. Seeing him now, he appeared eternally entwined with thoughtful concern, and she wondered if he ever told anyone the hidden thoughts and dreams of his heart. Even without Sergej's kind description of Ivan, in all his complexity, Ivan had a supreme air of importance about him that she momentarily lacked the proper vocabulary to describe.

Looking at Tess, Ivan noticed her perplexed gaze. Yet, when he looked deeper into her eyes, he saw tenderness directed toward him and this lured him. "I'm sorry it is not better here, but you will be safe here," he said.

"It's not the house that matters; it's the people within the house that count. I just don't understand war is all. I guess I can't comprehend what possesses people to hate others so deeply. But not only hate, but act upon that hate."

Ivan more than understood her words, which precisely echoed his sentiments; he believed their truth. Staring at the tabletop, she was lost in her thoughts. He held out the plate he had prepared for her, but she shook her head. Not taking it, she continued staring at the tabletop.

"Aren't you hungry?" he asked, hoping his voice would make her exit her privacy.

His voice did pull her from the hidden corners of her mind. And when she looked back at him, he could see she was concerned with some frustration over past memories that still appeared to haunt her present.

"No, not really," she answered.

He placed the plate down in front of himself and stroked her arm lightly as he said, "Eat something. We had a long day and you need to eat. Then you can rest."

Not wanting to upset him, she reached for a small piece of bread and a thin slice of cheese. He smiled at her compliance to his request.

By the time they finished eating, several of the men had gone to their rooms on the upper floors. The remaining men sat at the table, curious about Tess as they talked with Ivan. One of the men, Alek, sat next to her and began conversing with her.

"Where in America are you from, Tess?" he asked, even though he knew the answer.

"I live in New York City, in Manhattan."

"I have never been to America. What's it like?"

"It's the same as anywhere. There are a lot of people there."

"Is there a lot of crime, like in the movies?"

"Sometimes there's crime; the same as anywhere, just more of it because there are more people there," she said. Not wanting to remind anyone of the situation surrounding them, she added, "But there are good sides. There's a lot to do in Manhattan, many things to see: museums, historic sites, cultural events, good restaurants, and one very large and beautiful park."

"Are all the women in New York like you? Are they all pretty?"

Ivan heard Alek's question, and he noticed Tess laugh to herself, slightly embarrassed by his compliment, as she said, "Far prettier. New York is a place you should visit one day."

From her answer, Ivan detected that she did not consider herself pretty. But looking at her, anyone could see that her self-opinion was erroneous. As Ivan watched her conversing in the soft glow of the lamp's light, he felt she was the perfect description of what he thought the gentler sex should be. He knew not all women were that way and, actually, few women he met fit that description as completely as she did.

After an hour of talking and giving his men a chance to get to know Tess, Ivan stood. Taking Tess by the hand, he led her toward the kitchen, though he paused when she turned back to the men at the table. "Good night, gentlemen. It was a pleasure to meet all of you," she said.

Standing behind her, Ivan smiled at her courteousness. This was something they were not always privileged to while living in war. They smiled at her, and wished her a pleasant evening. She then turned back toward Ivan, and they disappeared, hand in hand, into the kitchen.

Once they were out of sight, the men began talking amongst themselves about the attractiveness of Ivan's "girlfriend," as they now called Tess. Not meaning any offense to Tess, they joked if Ivan would really sleep in the small bed they placed in the room earlier that day.

"Why would he sleep alone when he has a beautiful woman to be with?" Rurik commented as he smiled at Sergej; however, he smiled at the wrong man.

Sergej stood up. Slapping his hand on the table, every man in the room was startled to attention. "One more comment like that and all of you will go to sleep at the camp!"

"We're not saying anything about Tess. We're talking about Ivan. You know Ivan as well as us," Rurik stated, and smirked to the others.

Sergej placed his hands on the table and leaned toward Rurik. "Yes. I do know Ivan, and much better than you. He obviously has more respect for women than you do," he said. He then pointed at each man at the table, and now he had their undivided attention. "Whatever Ivan does is no one's business. Is there some reason he shouldn't be happy?" With a final disgusted glance around the table, Sergej left and walked into the kitchen to wait for Ivan's return.

CHAPTER TWENTY

Ivan led Tess from the kitchen and down a duskily lit hall. Stopping at a door to the left at the hall's end, he opened it. A soft light came from inside the room, and he allowed her to enter first. A low fire burned in a fireplace in the middle of the opposite wall. Strategically placed candles filled the room with flickering light, creating a wistful and romantic atmosphere as she entered.

Stepping further into the room, to her immediate right, was a double sized bed; her luggage and briefcase were at the foot of it waiting for her. To each side of the bed were small, square tables with candles on top. To the left, against the wall, was a small wooden table covered with a lace cloth. This was set up as vanity with a small stool in front of it, and above it was a mirror attached to the wall. On each end of the vanity were tall, thick candles burning brightly.

Straight ahead from the entrance was a small doorway with a drape pulled across it that she imagined was a closet. On the wall adjacent to the fireplace sat a small cot-like bed. Next to that was a tall, four-drawer dresser, and on the same wall as the fireplace, was a low, long dresser.

She walked to the bed as she continued to look around. Ivan closed the door and walked up behind her. "This is where you will sleep. This is the room I use when I'm here," he said in a soft voice. He then walked to the window, pulled the curtain aside, and looked around the grounds of the house.

For a moment, she watched him, wondering what he was thinking. "And if I am to sleep in here, where will you sleep?" she asked.

"In here with you, of course. How else can I protect you?" he answered. Letting the curtain go, he turned to see a curious look on her face. Should Tess be the spy, now would be the perfect time for her to start an orchestrated seduction, for he had set it up for her perfectly.

She said nothing, only nodded and looked to the floor.

He could tell she thought sleeping in the same room was a bit suggestive. He smiled and pointed to the far wall. "I will sleep on the small bed," he said, then he walked toward her and placed his hands on her shoulders. "The only other bedrooms are upstairs. If something should happen, I wouldn't hear you calling me, or crying, if you were frightened."

"I told you I wouldn't cry and I won't. That's a promise."

As he gazed at her in the soft glow of the candle's flickering light, her determination matched the intense passion he now witnessed in her eyes. At that moment, he would sacrifice all he had to positively know that she was not against him. Then he could fulfill the ideas racing inside his head. If he kissed her, would it be the kiss of death, or would she become his alone, the way he longed for her to be? He wondered if the passion he witnessed in her eyes was for him, or for whatever issue led her to Sarajevo?

His stare made her uncomfortable and forced her to look away. She took a step back, then turned her attention to her luggage at the foot of the bed.

"Just one kiss," his mind echoed as he secretly betrayed his higher purpose. In her kiss, he knew he would find his answers. In his arms, he would make her tell him the truth. He stepped closer to her and put his hands on her shoulders. "Tess," he whispered as the depth of his breaths increased the longer he looked at her.

Hearing the tone of his voice, she moved away from his grasp. "Yes, Ivan," she said.

He stood in place watching her. He knew he should go to her and do what his heart screamed for, but he could not, now that she had moved away. And he knew, if he did kiss her, it would not stop there, so he changed the subject. "Will you sleep now?"

"If you don't mind, I think so. I'm a little tired."

He lifted her suitcase and placed it on top of the low dresser. Seeing her wallet and passport on the small bed where Sergej had left them, he took them and placed them next to her suitcase. Placing more wood on the fire, he walked to the door. Then he turned around and looked at her. "Good night, Tess," he said, feeling inhibited.

When she looked at him, she noticed his repressed demeanor. "You're not going to sleep now?" she asked in a worried tone.

"Do you want me to stay with you?" he asked, taking a step toward her. In the back of his mind, he longed for her to say yes. Even if it was only to sit on his bed and watch her as she slept.

"I don't want to keep you from what you need to do. Don't worry about me, I'll be fine," she answered, then she turned away.

He sighed, looked to the floor, then back at her. "I'll be in later. I'll be quiet, so I don't wake you. Just call if you need me. I won't be far," he said, and opened the door to leave, but when he turned to close the door, she stood in the door's path.

"Ivan, thank you for taking care of me, again, today; for saving me from whatever fate waited on those tracks, and for taking me to see those children," she said. Then she smiled, moved toward him, and kissed him on the cheek. Stepping back and away from him, she whispered, "Good night."

He felt she wanted him to kiss her, but he did nothing; he did not want her to turn him away again. He felt that perhaps she was tired and his persistence would only insult her. Looking into her eyes, he did not want to offend her, despite who she really could be.

"Sleep now, Tess," he said, then stepping into the hall, he closed the door.

Shutting his eyes, he swallowed hard. With his hand still on the doorknob, he shook his head at his lack of courage. He wanted to open the door, walk back inside, and take her in his arms. If she were against his Cause, he would convince her to be on his side. As he would make love to her, he would convince her of the truth: not only the truth of the situation with the war, but also the truth of what he felt for her, because with the way he now felt, he would do anything to be with her. Anything, except ask her to tell him the truth. He feared what her answer would be, just as he feared that she would turn him away if she knew he was Idy. He also feared that she would shun him if she knew what part he played in this war. Too often he had stared down the barrel of a rifle and that did not frighten him, but to look into her eyes and hear the truth, for that he lacked the courage.

Pausing briefly, he knew that his loneliness caused his momentary lapse in valor. Then he heard Sergej calling, and with a troubled, but hushed sigh, his hand came from the doorknob, and he slowly walked to the kitchen.

"She's not the one. She's not the spy, if there even is a spy to begin with," Sergej said, not giving Ivan time to speak first.

Ivan looked at Sergej strangely and his expression questioned Sergej's statement; a statement that unfortunately erased his previous fantasy of possessing Tess. "What makes you so sure?" he asked.

"She's just not, I feel it. If you think she is, why didn't you let her stay on the train? Why did you get her off?" Sergej asked, but he knew the answer. He also noticed Ivan's changed disposition when he had entered the kitchen. Sergej could tell that Ivan's mind was on things other than the war. His mind was on only one thing, the woman in his bedroom.

"Put them together? Why should I make it easier for her, *if* she's the one? And what *if* she's not? Those men looking for her would have killed her, and that's only after they would have done other unspeakable things to her." He paused and thought of the look in Tess' eyes only moments before. Looking at Sergej, Ivan's gaze questioned his motives, and he asked, "What did you want me to do?"

Sergej's eyes widened as he looked past Ivan. At once, Ivan turned to his left and saw Tess standing in the doorway. She was holding the side of her head. Ivan's first reaction was anger for her leaving the bedroom and not calling him as he requested her to do, but as he looked at her, he saw she was not well and he went to her.

"What's wrong? Don't you feel well?" he asked softly as he bent sideways to see her face.

"May I please have a glass of water?"

"What's wrong?" he asked again.

"I have a small headache. I would have called you, but that would have hurt too much."

Ivan smiled. He then thought that she may have turned him away because of this, not because she lacked affection for him.

Hearing her request, Sergej poured her a glass of water from a gallon jug on the counter. Then he handed it to Ivan and said, "I'll be in the dining room when you're ready."

"Good night, Sergej," she said quietly, then smiled at him.

Ivan looked over his shoulder at Sergej, who smiled at Tess. Then Sergei looked at Ivan. His stare told Ivan that she was not the one, and that he knew she could not betray anyone, especially Ivan.

"I'll be there shortly," Ivan said.

Sergej nodded, then pushed through the door to the dining room and left them alone. Returning his attention to Tess, Ivan handed her the glass.

"Thank you," she said, taking it from him. Then slipping a pill into her mouth, she took a mouthful of water and swallowed it.

"What is that you're taking?" he asked.

"Aspirin. Now go to Sergej. I can manage. I'm going to bed." Handing him the glass, she walked back down the hall.

He stepped into the hall and watched her. At the door, she turned and gazed at him. "Good night, Ivan. I promise not to bother you again," she said, then she entered bedroom and closed the door.

Now she was gone and he stood helpless as, again, he watched his chance walk away from him. Expelling a disgruntled sigh, he turned and walked into the dining room as he sentimentally carried her glass.

Sergej and several of the men waited at the table for Ivan. When he was seated, the men started questioning him about his somewhat silent and extremely attractive companion. He explained who Tess was, or whom she appeared to be. He told them about her search for Mara and ordered them to pretend they did not know Mara; however, Sergej had already informed them of all this. Ivan also told them not to talk about Mara's brother or her parents. Mara's safety, their safety, and the safety of the people depended on their silence.

They agreed, but not all of them approved of Ivan's motives to hide Mara from Tess; some of the men's opinions of Tess were the same as Sergej's, which confused Ivan. He wondered how they could form such opinions from their brief amount of time spent with Tess. However, because of Ivan's efforts, they had the privilege of trust more so than Ivan had.

After a short while, the conversation shifted to other topics, mainly the purpose of the Serbian military police's search and seizure on the train that day. None of the men knew the truth of why the trains were being searched. Ivan surmised that it was solely based on a rumor started by either the Croats or Bosniaks or both to distract the Serbians, but the truth was that someone had to know about Tess and why she was there.

CHAPTER TWENTY-ONE

After Tess was back in Ivan's bedroom, she took another look around. The room was not as desolate as the rest of the house. "It's quite comfortable," she thought. As she sat on the bed, she realized that someone went to a lot of effort to make her stay special. She knew Ivan cared that much to welcome her so graciously. Lying back on the bed, her head touched the soft pillow and, though she wanted to get up to change clothing, she fell asleep on top of the covers.

It was after eleven o'clock when Ivan concluded the meeting. At that time, the men retreated to the upper floors to sleep. Ivan then made sure the house was secure, knowing three men would stand watch from upstairs until they were relieved in the early morning.

Walking through the kitchen and down the hall, Ivan knocked softly on the bedroom door. He waited, but hearing no answer, he slowly turned the handle and carefully opened the door. Looking into the room, he saw her lying on the bed. He stepped inside, then closed and locked the door.

Walking to the bed, he saw her sleeping on top of the covers, still dressed, and still wearing her boots. Gently lifting each foot, he slid them off. Slipping the blankets from under her, he covered her to her shoulders. She was so tired that she did not move, nor did she feel him kiss her lips as she lay there unaware that he watched her. He moved his lips to her ear, and whispered, "Please tell me the truth. I need to know, my beautiful, Tess," then he closed his eyes and kissed her a second time.

He put more wood on the fire, then sat on the smaller bed and continued to look at her. So many questions raced through his mind as his eyes moved off into space. Pondering Sergej's statements, he knew he should give her the benefit of his doubt, but debating the possibilities of destruction pulled him away from her innocence.

If she were the spy, he found it difficult to believe that she could take such an aggressive side, but all sides in this war were aggressive. Still, he could not imagine what her motives would be. But time would tell the truth and he hoped that the truth would oppose his suspicions. He wanted nothing more than for her to be that beautiful and gentle woman for whose arrival he had prayed.

Every time he looked into her eyes, he saw nothing of deceit or betrayal, only kindness and affection for all she encountered. Even when she was angry, she was kind. Ivan wanted the privilege of always being able to look into Tess' eyes and see those emotions. In his wildest dreams, Ivan could not imagine Tess ever fighting for something that would bring about the deaths of so many people. And though he had not known her for long, his comfort level with her made him feel that he had known her his entire life. Despite this, he had to be careful. Perhaps she was chosen for her natural ability to draw people out, then draw them to her.

As usual, so many questions with so few answers. All in good time, Ivan would find the answers, but for now, Tess slept and the Black Rebel was safe. In the back of his mind he knew, even if they had sent her to find him, she could not betray him. But for now, the question he needed answered was: could she love him? If so, then he knew for certain that God had heard and granted his prayer. With that thought in mind, Ivan smiled, closed his eyes, and surrendered his mind to dreams of Tess.

CHAPTER TWENTY-TWO

Ivan awoke the next morning to find Tess had already risen. The scent of her perfume lingered in her absence and made him smile. It was the first time he woke up happy since the war began, and it was the first, in a very long time, that he woke up knowing he was not alone. Seeing a woman's things in his room gave him a strange feeling, a strangely comforting feeling to which he wanted to become accustomed.

Sitting up, he saw that she had neatly made her bed. He then noticed that there was an extra blanket over him, and he imagined that she had taken it from her bed and covered him with it. Somehow, she must have also tried to slip another pillow under his head, because her bed should have had two pillows, but now there was only one there. Though when he had awoken, he had his arms wrapped around it as though he was holding someone. Tess, he imagined.

Looking toward the window, he presumed it was half past six. Standing up, he stretched, then walked to the dresser. He shaved with warm water from a thermos left there from the previous night, then he changed clothes. On his way out of the room, he passed the vanity, but stopped. Walking back to it, he saw she had placed several things on top. He lifted the end of her brush and smiled, as he imagined her sitting there brushing her hair. He was sorry he missed seeing her do this. From on top of the vanity a sparkle of light caught his eye. He looked and saw her ring and earrings on top. Picking them up, he then left the room.

Entering the kitchen, Ivan found Tess helping Sergej's mother prepare breakfast. Tess was learning to make coffee the way the men liked it, very dark and very strong. Stefan was sitting at the far end of the room translating for them. Ivan's expression brightened seeing Tess attempting to communicate with Mrs. Tomić, who spoke English, but when she was overly happy, excited, or upset, she only spoke Serbian because she expressed herself best in her native language. Right now she was very happy, because she imagined Ivan brought Tess home to meet her, for her approval of course, because he planned to marry Tess.

Politely interrupting their conversation by clearing his throat, Ivan walked toward them as Stefan looked up at him. "Hey, Ivan," he said as he stood, raised his eyebrows, and gave Ivan a pat on the arm. He then walked toward the door to the dining room and left, grinning as he exited.

Ivan smiled at him before turning his attention to the women. "Good morning, Mama," he said in Serbian. Then he turned to Tess. "Good morning, Tess," he said in English, and smiled at her.

Mrs. Tomić held out her arms, hugged Ivan, and kissed him on each cheek. In Serbian, she said, "Ivan, you're home safe again. Thank God."

She was always happy to see him. Ivan was like a son to her. Having raised him from age ten, every time she looked at him, she saw the boy she loved, who had now grown into a magnificent man.

Smiling at Ivan, she looked at Tess from the corner of her eye, then back at Ivan. Leaning toward him and speaking in a whisper in Serbian, as though Tess would understand, she patted his arm and uttered a single word of approval: "Perfect!" She gave a small laugh, indicating it was time he had something else in his life other than war. Turning to Tess, Mrs. Tomić gave her hands an affectionate squeeze, then she left the room so they could be alone.

Tess watched her leave, then she looked back at Ivan. She stood there staring up at him. He looked different from when he was in Belgrade. Again, his attire was slightly militaresque. "Good morning," she said, smiling at him.

He stepped toward her and kissed her on both cheeks. "You're awake early. Did you sleep well? Is your headache gone?"

"Yes, and yes, all better now. Are you hungry? Mrs. Tomić made breakfast," she said as she glanced at the wood burning stove in the far corner of the kitchen.

"Wear these. Don't leave them in the room," he said as he held out his palm with her jewelry resting in it.

She set the plate on the counter, then reaching for her earrings, the tips of her fingers tenderly grazed his palm, and he smiled from the sensation. She quickly put them on as he looked at her ring and noticed the design. He had seen it before and recognized it to be Irish in origin. Hers was a band of white gold with a pair of carved hands holding a heart with a crown on top. She waited for him to finish examining it, but when he was done, he did not give it back to her.

"Tell me about this ring. It's Irish, isn't it?"

"Yes. It's a Claddagh."

As she pointed out the three shapes that made up its design, he carefully watched and listened. "The hands represent fidelity, the crown loyalty, and the heart love. It represents strong friendship, but it's also used as a wedding band in Ireland. The story tells of an Irish sailor, who was to be married after he returned from his last voyage. On this voyage, pirates captured his ship, took him prisoner, and he was eventually trained to work as a goldsmith. He swore that someday he would escape, and while he was in captivity, he designed this ring for the woman he loved. Some eight or ten years later, he did escape, or perhaps his captors released him, and he returned to Ireland to find her. After all that time, and probably many opportunities to marry another woman, he still loved her with all his heart. She hadn't married, she loved him too desperately to be with anyone else. So, after all those years of waiting, they were married using that ring, and that was the birth of the Claddagh. At least how I've heard it told," she said.

"A beautiful story for a beautiful ring."

"Actually, there's a trick to wearing it. The direction and the hand you wear it on shows your availability. If you're not married and not involved with anyone, you're supposed to wear it on the fourth finger of your right hand with the heart point facing toward the fingertips. If you're involved with someone, but not yet married, you wear it on the same finger, and turn the ring around with the heart point facing away from the fingertips. If you're married, you wear it on the left hand, but I can't remember which way the heart faces." She frowned slightly. "In, I think," she said, then smiled.

When she reached for the ring, he pulled it back. He then did something odd, although particularly right for the way he felt. He held out her ring for her to slip onto her finger. Smiling at him, she went to slip the fourth finger of her right hand into the ring, where she had always worn it.

Again, he pulled the ring away. "No, wear it on the other hand," he said. Without waiting for her response, he lifted her left hand. With a smile, he slid the ring on her fourth finger with the heart point facing in.

"It points in and is not supposed to be removed except by the man who placed it there," he said in a romantic whisper.

Looking down at his hand holding hers, she admired the affection of his gesture, but could only wonder what thoughts passed through his mind. She looked back up at him. How gentle he was and how dedicated he was in his action.

"That's better," he said. Then sighing contentedly, he looked at her, lifted her hand to his lips, and kissed the ring and her hand simultaneously. After that, as if nothing had happened, he took the plate from the counter and walked to get her breakfast. Preparing the plate, he held it out to her. She stood still, staring at him and trying to figure him out.

"Here," he said, attempting to pull her from her thoughts.

"No, thank you. I don't usually eat breakfast," she said, but even if she were hungry, she could not eat after his overt display of affection, for she did not know what to make of it.

"Eat something. We'll have a long day today and a lot of driving."

"I'll be fine," she answered, then she walked to the kitchen door, and pushing it open, she waited for him to follow her into the dining room.

He hesitated for a moment, but then he walked after her. Sitting at the head of the table, he could hear his men coming down the stairs. One-by-one, she greeted them by name before they entered the kitchen. Exiting with their breakfast, they took their places around the table, and once settled, their attention immediately focused on her. As Ivan finished eating, they asked Tess questions about America, but mostly about American women. She politely answered every question they had and sometimes made them laugh with her answers.

Watching them carefully, Ivan saw Tess affecting them with her kindness. Though he was pleased that they found her comfortable to be around, his lingering suspicion queried her purpose. Then, speaking in Serbian, Ivan interrupted their frivolous conversations. At once, the men's attention turned to him as he distracted them from her. But did he do this because he suspected her of treason to his Cause, or was it because he wanted her attention to be his alone?

When the conversation became thick in debate, she stood, and reached to remove Ivan's empty plate from in front of him. Noticing her do this, he affectionately stroked her hand, then smiled at her before she turned and walked into the kitchen. Then he continued his dispute with one of the men regarding their opinion on the cease-fire, a cease-fire that Ivan knew would not last long. Something always happened to activate hostilities. Peace was a concept long forgotten in Sarajevo, and many wondered if they would ever feel it again in their lifetime.

When Ivan noticed that Tess had not returned, he called their meeting to a close. He walked from the table and into the kitchen. Not finding her there, he then made his way to "her bedroom" as he now referred to it, but what he really meant was that it was now "their bedroom." There he found Tess sitting at the vanity and brushing her hair. He smiled, seeing the image he had envisioned earlier that morning.

"Are you ready to go?" he asked as he entered.

She turned to face him. For the first time, he noticed the diamond cross she wore around her neck. He stood staring at it. Why it affected him, he did not know.

"That's very pretty. Was it a gift?" he asked, motioning to it.

She lifted it as she looked down at it, and said, "Thank you. Yes. It was a gift. I bought it when my first novel began to sell. I gave it to myself as a reminder that it wasn't my efforts alone that forged my success. As a matter of fact, I had very little, if anything, to do with it. I owe my success to God."

She stood up and walked to him as he continued to look at it. In his mind, he thought it was very appropriate for her. At the doorway, she stopped in front of him. "Ivan?" she said in a soft questioning tone, then she pulled out her identification and other personal documents from her purse and held them out to him.

"What?" he said as he looked at her, not comprehending her actions.

"I would feel better if you held onto these for me," she said.

He looked at her. Shaking his head, he rejected her request.

"What if someone stops us? I don't want to get you into trouble. A woman's handbag is an obvious place to search, isn't it? This way, I have no identification, and I can play the mute again," she said affectionately.

He gave a small laugh. He had already forgotten the previous day's events, but her depiction of the situation in the tunnel of trees amused him. He knew she was right, but he still asked, "Are you sure?"

"I told you that I trust you, and I truly do," she answered, then she placed her documents in his hand.

Taking her hand, he walked her back to the bed and sat her down, where he placed her documents next to her.

"What is it? What's wrong?" she asked.

"Do you have a piece of paper and a pen?"

"In my briefcase." Looking to the dresser where her briefcase lay, she was about to stand.

He touched her shoulder, stopping her. "I'll get it." Then he brought her briefcase to the bed.

At once, she opened it, pulled a notebook and pen from inside, and handed it to him. He sat next to her and began writing. When he was through, he tore out the sheet of paper, closed the notebook, then handed it back to her along with the pen. She sat there wondering what he was up to as she put them away and pushed the briefcase to the other side of the bed. He looked at her in a strange way, slightly serious and extremely loyal. He appeared cautiously devoted to her for reasons she could not fathom, then he handed her the piece of paper and smiled. "Here is the address of this house," he said, then he was silent as he watched her.

She did not move, nor did she say anything.

"Take it," he said, holding it closer to her.

She took the paper from his hand, glanced at it briefly, then looked back at him. "What do I need it for?" she asked.

"When you return to America, where will you tell people you stayed? You have no idea where you are, or who you're with."

"I know I'm in Sarajevo, and I'm with you. What else do I need to know?"

"You should know where you stayed. It's enough that you've walked into the middle of a war. If you returned and didn't know where this house was located, people would think you'd lost your mind," he said, smiling slightly.

"That would be nothing new. If you knew half the things I did in my life, you'd think I'd lost my mind, too. Besides, I don't answer to anyone. Don't get me wrong. It's just, there's no one back home to answer to."

"Keep it anyway, it will remind you of Sarajevo."

"No, it will remind me of you," she answered in a sentimental tone.

Again, something so simple would remind her of him. Because of that, he wanted her. There it was, that familiar feeling rising in him: the touch, the embrace, the longed for kiss, and the desire to possess her, and he wondered if she felt it. Shaking off this feeling, he could not imagine that she was so naïve to be so trusting. However, he hoped that she did trust him as much as she said.

She quickly slipped the piece of paper into her wallet, and held it out to him along with her other documents. With a smile, he took them and placed them in the top drawer of his dresser, then returned to her and said, "Let's go now."

They left the room. Passing through the kitchen, then the dining room, both were empty. The men had gone and the house was silent. He helped her with her coat, then put his on. When he opened the front door, she saw a car parked at the side of the house. They walked rapidly toward it as she recalled his warnings about snipers. He opened the passenger door and helped her in. As he walked to the driver's side, he looked around; scouring the immediate area, he then looked up toward the mountain next to the house. It was all too quiet, and an eerie chill crawled up his spine. It was as if he knew he should get her out of Sarajevo, but he entered the car, started it, and drove them from the house.

CHAPTER TWENTY-THREE

Now that it was morning, she could see the devastation of the city Americans only remembered when the evening news cared to report on the divided nation of Yugoslavia. From their elevated location, she felt she looked into a ditch where someone had thrown away once beautiful things that carelessness had now destroyed. She understood that war made everything and everyone expendable, proving that there was no reverence in conflict.

Alert and attentive for any sign of movement on the road before them, Ivan drove in silence to exit the city. He did not want to be the target of a break in the cease-fire, he wanted no casualties. Thus he tried to take her down streets that had the least destruction, so she did not have to see all that this city had become; however, the main thoroughfares were the only cleared ways in or out of the city.

As he drove, he watched her while she saw the devastation first hand. She saw buildings, small and tall, that were riddled with holes from gunfire, buildings that were burnt and had collapsed from explosions. She saw vehicles that had been on fire, landmarks that had been destroyed because of their national heritage, children's bicycles crushed and lying dormant in the streets. Trash and debris were scattered everywhere, although it appeared that someone had tried to clear the side streets of it.

He wanted to talk to her to distract her when they passed the area where many unclaimed body parts had previously been discarded, but she saw that as well. So much destruction, almost too much to take in for one passing.

She looked up at the buildings and their shattered windows, and he saw her shake her head at what she witnessed. She closed her eyes and tried to imagine what life was like there before the war. She tried to imagine what those same streets would sound like with residents milling about, getting on with their daily lives. What would those same streets sound like with children playing and living their innocent lives? As she saw what little was left, on their way out of town, she wanted to scream, but what good would that do? Who would that help now?

Once out of the city, the wreckage of demolished buildings was absent, but the brutalized and unnatural landscape clearly reflected the current hostilities. Scattered, torn pieces of earth from bombings, and capsized trees that once stood tall and strong, littered the surrounding ground. Trees that bore green leaves in summer, now appeared blackened from fires. Below them, and peeking from beneath the snow, was the suffocated and scorched earth that lay there innocent of its predicament.

The silence of death surrounded them as they passed the multitude of landmarks the war had left behind as reminders that hatred had been there. Although its essence was visible during the day, even at night, you could feel the threatening presence of death. It was like a penetrating fog from which there was no escape.

She was at a loss for words. What could she possibly say to describe the squander of a countryside, which once flourished, that she now witnessed? She felt that all civility there had been mercilessly destroyed. "But would it return?" she wondered.

He noticed her disturbed expression and he knew exactly what she thought. It displeased him that she had to see his country, for the first time, during a time such as this. How he wished he had met her years before the fighting. He wondered how different things would have been between them then.

"You'll get used to it. After a while, it all becomes normal," he said.

She turned her attention to him and noticed his detached demeanor as he drove and watched the road ahead. He obviously remembered things that he preferred not to think about just then, if ever.

He sighed despondently, then whispered, "War."

She felt his disappointment from that single word. War was a concept that she did not completely understand, and it was obvious that neither did he. He understood the fight, but not the reason causing it. Whether reasons or excuses, his countrymen used ideals to tear apart a mostly peaceful existence, and these were concepts of a foreign nature to him.

Seeing his distress, she felt accountable and attempted to change the subject. It was because of her that he remembered.

"Ivan, why do you call Mrs. Tomić 'Mama'?" she asked.

He smiled and said, "She's like a mother to me."

From his expression, she saw that he clearly loved Sergej's mother as he would his own. She smiled at his sentimental demeanor, even though she had no idea why he felt that way. Then his smile faded as unpleasant thoughts replaced Mrs. Tomić, and to Tess' surprise, he revealed something about himself that she surmised he would normally have kept private.

"My parents died when I was young. They were killed in an automobile accident, or so I was told."

He shook his head. And though his brow crumpled, a melancholy smile attempted to force his frown away. Lost in thought, he remembered the events of that time, and they were as painful now as when they had happened.

"My father was an attorney, but he worked for the government as a land arbitrator. He traveled around the country settling property disputes. The year that they died, I was ten. Also, that year, he was out of Serbia a lot, so the family traveled with him as often as possible. In spring of that year, we were near Sarajevo. He had one last dispute to settle before we went on holiday. It was a simple day trip, so he had taken my mother with him. The car drove over a land mine buried on a dirt road. It was not meant for them, but they reached it first." He shook his head and frowned.

She gasped silently, and from his expression, she could tell that he still wondered why.

"At the time of the accident, I was at school. The local authorities came to the school, told me that my parents had died in an automobile accident, and took me to an orphanage outside Sarajevo."

"They just took you there? What about other family?" she asked.

"There was nothing they could do. I had no other relatives, so they had no choice. Later that year, I ran away from the orphanage. I would take care of myself. I was a big man in my mind. So, I found my way to Sarajevo and lived on the streets. I had nothing and no one, and…well…not to starve, I stole food. Then, one cold day, I found out I wasn't such a big man." He shook his head, remembering, as a shiver ran through him.

Tess watched him, wondering how many times he was alone in his life and how that affected him as an adult. When he continued, her mind could only think of how she could be kind to him and make him feel that he was not alone.

"You see, I ran away from the orphanage during summer, but soon it would be the end of autumn, and then winter would be rapidly approaching. Well, I had not eaten in about three or four days and Mama, Mrs. Tomić, came out of the bakery where she stopped to talk with a friend. In her basket, I saw two fresh loaves of hot bread, and I thought I was going to die looking at them. The aroma was so unbearably delicious that I could already taste them. Being the little thief that I was, I casually walked up behind her, pulled one of the loaves from her basket, and ran in the opposite direction. I thought I was smart until she called for the police, and they caught me. But they would not have caught me if I did not try to eat while I was running. The more I stuffed into my mouth, the slower I ran." He laughed at himself as he remembered it so vividly.

Tess smiled and tried to imagine him as a small boy. Then she tried to imagine him as a small boy doing something wrong and she could not.

"The policeman brought me back to her and made me return the bread. I was terrified, so terrified that I almost choked on the bread still in my mouth. You see, I had never been caught before and I didn't know what would happen. I expected a good slap across the face from Mama and, of course, for the police to execute me immediately." He grinned slightly. "You know, death by a firing squad."

"But you were just a hungry little boy!"

"Yes, and little boys, hungry or not, have very grand imaginations." He chuckled, and shook his head. "But boys that are thieves grow up into men that are thieves, and there is no honor in theft," he added very seriously.

"So what happened then?"

"I guess Mama took a good look at me and felt sorry for me. So she took me home, kept me, fed me, and loved me. I never told anyone about my parents other than her. Everyone thinks I ran away from home, that I'm some sort of *rebel.*"

He paused and looked at her, wondering if the title *rebel* would cause any special reaction from her. Not seeing any, he continued with his story.

"Sergej and I grew up together along with the rest of the men you met last night. Sarajevo is *their* city. It belongs to the people who live there, not these warring land mongers."

Again, he paused, and when he continued, his voice revealed sadness. Watching him, she saw his eyes mist ever so slightly with tears, and she sensed there was more sorrow to his story.

"I've never told anyone this. I never even told Mama, but I'm telling you now, Tess. Everyone thinks I was an only child, but I had a baby sister, and she was in the car with my parents. She died that day." He paused reverently for a moment. "Her name was Mara," he said, then he was silent.

Hearing his sister's name, Tess' heart skipped a beat, and her eyes welled with tears that she quickly wiped away. What must he have felt every time she said the name Mara? What he must have suffered in his life, she could only imagine. At that point, all she wanted to do was be kind to him, but she was unsure how.

Leaning toward him, she placed her hand on his arm. "I'm so sorry, Ivan. I didn't mean to remind you," she said in a soft tone.

"That is the past. I am happy they are not here to live through this. Besides, forward is a better direction than backward," he said. Turning to look at her, he noticed the delicate concern for his loss in her gaze, and he saw her holding back her tears. How he wished she did not fight them so mightily. He smiled at her, then he looked back to the road in front of them. He imagined his story reminded her of her quest. Though he had lost his little sister, he now had Mara Jovanović to care for.

After hearing Ivan's story, Tess began to understand his logic. And, as kind as she thought him to be before, she now saw him as kinder and gentler than any man she ever knew. From the people she had met in her short time in his country, she found many to be receptive to the tragedies of others. They did not linger on their sorrow, but reached out to help those they encountered. His people were deep thinkers. They felt things passionately and remembered them for a lifetime.

Out of respect for his loss, they drove several miles in silence. He wanted to relieve her anxiety over his life's tragedies, and any other troublesome thoughts that he felt were present, so he broke their silence. "Today we are going to three towns: Visoko, Podlugovi, and Semizovac. There are several locations in each. We can't stay long at any of them. We must look and leave." He paused, and reached for her hand and held it, then he sighed.

She looked down at their hands, thinking how comforting it was to have his hand holding hers.

"There are many shelters. I don't know if we will be able to see them all. At any time the cease-fire could end. It will end. It always does, eventually. Still, we will see as many as we can."

She looked at him as he finished speaking; her expression made him curious and he wanted to dispel any fears she may have. "Tess, sometimes you look at me with uncertainty. Do I confuse you?" he asked.

"Well, if you do, it doesn't have anything to do with you. It's only because I'm easily confused," she said, and smiled to herself.

He smiled at her comment, which respected him and accused her. Through her kindness, she turned the situation around, where she could have been defensive.

"Seriously though, I wouldn't call it confused, more like amazed."

He smiled again. Her depiction of him obviously intrigued her. Though the people he helped during this war saw him as superhuman, he did not expect anyone from America to find him that interesting, let alone worth their time. And now, he was curious to know what amazed her about him. "Amazed? At what?" he asked.

"You seem to take everything that happens in stride. You have an uncanny way of organizing it all, and explaining it with logic and reason. And still, it's not that you accept the circumstances as much as you abhor the consequences."

He thought about her words, and sensed she understood him better than he had imagined. She thought carefully now to choose the right words to phrase her next question in order not to offend him.

"Does nothing frighten you, Ivan?"

"Fear does," he answered, and he smiled at the individual thoughts that defined fear. It was so different from one person to the next, and that made him curious about what she feared.

"Tess, I believe to fear is to surrender. And when you allow that type of surrender into your life, bad things happen. Of course, there is no way to stop every bad thing from happening. If so, war would not exist. I think fear comes from the unknown and the lack of knowing right from wrong, or better said, caring about what is right and what is wrong."

She said nothing. She only looked at him and waited for his next words.

Glancing at her, he saw he had her undivided attention. "I am like you as *you* strive to help children become educated with *your* money, not money from a foundation." He paused because he wanted her to understand the meaning behind his words. He also wanted her to be ready for what he would say next. "I agree with you when you say, *'If you can write, you can read. And if you can read, you can better understand the world and its different societies. Knowledge is the key to destroying prejudice and individual hate, which always culminates in violence against the innocent,'*" he said, quoting her.

She stared at him. His verbatim quote hinted that he believed her efforts were not in vain. It was his way of showing her that he respected her, besides listening to her when she spoke.

"I can't believe you listened so carefully that you can quote me. You are a most amazing man," she said, evermore astonished by him.

"I hear everything you say. I enjoy talking with you," he smiled, "and debating with you."

She smiled, remembering the silly arguments they had that had upset her. Arguments in which his opinion always made perfect sense when she thought about it.

"And now, we are here," he said, as he turned from the main road and parked behind what appeared to be another abandoned church. Then they entered the old building and walked amongst the multitude of children who played, ate, slept, and often cried without their parents.

As before, he saw she was devastated, sorrow was her staggering emotion. She tried to smile at the children that sought her attention, although in her defeat, her only option was surrender. But her surrender was not to fear, but to the hopeless cries and needs of those around her. In Ivan's eyes, Tess was just as she thought his people to be. She did not linger on her sorrow, but reached out to help those she encountered.

And though he had told her there was only enough time to look and leave, when she stopped to spend time with the children, he did not have the heart to pull her away. However, it was at the fourth shelter that Ivan realized something about Tess, and that something was her generosity of spirit. The entire day she paid complete attention to every child that demanded her notice. Sometimes, she sat in the snow and played with them, and sometimes, she would simply get out of their way as they ran past her, playing with one another. He saw that the children were equally fascinated with her as she was with them, despite that none of them really knew what the other was saying.

She no longer bothered Ivan to translate for her and, seeing her now, he knew there was no real need for his help. Examining her from his distance, there was an unreal amount of communication between these people from different world. The name of the language they spoke was love, of which, he now saw that Tess had in unlimited quantities. He knew she came to find Mara, but she gave complete attention to every child she met in her search.

Between picking up dropped mittens and wiping running noses, Ivan watched the children become instantaneously attached to Tess, but there was one thing in particular she did that stood out. She noticed a little girl who appeared cold. This child wore a large and poorly fitted, slightly tattered coat over a sweater, and pair of pants with the bottoms stuffed into her boot tops. She had mittens, but no scarf for her neck or hat for her head. Tess saw the little girl shivering and when Tess held her, the child still shook from the cold.

At once, Tess removed her coat. She unbuttoned and removed a sweater she wore over a second sweater. Then she quickly unbuttoned and removed the child's coat and slipped her sweater onto her. She buttoned the sweater and put the child back into her coat, and rolled up the sweater's sleeves over her coat cuffs until the child's mittens showed.

Removing the scarf from around her neck, Tess wrapped it over the top of the child's head and tied it in a loose but secure knot beneath her chin. She then placed the ends of the scarf inside the front of the coat. Buttoning the child's coat, Tess pulled the small collar up high around her neck. Then Tess sat back in the snow and smiled. The little girl threw her arms around Tess' neck, and with a kiss on the child's cheek, Tess sent her off to play with the other children, for now she was warm enough to do so. After a minute, Tess put her coat back on. Then she stood up and walked away from the play yard, away from Ivan.

Ivan saw Tess wiping her face. He knew she cried as she imagined that child could have been Mara, but had no way of knowing. One of the women from the facility stood next to Ivan and saw Tess' gesture. When Ivan looked at her, the woman smiled, though neither of them approached Tess. Ivan knew Tess needed a few moments alone.

After another fifteen minutes, the woman called the children inside and invited Ivan and Tess to join them for lunch. Ivan said he would ask Tess if she wanted to and, if so, they would come inside. If not, he thanked her for her offer and for allowing them to see the children.

When the children ran to the door, the little girl with Tess' sweater and scarf ran back across the play yard to Tess. Placing her small hand inside Tess', the little girl pulled her toward the building. Tess lifted the girl into her arms and carried her to the woman who waited to take her inside. Setting the little girl down to the ground near Ivan, Tess kissed the child again and handed her over to the woman. The little girl waved good-bye and walked inside the building as Tess stared at her tiny footprints in the snow.

Seeing Tess sad, Ivan stepped toward her. He placed his arm around her, but she did not acknowledge him, as he whispered, "Now you will be cold."

"I won't be cold. I have this beautiful coat to keep me warm," she answered, then pulled slightly away from him.

"You can't keep giving your sweaters and scarves to children," he commented, while trying to decipher her mood.

"Why not? I have a closet packed with clothes back home," she answered, and she answered that way because his comment made her feel stupid, although that was not his intention. By her response, he could tell that her mood displeased her; it was slightly defensive and, again, she tried to walk away from him.

To prevent her walking away from him, he held her by the arm and looked at her. "I didn't mean to tell you what you can or cannot do. I just don't want to see you personally suffer for a problem caused by others. I think this search is affecting you. I see you sad when you just did a good thing and should be happy," he said, and loosened his grip when he felt her stop pulling away from him.

But she felt helpless. Was what she had just done good, or was it patronizing? Through her sadness, she could not tell.

"Be happy? How could anyone be happy? Seeing the devastation of war makes you feel like the biggest sinner just because you're safe from it. What is a scarf, a sweater, fifteen thousand dollars, or anything I have compared to the life of a child? Aren't human beings worth more than things?" she asked.

When she spoke, she had not looked at him as he wished that she would have. Again, he moved close to her. Not speaking, he watched her, hoping she would look at him. To his disappointment, she only stared at the child's footprints.

"I'm sorry, Ivan. I'm not upset with you. It's me who upsets me," she said.

"Let's go home now. It's been a long day," he said, as he stroked her hair, then tried to walk her from the yard, but she did not move. He stepped back to her. Placing his arms around her, she rested her head against the side of his face, and he heard her whisper, "Thank you, Ivan."

Her whisper affected him. It carried the same affection she displayed for the lost children of his country. Moving to her side, he kissed the side of her head. Keeping his arm around her shoulder, they left the grounds of the shelter.

Once they were on their way home, he was the first to speak when he noticed her blank stare out the window. "Tess? Tell me something," he said.

"What would you like to know?" she asked as she turned to look at him.

"What really made you start your children's foundation?"

The sweetness of her smile faded as she turned her face away slightly. Briefly reflecting on his question, she remembered, and after a moment of frozen posture, she looked at him.

"I wanted to do something for children, but the idea came to me when I was sitting at my computer one day and I had just received my first royalty check from my first novel."

She paused and looked at the dashboard of the car. Taking a deep breath, she described the scene playing in her memory.

"I was working on the final edit to my second novel and, I don't usually listen to the radio, but it was on. The front page of the Chicago Times was staring me in the face. The cover story was about a boy, seventeen years old, who had stolen a car at gunpoint. Shortly after the theft, he was cornered by the police in a vacant lot, and they shot him. He was trying to surrender, but the police shot first because he had a gun in his hand. The article was very emotional, and I found it difficult to finish. The crux of the story was that the boy had applied for a scholarship to go to college and it was denied. He wasn't a fantastic athlete, a whiz kid, or the heir to a great fortune. He was just an ordinary boy from a poor neighborhood of Chicago. Just an ordinary boy that made a horrific mistake in a moment of weakness. Just an ordinary boy, who wanted to better his life, but was denied the opportunity, and, most likely, because of politics. Scholarships are very political. What school just wants an ordinary boy who wants to become an artist, musician, or an English teacher? But, what if this boy wanted to be a doctor when he grew up? What if he would become the doctor that would find cures for horrific diseases? Who would give him the chance? Schools want star athletes, geniuses, or children of rich parents that make donations to schools to take their kids in, whom sometimes don't even want an education."

She paused again. Shaking her head, she relived the incident as if it had just happened. Periodically, Ivan looked at her, but he had no idea where her story would lead.

"Anyway, I had placed my check for one hundred and seventy-five thousand dollars on top of this article. As I said, I had the radio on and, ironically, this song by Elvis Presley came on. It's called "In the Ghetto" and it's about a young boy in the ghetto who doesn't have a chance. He steals a car in an attempt to escape, and gets shot trying to leave his old life behind." She shook her head. "Was it coincidence that song played just then?" She was peculiarly silent as remembered.

He noticed that she held her breath. He touched her hand, and she started to breathe again. "It's alright, don't continue. I get the idea," he said softly, not wanting memories to torment her further.

"No. I want to tell you the rest. It needs telling. It's the reason behind the Children's Writing Foundation," she said, then turned and smiled at him. And when she continued, he did not try to stop her.

"So many deaths are reported in so many daily papers, but this one did something to me that I can't explain. As I listened to this song, I picked up my check and stared at it. I worked hard and waited a long time for this money, but the next thing I did was to go to the bank and cash it. I found out the boy's parents had no way to bury their son. So, I bought a cemetery plot for the boy and paid for the funeral arrangements. I asked the funeral director to contact the parents, which he did, and they accepted. I also asked that he not tell them who gave this to them, and he complied. After a few months had passed, and the investigation was closed, I purchased the vacant lot where the police had shot the boy. I had a park made out of it. In the center, I had landscapers plant a seventeen-year-old oak tree. At the entrance to the park, there's a bronze archway with a plaque bearing his name. Well, as you can imagine, that blew that check quickly."

He frowned at her. Thinking her story was finished, he held her hand, although she was not through.

"You want to know the funniest thing? The day after the park was dedicated, I received word from my publisher that an order for one hundred and seventy-five thousand copies of my next novel had just come in," she paused briefly, then concluded, "prepaid."

They were both silent now. He wondered if it was luck or a miracle, and he opted for the miracle. He sighed and gave her hand a gentle squeeze. "What a story and a beautiful reason behind your foundation," he said.

"Well, what's the use of going to the beach if you don't make at least one footprint in the sand?"

He did not comment, he only looked at her, then looked back to the road. From what he had experienced of her so far, he knew that she had made many footprints in the sand.

"Just a little affection, that's all. Someone has to give back more than they take. If not, there is no hope," she concluded.

As they made their way back to the house, she said no more. Again, in the back of his mind, and in the depths of his heart, he hoped that she would give him the same affection others had received. Just as the children did that day, he wanted to tug at her coat, and seek her notice. He wanted to lay in her arms as did so many of them that day, but not let her go as the children did when she had to leave.

Many times the needs of his people were an unbearable burden. The people had him to release their troubles and fears to, but he had only that invisible Higher Power, and he now wondered if that Power had sent her. He longed for someone that he could confide in, someone whose arms would always welcome him when he felt lost. The more Ivan was around Tess, the more he understood that he was only a man. Then he remembered the saying, "For every man, there is a woman."

But, still he wondered, what was Tess' real purpose? He certainly risked his life taking her to these shelters. Did she know this, or did she merely think that war and death were something that only happened to others? That somehow neither could touch her. And so it was up to Ivan to make sure that the death Mara wrote about in her story, that death that chased her, would not find its home with Tess either.

CHAPTER TWENTY-FOUR

The next three days' search yielded no more than any previous day. Luckily, the cease-fire continued and Ivan was able to take Tess away from the city every morning without sighting snipers, though their threat was ever present. It was only a matter of time before one side became impatient, their actions adding to the death toll and the mass of homeless, unclaimed children that waited for parents that would never return.

Shelter after shelter, Tess searched for a child she could not identify. With no photograph or even physical description of Mara to compare to the children she encountered, she felt lost. Time after time, she recalled Ivan's words from the first shelter as she witnessed, firsthand, the devastation of children lost and alone. And as he had said she would, she saw the sadness in the eyes of the children who waited for parents that were most likely gone forever, as were Ivan's.

Perhaps now she understood the likeness she felt between herself and Mara. They were both, in essence, lost and alone. Maybe in Mara's words Tess found refuge, a soul mate that understood the tragedies of life all too well. But that would make Ivan part of their partnership, for he too knew the tribulations of life. He too longed for the sanctuary that true love provided. Now, when Ivan looked at Tess, his suspicious eye was becoming blind to all he had previously seen in her. He was allowing himself to be seduced by all that she was, just as the children were.

Still unbeknownst to Ivan, Tess felt the urge to cry many times, but she refrained in order to keep her promise to him. If she broke her promise, he would continue to see her as an inappropriate American, or so she imagined, and she did not want him seeing her that way. She wanted him to care for her, so she refrained from crying until she was alone in the bedroom at the house. Alone in the dark, she wept every night in forsaken silence before Ivan came to sleep.

As the week progressed, she became more desperate in her search; lost hope seized her heart every night before she slept. But every morning, before she awoke, she felt the strange and beautiful sensation of someone kissing her lips. After which, she would hear the sound of the bedroom door closing. With that, she greeted the morning with the hope that she would find Mara that day.

The Monday and Tuesday of her second week, Ivan did not take her from the house, icy roads kept them inside and away from their quest. On both days, he stayed at the house with her. He found no reason to try to visit the Rebel camp. The weather had curtailed any would-be breaks in the cease-fire, and staying at home with Tess was preferable to traveling back and forth through inclement weather.

For most of Monday, Ivan, Tess, and several of the other men spent the day talking. Because the majority of the conversation was in Serbian, eventually Tess would leave them to talk amongst themselves. Ivan knew he would find her writing in their bedroom. When it was time for their meals, she could be found helping Mrs. Tomić in the kitchen—a most welcome pair of hands in caring for so many men.

On Tuesday, the men ventured out to pick up supplies from the camp, and Tess and Ivan were alone in the house. Late in the afternoon, Ivan sought Tess. He found her sitting on the bed, writing in her notebook, and he knocked on the half-open door. "Tess?" he said, then waited for her acknowledgment.

She looked at the door. "Come in, Ivan."

"And what if it wasn't me? What would you do?" he teased as he entered. Closing the door behind himself, he walked to the bed and sat at the foot. Watching him, she smiled at his comment, and he noticed that she appeared particularly amused with him.

"Who else would it be? Besides, I would know your voice even if you were behind the screen of a confessional."

"Perhaps I should have been a priest."

"A priest?" She laughed quietly. "You? A priest? You must be joking."

"What's so funny? What's wrong with being a priest?" he asked, trying to be serious.

"Nothing for anyone else, but for you? That would be the world's biggest sin against women. Women would be killing themselves just to get into your confessional." She paused and smiled, then added, "Father Ivan."

"And what's so bad about that? I'd reform them," he said, and laughed.

"You couldn't be a priest. God had no intention of you being that. If He did, you wouldn't be so extraordinarily handsome," she stated, then she was suddenly silent; she had revealed her appreciation of his flawless attractiveness. Slightly intimidated, she looked at her notebook to avoid his attentive gaze.

He smiled. It pleased him that she found him to be *"extraordinarily handsome."* And though out of his true feelings he wanted to return her compliment, again, he saw the effect of her own words on herself as they made her unsure of the situation. "Thank you, Tess," was all he said, then he placed his hand on her shin, acknowledging her feelings.

She smiled as she glanced up at him, then immediately back to her notebook. As they sat there in the silence of this delicate moment, they heard the men enter the house as someone called to Ivan. Since Tess had arrived, none of the men would approach the bedroom without a direct order from Ivan. Out of respect for Ivan, they never bothered him when he retreated to that room even before she was there.

Hearing them call Ivan's name again, Tess looked toward the door, though he stared directly at her, ignoring them. Feeling the intensity of his gaze on her, she slowly turned and saw him smiling at her. Strangely gentle was the look in his eyes as he watched her.

"Someone's calling you. Someone needs you," she whispered.

His eyes did not move from hers. To him, nothing could be as important as prolonging that moment alone with her. He wanted to live in the affirmation of her appreciation of him. As he heard her words, "Someone needs you," and looked in her eyes, he saw that she needed him more than his men did. He wanted her to need him. Perhaps if she needed him enough, she would be his the way he longed for her to be.

"Ivan?" Miloš called from the kitchen.

Tess' frown questioned Ivan as he continued to ignore the men who sought him. Shaking her head at his insistent stare, she placed her notebook on the table at the side of the bed. "You don't have to sit here with me. Go to them," she whispered, then she attempted to move her legs from the bed, but he held them in place, not allowing her to leave. She looked at him, questioning his action, then she looked at his hands.

He immediately let go of her legs. He gently pushed them out of his way, turning her, so she was sitting at the edge of the bed and facing the door. He then moved toward her. Grasping her arm, he pulled her the rest of the way to him, and held her nearer to him. "The other day you asked me if anything frightens me. I ask you the same question now. Does anything frighten you? Is there anything that I should know about?" he said in a secretive tone.

She lowered her gaze to the floor, then turned toward him. Still, she did not look at him. She could feel him staring at her and waiting for some answer to appease his relentless curiosity.

"You said, 'to fear is to surrender.' If that's so, then I'll be strong like you and not surrender. But fear isn't the only thing there is to surrender to. Sometimes—"

She stopped abruptly as she looked up and directly into his eyes. She felt his passion as he held her from leaving. Except it was not his physical strength that held her there, it was his emotional strength binding her to him. And she witnessed his affection for her in his eyes and, suddenly, it was difficult for her to breathe.

"Sometimes, what? What must you, Tess, surrender to, sometimes?"

She could not answer. Looking away, she attempted to stand up, though he held her there, waiting for her response. And again, she looked into his eyes, but this time the gentility she had witnessed before had vanished. His eyes reflected the essence of his soul as she now saw a wild intensity that consumed him. She briefly wondered if it was for her, or for someone or something else.

Ivan knew what she would say, and he wanted to hear her say it. He wanted to hear her say that sometimes everyone must surrender to love. But in her case, he wanted to hear her say that she would surrender only to his love.

"Can't you tell me? Don't you trust me with this secret?" he asked as his lips moved within inches of hers.

She glanced at them as they called to her. Then she looked back into his eyes. With a sudden burst of strength, she stood up and walked to the door. Before she opened it, she turned around, paused, and looked at him. With distance between them, she felt safe to answer his question, as she whispered, "Surrender to love." Then she opened the door and fled the room.

He knew that her feelings for him frustrated her. He remembered the morning in Belgrade when he delivered her breakfast. He found it hard to believe a woman like her would be waiting around for a man to find her. Perhaps she was involved with someone in America. Perhaps he overstepped his bounds and forced her to do something, or feel something, that was not right for her. If that were so, then why did he imagine he saw love for him in her eyes? Not knowing the answer, he sighed, stood up, and went to find Miloš.

CHAPTER TWENTY-FIVE

Immediately after dinner, Tess returned to the bedroom instead of sitting at the table with the men. Ivan discussed strategies with the men for a short time, then he sought her. He felt his actions had offended her earlier that afternoon and that was why she ran away from him. He knew she chose not to surrender to what he hoped she felt. He knew he had made her uncomfortable, and he did not want her to feel obligated to be around him.

Without making any sound, he walked down the hall to the bedroom. The door was open and he waited there and watched her momentarily. Dressed in her floor length black cashmere robe, she sat at the vanity and brushed her hair. She did not notice him at first. And as he watched her, her actions made him smile.

"Tess, it's Ivan, may I come in?"

"Yes," she said as she paused momentarily, but then continued brushing her hair.

Walking into the room, he sat on the bed in her direct view from the mirror. "Tess, perhaps Sergej should take you to the shelters from now on. Maybe you would enjoy his company for a change," he said.

She stopped brushing her hair and looked at him in the mirror. Then glancing half way over her shoulder, she stared at the door as she analyzed his words. She shook her head, rejecting his suggestion. "No. I don't want to go with Sergej. Not Sergej or anyone else. I want—" she said, stopping herself from saying what she truly felt.

Ivan stood up and walked to stand behind her. He knew she wanted to be with him. He also knew that it was only a matter of time before she would surrender to the feelings causing her uneasiness. Bending down, he looked at her in the mirror as his hand moved to the brush she held. "May I?" he asked, then waited for her permission to brush her hair.

She nodded, then he took the brush from her hand and delicately began to pull it down her hair in long, smooth strokes. As she watched him, he was strangely proficient at how he handled it. It was as though he did this regularly.

Stroke after stroke, he watched the brush move smoothly through her hair. Her hair reminded him of Mara's, which he would brush every night before putting her to bed. That was before it became too dangerous for her to remain in the city. But he did not do this now because he missed Mara. Although the act was similar, the emotion behind the act was at opposite ends of the spectrum. This was the only form of affection he felt that Tess would accept under the circumstances. Though he wanted so much more from her, he took great pleasure in this small gesture of her trust in him.

"Tomorrow we will go east of Sarajevo. Perhaps we will have luck there. The weather should be better tomorrow, no ice," he said. Then he smiled at her and placed the brush on top of the vanity. Reaching for her hand, he grasped it gently and pulled her up and toward the bed.

In awe of his possessive, but gentle, display of affection, she willingly followed him.

"Sleep now. We will be up early. We will try to see five locations tomorrow," he said. Then pulling back the blankets, he waited for her to lie down so that he could cover her.

She only stood there, looking into his eyes. Then she moved toward him and kissed the corner of his lips as her eyes closed briefly. The suddenness of her actions surprised him, and his lips moved slightly at her touch.

"Good night, Ivan," she said, then she lay down and pulled the covers over herself.

He felt helpless as he stood above her, looking at her with deep longing. In his mind, he wondered many things. "What would she do if I lay next to her? Would she leave the bed? Or would she lay in my arms if I pulled her to me?" he asked himself. He smiled at his thoughts and remembered her words from earlier that day: "Surrender to love," she had said.

"Good night, Tess. Sleep well," he said, then he left the room.

As she watched him go, she longed to call him back to her, but did not think he would return. Though she had normally cried at night over her inability to find Mara, this night, she was saddened by his absence. She lay there in the silence of that lonely room, analyzing his actions from that afternoon. Finding no true answer, she imagined that war made people do strange things. Things they would not normally consider doing if not for war. Thinking about this, she finally surrendered to sleep.

CHAPTER TWENTY-SIX

The next day, as promised, Ivan took Tess east of the city. Despite his plans to see five locations, they only saw three shelters, all in a town known to the locals as Morko.

It was early morning when they left. Since Ivan had not been to the Rebel camp in several days, he was unaware of the changed conditions in these locations, of which all resembled infirmaries more than shelters. At the first two shelters, the children were all war casualties, with various types of wounds and broken limbs, but it was no less devastating to see injured children, regardless that they would recover.

At the third shelter, the children were very young and very ill, all quarantined with viral infections of various origins. Ivan tried to convince Tess not to enter the sick rooms. However, despite his most valiant attempt, she ignored his warning and walked amongst the parentless children who were elated to see someone new. For because of their illnesses, they were all but forgotten except for those attending them.

It was at this shelter that she wanted to spend the most time. They had arrived there at approximately two o'clock that afternoon. And though he preferred not to drive after dark, fearing what surprises they could encounter on their way home, for some unknown reason he could not pull her away from the children once the sun began to set.

When they first entered the shelter, Ivan had commented about the orphans to Tess saying, "These are the lucky ones." What he meant was that they would all pass on from their illnesses and not be left parentless. Looking at him, she did not know this and she wondered what worse evils befell the others.

She walked into the room as he stood in the doorway, watching her as she sat with every child; she sometimes fed them, sometimes brushed their hair, or washed their faces. She tried to tell them stories, although the majority of them did not understand English. Nonetheless, she made them laugh with her animated gestures. One by one, every child received her undivided attention and more love than they had experienced in a very long time.

As he watched her circulating amongst these children, he saw she had a deep need to do for others. Not being able to do for others appeared to sadden her because she was not the type of woman to sit back and allow bad things to happen. And again, he wondered about her life in America. What was it like to be Tess Fordel? Still, the question that overpowered all others was, what would it be like for a man to share a life with Tess Fordel?

As expected, Tess had picked out the child who needed her attention the most, a small girl about Mara's age. After talking to one of the women attending the children, Ivan knew the girl would not live out the week. He wondered how Tess knew which child needed her attention more than the others did. He could only imagine she possessed some strange, unearthly ability for detecting varying urgency of need. He found that quite incredible, considering all the children at this facility were critically ill. He understood that in order to know that type of desperation, one must have experienced it. If not, it would be unperceivable. That made him wonder what she may have gone through in her life.

As he continued to watch her, he wondered if she were attempting to make up for some great wrong she felt she had committed. Or was she only acting out something that was missing from her life? He wondered if he would ever know. What he did know was that he wanted to understand her and know her completely.

He was silent as he stood in the doorway of the small, makeshift infirmary. The room was dark with its sparsely placed kerosene lamps that flickered with the slightest stir to the lifeless air. Old stone walls encompassed the children who slept, unaware of the bleakness of their surroundings. The only sounds he heard were their moans, constant coughs, and traces of Tess' soft voice whispering to the little girl she held.

Almost two hours had passed as Tess held the same child. At first, she spoke as she cradled the child in her arms. Trying to convince her to sleep, Tess stroked her face, smiled at her, and spoke to her in a whisper. To Ivan's amazement, this little girl spoke some English, and though Ivan made out only a few words that Tess spoke, the child's relaxed expression told him exactly what was happening.

Seriously infected with pneumonia, there was no hope for this child. She was past being cured by the simple medicines supplied. He could see the child hid her struggle. Trying to breathe silently, she strained to hear every word Tess spoke, and each attempt was a vain denial of the death that awaited her in the shadows.

Despite that, Ivan saw true love's effect on the child, who smiled at Tess with a fearless expression before she closed her eyes. Ivan thought that the child had finally fallen asleep, though Tess knew the truth as she held her tired body and spoke lovingly to her. The child's last experience of this world was Tess' caring smile, tender words, and her arms that comforted and reassured her.

Tess felt her little body become limp and heard her last breath rush forth from her lungs with a serene, but strained sound; a sound only God and Tess heard. For a long time, Tess continued to hold the girl, and when the child had passed, she was smiling from Tess' unselfish and earnest affection.

Shortly after, Ivan saw Tess talking, though the child did not respond. He did not know what she was saying as shadows covered her face and her were eyes closed. When she finally laid the child back, and stood up, he imagined she had said a prayer with the child because Tess crossed herself. Then she stared off into space, and Ivan wanted to go to her, thinking that she would definitely cry. In the broken sorrow of her inability to help this child, she would need him, and he desperately wanted to be there for her. When she did not cry, he remained in his place at the door, but she could not cry because the situation was well beyond tears.

With a loving expression, Tess straightened the child back against the pillow, and positioned her small hands on top of her chest. Then she bent down and kissed her on the forehead as though she were putting her to sleep for the night. However, it was when Tess pulled the covers over the child's peaceful face that Ivan realized the child had not fallen asleep, she had died.

Ivan hurried into the room. Tess briefly placed her hand on the child's head. As Ivan neared, he heard her next words. As she looked toward the ceiling, she made a fluid hand motion upward as if directing the little girl's spirit toward heaven. "You're free now. Fly away little angel," she whispered, as she closed her eyes, bowed her head, and rested her hand on the child's shoulder.

At a loss for words, Ivan stood at the foot of the dead child's bed. He waited for Tess to move her hand from the child, but she did not. He went to her side, placed his arm around her shoulder, and tried to turn her away—she had endured more than enough for one day. Only when he pulled Tess firmly did her hand move from the child, though she looked back at her as he led her from the room.

He knew what question passed through her mind. She wondered if that child was Mara, especially because the little girl spoke English. If so, then it was too late and her efforts were in vain. But Tess would never know who that child was. Ivan could see it in her lifeless expression. He could feel it in her stride as she appeared to hesitate leaving the child, though there was nothing else she could do.

As they exited the room, one of the women called Ivan back to ask what had happened. Letting Tess go, he turned around and explained the situation. He thought Tess would have stopped and waited for him, but as questions flooded her mind, she continued her dazed exodus down the hall. She was completely unaware of Ivan's absence as he stood talking with the woman in the doorway to the sick room.

It took every ounce of strength she had not to break her promise. She now wanted to cry more than any other time, to shed tears for what had just happened, and to mourn the death of a child that she did not know. If not to shed tears for the child, then for herself and the helplessness that consumed her. For the first time since she was there, she felt the war creep into her very soul. It laughed and clawed at her, mocking her, as it had dangled a helpless life in front of her, only to extinguish it without concern or remorse. Greed prevailed, wiping out all that stood in its path, and all she could give into was the anxiety that seized her heart.

Without warning, and as though every drop of blood had escaped her body, she saw nothing but blackness. Her hands reached helplessly out in front of her for something to steady herself, and her breaths came in a strained rhythm. Finding nothing to hold for balance, her hands dropped to her sides as if she no longer cared.

The woman speaking to Ivan looked past him. Seeing Tess' weakened state, and lack of balance, her eyes widened as she gasped. At once, Ivan turned around to see Tess plummeting sideways to the cold, tile floor. He heard a thud as the side of her head hit the ground, knocking her unconscious.

"*Tess!*" he said as he rushed to her. Panicking and kneeling by her side, he gently rolled her onto her back. When he turned her face toward him, he saw blood on the floor, and her cheek and brow were cut open.

Another woman rushed to them with a clean rag and handed it to him, although he refused it, feeling it was not sanitary enough to touch her open wounds. Instead, he pulled a clean handkerchief from his pocket and used that to blot the blood from her cheek and brow. Quickly shoving it back into his pocket, in one swift movement, he lifted her up as her head and arm slipped toward the ground, limp and lifeless. The first woman approached and wanted to show him to a vacant bed where Tess could rest. He refused, not wanting her to be there any longer. All he could think about was getting her back to the house and to the safety his men provided, back to the room they shared so he could be alone with her.

The woman helped Ivan to the car where he placed Tess in the front seat with her head leaning back against the headrest. Going into the trunk, he grabbed two blankets and closed it. Then quickly getting into the driver's seat, he closed the door to block the cold. He started the car, then he pulled off his coat, folded it, and placed it between the seats. Moving her toward him, he lowered her across his coat, so her head would come gently to rest on his lap. He covered her with the blankets, and smiled sadly as he brushed the hair back from her face. "Tess," he whispered and, with a deep sigh, he headed back to Sarajevo.

At half past seven, they arrived at the house. Ivan stepped from the car and hurried around the front to the passenger side as Sergej walked out onto the porch to greet them. He had been worried when they had not returned earlier. Once Sergej saw Ivan carrying Tess, he ran down the front steps, half-slipping in his panic. He could only imagine that something terrible had happened.

For a moment, in the dim glow of the light coming from inside the house, Sergej thought he saw tears in Ivan's eyes. Sergej's mind flew in all directions. He thought that definitely Tess was dead, and he panicked. "Ivan? What happened? What's wrong? Is she hurt? Is she—" He stopped himself and looked at her. Noticing her blood stained skin, he could not bring himself to ask if she were dead. Hearing Sergei's questions, the other men from inside came to see what was happening.

Ivan shook his head and continued walking in the snow toward the front door. As he walked up the front steps, he issued his order. "Have someone get my coat out of the car, then have someone put the car away."

Sergej imagined Tess was seeing the war for what it really was: up close and real enough to touch. The color of her skin told him she was not dead, but he wondered how she had gotten bloody. He then called for Dragan to drive the car around to the back and secure it for the night, and bring in Ivan's coat.

With deep concern, the men crowding the front door moved from Ivan's path. Without acknowledging them, Ivan walked through the living room, then through the dining room and kitchen, and directly to their bedroom. Entering the room, no candles were lit, although Ivan was happy to see a fire started, which was usual for his men to do for him.

Carefully laying her on the bed, he then closed the door. He quickly slipped her out of her coat and pulled off her boots, which he put near the fire to dry, then hung her coat by the door. Returning to the bed, he pulled the covers from under her, then up and over her.

Quickly glancing around the room, he saw what he was looking for—a thermos of warm water waiting on the dresser. Hurrying to it, he wet a towel and returned to her. Sitting gently on the bed, he softly blotted her cheek and brow, and wiped her forehead. Looking at her, he could only imagine that she had collapsed from fatigue after their long day. That, and the obvious thought that the child who died could possibly have been Mara. He could only imagine the multitude of unanswered questions that plagued her mind, but for now she was peaceful, or so he hoped.

Regardless, the next day Ivan was going to make sure Tess rested. He would care for her in the same tender fashion she had cared for the dying child. He would attempt to comfort her for that compassionate act. With that thought, he looked at the bloodstained cloth in his hand. Pulling the covers up to her shoulders, he leaned toward her and, as every night, he kissed her lips then whispered, "Rest now, my beautiful, brave, Tess." Still carrying the cloth, he left the room to speak with Sergej, who paced nervously at the end of the hall.

CHAPTER TWENTY-SEVEN

Ivan awoke at half past six the following morning. When he sat up, he saw Tess was not in bed. As on those rare occasions when she woke up before him, she had made her bed, and her perfume lingered in the stillness of the morning air. Wanting to find her, he walked to the dresser, rinsed his face, shaved, then changed his clothes.

Walking from the hallway into the kitchen, he expected to find Tess helping Mrs. Tomić, but she was not there. Greeting her with a kiss on each cheek, Ivan inquired where Tess was. She pointed out the kitchen window. Then she grasped Ivan's arm, pointed to her own face in the spots where Tess had been injured, and asked, "What happened?"

Attempting to make light of Tess' abrasions, his response was somewhat less than convincing. "She was too tired yesterday. She fainted. I couldn't catch her in time."

"Keep her home today. Stay here with her. What are the two of you doing here anyway? Go back to Belgrade and spend time with her there."

Ivan had not told Mrs. Tomić what Tess' purpose was for being in Sarajevo, so she was under the impression that Tess was there to be with him. She knew that Ivan would not have brought Tess into her house if he did not have serious intentions toward Tess. None of the men would tell Mrs. Tomić the truth; those were Ivan's orders and the men obeyed them. But she did not even know where Mara was, and she agreed not to mention Mara to Tess as Ivan had requested. She trusted Ivan, knowing that he would protect Mara; however, she also did not know that Ivan was the Black Rebel, but she had her suspicions.

Giving her a brief smile, Ivan walked outside and momentarily observed Tess standing alone in the snow near a row of dormant lilac bushes. He noticed her shivering. He walked toward her, placed his arm around her, and delicately kissed her bruised cheek. The cold made her tremble, but she smiled at him when he whispered, "Good morning." He then tried to lead her back to the house, although she stood still, not moving with him. She stood firm as if she were a beautiful statue to be admired from a distance.

"Why do you stand alone out here? You shouldn't be out here. It's not safe. Come inside," he said softly. However, looking back at the house, he noticed two of his men in two of the upstairs bedroom windows, poised with shotguns as they watched over her.

She reached for the frozen limbs of the lilac bush in front of her. Looking at the row of bushes, she tried to smile, but only heaved a sigh.

"What are you thinking?" he asked.

She shook her head. Lost momentarily in private thoughts, she expelled a smaller sigh. Then she looked back to the limb she still held in her grasp. "Even during periods of harsh conflict and confrontation, the delicate beauty and fragrance of the lilac have been faithful annual reminders of the lovelier aspects in human relations," she quoted.

"Did you write that?"

"No, someone named Nell Singer did."

"Is that a friend?"

"No. I read it on a plaque at the east end of Lilac Walk in Central Park." She was momentarily silent as she thought to herself. "It makes you wonder if any lovelier aspects remain to human relations," she said, letting the limb go.

"Perhaps not at this time in this country, but I think so," he said. Then he turned her around, and with his arm still around her, they walked back to the house. Entering the kitchen, Mrs. Tomić held a tray with their breakfast. Ivan immediately took the tray from her and carried it into the dining room as Mrs. Tomić followed. Once they passed through the door, Tess walked down the hall to the bedroom. Removing her coat, she sat on the bed with her notebook and began to read.

Ivan called to Tess, thinking she had followed them and perhaps was putting her coat in the front room. Looking for her there, he did not see her. Then he walked back into the kitchen, and when he did not find her there, he proceeded to the bedroom. Finding the door halfway open, he knocked softly and said, "Tess? Are you alright? May I come in?"

"Of course," she answered.

He pushed the door open and saw her sitting on the edge of the bed, facing the door, and reading from her notebook. She looked up at him as he approached. Taking the book from her, he placed it at the bottom of the bed, then he crouched down in front of her. She looked directly into his eyes as though she searched for hidden answers that only he had, and her smile was melancholy as if she were waiting for something to happen.

Gazing up at her, he noticed serenity emanating from her stare. It was as though she was better understanding the war that, in the past, she had spoken of with somewhat disbelief. The child that died in her arms made everything more personal to her. Now it was no longer something reported on the evening news. Being there in person, she could not turn it off as she might have back in America. This war was a constant factor of life that she was learning to cope with and, under the circumstances, he felt she was coping very well.

He reached for her hands and held them. "How do you feel today? Better?"

"I'm sorry about yesterday," she said, then looked away. "I was more tired than I thought." She could not look into his eyes when she said she was tired because she knew it was not the truth. She did not want him to see what she really felt, but after a moment of silence, she looked back at him and tried to smile.

"We should stay home today. Yesterday was a very long day. You made many children happy, one especially happy," he said.

"I don't want to stay home."

He did not respond right away, he only observed her. Still holding her hands, he stood, and pulled her up with him. "Alright! If you want to go out, you must eat breakfast," he ordered.

Walking with her to the door, they left the bedroom and went to the dining room. Sergej and several of the men were already eating at the table, but when Ivan and Tess walk in, they all stood, greeted her, and inquired as to how she felt. They tried not to look, however, they saw her cut and bruised cheek and brow, and they had heard a vague version of the truth from Sergej about what had happened.

With a possessive gesture, Ivan pulled Tess' chair close to his as he sat her at the table. By now, the men were used to Tess praying before eating, and, out of respect for her, they waited until she did. Only then did they continue eating and talking with her. Shortly after sitting down, Ivan became lost in conversation with Sergej regarding Rebel matters. Tess spoke with Alek and Miloš as they told her the story about both of them slipping down the front steps of the house. The way they attempted to re-enact the event from their seats made Tess laugh. They hoped their story would make her forget her fall from the day before, if not forget, at least not feel so bad about it.

"And then Alek fell on me like an enormous elephant, and I thought," Miloš said as he dramatically put both hands to his chest as if he were out of breath. "*OH! I'm dead!*"

"*Fell?* You grabbed me as you slipped down the steps!" Alek said as he shook his head and rolled his eyes. As Tess laughed, she held the side of her face because smiling made it hurt, but they accomplished their goal of making her feel less awkward.

CHAPTER TWENTY-EIGHT

After breakfast, Ivan and Tess left the house and ventured east of Sarajevo again. They returned to Sokolac, then went to Obrtići. Sergej informed Ivan that these locations housed only healthy children. Regardless that Ivan did not tell Sergej exactly what had happened, Sergej knew something profound had happened the day before when Ivan insisted, "No more infirmaries." From Ivan's firm tone, Sergej could only imagine that Tess began to experience death as she searched in vain for Mara. Sergej tried not to question Ivan's motives; however, Sergej's gaze displayed his disapproval of the lie Ivan continued to tell Tess.

Ivan and Tess returned home by half past four that afternoon. Their efforts that day yielded nothing, as did the following day. The more Ivan saw Tess surrounded by children, the more he doubted her ability to betray anyone. In his mind, he continued to rationalize his suspicions farther and farther into the background, pushing them aside as his love for her grew stronger. The only troublesome thought that lingered in Ivan's mind was Tess' suggestion to take Mara back to America. Even though she had mentioned that she would gladly take Iđy with her, Ivan did not know what she would do when she found out that he was Iđy. What would she do when she found out that he had kept her from finding Mara?

"Why did Tess come along now? Why not ten years ago, or even five, when I could have taken her and run off to some faraway place. Why not before I was involved with the war?" he thought, but who would answer his questions?

He felt cheated out of life; cheated out of love. Every time she looked into his eyes, he saw such trust in him that the thought of telling her the truth was becoming ever more unthinkable. The longer he waited to tell her, the more absurd the situation became. Then there was the thought of his making a single mistake, and telling her the truth only to discover that she was a spy. Those who depended on Ivan would be lost if he did not choose wisely. As usual, he kept up the pretense of the search, sacrificing his needs for the needs of those who depended upon him. In the end, he would do what was expected of him, what was expected of the Black Rebel.

CHAPTER TWENTY-NINE

On the following Saturday, after going to Kiseljak and Gromiljak, the last shelter Ivan and Tess visited before heading back to the city was in Fojnica, to the west and slightly north of Sarajevo. After looking at the children, Tess walked back to Ivan and shook her head. Nothing seemed familiar about any of them except the common denominators of lost dreams, lost families, and lost hopes.

Walking from inside the children's quarters, Ivan stopped to thank the man who headed the facility. Tess did not wait, but instead, kept walking. Passing through the gated entrance, she crossed the road and proceeded to enter a makeshift cemetery she had noticed when they arrived. One by one, she examined the graves with only white wooden crosses for markers. "Even in death, the war has stripped away their identity. Who prayed for them on their journey to wherever they were headed? For certainly heaven was their destination after the suffering they endured," she thought.

Walking further, she stopped at a small grave. From its size, she imagined it belonged to a child. The cross at this grave had fallen over to the ground. She knelt in the snow, lifted it, and tried to secure it at the head of the grave. Despite her efforts, it fell over again. She sighed, but did not rise immediately, nor had she noticed that Ivan stood a few feet away, watching her.

Seeing her sorrow for the people of his country, people she did not know, he wished she would break her promise and cry. He wanted a reason to hold her and comfort her. A reason his suspicions would not deny, but was it his suspicions that stopped him when he wanted to hold her and tell her what he felt? Or was it his fear that she would reject him as a foreigner, a Socialist, as he imagined any American woman would see him as.

She lowered her head and closed her eyes. Though she made no sound, he saw a tear tumble from her cheek and fall to the snow where she knelt at the unknown child's grave. He felt her suffering, although she continued battling her feelings in order to keep her promise to him. Seeing her now, it was as though that simple promise meant more to her than anything else did; she would keep it as long as she could.

"Don't cry for this child; it's not Mara," he said, trying to console her.

She quickly stood and turned away from him. Walking out of the cemetery, she looked over her shoulder and said to him, "Why would I cry? I'm a Capitalist, remember?"

Ivan could tell that she was angry with herself at her loss of control. He knew that she did not want to be that crying woman he said he would not tolerate. He followed her as she walked through the high snow toward the road. At the entrance to the cemetery, he caught up to her. Grasping her arm firmly, he roughly pulled her back to face him, as he said, "What brought that on? Why do you speak to me like that? Did I do something wrong? Because I don't think I did."

As he waited for her answer, his stern disposition forced her to look away from him. She knew she was wrong for snapping at him, but he was equally wrong when he had insisted that she not cry, and he knew it.

"We'd better leave now. You don't want to drive in the dark," she said.

He did not let her go, and when she still did not look at him, he lifted her head by her chin and forced her to look at him. Seeing regret in her eyes, his anger vanished. He knew he was the root of the provocation that caused her sadness. He was the one at fault, not her.

"If you're angry with me, tell me. Perhaps you would rather have Sergej take you to look for Mara," he again suggested.

Looking up at him, she could see he feared her answer. She gave a brief smile, and shook her head. "No. I don't want to go with *anyone* but you. It's just, well, I don't like you wasting your time," she answered.

He smiled. Hearing her need to be with him made him happy, and he let go of her chin and pulled her closer to him. "Don't worry about that. Your search is not a waste of my time. I want to help you, so don't think about it," he said, as he sadly thought that it was not a waste of his time to search for Mara, but a waste of hers.

He moved even closer to her, still looking into her eyes that called him to her. There were moments when he felt himself lost in her mossy-green gaze, lost in all that lingered there. He felt as though she had been waiting all this time just for him. Such depth of emotion and caring was one part of her that held him captive, one part of her that he wanted for him alone. As he continued to look at her, it appeared that she existed for the simple purpose of being with him, but when she pulled away, that feeling dimmed with her movement.

"Can we go now?" she asked as she looked away from him and toward the street.

Taking her hand, he led her to the car. Once inside, they headed back to Sarajevo. They did not speak on their way; he could tell she thought about something, but not Mara. She periodically looked at him, then looked away before he could turn to see her. From this, he knew she questioned something about him. He imagined that she began to distrust him. He tried to hide his lie to her about knowing Mara, but perhaps she could tell that he hid things from her. Perhaps she could feel his insincerity. Maybe that was why she pulled away from him when he tried to be close to her, when he tried to kiss her. He could only hope that she would talk to him, for the meaning behind her words would tell him what she felt.

CHAPTER THIRTY

When they arrived back at the house, they were greeted with shocking news. Alek immediately approached them and spoke uneasily in Serbian, so not to upset Tess. "Unknown troops have broken the cease-fire. Kiseljak, Gromiljak, and Fojnica shelters were attacked. Everyone was killed!"

"Get the men together!" Ivan ordered in Serbian. Then his expression grew angry and, grabbing Tess by the wrist, he pulled her behind him through the kitchen and onto the bedroom.

"Ivan? What is it? What happened?" she asked as she walked quickly behind him. He ignored her, still pulling her to the bedroom. Opening the door to the bedroom, he forced her inside and roughly sat her on the bed. Without a word, he walked back to the door. She stood, walked after him, and touched his arm. "What happened?" she asked again.

Turning around quickly, his expression was angry as he came close to her. Seeing the look on his face, she stepped backward. As he stared down at her, his appearance threatened her. He resembled a mad man as his eyes reflected his anger. Again, she stepped back, though every step she took, he took one toward her until she was next to the bed. Placing his hands on her shoulders, he pushed her to sit down and she could tell his thoughts were hostile as he leaned toward her.

"The shelters we visited today were attacked. Everyone was killed, all of the children. Wherever Americans go, death follows. Amazing, isn't it?" he said in a low and menacing tone.

"Why?" she asked, observably confused.

"Why? For reasons you could never understand!" he said, then he walked to the door and roughly opened it. Pulling the key from the latch, he pointed his finger at her, and said, "You stay in this room. You don't come out until I let you out! Don't try to get out either!" Then, without another word, he stepped into the hall and slammed the door.

She heard the key turn in the lock and she knew he had locked her inside his bedroom. For several minutes, she sat there hearing the men's elevated voices from the kitchen. Then she heard them leave through the kitchen door. An eerie silence filled the house, *except,* for the sound of one man's boots approaching the bedroom, and the clack of a shotgun being chambered. In that instant, she went from guest to prisoner.

Walking to the window, she moved the curtain aside ever so slightly and peeked out at the rear grounds of the house. She saw Ivan with the men surrounding him. They all held rifles or sub-machine guns of various calibers. Even Ivan had a rifle in his hand. She heard his muffled voice through the window as he appeared to order the men while he pointed in the directions they were to go. When he had finished talking, the men left. She heard car engines starting, and Ivan, Sergej, and Tomo got into a car and drove away, leaving a swirl of white exhaust trailing behind them.

Stepping away from the window, she recalled a statement from Mara's book: *They call him the Black Rebel. He fights for the lost people of Sarajevo. He fights for people like my family and me. God bless the Black Rebel.*

"God bless the Black Rebel," Tess whispered, then she released a small breath. Seeing Ivan armed, then seeing the men with their weapons, changed the situation. How they listened when Ivan spoke. How they appeared to hang on his every word, perhaps words that sent his commands to countless other men waiting for his instructions. From all she had witnessed since meeting Ivan, she now knew that Ivan and the Black Rebel were one and the same—she was sure of it.

Ivan was the man who commanded the army of freedom fighters that suppressed Nationalist aggression. She understood that he was the man who protected and saved as many of his countrymen as possible. But what she could not understand was why a man so important to his people would waste his time helping her find a child? What was it he wanted from her to take so much time to assist in her search? His responsibility to his people was great. He fought for a nation divided, a people divided. He fought against all attempts to capture and further destroy the people of this dismembered region that was once Yugoslavia.

"Ivan," she whispered with a strained sigh, and without any choice, she removed her coat and awaited his return. For hours, she waited. Alek stayed in the house with her, sitting right outside the bedroom door. However, he was not there to make sure she did not get out, he was there to keep her safe. In Ivan's absence, Alek was her bodyguard. He spoke to her through the door, offering her dinner, but with few words she declined. As she waited for Ivan to come home, she wrote about the Black Rebel. She wrote of Ivan as the Black Rebel, and wrote about all that she felt for him. She wrote until she had transcribed the convictions of her mind about him, and the passion in her heart for him. Then it was late and she grew tired. Changing into her robe, she put her notebook on the bed stand, slid under the covers, and fell asleep.

CHAPTER THIRTY-ONE

It was two hours before sunrise when Ivan and his men returned to the house. After securing further reports, he and Sergej discussed the intel on the attacks. They learned that several other locations east of Sarajevo were attacked and people there were killed; however, not all civilians were fatalities at these locations. The ones that survived the attacks were taken to the Rebel camp for their safety.

Before Ivan knew about these other attacks, he felt perhaps Tess had contacted whomever it was that she sided with. He felt that perhaps they had killed these innocent people as a warning to him that they knew his moves. At this point, he was not sure of anything except his hasty accusations. Now that he knew the randomness of the attacks, he regretted treating her so harshly. With few words, he had accused her of betraying him, though he could not figure out how she could have sent a message to anyone. He now knew these attacks were indiscriminate acts of violence by unknown radical militant groups hiding in the hills surrounding Sarajevo. Their method, hunt and peck, as they sought to wreak havoc on anyone in their path and, in the process, take all they could.

His identity was safe, but he wondered how he would explain his actions to Tess. Would she believe him when he bent the truth and told her that his anger was for her own good? When he apologized, would she reject it and see him as the tyrant he felt he was?

Carrying an oil lamp to light his way, he left Sergej in the kitchen and entered the hall to the bedroom. Seeing him approach, Alek met him halfway and placed the bedroom key in his hand.

"Did she eat?" Ivan asked.

Alek shook his head.

"Did she try to get out? Did you hear her crying?"

Again, Alek shook his head. "She refused food. She was silent for hours, and finally the light went out. She must be asleep."

"Thank you for staying with her. Sergej will fill you in," Ivan said.

With his shotgun in hand, Alek walked from the hallway and retreated to the upper floor. Ivan looked at the doorway as he walked toward it. With only the slightest sound, he unlocked the door and stepped into the room. He then closed and locked the door behind himself. The moon shone brightly through the split in the window's drape. He walked toward it and looked outside as he listened to the wind rushing down the chimney.

Pulling the drape shut, he lowered the flame in the lamp he carried so not to wake her with its light, then he walked to the bed. She lay sleeping under the covers with her knees pulled up toward her chest. The room was so frigid that he could almost see his own breath. With all the excitement, he neglected to make a fire for her. And since there was no wood in the room, she could not make one for herself. Now he knew that she was locked in that cold room all night with nothing to keep her warm: no coffee, no food, no fire, and no Ivan.

Setting the lamp down on the table next to the bed, he unlocked the door and walked to the kitchen. He saw extra wood near the stove. Filling his arms with enough for a fire, he returned to the bedroom and kindled a fire immediately. The glow from the flames illuminated the room as its warmth reached out from the hearth, seeking every corner. He returned to the kitchen and placed enough wood in the stove for the next morning. Then he brought the rest of the wood to their bedroom. Placing it down on the floor next to the fireplace, he walked back to the door, closed it, and locked it again. He walked to his small bed and pulled one of the blankets from it. He returned to her and pulled the covers higher over her shoulders, he then placed his blanket over her. Still wanting her to be as warm as possible, he retrieved her coat from the hook on the wall and placed that over her as well.

Bending down to her, he kissed her cheek; it was chilled to the touch, but in her sleep, she smiled as if she knew he had kissed her. He knew that he was free to kiss her when she slept. She would not turn away from him then, so he seized every opportunity.

"Forgive me, Tess," he whispered as if she would hear him, then he kissed her again. Taking the lamp, he set it on the dresser, then he sat on the small bed. He removed his wet boots, though left on his coat, then he lay down and pulled up his blankets. His head rested on the pillow as he stared at the ceiling. Even if his mind should have been on the people that perished at the shelters, his last thoughts were of Tess, and he questioned himself, "What will I say that will make up for my inappropriate behavior last night?" Not knowing the answer just then, in his exhaustion, he slept.

CHAPTER THIRTY-TWO

It was around half past seven the next morning when Ivan awoke. Having only slept a little over two hours, he forced his eyes open. Seeing Tess sitting at the vanity, he took a silent breath. He sat up and ran his fingers through his hair. For a few moments he watched her, as, again, she read the papers about Mara; her reflection told him so. In the mirror, he saw her heartache as tears slid down her cheeks. Running his hands through his hair again, he stood up while his gaze did not leave her. She suddenly looked at him in the mirror, but then quickly pretended not to see him rather than have him catch her in a moment of weakness. Placing the papers to the side, she immediately wiped the tears from her face then began to brush her hair.

He walked to the dresser where a thermos of water waited for him. The water was tepid, but he rinsed his face, quickly shaved, then dried his face and hands. With no words passing between them, he could only wonder what she was thinking. Looking at her, he saw her braiding her hair. She was aware that he watched her, but she said nothing. Her indifference to him was upsetting, and he frowned as he walked to her. Placing his hands over hers, he stopped her from continuing. She looked down and moved her hands to the vanity top as he pulled the braid apart, allowing her hair to fall against her back. And though his smile told her of his affection, she ignored it.

"Don't wear your hair that way. Leave it like this. This is how it was when I first saw you," he said. He watched her in the mirror as he smoothed out the last waves of the braid.

Not moving, she did not look at him. She allowed him to finish, then she asked, "Am I allowed out of this room yet?"

His shoulders slumped from pride to despair. When he fell asleep earlier, he had hoped that she might not be angry with him this morning. However, now he could see that he was wrong, and in his heart, he could not blame her.

Crouching down by her side, he gazed up at her. "Last night—" He stopped and heaved a deep sigh. "That's the way it is here. Things happen for no reason. Things happen without warning. I knew if you were in here, you'd be safe," he said in a matter of fact tone.

"I'd be safe? Or someone else would be safe? Safe from me," she said. Then she turned in the opposite direction and stood up.

He was shocked when she walked away from him, but what did he expect? He tried to smooth things over, by saying, "What I meant was—"

"What you meant is what you said last night. I know your actions were a direct result of the situation, and you did what you felt was best. But at this point, any explanation would only rekindle your mood from last night."

Ivan stood up, walked to the bed, and stopped behind her. Searching his mind, he could not find any words to explain. She was right, and she caught him trying to compensate for his behavior for which there was no compensation.

She looked over her shoulder toward him. "If I may be permitted, I promised Mrs. Tomić I'd go to church with her this morning. It is Sunday. May I go? If all else is to be stripped from me under your martial law, I beg you to allow me to keep my promise."

"You know it will be a Serbian Orthodox Mass," he said.

"I'm asking your permission if I may keep my promise," she said, ignoring his comment.

Feeling her defenses were heightened, and her opinion of him was diminished, he stroked her arms softly hoping to reassure her. "You don't need my permission. I will take you and Mama to church. I'll change my clothes and we'll go."

As he walked to the dresser, she walked to the door and pulled her coat from a hook on the wall. "Please don't bother yourself, it's not necessary. Yesterday morning Sergej said he would take us."

"I want to take you. Wait for me, please," he insisted.

"I'd prefer you didn't. I know you're a busy man, and I don't want to distract you from your business," she answered.

"Tess—"

"We'll be back right after Mass. I'll come back to the room so you can lock me up again. This way you'll know exactly where I am, and you'll be safe." Without another word, she gently opened the door. Stepping out into the hall, she closed the door without looking at him, then she was gone.

He stood there stunned. She was right. He had locked her in the bedroom so he and his men would be safe from her. He had hoped she would not have seen it that way, but now he knew that she did; it was not for her own safety. Because of this, he knew Tess realized that he did not completely trust her.

Quickly changing his clothes, he grabbed his coat off the hook near the door and rushed from the room. He wanted to catch them before they left, but they were gone by the time he walked from the kitchen into the dining room where Rurik, Alek, Tomo, and Miloš sat talking.

Feeling she was safe with Sergej, Ivan did not rush after her. Instead, he tossed his coat on the sofa as he thought that perhaps some time away from him may help her not feel so mistreated. He walked back to the table, sat at the head, and they discussed the attacks from the day before. The men looked to him for answers that he did not have. The military police had not acted on the attacks and that confused matters. It was a violation of the cease-fire, but no one did anything. Listening to his men's opinions, he tried to formulate a plan to protect the orphaned children in the immediate area. His only choice was to split up the men at the Rebel camp south of Sarajevo, then distribute them amongst the shelters. In the back of his mind, he debated taking Mara from Saint Michael's and sending her away. Where he would send her, he did not know, but instead, he would reinforce the men he had placed there to protect her.

For half an hour, Ivan sat quietly as he thought and listened to his men. Then suddenly the front door opened and the sound broke his concentration. Lukáš hurried into the house. Out of breath as he approached the table, he spoke of more trouble. "Three Serb soldiers are on their way to the church. They are searching for an American woman. The men are on their way," Lukáš said as he looked at Ivan and waited for his command.

Ivan sat there as thoughts of Mrs. Tomić and Sergej flashed in his head, then he thought about Tess. This was the third time men searched for her. In haste, he stood, causing his chair to drop back toward the floor. Grabbing his coat from the sofa, he put it on. His men followed and, all together, they exited the house and got into two cars. With great caution, they drove to the church. He searched the side streets for signs of any one out of the ordinary, but for war, everything appeared normal. Then again, it was almost too quiet. Hardly any citizens walked the streets any more in Sarajevo for fear of snipers. Even with major streets having been cleared of debris, only a few moving cars were ever seen that did not belong to military forces.

Lukáš drove with Ivan riding shotgun. The car stopped at the back of the church and Ivan stepped out. Walking briskly to the door, he entered a side vestibule. Mass had concluded and the few people who attended were cautiously exiting the front of the building.

He approached Sergej and Mrs. Tomić. "We have to get out of here. The men are here. Take Mama out the side door."

Sergej saw his concern, but was afraid to ask what had now happened.

"Three men are searching for Tess," Ivan whispered. Then looking past Sergej, Ivan did not see Tess. "Where is she? Where did she go?" he asked as he looked around for her.

"She's right there. She wanted a few minutes alone before we left," Sergej said as he moved to the side and motioned toward the altar.

Ivan was relieved to see Tess safe. He then motioned Sergej and Mrs. Tomić toward the side door where he had entered. "Miloš will take you and Mama home. Radio the camp and have the men on standby. Come on. Out this way," he said, then he led them to the side where he had entered. Opening the door, he looked out. Signaling to Miloš, who stood by the car, Ivan waited for him to approach. Then Sergej and Miloš escorted Mrs. Tomić to the car.

Ivan walked back inside the church. Looking around for Tess, she was not there. No one was there. He looked toward the entrance and saw her pushing the front door open. He started walking after her, but before he could call to her, she stepped outside, and the door closed behind her. As he neared the front doors, he heard a noise from behind the altar. Turning around, he saw them: two men holding pistols had entered from behind the altar. Not seeing Ivan, they looked toward the side entrances.

Ivan quietly slipped out the front door and walked to the street. Where was she? He walked toward the right of the church and looked along the outside of it. Not seeing her there, he walked to the left and looked down a narrow walkway leading to the back of the church. Standing in place, he saw a familiar figure walking to the side entrance; it was Tess. He wanted to call out to her, but again, she entered before he had the chance. Running down the walkway, he expected to hear gunshots or her screaming, but as he approached the door, he heard nothing.

Reaching to his ankle, he pulled a double-edged knife from a sheath strapped to his leg. When he was about to enter, he felt the door pushing toward him. He could only imagine one of the unknown men would exit and possibly have Tess. Moving back as the door opened, he stepped out of sight as he allowed whoever was inside to come out. At the first sign of the unknown person, he stepped forward, roughly reached his left arm around the figure, and covered the person's mouth with his gloved hand. Then he pulled the person behind the door as his right hand lifted the knife to the person's throat. He responded so quickly that his reflexes blocked his recognition of Tess, whom he now held threateningly in his grasp.

Once backed against the wall, he quickly lowered the knife, and expelled a heavy breath, then whispered, "Tess, I told you never to walk alone." Then he moved his hand from her mouth and wrapped it around her shoulder. Closing his eyes, he held her securely to him and expelled a second, less worried breath.

She stood still, trying to regain her breath. Through her coat, he could feel her heart pounding. After a moment, she pulled away from him and turned around to face him. "What's wrong with you? Are you trying to scare me to death?" she asked, hitting him in the chest. Then she turned around, and without looking back at him, she started to walk down the path to the front of the church where she was supposed to meet Sergej and Mrs. Tomić.

Her reaction angered him. He was there to save her life and she was upset with his efforts. Sheathing his knife, he hurried after her. He pulled her back to face him and she saw his expression, which simultaneously questioned and accused her. "Is that all you have to say to me? I came here to save you, *again.* Your *friends* are here searching for you. *Again,* they seek you. Why? What do the Serbians want with you?"

Jerking her arm from his grasp, she stared at him for a moment. "I don't know. Maybe they like Americans. Perhaps they want a date!" Again, she walked away.

As Ivan watched her, he saw a man walking down the path toward them. Seeing them, the man's pace quickened as he removed a pistol from his coat pocket. Ivan ran up behind her, grabbed her arm, and pulled her back to the side entrance of the building.

She had been looking at the ground and had not noticed the man approaching, so she resisted Ivan. "What are you doing?" she said, attempting to pull away from him.

Ivan managed to get her inside the church. Pulling the door closed, he reached up and pushed the bolts into the doorframe just in time to lock the man out. At once, the doors shook as the man on the outside tugged at them. Ivan heard the man speaking in Serbian to someone else. "She's inside! She's with someone! This door is locked. Go to the front!" the man said angrily, then he kicked the door.

Ivan then heard the men running away. Tess watched in confusion as he hastily reached for her. Roughly his hand clenched around her right wrist, as he hurried across the interior of the church, pulling her behind him. With his eyes fixed on the front entrance, he watched for the men to enter, while his grip crushed her wrist as they moved rapidly toward the door on the opposite side.

"Ivan, let me go. Quit pulling me," she said.

Reaching into the back waist of his trousers, he pulled out his pistol and flipped off its safety. *"Don't talk!"* he ordered in a whisper, as he kept moving and looking back at her with the same menacing expression from the night before. He continued through the pews and his grip did not loosen when they neared the door. He pushed the door open enough to look around, but then he heard the front door open. Looking in that direction, he saw two men enter. Both were armed and, just then, Tess saw them and understood what Ivan was trying to do.

The men spotted them. "There! That's her," the one man said in Serbian as he pointed his pistol at them and started moving in their direction.

Ivan aimed and fired two rounds at the first man. They broke the sacred silence, piercing the serenity of the church. The first man fell backward, shot in the side of the neck. The sight of his dying associate startled the second man, who was younger and less experienced.

Tess stood watching as if she were at the movies. Regardless that this was real, it did not register with her. Then, with a single thrust, Ivan forced the door open and they ran from the church; now she followed him willingly. Running down the snowy stone path, they reached the back of the church. He looked for the cars, but the men had moved them. He heard the side door of the church open. The second man stepped out just as Ivan pulled Tess behind the stone wall. Holding her close to him, he looked at her as she nervously looked around the street. He heard the distant sounds of car engines and placed his pistol into his coat pocket. He glanced past the church and saw cars approaching in the distance.

"Come on. This way," he whispered, then grasping her hand again, they ran across the street and headed for a narrow side street. Once on the other side, they darted out of sight. Running to the street's end, he stopped to look out to the next street. Then standing with his back against the wall, he looked back toward the church. The cars came to sliding stops in front of the alley as uniformed men with rifles exited. It was as if these men knew where he and Tess had been as they ran to the side entrance of the church.

Tess stared at Ivan. Her heart raced and her breaths were short and strained. Seeing her fear, he pulled her to him. Feeling her trembling, he stroked her hair, and said, "It's alright. I won't let them take you from me. I won't let them hurt you, even if I must kill them."

Out of fear, she wanted to break down and cry. Looking at him, she knew he meant what he said. She imagined that he had just killed that man in the church and she knew this situation was not a game. When she looked away, he wanted to tell her that he cared, but he thought his words had already portrayed his feelings—he cared enough to kill for her. He wanted her to know that no matter what trouble she may be in, he would understand and he would help her. He wanted her to know that it was not too late to stop whatever she might be doing; that was, if she were doing anything. If she were not doing anything wrong, then why were these men searching for her? Who in this area knew her? Who was it that wanted her so badly to hunt her down?

Tess looked back at Ivan, and he gave her a brief, but affectionate, smile. She looked down and turned her face away from him. She did not know why these men wanted her. She could only surmise that they searched for her to find the Black Rebel, who was the same man holding her close, the same man who promised to protect her, and the same man that had just killed for her. Then she looked back up at him and his gaze was still determined. She saw so many unasked questions in his eyes. Questions he pushed aside while he protected her. Then he looked away from her as he heard a car entering the opposite end of the narrow street. It drove slowly while the men in the front seat looked into doorways with their guns drawn.

He grasped her hand, then he quickly looked out into the adjacent street. No one was about, so they rushed across it. Running down the sidewalk, they moved swiftly down the next street just before the soldiers' vehicle exited the alley. Hearing the car following them, he stopped at the entrance to an abandoned shop. He began trying to push open its broken door, but it was stuck from the cold and lack of use. Not knowing what else to do, he moved her behind him to shelter her as he kicked in the remaining long window pane to the right of the door. Frozen fragments of glass flew inward and back at him, as he turned his face away. Then the remainder of the windowpane fell like the blade to a guillotine—long splinters of jagged edged glass that stood on end in the debris under the snow. He kicked the remaining glass from the bottom of the frame, knocked over the upright pieces of glass with his foot, then stepped hurriedly through the window. Reaching back to her, he helped her through the opening as he heard the car rounding the corner and driving down the street; he knew the men would be looking into the doorways.

Stepping over debris left behind from bombs, then looters, Ivan and Tess hurried to the back of the shop. She held his hand as he pushed through a door to a storeroom, then led her inside. It was a small, dark room; their only light came from the main room via a knocked out hole in the wall. Looking through it, he saw the car had stopped in front of the shop. Ivan removed his pistol and looked back through the hole in the wall. Straining to listen, he heard a second car stop.

The two drivers conversed in Serbian, and he heard one of them say, "Check the streets. Clear the area of stragglers." Then one car drove away and, after a moment, the other car drove away.

Ivan released a long breath and placed his pistol back into the back waistband of his trousers. Tess stood speechless in the darkness. He turned to look at her and he saw her fear as the dim light, coming through the hole in the wall, softly illuminated her face. His main concern was how to get her back to the house without a car. He needed to keep her out of sight and bring her safely home at the same time.

"Ivan," she whispered.

Reaching out his hands to her, he stepped toward her. Then his head jolted to the right as he heard a car driving down the street. He immediately raised his hand to her lips as he looked at her and shook his head, indicating she should not speak. He smiled quickly as his hand moved to her cheek, then to her shoulder. Listening carefully, he heard a knocking sound, like someone's hand beating against the side of a car: three knocks, two knocks, and a pause, then again, three knocks, then two. He smiled. "Stay right here," he said, then he left her alone, and walked to the front of the store.

The car passed slowly as the driver looked into the shop windows. It was Lukáš. He was searching the streets for them, signaling that he was there.

Ivan stepped out into the street and whistled for him. At once, Lukáš stopped the car and backed up as Ivan returned to the shop. "Tess. Come here now," he said.

She quickly exited the back room and approached him. Holding her by the hand, he helped her back through the broken window. His eyes searched the streets and the buildings for signs of anyone. Seeing no one, he walked her from the shop to the car as Lukáš reached to the back door and pushed it open. Ivan let her in first, then he followed. Once he was inside, he closed the car door as they drove off.

"The police have one of the men from the church and one is dead. We have two others. There were four, not three. That's why the cars weren't there when you came out of church. Regardless, none of them deserve to live past the night," Lukáš said in Serbian as he looked at Ivan in the rear-view mirror.

Ivan nodded as he placed his arm around Tess. He then pulled her head to his shoulder while they sped home in silence. Within five minutes, they were back at the house. Lukáš pulled to the rear of the house and stopped the car. Ivan helped Tess from the back seat, then they walked into the kitchen. Lukáš turned the car off, walked into the house, and went to the dining room to wait for Ivan.

From the kitchen, Ivan could hear his men talking in the next room. Tess looked at Ivan, and he knew that she was puzzled about everything. "Wait here for me," he said, and stroked her cheek. He then walked into the dining room, and she heard him speak in Serbian to the men who waited for him. "What did the other two men from the church have to say?"

"They say nothing," Miša answered.

"Where are they now?" Ivan asked.

"They're on their way to the camp," Miša said.

Ivan quickly glanced at the other men at the table, and the menace in his eyes told them that he would personally take care of the two other men from the church. "Wait for me. I'll go with you," he ordered, then he returned to Tess.

Gently taking her hand, he led her to the bedroom, and once they were inside, he closed the door. He helped her with her coat and gloves and sat her on the bed. Removing his gloves, he walked to her and crouched down in front of her. Holding her hands, he looked up at her. "Tell me the truth. What do those men want with you? Don't lie to me. I need to know, Tess. If I am to help you, I must know. You *must* trust me," he said quietly.

"Ivan, I trust you completely, but I don't know what they want. I don't know them. I've never seen them before in my life, and that *is* the truth."

He did not know what to believe. He stood and walked to the window as he debated her answer. Passing his fingers through his hair, he paused as he thought for a moment. He would try again, with even more kindness. Taking a deep breath, he walked back to stand in front of her. "Please, tell me the truth, Tess. I promise I won't be angry with you. Everyone gets into situations and they need help. This war is confusing. People make mistakes and bad choices. I will help you if you're honest with me. So, please, tell me the truth. What do those men want with you?"

"I have told you the truth. I don't know what they want with me," she answered again.

Staring down at her, his temper flared as he pulled her up from the bed. As his grip strangled her arms, his tone was insistent and intimidating. "Why do you lie to me? This is life and death here. This isn't a game to play with one of your boyfriends back in America, and this isn't one of your books. This isn't fiction! This is real, Tess! Now tell me, what do those men want with you? Because they mean to kill you!" he said.

She could see the desperation in his eyes, and she could also see his suspicion. Confused by it all, she examined his expression a bit longer, then said, "I have no idea why those men would want me, but from the tone of your voice, I have a feeling that you do. Why don't you tell me why they want to kill me? Who are they? Why don't you be honest with me? Why don't you tell me who you really are?"

Stunned by her statements, he did not answer as he released her and walked back to the window. He wondered what she meant by "who you really are." She obviously suspected him of lying to her, just as he felt she refused to tell him the truth. With all that he felt for her, her words now made him feel rejected. He thought she trusted him, but now he felt differently.

"What is it you want from me, Ivan? Whatever it is, you must want to know so badly that you brought me to Sarajevo, when Sergej told me that you only take people out of here." She paused as her thoughts wandered into a sickening daze. In her mind, she quickly reviewed his actions since the night they met, but she found no answers there. "Why did you ask me to dinner that night in Belgrade?" she asked.

Although he avoided the full truth, he could not lie about his feelings for her. She could see that in his eyes, or so he believed. He turned his face halfway toward her, but from that, she could not see his affection for her.

"I asked you to dinner because you are very beautiful, and I was very lonely. From the moment I first saw you, I wanted to know you, to spend time with you. That's why I asked you to dinner that night in Belgrade," he said in a low tone.

He wanted to tell her the truth, but he felt that she would not understand just then. Despite that, he was a man with a high price on his head: wanted dead or alive, it made no difference. Others regarded the aid he provided as interference with the plans of their higher order. However, he followed the will of the Highest Order, that of his conscience, and for most women, that would be enough to make them leave him. At that moment, he surmised that she would not believe him regardless.

"Why though? Why an American? You think so little of us. That would mean you only wanted one thing from me," she said sadly as her gaze moved to the floor.

He turned toward her. Her words were direct, and he was upset with her misconception of his feelings, but looking at her now, he felt her abused emotions. She thought he considered her a temporary pleasure to be disposed of once he lost interest. She felt that he did not care for her because she was an American. Recalling his past statements, he now felt that she took them to mean that she was somewhat less than human to him. Considering the way he had treated her the previous evening, his actions confirmed this inference. Yet, if that was true, why was he protecting her?

Still stronger than all of this, again, there was that overwhelming urge twisting his thoughts and ensnaring his heart: the touch, the embrace, the longed for kiss, and the desire to possess her. Yet, he felt any physical pursuit just then would only confirm her fears, so he refrained. Not denying his opinion of Americans, he walked to the door and opened it slowly.

She did not acknowledge him leaving; she only looked the other way, as he said, "My intentions that evening were not dishonorable." He paused. "Nor are they now." Wanting to say so much more, but knowing then was not the time to have this conversation, Ivan held his tongue as he stepped from the room and closed the door.

CHAPTER THIRTY-THREE

Ivan left four men at the house to protect Tess. Then he and his remaining men left and headed to the Rebel camp to question their prisoners. As Sergej drove, Ivan stared out the front passenger side window as he mulled over the situation. He could not imagine that she would not tell him the truth. He felt it was more than obvious that he had risked his life for her, but perhaps she did not see it that way. Perhaps she actually believed that he was with her for a sexual encounter from a momentary lapse in his judgment.

Despite the cease-fire, and the potential peace treaty, this war created a populace separation that would cause lingering discord. Maybe Tess felt sympathetic for one of the Nationalist causes. Did she see the unbiased citizens of Sarajevo as the villains of this war? None of it made sense. But to further confuse the issue, when he looked into her eyes, he saw no disloyalty, only attentiveness. The only times he saw desperation in her disposition was when he imagined that she thought about Mara. The rest of the time her disposition paralleled the situations she encountered.

Preoccupied by his thoughts, he had not noticed that Sergej had stopped driving. They were at the camp, and Sergej was looking at him and prompting him. "Ivan? Ivan? Come on," Sergej said, then he stepped out of the car and closed the door.

At once, Ivan looked around. With a deep sigh, he opened the car door and stepped out to see his men waiting for him. Closing the door, he said nothing as he looked at them. He then proceeded to the tent where they detained the prisoners. Armed men stood outside the tent guarding the ongoing events inside. As Ivan approached, he heard Tomo questioning the prisoners in a violent tone. When Ivan neared, his two men guarding the entrance stepped aside and pulled the tent flaps open for him to enter. Once he and Sergej were inside, the flaps closed, blocking the winter wind's constant pursuit.

Seeing Ivan, Tomo immediately stopped speaking. Then he and Rurik stood at attention in Ivan's presence. The two prisoners looked at Ivan. From the respect his men paid him, the prisoners deduced that they were in the presence of the Black Rebel. Not certain of what to do, they looked at each other as they knelt in the dirt with their hands securely bound behind their backs.

Ivan did not speak right away. Instead, he walked around them as he examined them. Stopping behind them, he tried to suppress his anger. "What are your names?" he asked in Serbian, for he wanted them to understand every word he said.

Since they did not answer, Rurik handed Ivan their identification and a list of names from one of the men's pockets. The list detailed the men these two dealt with in the Serbian armed forces. Ivan quickly reviewed the list. He then looked at the men's identification that read Marko Milić and Jasa Burić. He walked around to face them and, for a moment, he did nothing other than look at them.

"Burić." He paused. "I went to school with someone named Burić." He paused again. "Josip Burić. I didn't like him very much. He was disrespectful," Ivan said, as he examined Burić's expression. Heaving a pestered sigh, Ivan handed the wallets and list of names back to Tomo.

The two men only looked at him, not speaking. This made Ivan wonder what they were hiding, or were they just afraid of him?

"Why do you search for the American woman? What do you want with her?" he asked. Waiting for their response, he imagined he would receive none, and he was right, they did not answer. "You want to find her, so you can find me, is that correct? What were you to do when you found her? Kill her if she couldn't lead you to me? You wouldn't hurt an innocent woman to find me, would you?" he asked, as he noticed the prisoner named Milić seemed confused and looked at Burić, then looked away.

Ivan started walking again and, when he stopped, his right side was toward them as he stared straight ahead. "So, now you've found me. What happens next? You are to kill me?" he asked, still not looking at them, but he did not have to look at them for them to know there was no escaping him.

Yet, he differed from his reputation; he appeared more genteel. He did not appear to be the wild dictator the Serbians presumed he was. As they saw him now, he was every bit the leader they had hoped he was not. They had hoped that his success was due to luck, or chance, not to experience and strategically planned military maneuvers.

He stood there staring in silence, as he thought about the situation, while his presence commanded their total attention. And though there was something valiant about him, they could sense his anger building the more their silence persisted. But it was his controlled emotions that frightened them most, for they knew he was capable of more than he revealed.

"How do you know who she is? How did you know where to find her?" Ivan asked.

"I saw a photograph of her," Burić answered, finally, breaking their silence. Though he spoke out of fear of Ivan, one of them eventually had to start talking. Ivan then noticed Milić's expression, which showed he had no idea Burić had seen a photograph of Tess.

"Who gave you a photograph?"

"Her driver in Belgrade, Bora Oddelek. He received it from her travel agent, so he would know her when she arrived in Belgrade," Burić said.

Ivan remembered Oddelek with Tess at the train depot. This answered the question as to how the Serbians knew what she looked like; however, *why* they wanted her was still to be revealed.

"And when you found her, what were your orders?" Ivan asked.

"We were told to take her to the camp at Kraljevo. That was all we were to do," Burić answered.

Hearing this farcical lie, Ivan's temper grew. The anger they saw lurking in his eyes now came forth. Rushing toward Burić, he grabbed his head by the ears, and his eyes were wild with hatred over their hidden intentions, and his voice was overwhelmed with menacing fury. "But not all you would have done to her! Then what? Beat her? Rape her? Sell her to the highest bidder?" he said, then he let go of Burić's ears with a violent shove that forced Burić's head backward. After that, as suddenly as his outburst appeared, it disappeared, and complete composure replaced it. "Why would you bring her to a refugee camp? You know what happens to women at the camps," he said, then he was silent.

He began pacing, this time in the other direction, then back again. It was not that Ivan did not know what to ask them. This delay tactic gave them time to think, time to volunteer explanations. To get answers, Ivan could have treated them as detainee camp officials treated their prisoners. But Ivan knew that tortured men would confess to anything, which made discerning truth from fiction difficult.

Roughly five minutes passed as he paced in front of them with his hands casually clasped behind his back. All the while, he periodically glanced at the man named Milić. Then he stopped and looked at both men. "Who ordered you to find her?" he asked.

The men looked toward each other, but only continued their silent act. He walked behind them and stopped. They could feel him there, breathing impatiently, yet silently, then he took a single step toward them.

"Cravst, a man named Cravst," Burić answered, not knowing if Ivan would strike him.

"What is his first name?" Ivan asked as he walked around to face them.

"I don't know. Everyone calls him Cravst," Burić answered.

Ivan looked at Tomo, who motioned to another list of names previously received from one of their informants indicating Cravst's name was on that list. The list also cited his high position in the Bosnian Serb army.

Ivan now turned his attention to Milić. "Is this so? Did the same man order you to find the American woman?" he asked.

"Yes," Milić answered in a semi-question.

"On the list of names we found on you, there are addresses. Are those the meeting locations for those who give you orders?"

Milić hesitated momentarily. "Yes," he answered, but Ivan could see that he had no idea what he was acknowledging.

"Who are you to meet with?" Ivan asked.

"Cravst," Milić answered.

"When?" Ivan asked.

"Tomorrow afternoon," Milić answered.

"Regardless of whether you have the American woman or not?" Ivan asked.

"Yes," Burić interrupted, as he motioned Milić to stay quiet.

Ivan nodded, then expelled a heavy sigh. He looked back and forth between Burić and Milić, but his expression displayed no emotion and gave no clues to his thoughts. He then asked, "Do you have anything else to say?" Again, he looked once at each of them, but they said nothing.

Shaking his head, Ivan walked to the entrance of the tent. Without looking back, he issued the final order as he looked at Rurik. "Take them to the south east hills and shoot them. Leave them as a message from me," he said, then without another word, he pushed the right flap of the tent open and walked outside. He stood at a distance from the tent as Tomo and Rurik led the prisoners to a nearby cargo truck. Sergej walked to Ivan and stood next to him, not speaking, only waiting for his orders.

Then, from their distance, they heard Tomo yelling. Burić had jerked away from Tomo and was running through a clearing, making his way to a dense section of trees.

At once, Ivan approached as he ordered his men to stand down. Grabbing Rurik's rifle, he hurried to the edge of the camp where Burić had run through to escape. He lifted the rifle into position and looked through the scope as his eye fastened on the running target. Shrill and piercing, the shot rang out as the round left the rifle and, within seconds, the bullet entered the back of Burić's head, thrusting him forward, as his body slapped down into the now blood-speckled snow.

The chilling ring of the fired round lingered briefly in Ivan's head. As the sound faded, he saw that he had accomplished the required task and he lowered the rifle to his side. Then turning around, he walked back to Milić. At twenty paces away, he stopped. He motioned for his men to step away from Milić. With hatred for these men's intentions toward Tess, Ivan lifted the rifle to his shoulder, but hesitated for a moment. The vision of the other two men chasing him and Tess through the church came back to him. Thoughts of what they would have done to Tess, had they caught her, tore at Ivan's heart.

Milić fell to his knees, begging for his life, but the words Ivan had told Tess earlier that day came into his mind: "It's alright. I won't let them take you from me, even if I must kill them."

Remembering her trembling in his arms, he stood there for a moment, and his soul was torn, as he looked at Milić through the sights of the rifle. In Ivan's mind, something about Milić told him that he was only doing what he was ordered to do. Even though that was no excuse, he felt that if Milić was ordered to do the right thing, he would not become like those who had sent him. Milić was a boy, only eighteen years old, or so his identification read, but Ivan knew he was younger. How could he know that his part in this war was so detrimental? Then Ivan thought of Tess and what she would say if she knew he had killed a boy to protect her. After that, he remembered when he was a boy and lived on the streets, stealing food, and hiding so not to be caught. He remembered the lost feelings that consumed him. He remembered how Mrs. Tomić showed him kindness, even after he had stolen from her. And, with those memories, God softened his heart to this poor lost boy.

He lowered the rifle and stared into Milić's eyes. "Help him up," he ordered. His men did not move; they only looked at him as if he had lost his mind. Ivan turned and looked at them as they stood staring at him, and his temper flared. *"Help him up!"*

At once, his men walked to Milić and helped him to his feet.

Ivan walked closer to the boy and looked at him. "If I untie you, will you run?"

The boy shook his head.

"Untie him," Ivan ordered.

Sergej looked at Ivan, then untied the boy's hands.

"Are you hungry? Thirsty?" Ivan asked, because Milić was thin, and looked as if he had not eaten in a while.

Milić nodded.

"Come with me," Ivan said, then he headed back to the same tent they had just exited. Turning to Sergej, he said, "Bring food, water, and a pack of cigarettes," then he pulled the right tent flap open, turned around, and waited.

Milić stood in place and looked at Ivan. Then he looked at the other men and his expression was petrified, like a trapped animal, with no means of escape. He did not know what to expect, but surmised this was a trick.

"Come on," Ivan said, then entering the tent, he let the flap go.

Sergej walked up to Milić and looked at him. "Go. He won't ask you again."

At once, Milić walked toward the tent and went inside. Sergej told Tomo to go and get the boy some food, water, and cigarettes, then Sergej stepped inside the tent.

Ivan was standing near Milić, who sat at a small table. Milić was apprehensive and he wondered what would happen next. Ivan walked around the table and pulled out one of the folding chairs. Then he sat and leaned forward as he rested his elbows on his knees.

"Marko, that is your name?" Ivan asked.

Milić nodded.

"How old are you?"

Milić looked away for a moment, then he looked back to Ivan. "Eighteen," he answered.

Ivan frowned at him. "You're tall, so you can pass for eighteen, but aren't you younger?"

Milić looked to the dirt floor.

"It's okay. You're what, fourteen, fifteen?"

"I'll be fifteen next month."

"What are you doing?"

Milić frowned, not understanding what Ivan meant.

"What are you doing in the army? What were you doing with a man like Burić? Do you know what kind of man he was?"

"A bastard," Milić answered.

"So you're not angry that I killed him?"

"No. I'm happy. If I could have, I would have done it myself," Milić answered, and that made Ivan wonder what he had been through to want a comrade dead.

Tomo entered the tent with a gust of cold wind, and Ivan noticed the boy shiver. Tomo set a bowl of stew, and a half loaf of bread, down on the table in front of Milić. He placed a canteen of water down next to it. Reaching into his pocket, Tomo pulled out a pack of cigarettes, and set them next the canteen, then he looked at Ivan for further orders.

Ivan stood, motioned to Milić, and said, "Start eating." He then walked to the tent's opening with Tomo. "Go find my other jacket in my tent and bring it here. Then make a place where this boy can rest," he ordered.

"This is a bad idea," Tomo commented, looking from Milić back to Ivan.

"Why? He's only a boy. He's not even fifteen."

"He will kill someone, then he will tell what he knows."

Ivan shook his head. "No, he won't. Now go get my jacket." Then he returned to the table and sat back down. Milić had torn off a piece of bread and was eating it, but he then did something Ivan did not expect. He held the larger piece of bread out to Ivan. Ivan took the piece from Milić, tore off a small piece, handed the rest back to him, smiled, and said, "Thank you," then he ate the piece in his hand.

Sergej stood there watching Ivan and this young boy as they began to talk and become acquainted. There were times when Sergej could only stand in amazement at Ivan's keen judgment and kind heart. At that moment, he wished Tess were there to see exactly how good a man Ivan truly was, how good a friend he was, even to someone whom he presumed to be his enemy.

Ivan took a deep breath. "Where is your family?"

Milić looked down at his bowl. "Dead."

"I am sorry for that. So because of that you joined the army?"

Milić shook his head as he set down his piece of bread. "No. They came and cleared us out of a shelter. There were eight of us, and they took us and made us fight with them."

"Don't stop eating," Ivan said, then asked, "Who are they?"

"Serbian army from Belgrade now stationed in Pale."

"Where was the shelter?"

"In Gora."

"Are you from Gora?"

"No, from Sarajevo."

Ivan nodded. "And how long ago did they take you from the shelter?"

"Eight months ago."

"When they took you from the shelter, where did they take you to?"

"Back into Serbia, just across the border."

"You don't know where?"

Milić shook his head. "We always rode in the back of the truck. There were no windows, so we couldn't see where we were going. They didn't want us to know where we were so we couldn't escape, but it was up in the mountains."

"Did they ever talk about other shelters where they took boys from?"

"No, but there were many there my age; some younger, some older."

Ivan nodded. "How long since your family is gone?"

"A year."

"Was Burić one of the men that came and got you from the shelter?"

"Yes, and his brother."

"Josip?"

"Yes."

"Who else? Anyone else from the list of names?"

"Yes. Cravst was there. He decided which troops were allotted which boys. He said we are Serbian and we must fight for greater Serbia."

"Are you Serbian?"

"Yes," Milić answered, but looked away, and Ivan could see he hid the full truth.

"One hundred percent Serbian?"

"No. I am half Croatian."

"But you never told them that."

"No. They would have killed me because of it."

Ivan nodded, then he frowned slightly. "Do you feel you need to fight for Serbia?"

Milić thought for a moment before he said, "If I don't fight, I die."

Again, Ivan nodded. "So if I let you go, you will go back to the army and fight more? You will join another team, then try to come back and find me and kill me?"

Milić shook his head. "No."

"If you go back to them and they send you out to look for the American woman, you will search for her? And then you will take her to some dirty camp someplace where they will torture her and do ungodly things to her?"

"No!" Milić answered; he was obviously upset.

"But you were here with Burić, and that was what he was going to do, so you were going to do that along with him."

"NO! I would not have hurt her!"

"Did they order you to go on this mission today?"

"No."

"Then why were you out with Burić? If you did not mean to go along with their plan," Ivan shrugged, "why go?"

"They said she is very beautiful. I wanted to see her. I have never met an American."

Ivan smiled at his simple ideas. "What do they want with her? Do you know?"

"They never said why they wanted her, just that *someone* wanted her."

"They never said who that was?"

"No."

"Did they tell you her name?"

"No."

"Did they tell you what she looks like?"

"No."

"Did you see this supposed photograph Burić mentioned?"

"No."

"Do you know why?"

Milić shook his head.

"Because there is no American woman."

"But they said—"

"They lied. Just as they lied to you, being not even fifteen, and they told you that you needed to fight for greater Serbia. You need to be young while you are still young, because too soon you will be old. That's what they needed to tell you. They needed to feed, clothe, and protect you, not put you out in front of them when they're being shot at," Ivan said in a slightly elevated tone.

"But what do I do now?" Milić asked.

"What do you want to do? Do you want to go back to the army?"

"No," Milić answered.

"Do you want to stay here? You can if you wish to, but if you do anything to harm anyone, try to escape, betray me or the people here, you will be killed. That will be my order," Ivan said. "So, do you want to stay?"

Milić looked at Ivan, and Ivan could see in his eyes that he wanted to stay. His expression displayed that this was the first true kindness he had received since his family had been killed. Just then, Ivan remembered Tess having said: *"People need kindness more than anything."* In the back of his mind, Ivan wondered how many other boys had been taken and made to fight in armies.

At that moment, Tomo entered the tent, carrying Ivan's extra jacket. Standing up, Ivan took the jacket from Tomo and walked around the table to Milić. Holding the jacket out to him, he said, "Here, put this on. It will keep you warm."

"Whose jacket is it?" Milić asked, as he took the jacket and slipped it on.

"Mine," Ivan answered, then asked, "So are you staying?"

"Yes," Milić answered.

"You remember my warning, because I won't give you another chance." Milić nodded his head.

"Once you're finished eating, you will be shown to a tent where you can rest. Then tomorrow you will follow orders and help keep this camp going. You will tend to the sick, cook, clean, and do whatever you're told, *but* at no time will you be told to hurt another person. Once this war is over, you will say nothing about anything or anyone related to this camp. If you do, it will not end well for you. Do you understand me?" Ivan said.

"Yes," Milić answered.

Ivan nodded and, as he walked to the tent's opening, Rurik stepped inside the tent and whispered to him. "The other man from the church is dead. Miloš slit his throat after he left the police station." Rurik paused and studied Ivan's ominous disposition. He then saw the boy sitting at the table and wearing Ivan's jacket. "What's he still doing alive?" he asked.

"He will be staying here. He's another orphan, kidnapped from a shelter. He'll stay here along with all the others," Ivan said, but the only thought in his mind right then was Tess, an image that completely consumed his heart.

"So did he say why they want Tess?" Rurik asked.

"He doesn't know anything."

"Tess only came to find Mara, right?"

"I don't know," Ivan answered, then he exited the tent and walked back to the car. Opening the door, he paused before he entered to speak with Sergej, who had followed him outside. "Get Oddelek. Find out what he knows, then get rid of him. Question, then get rid of any outsider mentioning Tess. Then try to get a location on Cravst."

"You want to talk to Cravst?" Sergej asked.

"Perhaps," Ivan answered as he got into the car and closed the door. The men in his path made way for him to pass, then he drove alone from the camp and back to the house to Tess.

CHAPTER THIRTY-FOUR

It had been one week since the incident at the church. During this time, Ivan kept Tess inside the house for her protection, but he did not expect her to spend every day in the bedroom. He stayed at the house with her most of the time. Though he wanted to spend every waking moment with her, he did not interrupt her when she spent her days sitting on the bed, writing. He would periodically walk down the hall and watch her through the half-open door. He could hear the low sound of music coming from the room and saw she wore headphones as she listened to one of her compact discs. If not for the sound of her music, he would have sat with her. However, when she played music, he felt that she wanted to be alone, and he could only hope it did not mean that she wanted to be away from him.

The few times she left the room, mostly to step outside the kitchen door for a change of scenery, he would turn on her disc player. Holding the headphones to his ears, he could hear romantic, orchestral music playing—music with sweet, wonderfully baroque and quixotic undertones—mostly Mozart, which he surmised was her favorite. But he also heard more dramatic and tragic pieces from Wagner, and sometimes, Celtic laments played on a harp. He wondered if her writing would reflect the mood of this music, or did she play it to shut out the rest of the world, to shut him out?

It was the afternoon of the fifth day, and she had not left the bedroom to step outside as she had in the days past. The house was quiet and she remained in the bedroom thinking about Ivan's explanation for wanting to meet her in Belgrade. She could have presumed that he was like other men she knew, wanting only a few things in life: sex, money, and power. It was always one or all of those with other men. Nonetheless, from his last words, she knew he was different.

The more she thought about it, she also felt that he was aware why those men wanted her, and she wished he would tell her the truth. She wished he would tell her that he was the Black Rebel, though he did not appear to trust her enough to do so. Perhaps he truly saw her as a selfish American, and, if so, she could not fathom how to prove otherwise. He was a man of definite convictions and little swayed him from his opinions, which were usually right, but what are opinions other than realizations based on observations?

Tess tried to think of how she could change the facts so that he would see her differently, even if he could not see her as a woman who cared deeply for him. However, she knew that a suspicious man was difficult to persuade, and she felt that Ivan was too preoccupied to be convinced of anything that interfered with his vision. She imagined Ivan's vision was for peace, not love; for he was certainly handsome enough to find love in the arms of any woman he favored.

He was not an ignorant man either. On the contrary, his intelligence far surpassed the situation. His intelligence led him to his suspicions. She knew that, being the Black Rebel, he had the lives of his people in his hands, a responsibility he appeared to accept without question, but did he deserve that? Did he deserve to sacrifice his life for those he helped when others sat, watching their destruction? Whether rebel or avenging angel, he accepted the task of protecting his people without a second thought, or so it appeared. He did what he felt he must do, but when would he stop to examine his needs as a man? Perhaps he denied himself for so long that he no longer knew how.

Tess saw Ivan as a very understanding and accepting man. He would help her, even kill for her, if she were involved in something perilous, and he would do it because it was right, or so she surmised. But he had killed for her for reasons other than it just being right. He had killed for her because it was the right thing to do for him as a man. He needed to protect her because he saw her as his.

She wanted to help, but what could she do? She did not understand all that was happening. Nevertheless, it appeared that she brought danger to Ivan and his men by being in Sarajevo, a thought that upset her greatly. She felt she should leave and stay elsewhere. If he were going to protect his people, he did not need to waste time with her, she could struggle on her own. She now believed in Ivan as the Black Rebel so greatly that she did not want to be the cause of his failure.

On that fifth day, the men had left the house and Ivan sat alone at the dining room table. He stared at the map he had laid out there, and thought about moving the Rebel camp. Tess left the bedroom and, instead of walking out the kitchen door for a change of scenery, she walked to the dining room. Pausing in the doorway, she saw Ivan lost in thought.

When he looked up at her, he smiled. He saw her loveliness as she stood waiting for permission to join him, and he appreciated her respect toward him as a man. When he saw her standing there, he felt she had many questions that she would not verbalize, but finally, he saw her trust in him again. "Please, sit with me," he said as he stood and pulled out her chair at the table.

Walking toward him, she stopped next to him. As she looked into his eyes, he noticed a certain innocence to her expression. He stared into the softness of her mossy green gaze and, in his mind, he tried to guess her questions. Then she looked away and sat down. He also sat, and much to his surprise, she began to reveal the questions concealed behind her gaze.

"Ivan, please tell me the truth about what's going on here," she said.

At first, he was not certain as to what she meant. For a moment, he thought she might know that he was the Black Rebel. "What do you mean?" he asked.

"What is this war really about? Why does it keep happening? Even Capitalists, like me, understand that war destroys. Even if it helps solve one problem, so many others are created from it. Is it just to destroy the country because of the differences between its citizens, or is it still centuries old hate and religious differences, or is it something else?" she asked.

He was slightly shocked by her brief summation, but he was also relieved. And though this question was not easy to answer, he felt explaining was possible because her comment revealed that she already knew the truth. Yet, before he explained, he wanted to address her first comment.

"Don't call yourself a Capitalist," he said as he reached for her hands and held them.

"Why not? I am, aren't I? America is a Capitalist country, just as Yugoslavia is a Socialist country. I am a Capitalist and you are, I guess, a Socialist. Of course, these are generalizations, and as with all generalizations, some are true and some are not. Sometimes you can't help but look at the generalizations before you see the finite detail. The closer you get to situations, the more you learn and, hopefully, the more compassion you have for those involved in the situations," she said.

Feeling her pull her hands from his, he held them tighter until she relaxed. Then he shook his head and addressed her questions. "You ask what the war is about and why it keeps happening. I will try explaining as briefly as I can, even though there is no single explanation. In part, it is about hatred and past atrocities. Another part is about longing for freedom, but foremost, it is about greed. Part of the reason goes back to the Holy Wars, Christianity against Islam. Part goes back to the Second World War between Croatian Nationalists and the Serbian population. Part is caused by the hatred of the individual republics for not being allowed to independently govern themselves; however, it's always about who has power. All sides use the media and propaganda to plead their needs to the world, and this adds to their power. Their propaganda has kindled the flames of hatred and reminded people of many past atrocities. Then people get angry, and there is nothing more frightening than an angry mob, except a well-armed angry mob. Were some citizens of the individual republics still holding grudges for the past? Of course, but for the most part, the country worked, even if by force. And if the country was to split up, there were better ways to accomplish this split than to destroy it. This all started as a civil war, but due to greed, and to Super Power/Peacekeeper interference, it has become a disgrace.

"The issues this time started in Kosovo and will most likely end in Kosovo. You see, Kosovo was the cradle of Serbian civilization until the fourteenth century when the Serbian's lost the Battle of Kosovo to the Turks. Serbians will not forget this. So many ethnic and religious differences have to resurface at some time. So much hatred and death passed between these groups making up Yugoslavia that, even after hundreds of years, for some, it cannot be extinguished. Because of grudges, hatred, and pride, Nationalism surged after Tito's death in 1980. By then, the major regions—Serbia, Croatia, and Bosnia—were ethnically diverse, and each region wanted to be ethnically pure, as much as was possible. Because of the propaganda from each side, neighbors that once lived peacefully together took up arms against each other."

"Because of all that has happened here and all the misuse of propaganda, now the world needs a scapegoat for this war, and the Peacekeepers point the finger at the Serbians. However, if the same situation happened in any of the Peacekeeper countries, their military would suppress it by use of extreme force, and the rest of the world would cheer them on. Quite the double standard," he said.

"The media reports the Serbian military caused atrocities, but they ignore the Croatian and Bosniak military caused atrocities, which are also horrific, just not as plentiful, at least not this time around. This is war, and people do things in war that they would not normally do, but war is not a tool, nor is it an excuse. War should be about the goals to be attained, not the persecution and torture of civilians. Civilians are not pawns, but they are routinely used as such. Because of these publicized atrocities, the entire world is pointing the finger at Serbia. Then the world pats the Peacekeepers on the back and gives them free rein to do what they want in a country that does not belong to them," he said.

She shook her head. "The media does paint the Serbians as the demons of this war because of the atrocities, as you say. Maybe it's also because they control the army. But didn't the Slovenians and Croatians turn to Germany and Austria for backing when they declared their independence?" she asked, then added, "At least I thought I read that somewhere."

"You've been reading independent news, not mainstream," he said.

"Well, anyone with half a brain knows that mainstream is government regurgitation, not truth. Governments control their populace through media and, like chattel, the populace believes, because their government wouldn't lie to them," she said, slightly sarcastically, then shook her head at the absurdity of that thought.

For a moment he stared at her. He never thought she would see things this way. She noticed his stunned expression, and said, "What?"

He smiled at her. "Nothing," he said, then he shook his head, and asked, "So what does your friend George Preston think of this war?"

"He's disgusted. He's been trying to get over here since Slovenia declared its independence, but the Times wouldn't let him," she said.

"Why not? He's an exceptional journalist."

"They wouldn't print what he would write because it would disagree with US/Peacekeeper opinions. The Times didn't mind when he reported truths from China, but they don't want the US government on their back because of an independent journalist's views about a war in which they are so deeply vested," she answered.

"It's unfortunate that the truth opposes their agenda," Ivan commented.

"If you came to New York, George would love to talk with you."

"Perhaps," he said, then asked, "Would you want me to come to New York?"

She smiled. "If you wanted to."

"No. Would *you* want me in New York to *be with you?*" he asked.

"Yes, if you would be happy to be there with me."

Her answer made him smile. She did not know what he was thinking, but she momentarily looked down to the tabletop. When she looked back at him, he was still smiling at her.

"So, back to what you were explaining. Each side's propaganda gave power to individual Nationalism," she said, as she looked at the map.

He did not answer immediately. He continued looking at her, thinking about being in New York with her, thinking about being anywhere with her other than where they were just then. Waiting for her to look directly into his eyes, he finally continued when she did.

"Yes, it did. In some instances, you cannot resurrect something that does not exist, so propaganda creates it. Whoever has better propaganda wins. If we know anything about Nazi Germany during the Second World War, we all know how successful propaganda can be. Rarely is propaganda truthful. Propaganda desensitizes people. It creates savage, careless robots from human beings, willing to do anything for the approval of a false god. All sides have their national propaganda, but in this war, the Croatian and Bosniak governments have better *international* propaganda. That's one reason that feeds the labeling of Serbians as demons in this war. The atrocities perpetrated on the Serbian military's behalf are being discovered daily and publicized globally." He paused briefly. "And, yes, many atrocities perpetrated by the Serbian army and others of Serbian descent, such as rape and forced impregnation of non-Serbian women, is a sin. However, it makes one wonder if there was no propaganda, and no finger pointing, would these acts be so plentiful?" he said, and paused again.

"So your saying, it's like the question, 'What came first? The chicken or the egg?'" she said.

He smiled and nodded at her explanation. "Yes, like that, but regardless, confusion does not erase the sin," he said, and again, he paused as he looked at the map. Then looking back at her, he continued. "And so, wars are not only fought between armies, they are fought in the media. Then the Peacekeepers come in and act like the saviors in a fight between three armless children. That's a smokescreen for a larger agenda, because to them, Capitalism is *their* nationalism, their religion," he said.

"No matter how many Peacekeeping troops come to help, the fighting always starts again. Tens of thousands of people killed, countless women raped, children orphaned, cities destroyed," he shook his head, "useless destruction. That makes you wonder if Tito should have created the Socialist Yugoslavia that is now dissolving. Of course Serbia's answer is yes because it means more land for Serbia, and more land is more power, considering they held the seat of power while Tito was alive. They want Yugoslavia just the way it was because to them it was strong. They're not wrong. It had the third largest army in all of Europe, and that *is* a lot of power, but that is one side's opinion. To the other provinces, the answer is no. They want to be free, and they want to rule themselves."

"In retrospect, none of these regions should have been joined to form the Yugoslavia that is now disintegrating before our eyes. Regardless that it may have worked for a while, there was too much discord to push these regions together—like siblings with nothing but contempt for each other. But everything was left for the taking after the Second World War and the fall of the Third Reich. And now, with this war, all sides involved are simply fighting for what they believe rightfully belongs to them."

He sighed as he remembered his country's tumultuous history. So many conquerors and so many rulers had controlled the land that was known as Yugoslavia.

"Now the Peacekeepers come in with their treaties and will chop up the country and give it out to the wrong people. And once they depart, in time, the war will start up again. The criminals of this war keep emerging and most of them will go unpunished. No one knows the changes made to innocent lives by the Peacekeepers and the propaganda. No one sees the Peacekeepers for what they really are. *They* are the war mongers," he said, then his gaze moved to Belgrade on the map, and sighed. "War is fighting for your beliefs, but the side effects of war: torture, rape, and murder," he shook his head, "those are sins against God. If wars are truly unavoidable, then they must be waged without dehumanization."

"So, since Yugoslavia was already united for all these years under Tito, do you think it should have stayed united? Do you think it was better united?" she asked.

"Perhaps," he said, then shook his head again. "Innocent people would still be alive, along with all the hatred for each other, but alive."

"Some people will do anything for freedom," she commented.

"Freedom is a wonderful thing, but it's hardly free. And no one is free from the law of God, though these war mongers try to be. Either you are

God's servant or you are the devil's, and this world belongs to the devil."

"It's unfortunate that so few realize that obeying God's law is the only way to have true freedom," she said, then added, "It makes you wonder what people are afraid of."

"Here? Fear of failure, which is staring them in the face. Because of this war, in ten, fifteen, even twenty-five years, the new countries formed from Yugoslavia will be steeped in unemployment, inflation, and devaluation of everything related to their new countries and their citizen's daily lives. They will not automatically be taken seriously by the world because they were the victims of a useless war. Unless they make a tremendous effort, and prove they are worthy for world commerce, just as Yugoslavia did, their countries will suffer. Serbia will survive. It will have a horrific reputation to live down, but, yes," he paused briefly, "it will survive. Serbians know how to get their hands dirty and make work what is irreparably broken to others. They are an earthy people, with a great deal of tenacity and intelligence, that aren't easily swayed from their beliefs." Again he paused. "Unfortunately, they are not portrayed or seen that way by the rest of the world. Unbeknownst to the common world, for centuries, they have fought for right, even if their methods during this conflict are wrong. But still, there is one fact that the majority of the Christian world does not know, and that is that Serbia fought and persevered to stop Islam from spreading to western Europe, and further."

She looked at him as he paused. She knew this history he spoke of was true, and she wondered why more people did not know of it. Then she heard him take a deep breath, and he changed the subject.

"Yugoslavia took decades to build. It was far from perfect, but it worked for the most part. No government works perfectly, but in this instance, a slow transformation, giving each of the provinces more control, would have worked better; but, people are impatient. In time, many of the citizens of the former Yugoslav regions will wonder why their lives are not better as their Nationalist side's propaganda had proclaimed," he said as he looked at the map again.

"Is that what you really think?"

He looked back at her. "It is what I know. It is what I live."

"So each side is responsible for its own demise," she said.

"Yes, they are. But when you look at each of the sides involved, and their need for freedom, each perspective is right to each side. Despite differences in opinion, it is how those in command executed their opinion, and exerted their authority, that has caused the evils of this war. That is their sin. They lay waste to everything they touch. I cannot understand waste, especially waste of human beings," he said.

She looked away for a moment, then back at him as she remembered that George had said the exact same thing about the Black Rebel.

Ivan stared at the tabletop. Then he looked at her and saw concern radiating from her gaze. "And here you and I sit in the middle of a war caused by greed and hate," he said as he secretly recalled the devastation he had seen since the war began. If she knew all that he had experienced, and all that he had done, he felt that she would run so far from him and never want to know him. Thinking of all this, he was silent as his gaze returned to the table top.

For a moment she watched him, wondering what he saw in his mind. "How do you tell this truth to the world?" she asked.

"You don't," he answered, still halfway lost in private memories.

She reached for his hand and cupped hers over the top of it. He turned his hand upward and placed his other hand on top of hers. This gesture proved that, even though he suffered, he would still protect and comfort her.

"It's a curse that so many have to suffer for the actions of so few. It makes me wonder if the Peacekeepers did not get involved, would so many have died here," she said, then added, "So much suffering. So many questions left unanswered. So many *ifs* to be accounted for."

"There are evils in this world that no man or nation can subdue. Perhaps they were created in the Garden of Eden, but only God has dominion over them," he said, then smiled slightly at her.

For a moment, he only looked at her, wondering what she was thinking. He was happy that she had joined him to talk with him, but he then let her hand go. "The land of my childhood is no more and never will be again, and all because of greed and hate. Fighting brings about desperation and lost hope, but even with such lost hope, the fighting continues. The problem is that no one stops *people* from becoming casualties of war. This war is about Nationalism, ethnic purity, land, and power, but it is based on the personal ideals and hatred of its participants. Instead of following God's law, they follow man's law, and that is not right. And this war, and all that has happened, only carves the hatred deeper, giving it more power."

"Sergej told me that you won't turn your back on a friend. A friend is a friend until that friend proves otherwise," she said.

"If I do not keep my word, what sort of a man am I?" he asked, briefly reflecting on private thoughts. "Even if no one else mattered, how could I turn my back on the one person that took me in when I had no home? How could I turn against the one person that gave me everything when I had nothing, even after I stole from her? How could I ever turn my back on Mrs. Tomić?"

When he looked at Tess, she appeared to understand his thoughts and respect his views. He smiled and stroked her arm, and though she had smiled at him, now her smile lessened, and he wondered what troubled thoughts took away her smile.

"Tell me about President Tito? What sort of leader was he? Did his people love him?" she asked.

Again he smiled at her. Her interest and knowledge of his country caused him to pause before he answered. "To some he is a hero and to others he was a villain. He was a man, like any other, except he had dreams that no one could take away. He loved this country, but he loved power far more. And like any man, he was not perfect and made mistakes attempting to do what he thought was best, *and* do what he wanted. Trying to fulfill a vision is never easy. There are always personal sacrifices. There are always opponents to any plan. Someone always thinks that they know better, and in their attempt to overtake a man's vision, the vision fails. But sometimes failure comes when there is no one to carry on your ideas once you're gone," he said, and, as before, he stared at the table and exhaled a deep breath, remembering the war again.

"In 1992 I was at the library and I took home a book about President Tito. The title was *The Red Rebel.* If this book about Tito was called the 'Red Rebel,' who is the Black Rebel?" she asked.

Dead silence filled the room. His stare moved toward her, though he said nothing. However, the look in his eyes confirmed her suspicion.

"They say he's a tyrant. Is that so, Ivan?" she asked, trying to provoke him into telling her that he was the Black Rebel. She knew he was no tyrant, only a kind and concerned man, who carried the life and safety of those he helped in his palm.

He was curious to know exactly how much she knew about him, other than what Mara had written in her story, but more than that, he wanted to know what she thought about him. Would she hate him if she found out that he was the Black Rebel? And so, he attempted to satisfy her curiosity with as little information as possible.

"From what *they* say, whoever *they* are, do you think he's a tyrant?"

"I don't know him. I only know of him from Mara's book. I could only tell you what I thought if I looked into his eyes," she said, then she looked straight into his penetrating gaze.

He sat there proudly as she became consumed in his unwavering stare. She saw his strength and determination staring back at her, although its persistence forced her to look away.

"Do you know him, Ivan?" she asked.

"Who can know a phantom?" he answered, still staring at her, trying to gauge her response.

She looked back at him and recalled that her friend, George, had called the Black Rebel a phantom. Was it coincidence?

Just then, Ivan noticed the change in her expression as if she questioned something about him. "Rumors say that he does not let anyone know him. Though perhaps he would like to," he answered evasively, but purposely piqued her curiosity even further, because he wanted to know all that she knew of him.

"Why do they call him the Black Rebel?" she asked.

Leaning closer to her, he attempted to frighten her out of her curiosity as he whispered, "Black is for death and night strikes. He is like the wolf hunting at night."

"Wolves are so very beautiful, so perfect in every way. Don't you agree?" she said, hoping he would see the compliment in her statement.

He smiled at her. "As the male alpha wolf protects his pack and his territory, he kills those who oppose him and invade his land. He attacks those who attempt to conquer his pack and take away his land. He is a leader to his pack. When they cannot defend themselves, he protects them. He fights for their cause, not his. His cause is peace, but his people do not know peace, so he fights for that which may never come."

"So, he is real?" she asked.

"To his people, yes. Does this sound like a tyrant? Or perhaps you think he's nothing more than a murderer or a fanatic?" Ivan asked.

She took a deep breath and exhaled it silently. Then looking into his waiting gaze, again she saw his uncertainty of what her answer would be. "I like the wolf analogy best. Wolves only kill to survive, not to repress."

He smiled at her logic. She appeared to understand him better than he could have hoped for, but he needed to know what she felt, so he asked, "But do you think he is wrong?"

"Is there any right in this war? From what I know, I think he is a symbol to his people. A hero to those who accept his aid, and a villain to those he opposes. Like Tito, he does what he thinks is best, even if it isn't best to all. At times, it's better to do something that may not be considered, by all, to be the best, than to do nothing. Complaisance can be just as bad as advocacy. As for a murderer? He barely kills at all, compared to the opposition, and most deaths related to him are defensive not offensive, unlike the criminals of this war. As for a fanatic?" She shook her head. "All men with dreams are fanatics in one way or another. I'm also a fanatic, because my dream is to find Mara."

He was quiet as he thought about what she had said. As she looked at him, he noticed her inquisitive stare, and asked, "Is there something you want to ask me?"

"Can I ask you something," she paused a split second, "personal?"

He looked at her, smiled slightly, then nodded.

"On the train, I asked Sergej if he was Russian because Sergej is a Russian name. He told me he was Serbian. When I asked him about you, he said you should answer, not him. From your response about whether you were Serbian that first night, I take it you aren't Serbian," she said.

He looked at the tabletop thinking about why she would ask that now. He wondered if his ethnicity would matter to her.

Seeing his hesitation, she felt rude, and said, "Please forgive me, I shouldn't have asked."

As she stood to leave, he grasped her wrist and held her in place. Looking away briefly, he then looked back at her. "I thought you were going to ask if I were married," he said, then quickly added, "I'm not, in case you're curious."

She smiled at his comment. She had not considered that he could have been married, but was happy that he was not, and when he answered her question, she was genuinely shocked.

"I am Yugoslavian. But more precisely, I am Croatian. In the future, once this war dissolves what is left of Yugoslavia, I will have to say that I am from the former Yugoslavia, if that will be politically correct. I say I am

Yugoslavian, because I was born in Yugoslavia. Anyone that was born here and now chooses sides denies part of themselves. You may not like your past, but you cannot deny it, and you cannot run away from it regardless of how wrong it may have been. This dissolving country helped to make me who I am today. When someone asks where you're from, you answer 'America' because you were born in America. But what if your country dissolved and all that remained were individual states or a grouping of states?"

"From your physical appearance, it is obvious that you are not of Native American descent. Your ethnicity most likely originated in Western Europe. So how would *you* answer that question? What would *you* say? If America dissolved, would you leave your home in Manhattan and run off to the state you were born in? Would you suddenly run off to the land of your blood heritage and claim that as your country? What if your heritage was from two countries, and suddenly you were forced to choose one over the other? What do you do? It's the same as if you have two children needing to be saved, but you can save only one. How do you tell the other they must die?"

"Because of my father's position with the government, my parents lived in Belgrade, and so I was born in Belgrade. Does that make me Serbian? Perhaps. Is there Serbian blood in my ancestry somewhere back hundreds of years? I'm certain there is. But if you had talked to my grandparents, they would have vehemently denied it. In this part of the world, your ethnicity is patrilineal—determined by your father's ethnicity, not your mother's. In my family, all of the men have been Croatian, so all children are considered Croatian. Forced patrilineal descent is one of the main reasons for the continual rape of women during this war," he said.

He looked away, shook his head, and paused for a moment before he looked back to her. In her expression, he saw her sympathy for his plight.

"Even though I am Croatian, I have no plans to move from Belgrade to Zagreb or any other city in Croatia because my family came from there. I have lived much of my life right here in this house in Bosnia, but I have never claimed to be Bosnian. I don't know what the future will bring, but one day, I may not be welcome in Yugoslavia, what remains of Yugoslavia, in Serbia, or any other independent republic that once belonged to Yugoslavia. This war is very disorienting to so many. Still, if my country ceases to exist, what will I be?" he asked, then he shook his head and looked at her. He hoped that he had fully answered her question.

For a moment she said nothing, she only smiled at him. She wanted to tell him how honorable she thought him to be. She wanted to say something about how much love, kindness, and goodness she saw in him. Her gaze moved away from him briefly as she thought about it. Then she looked straight into his eyes, and asked, "Would love or honor by any other titles be less their virtue?"

By the way he smiled at her, she knew she had chosen the right words; he understood. Just then, interrupting their moment of understanding, the front door opened, and Alek walked into the house. He motioned to Ivan that he needed to talk with him, then he said hello to Tess. She smiled at him as she stood up. Then she walked through the kitchen and back to the bedroom as Ivan watched her leave him.

"Sergej said the package arrived," Alek reported.

Ivan nodded, then Alek climbed the stairs to the upper floor. Standing up from the table, he walked through the kitchen, then to the bedroom. The bedroom door was open and he knocked, waiting for Tess' permission to enter.

"Come in," she answered. She was sitting on the bed with her notebook on her lap. She had been writing, though she stopped and looked at him when he entered.

He closed the door. Then he walked to her and sat at the foot of the bed. "What are you writing about?" he asked as he moved closer to her and looked at her notebook.

Her gaze moved from her notebook to him as she held it out for him to read. "I was trying to capture all that you said. I want to relay the truth to whoever will read it. People should know the truth of this tragedy, not only what propaganda tells them."

He did not take the notebook from her. He felt that reading her writing would be an invasion of her soul. After lying to her, he felt he was not privy to that part of her.

She placed the notebook back on her lap and smiled. "I don't blame you. My books usually end up as romances, and what's going on here isn't romantic."

Again, he did not respond, he only looked at her.

She noticed his stress and changed the subject. "When will it be safe enough to leave the house?"

"Perhaps tomorrow or the day after," he answered, pausing as he looked into her eyes. "Tess, would you rather go back to Belgrade for a while? I could take you back if you like and, if you like, I would stay with you. I wouldn't leave you alone. It's not safe for you to be alone anywhere in these regions."

She thought for a moment as she tried to guess the motive behind his suggestion. Although she felt that he did not want her around anymore, his feelings were the opposite. He wanted to be away from the war and have time alone with her. He wanted to spend more time with her, than with his men. He felt that he was beginning to know and understand her, and the more he analyzed her, she was less American than he had presumed her to be.

"I'll go if you want me to. I don't want to overstay my welcome," she answered.

"That's not what I said. I thought you would like a break from the difficulty here, but it's your choice," he said.

"Then my preference is to stay. I came here for a reason, but that reason was not to burden you. If it makes you happy, I'll go elsewhere." She paused, then laughed to herself. "And give you back your bed. That small bed can't be comfortable for a tall man."

He smiled at her thoughtfulness. Looking over his shoulder toward the bed, he laughed, and said, "It's better than sleeping on the floor."

She laughed slightly through her smile, and he smiled again, curious at what she found funny. Was it something he said or something else? So he asked, "What's so funny?"

"I was just thinking back to my childhood of sleepovers at friends' houses where you spend the night sleeping on the floor in sleeping bags." She shook her head, and her laugh faded into a smile. "Children love it, but as an adult, it would never do."

"Children are children. Some have little to worry about. Maybe it is silly compared to the situation here, but to children, it is very important. And the children that have those opportunities to be happy should be happy, even if all children cannot," he answered.

Her smile faded as his words only reminded her of Mara. He saw her helplessness and, again, he wanted to hold her and comfort her. But his attempted pretense in finding Mara was becoming a growing chasm between them. It pulled him from his chance of being with Tess as more than what he was. As Ivan saw it, he was merely a friend; however, true friends do not lie to each other. Though he knew he should tell her the truth, he could not. The possibilities of their situation made his mind spin. The eventual outcome of her leaving for America, and never seeing her again, was the obvious conclusion to his thoughts.

"Tess, what if you don't find this little girl? What will you do?" he asked.

She looked down at her notebook. "I will have failed, and I will go back to America. What else could I do?" she answered.

With her statement, she testified to his obvious conclusion. This upset him, though he said nothing. Looking at her, he felt she would rather be alone, and he had to leave. Standing up, he moved toward her and kissed her on the cheek, then said, "I have to go out. Will you be alright? Alek will be here with you."

She nodded as she continued looking at her notebook, and he imagined she was hesitant from his show of affection.

"I'll be back for dinner. After dinner, we can plan what shelters we will see tomorrow. I think it will be safe tomorrow," he said.

She smiled, and he felt that he slightly relieved her distress. He walked to the door, and opening it, he looked back at her. He did not want to leave; he wanted to stay with her and talk more with her. When he talked with her, he felt he could tell her things that he could not tell anyone else, but he still could not tell her the truth, not yet at least.

"Ivan, be careful," she said, secretly worried for his safety since she knew he was the Black Rebel.

The concern in her tone called him back to her. Without hesitation, he walked to the bed and sat next to her. Taking her hand in his, he knew he should not be asking her if she wanted to join him, but he wanted her with him. He also felt that, after the night he locked her in the bedroom, she had spent her time in there trying to make him feel secure. As though he wanted her imprisoned, and contained like an animal that needed caging to prevent any deadly occurrences. And now her avoidance of his stare confirmed his skepticism.

"Come with me, Tess. You don't have to stay in this room all the time," he said as his thought, just then, was that he would tell her who he was once they were at the Rebel camp. And, of course, the next confession would be that he was Idy. "But how will she react to all this knowledge," he wondered.

"Thank you, but you have your work, and I have mine," she answered, as she turned to a blank page in her notebook.

"Alright. I'll see you later, but don't stay in this room all afternoon. Ask Alek to take you to Mama and Stefan's for a visit. They are only two houses away. It would be good for you to get out," he said. He then let her hand slip from his, but as he stood up, he knew she would not leave the house.

"Bye," she said.

Ivan took this as a sign to leave. He felt that her work pressed her to continue, and he did not want to disturb her any longer. He stroked her cheek and left the room. His last glimpse of her was of her looking down at her notebook. As he pulled the door closed, he thought he saw a tear fall from her cheek and hit the top page. Then the door closed completely, and he left the house for the Rebel camp.

CHAPTER THIRTY-FIVE

The package Alek had referred to was the dossier Ivan had requested Sergej to get on Tess. It had arrived, and Ivan would learn all about Tess today. Regardless that he wanted to stay with her, and felt he no longer cared about the truth, he knew he had to be loyal to his men. The contents of her dossier would be the proof he needed to dispel any doubt of her being a spy for the Serbians, or for anyone else, for that matter. He knew that the rumor of a woman spy was most likely propagated by the Croatians and the Bosniaks.

In Ivan's heart, he felt the report would read that Tess was just who she said she was, because he was not prepared for bad news. If she turned out to be a spy, he did not know what he would do. The men would expect him to get rid of her. If she were, he felt he could not do that and disregard his love for her. Instead, he would have to find another solution. He would find a way to convince her to be on his side. He had promised her that no matter what trouble she was in, he would help her. He would not let anyone take her away from him, even if he had to kill to make it so.

Riding out to the Rebel camp in the hills south of Sarajevo, the snow fell softly on the road in front of him as it blanketed the surrounding landscape. Ivan's mind raced as he wondered what he would discover about Tess. Once he arrived, he walked quickly across a snow trodden path, and into a tent at the center of the camp, where Sergej waited to place the envelope containing her dossier in his hand. Dismissing the other men from the tent, Ivan requested that Sergej stay.

Opening the sealed envelope, Ivan began to read about her life. She was born in Chicago and was the younger of two children, both girls; however, her parents and sister were deceased. Ivan paused momentarily and sensed that her life was very much like his, except that he had Mrs. Tomić to replace his mother, but from what he read, Tess had no one. Sighing as he thought about that, he continued reading that she had pursued a career in writing six years past. The report detailed her whereabouts from the time she was born. Scattered bits of information, out of order, and random, told of the successes and failures of her life and her writing career. From what he read, Ivan began to know that Tess was just who she said she was.

He read on and the report described, in detail, the foundation she started for underprivileged children. Her dedication to promoting the art of writing was emphasized in the previous two and a half years, and he wondered why the sudden burst of humanitarian efforts during this time. Then he skimmed over a court document—it was a divorce decree. This caused him to pause. He never imagined that she had been married; she had not mentioned it, and he had not thought to ask. Searching the page for a date the divorce was granted, he saw it was two and a half years past. That corresponded with her sudden charitable outlook. Then he read the name of her husband, Jacek Kralj. Ivan knew that name, and he wondered if it was a coincidence, or if it was the same Jacek Kralj he knew of.

Turning to the next page, he read a report on her ex-husband that contained a copy of his birth certificate. Jacek Kralj was born in Belgrade and was the son of Milan Kralj. Tess had been married to a Serbian Nationalist. Not a man who was just of Serbian descent, but a man born in Serbia, whose family was of the highest echelon in the Serbian Nationalist party of Yugoslavia for over three decades. Ivan's heart thumped in his chest. He had to reread the document to be certain what he read was real. Then his eyes moved up from the page as his gaze locked on the tent's frayed opening.

Sergej noticed his expression, then saw a silent rage building inside him. "Ivan? What is it?" he asked.

Ivan could not answer. He only shook his head and handed the papers to Sergej who read them, then looked back at Ivan in panic. Ivan's gaze was wild as he realized the consequences because of the woman he had brought into that house with his men.

"Ivan, burn this! Forget you ever saw it! It doesn't mean anything," Sergej insisted.

Ivan snatched the papers from Sergej's hands and shoved them back into the envelope as he walked to the tent's opening.

"What are you going to do?" Sergej asked as he grabbed Ivan by the arm to stop him from leaving in haste.

Ivan stared straight ahead. "What a fool I've been. She doesn't care about Mara. She's here to find me." He gave a sarcastic laugh. "The rumor is true."

"What if the rumor isn't true? What if they found out she was coming here and made up the rumor around her to find you? She doesn't know who you are," Sergej said.

Ivan only shook his head, but it was a possibility. For a moment, he gave Tess the benefit of his doubt, but that moment was short lived.

Sergej saw his expression and was worried about how Ivan would confront Tess with this information. "What are you going to do?" he asked.

"I'm going to get rid of her, but not before she admits it to me. I will make her admit she's a traitor, then I will—" He abruptly stopped. He was irate, but still, he could not bring himself to say that he would harm her in any way. He pulled from Sergej's grip, and leaving the tent, he walked to the car. Sergej followed Ivan, telling him that he should let it go. She had not done anything to prove that she was guilty of working against him, but Ivan did not listen. He got into the car and drove back to the house to confront Tess.

Sergej and several other men got into a second car and followed Ivan back to the house. Sergej knew Tess was not guilty of betraying Ivan, and he felt it was only right for him to be there to try to intervene against Ivan's imminent inquisition. He needed to be there to convince Ivan of the truth.

Sergej remembered when he was on the train with Tess. She had spoken about a man who had failed her, a man who did not love her. He now knew that man she spoke of was her ex-husband, and he recalled her words: "He was never my friend, though I was his greatest friend, and he threw me away." Sergej knew Tess was incapable of being anything but loyal to those around her. Because of her loyalty, he knew that she would tolerate Ivan's accusations.

Because of this, Sergej had to stop Ivan before he did something that he would regret. Because he knew that, with all of Ivan's conviction and love for his people, more importantly, Ivan was in love with Tess. If Ivan did not love Tess, he would not have brought her to Sarajevo. Sergej also knew that Ivan's future actions would only be those of a man who felt he was betrayed in love, not in war.

With those thoughts in mind, Sergej drove faster. He did not know what he could do to convince Ivan, but he had to try, just as Tess tried to find Mara, and while she tried, Ivan let her struggle in her search as his men had to watch. And though they did not know all of Ivan's reasons for this, they were loyal to him, loyal to their leader, loyal to the Black Rebel.

Now the truth Sergej would have to show Ivan was that Tess was no different from his men. She, too, was loyal to him.

CHAPTER THIRTY-SIX

Both Ivan and Sergej reached the house at the same time. Ivan walked inside, taking the envelope with him, and seeing Tess setting the table for dinner, he stopped in place and stared at her. She saw him and smiled at him. When she stepped away from the table to approach him, his upset expression stopped her in place. When Sergej walked in, she looked at him. Her gaze questioned him, though he displayed no sign of distress.

Tess could not imagine why Ivan appeared angry. When he left earlier that day, he was pleasant and sorry to be leaving her. Now, he was obviously agitated, but was he agitated with her, or with something that had happened after he left? Disheartened, she turned around. Then walking back through the dining room, she retreated to the kitchen to help Sergej's mother, feeling as though she were a mere scullion.

Looking at Sergej, then at his men, Ivan said, "Tonight we will speak in English; no Serbian, not unless you hear me speak it. Do you understand?"

The men agreed and, though they thought Ivan was acting strangely, they took their places at the table. Sergej stopped Ivan in place before he left the living room. "Ivan, this is not right. You torment her for no reason," he said, and his stare was firmly against Ivan's intentions.

"She was married to a Nationalist. She might cross herself when she prays and might go to church, but she was married to a Nationalist. If I have brought a traitor into this house, it is up to me to get rid of her," Ivan said.

"*Was* married! *WAS*, not *IS* married! We don't even know if Jacek is a member of the Serbian Nationalist party," Sergej said, shaking his head at Ivan.

"Like father, like son!" Ivan said sarcastically.

"Why don't you find out why she divorced him before you accuse her of doing something wrong? Being married to a Nationalist in America isn't wrong," Sergej said.

"Being married to a Nationalist anywhere is wrong when it's that family!"

"You know very well that she could no more betray you than I," Sergej said, then quietly added, "Talk to her in private. Show her the report and give her the chance to tell you the truth."

"You are so naïve to think she would tell me the truth," Ivan said.

"Has she lied to you yet?"

"She didn't tell me she was married to Kralj."

"Did you ask her if she was married, or ever had been?" Sergej asked.

Ivan said nothing. He had asked if she were "Miss" when he first met her in Belgrade, but he knew he had not asked if she *had* been married at any time.

Sergej looked into the dining room and noticed a few of the men staring at them and wondering what was going on. He then shook his head. "Ivan, you are angry right now, but do not accuse Tess. Do not speak to her in a way that you will regret."

Still, Ivan did not respond. He thought silently as he looked past Sergej toward the dining table, then at his men who stared at him. He knew all of this, yet his expression did not display this.

Seeing Ivan's stubbornness, Sergej uttered a grunt and roughly shoved Ivan out of his way. Talking under his breath, Sergej walked away and left Ivan standing alone in the living room.

Tossing his coat over the back of the sofa, Ivan walked to the table. Placing the envelope against the table's leg to his right, he took his place at the head, where he impatiently waited to be served by his American slave, as he momentarily saw Tess in his mind; however, his heart did not agree. His mind spun at his racing thoughts, and though he was angry with Tess, he still longed to have her seated next to him.

When the food was served, the men waited to eat until Tess prayed; however, Ivan did not wait, which showed his present disregard for her. The men looked at him and were shocked at his lack of respect. They knew something was wrong, but they had no idea what—in all their years of knowing Ivan, they never witnessed him being rude to anyone.

Ivan cautiously watched Tess. Realizing the truth in Sergej's words, Ivan had to know beyond all doubt whose side Tess was on. Why did she divorce the man she was married to? And for her sake, her answers had better not be lies.

Sitting next to Ivan, Tess felt uneasy. So uneasy that she did not eat; she only made sure the men had what they needed. She did not speak either.

She could feel something was wrong, but could not imagine what. Sergej sat across from her as usual, while several of the other men sat around the opposite end of the table from Ivan. Considering the strangeness of Ivan's mood, none of them wanted to be too close to him, or so it seemed. And though they truly had no idea what was going on, they kept their distance because they surmised it was a lover's spat between Ivan and Tess.

Ivan sat near to Tess and examined her closely. He appeared curious about something. Every time Tess smiled at him, he frowned, and she did not know what she had done to upset him. Sergej sat there, watching Ivan's exhibition, but he could only shake his head and smile at Tess when she looked at him. Nevertheless, soon after they sat down, she stopped looking at any of them, especially Ivan.

Her mind raced. She could only imagine that Ivan was tired of spending time with her and taking her to makeshift shelters. He was tired of looking at children. Tired of searching for the little girl she tried so desperately to find, but mostly, she felt that he was tired of being with her.

Ivan began talking to the men at the opposite end of the table and, as he said he would, he spoke in English. To everyone's shock, he began discussing Nationalism. Even though he used the term Serbian Nationalists instead of Chetnik, Tess still cringed with the memory of her ex-husband. Ivan's tone of voice made her feel strange, as she felt he directed his comments at her.

After he discussed Nationalism, he discussed the continual border disputes of the independent countries of the former Yugoslavia. He then spoke of living in the old Yugoslavia with Serbian Nationalism, but none of what he said was what he meant or what he felt about the situation. He only emphasized the extreme side of Serbian Nationalist opinions.

"Most people do not understand the ways of *Serbian Nationalists,* but some people know firsthand," he said, then turned to face Tess as he paused and waited for her reaction.

Her eyes gradually moved toward him, and he saw coldness in her gaze that he had not witnessed since he had known her. He was under the impression that her gaze was meant for him, but he was wrong. The mere thought of her ex-husband evoked dread, and his memory threw her back into a dehumanizing phase of her life that she thought she had long since left behind.

"Some people would live with them and even marry them," he said as he stared at her.

Just then, she understood the root of his anger. He had somehow found out to whom she had been married, and now, it appeared that he resented her for it. She slowly stood up from the table as her eyes moved from Ivan to Sergej, who looked at her sympathetically. Then, one by one, she looked at the rest of the men. They all stared at her, questioning the truth of the situation and, for the first time being there, she was truly frightened.

"Excuse me, please," she whispered, then she turned and stepped away from the table. Pushing through the kitchen door, she hurried down the hall to the bedroom and locked the door once she was inside.

Watching her flee, Ivan's temper flared. He felt she left because he had finally caught her. Snatching the envelope from beside the table's leg, he stood up quickly. So quick were his motions, that his chair fell back against the floor. He then stepped away from the table and pursued her. The men were frozen in their places as they watched him barge through the kitchen door. They looked at Sergej, who shook his head, then looked toward the living room.

Ivan's voice broke the silence in the house as he beat on the outside of the locked bedroom door. "Unlock this door, Tess!" he said in a low and intolerant voice.

Tess had her suitcase on the bed and was packing. She ignored him, hoping that he would go away.

When she did not comply, he persisted, louder and angrier this time. *"Tess! Open this door before I kick it in!"*

Still, she did not answer, so in his rage over her presumed guilt, he kicked the door open with one vicious thrust. The clothes she held dropped to the floor as she saw hatred on his face, and fearful of him, she began to back away.

He entered the room and slammed the door closed, although it opened on its own because the lock was now broken. He saw her luggage and surmised she wanted to leave because she was guilty. Despite that thought, he needed to discover exactly what she was guilty of. At that moment, he appeared capable of anything, and she now witnessed from where the rumors of the *tyrannical* Black Rebel originated. Seeing his anger, she felt she would not get the opportunity to leave.

Throwing the envelope to the floor, he rushed toward her. Grabbing her by the arms, he lifted her up so that her face was inches from his. When he spoke, his voice was so deafening in his anger that the men in the dining room could hear. And though they wanted to help Tess, Ivan was their leader, so they had no choice but to respect what he would do. Without him, where would they be? Knowing this situation was private, they retreated to the living room where they could not hear him as well.

"Why didn't you tell me in Belgrade that you were married to a Serbian Nationalist? Why? Did you think you could hide that fact forever? You're on their side, aren't you? Tell me the truth for a change!"

He paused briefly to give her time to answer, but she said nothing. She was without words from fear, just as she used to be with her ex-husband. And though she was right there with Ivan, part of her was back in her marriage, suffering again from all she had gone through then.

"No wonder why you looked so shocked when I introduced you to Jacek at the restaurant. Hearing his name must have reminded you of *him!*"

Again, she did not respond; she only tried to pull from his grasp, but he jerked her up higher, and continued questioning her. "Tell me? If you married him, why did you divorce him?" he asked, trying to curb his anger, but his relentless grip bruised her arms. He did not know his own strength, and the angrier he became, the tighter he held onto her. Yet in his heart, he held onto her so tightly, because he did not want to lose her. Even so, his voice became slow and deep. She could see his anger in his eyes, along with his desperation, and still, she was voiceless.

"Tell me, Tess, or I swear I'll—" Hearing his own words, he stopped before he could finish his statement. For a moment, he could not believe he could even think what had passed through his mind.

She froze and looked him in the eyes. He could feel her shaking in his grasp, and her terrified expression told him that someone else had treated her similarly in the past.

Then, as if provoked by a need to tell someone her secret, she finally responded. "You'll what? Kill me? That's something he used to say to me."

Ivan was correct. Realizing that his actions were no different from her former husband's, his grip loosened. He saw her vulnerability, and that made him feel like he was in a surreal nightmare.

"I divorced him because he treated me like you're treating me now: like a thing, not a person. And on two separate occasions he became violent with me as perhaps your rage will drive you to as well." She looked away, and her voice faded out, as she whispered, "No matter how desperately I try, I can't escape him."

He let her go as his shocked stare quickly moved to the floor. He walked to the window, pushed the curtain aside, and looked out. Did she see him as a violent man? What else could she think from the way he acted? He wanted to apologize, but he was quiet. His thoughts were scattered with disbelief, but was it disbelief of her, or of his behavior? At that moment, nothing made sense to him.

"Why did you marry him? What made you love him enough to marry him? You're American. Why didn't you marry an American?" he asked.

"I'm not that much of an American Nationalist," she said.

He looked at her, then quickly looked to the floor as she continued. "I was young. I thought he was a good man. I thought he was the right man, but deep down I knew he wasn't. He was just better than the others were, or so I thought at the time. I was stupid. I didn't wait long enough for the right man to come along," she said as she briefly looked at him, then looked away.

Coming out of his thoughts, he let the curtain go, then he turned to look at her. He noticed her rubbing her upper arms where he had grabbed her. From this, he knew he had hurt her, but before he could ask, she continued her story.

"I hadn't had any negative experiences with Serbians, nor did I know about Serbian Nationalism before him. To me, Serbian was a nationality, or a region, not a characteristic. Everyone told me how lucky I was to be with him, and he was pretty convincing that he was the right man for me. We met at a classical music performance when he was working on his doctorate degree in biochemistry, but I'm sure you already know all that. I'm sure you don't care about that either."

He frowned at her. He hated for her to think that he did not care about her past. Why else would he have gone through all the trouble to check into her background? But now he was voiceless to tell her otherwise.

"Now that I know what a Serbian Nationalist is, I can say he wasn't that when we met. I don't think he ever joined the party, only teetered on the edge of it. He didn't have much when we were first married because his father was upset with him for not returning to Belgrade, and so he stopped sending him money. I was the one with access to comforts because I worked, so maybe that's why he asked me to marry him. I'll never know because he was never honest with me."

She gave a laugh as she thought back to that time in her life. And though she knew Ivan was there listening, she continued as if she were alone and speaking to herself. "I never met his parents, and only after we were married a year did I meet his two brothers. One of his brothers, Goran, came to visit. He caused lots of trouble, but for some strange reason, he stopped Jacek's first attack on me."

Ivan looked at her as her words about her ex-husband's abuse sank in. She was silent as she stared at the floor. He saw her frown, and knew she remembered that day with vivid accuracy. And now he started to hate himself for having been violent with her and for having reminded her of someone who had hurt her so deeply.

"Just prior to that visit is when Jacek began to change. He stopped caring about the usual things he cared about. He was more interested in his Serbian heritage. If I showed any interest in his heritage, he became violently angry. He'd walk around the house and break expensive things, or take a baseball bat to my car. When Goran came, they were out together all the time, for several days at a time they'd be gone. I imagine when Goran returned to Belgrade he reported to Milan, their father, that all was fine with Jacek. After Goran left, Jacek apologized for the way he acted when he was angry and I forgave him. Everything appeared normal, and it seemed he had put on a show for his brother so his father would send money, which he did—lots of it. Once Jacek was bankrolled, he was then free, so free that he used to stay out all night most evenings. I knew where he was. I knew who he was with. I knew the truth."

She was silent as she looked toward the ceiling. Ivan stared at her and he could see tears forming in her eyes. He wanted to stop her, he wanted to apologize, but before he could, once again, she continued her story.

"After that was when he received his US citizenship from being married to me. His father was incensed that he had given up his Serbian birthright; he had found out from his youngest son, Stanislav, who was visiting. That was the second time he was violent with me. And like Goran, Stanislav intervened, although I can't imagine why he did either. Well, that was the start of everything all over again, all the bizarre behavior, and all the Serbian heritage discussions. But when Stanislav left, Jacek never apologized for striking me. That was the end for me, even though there really was nothing to end. His father sent him money again, and he took off with one of his girlfriends. Only this time, when he was gone, I filed for divorce. At this point, I'm not even certain that he knows we're divorced, because I had no address to mail his copy of the divorce decree to," she said, then she shook her head at the thought as she stared at the flame of the candle on the small dresser—for a moment, she watched it flickering in a draft from the open bedroom door.

Ivan knew she saw visions of her past in that flame. Just then, her statement about not getting a copy of her divorce decree to her ex-husband made Ivan think. He wondered if perhaps her ex-husband was searching for her. Now that the war in Sarajevo was winding down, and not going in the Serbians' favor, perhaps Kralj wanted to return to the safety of America. Perhaps Kralj imagined that Tess was there searching for him. This changed things completely. This complicated things, because Kralj's family had the power to find her, whereas a lower ranking Serbian Nationalist's did not. This thought sent a chill up Ivan's spine, and he contemplated getting her out of the country at once. Then, when Tess continued, he emerged from his private thoughts—thoughts he would sort out later.

"I sold the house, which he had no proof of ownership in, and moved to Chicago. He took off with his money and left the bills behind. The last time I spoke to him was on the telephone about two and a half years ago, which was before the divorce and just before the house sold. He had spent his money. His girlfriend, or girlfriends, had left him, and he wanted to come back to *his* house as he called it. I hung up on him and I haven't heard from him since, nor do I ever care to."

"When you spoke to him that last time, you didn't tell him that you filed for divorce?" he asked.

"No. I didn't want any opposition, fights, or any more violence. I just wanted him gone because I *needed* him gone."

She paused and looked back at the flame. She stayed quiet for a moment and waited to see if he would ask another question, although he did not.

"He had insinuated during that last call that his father had cut him off completely, again. I guess being married to an American was a disgrace, and Milan wanted Jacek to come home to Serbia. He said he would correct the error Jacek made in becoming an American citizen, or so Jacek said. I imagine Milan had plans for his son. I don't think his father ever approved of our marriage, but I wouldn't know because I never met him. He already had a wife picked out for Jacek, or so Goran had said; some political setup, most likely. I'm sure if Milan Kralj knew of the divorce he would be the happiest man in the world. I know I'm happy."

"Were you in love with him?" Ivan asked, but he was almost afraid of her answer.

"Looking back now, I know I wasn't *ever* in love with him. That type of love, being in love, doesn't happen for everyone, at least not mutually. I tried to love him for his good characteristics, but in the end, those were illusions. After not hearing from him, I imagine he went back to Serbia. He was a weak man and money was always his bait. So, you see, you're right, I learned what it was like to be married to one Serbian Nationalist. I soon understood that being a Nationalist, like his family, was his mentality. Thank God I lived in America and not some other country. I would have killed myself, or more likely, ended up decapitated in a shallow, unmarked grave," she said.

The accuracy of her last comment shocked him. She understood the violent side of Nationalism better than he had ever imagined she could, and much more than he would have ever wanted her to. But her ex-husband's behavior was not actually Nationalistic, but simply angry and greedy, because it was obvious that he was a spoiled and lazy man.

Ivan looked at her. His gaze moved to her suitcase, then back to her, as he asked, "Why didn't you tell me when we first met?"

"You didn't ask. Besides, he is my past, not my present, or my future," she answered.

"Then why didn't you tell me earlier today when I told you that I wasn't married?" he asked, thinking that would have been the best time for her to tell him.

"I didn't think it was appropriate just then. It's not something that you reveal out of nowhere. I knew you already suspected me of some sort of disloyalty. If you had asked, I'd have told you a less thorough story, but *I would* have told you the truth. Most men think when they see a woman who appears successful and is divorced, everything she has she *took* from her ex-husband. I don't want people thinking that way of me. He gave me nothing. I gave him everything I could and it was never enough. To me, making someone else happy is what marriage is about, but that's a two-way street. True love is about what is good for the other person, not what is good for yourself. To him, I was always wrong and he was always right. He was demeaning and self-gratifying, and he tried very hard to strip away my dignity."

She shook her head and gave a small, breathy laugh. "After six years, I had enough. That's why I filed for divorce. Being married to him changed my life forever. But I have to forgive him, just as God forgives me. Because of God's forgiveness, it is not my right to hold his offense against him, just as it is not my right to seek revenge against him." She paused and released a small sigh. "Forgiveness is something all Nationalists refuse to practice, because they don't really understand or grant mercy. It's always an eye for an eye, which seems right to them, but it's not right. In their quest for that simple revenge, they always take more than the equivalent of what was taken from them. That is, if anything was taken to begin with." She shook her head. "It's all covetous greed."

Ivan was frowning as he stared at her. Why she endured this man as long as she had was a mystery to him. The hows and whys of her life with her ex-husband were plentiful, and it was too confusing to think about just then. Her story astonished him. Her honesty humbled him. And, for a moment, his mind was still, except for his thoughts about all she had been through. Before she continued, he heard the muffled sound of the men talking in the kitchen, but he was so attentive to her that he ignored them.

"He took a lot and left wounds that sometimes don't seem like they will heal. I don't expect you to understand and I see no reason for you to care. Whatever happened, I'm sure it was no less than I deserved for having married him. Besides, why should you care? I'm just an American," she concluded. Then, unexpectedly, she turned and rushed out of the room as tears streamed down her cheeks—she did not want him to see her cry. As she entered the kitchen, the men crowded the room and blocked her path. Struggling against them, she pushed through them to pass through to the dining room.

Hearing the commotion, Ivan walked to the entrance of the kitchen as he heard Lukáš say, "The train from Zagreb with the supplies has been hijacked!"

"Where? Who?" Ivan asked.

"Two hundred kilometers west of Tuzla. We don't know who yet. Miša's finding out," Lukáš said.

Ivan gave his men their orders, then half of them walked to the kitchen door to exit, the others toward the main part of the house. Tess was in the living room, but heard them coming into the dining room. Having nowhere else to go, she rushed to the front door, pulled it open, and ran out into the frozen darkness.

Tomo had been upstairs on patrol and saw soldiers walking in the street. He was hurrying down the stairs to let Ivan know when he saw Tess rush out the front door, and yelled after her, *"NO! Tess, come back! Don't go out there! There are soldiers out there!"*

Ivan heard Tomo call her, then he saw Tomo dart out the front door. Sergej hurried after Tomo, who ran into the street trying desperately to catch Tess. As Ivan hurried toward the open front door, he heard the shot ring out as it pierced the night's silence, and instantly he panicked, thinking about Tess. Looking at Alek, he tore the rifle from his grasp. Checking that the rifle was loaded, he hurried to the front door.

Rushing out onto the snow-dusted porch, the full moon, peaking through the break of clouds, shone brightly down on the scene before his eyes. Ivan saw Tomo shot and lying on the ground. He stopped in place and suddenly, the hush from the freshly fallen snow surrounded him. Sergej stooped next to Tomo, and Tess was between Sergej and two Serbian soldiers, who both aimed their rifles at her. With her left hand held back toward Sergej and Tomo as if to secure them behind her, and her right hand held out toward the soldiers as if she could stop any action they could take, she spoke to them as she blocked their view of the men that were behind her. In fear of the deadly situation Ivan witnessed, he stood paralyzed as he heard her say: "Please, don't kill them. Please—" She stared at the first soldier, and then at the second. Then she shook her head and said, "Don't."

The young soldiers looked at her strangely and it was obvious they did not understand English. It was also obvious they did not see Ivan as he lifted the rifle to his shoulder and focused his vision through the scope. Tess stood directly in front of the first soldier and, from where Ivan stood, the only visible part of the second soldier was the left side of his head, which was just off to the right of her head. Ivan knew what he had to do, but she was moving and the shot was unclear. Then again, even if he took out the second soldier, what would the first one do? Would he fire, or would he freeze? Despite the volatility of the situation, Ivan had to do something. It was enough that Tomo had been shot, and Ivan refused to allow Tess and Sergej be injured. So, like a statue, he stood there deliberating briefly. Then Sergej turned and saw Ivan from the corner of his eye, and he knew what Ivan planned to do.

Ivan looked directly at Tess, and his voice froze her in place as he said in a low and authoritative tone, "Tess, don't move an inch."

Hearing Ivan's voice, the first soldier's curiosity piqued, and he moved around her to see who had spoken. As he revealed himself, the shot rang out. From behind her, she could hear its approach, and felt its looming danger singing through the bitter night air. Then a single round ripped past the left side of her head. The first soldier stared directly at Ivan as the world moved in slow motion, then he yelped in shock. She thought she saw the bullet pass by the side of her face, but it's passing was confirmed when she saw it enter the soldier's mouth. Then the back of his skull cracked open, and his sensibility flew out the exit wound.

Although muffled by the slight ringing in her ears from the first round, she heard the second round fired, and the same song approaching from behind. Only her eyes moved to the other soldier. Too slow, however, to see the bullet pass her, but she felt its wind shear graze her hair, and saw it pierce the second soldier's left eye. At first, the hot bullet punctured the eye, but in its searing journey, it pulled the iris back, imploding the eye into the socket. Then it vanished inside the man's head and exited the back of his skull with a fine red mist, taking his life with it on its way. In an instant, two soldiers lay dead at her feet, and all that remained was an overwhelming scent that seeped into the air: blood, gunpowder, and death. Frozen in the moment, she tasted it.

After seeing their comrades killed, the two remaining soldiers scurried away in an attempt to escape, but with the snap of Ivan's fingers, his men emerged from the darkness and pursued them. Then shoving the rifle back at Alek, Ivan ordered, "Go check on Mama and Stefan!" and Alek hurried to follow his command.

As Ivan rushed down the front porch steps and toward Tess, clouds drifted over the moon, and the snow began to fall again. The temperature dropped slightly, and the quiet became quieter as the snow hushed the sounds of the night.

Sergej and Lukáš helped Tomo back into the house. Several others picked up the two corpses, carried them around the back of the house, dumped them in the trunk of a car, and slammed the trunk shut. Then they returned to the street to erase the evidence.

Still frozen in place, Tess was silent, but her tears were gone. Ivan reached for her hand and gently pulled her toward the house. And though his gentle tug should have been sufficient to capture her attention, she appeared incapable of responding, incapable of movement.

"Tess, come on! Come inside!" he ordered, however, she did not move. She stood there, snow gently covering her, as she heard the distant sound of gunfire, which made her jolt, and she knew the fleeing soldiers were now dead. Desperately wanting to get her back in the house, he tugged again at her arm. But this time, she fell to her knees, just staring at the spot where the last soldier had fallen.

"Tess," he whispered and bent down to her. Lifting her into his arms, she rested her head on his shoulder as he quickly carried her through the deep snow and back toward the house.

Since the men had taken Tomo into the living room, Ivan carried her around and into the back of the house and directly into their bedroom. Setting her on the bed next to her suitcase, he then shut the door. Closing her suitcase, he placed it back on top of the dresser. He collected her clothes from the floor, placed them on top of the suitcase, then sat next to her.

Her silence spooked him, and he knew he had caused this situation, not her. His mind could not release the image of her standing between Sergej and a bullet. Her plea to the two now-dead soldiers was like a sharp slap across his face. Without a doubt, he now knew that she was not against him, she was for him. Her actions proved to Ivan that she was willing to sacrifice her life for those she cared about.

Looking at her now, he did not know what to say. As she sat there staring at the floor, a saddened and fatigued expression emanated from her. Ivan knew this expression was shock. He had brought her into the middle of a war. He risked her life because he suspected her of something he now knew she was incapable of, and that was betrayal. But he also risked her life because he was in love with her.

Tess could have easily let the soldiers kill Sergej, but instead, she did what she had to. It was obvious she felt responsible for Tomo being shot, and she was not about to let Sergej be shot as well. As if it were her only choice, she stood in front of those soldiers' rifles, more than willing to die for Sergej, whom she saw as her friend. Sergej deserved her friendship as he had given his in return. Yet, what did Ivan give her except his lies and harsh treatment?

As she faced death, she pleaded with the soldiers not to kill Sergej and Tomo. She could have told the soldiers that Ivan was the Black Rebel, even though he had no idea that she had figured out exactly who he was. She could have said anything to save herself, but she did not. Instead, she pleaded for the lives of the men she felt her presence had endangered. She was prepared to walk into the hands of the enemy to save the lives of Ivan and his men. In the desperation he had caused her, he felt she preferred death to being with him at that moment. Because he distrusted her, she could have been the recipient of a soldier's bullet, or worse, she could have been taken by the soldiers.

He stroked her face though she did not respond. Her ears were still ringing, and she sat there dazed and not certain it was over. At that moment, he did not know how to reach her. And though he sat next to her, his actions placed him on the other side of the world when she refused to acknowledge him. She could not see his desperate love for her, although he hoped that she would hear it in his voice as he whispered, "Are you alright? Are you hurt?"

She did not answer or look at him. Needing her attention, he slid from the bed and to his knees in front of her. Taking her chilled hands in his, he kissed them. He looked at her, but her stare pierced him with silent retrospect. The pain of his heart cried out to her as tears misted his eyes. "Tess, I am sorry for what I thought. I had no right to treat you the way I did. Please, Tess, please," he begged, but still, she did not respond. Then a knock sounded lightly on the door. *"What!"* he answered angrily in Serbian.

"Tomo is alright. It's only a flesh wound in the arm," Sergej said in English so that Tess would know that Tomo was not critically injured, then he switched to Serbian. "Mama and Stefan are okay." Without another word, he walked away.

It was then that Ivan noticed the torn threads near the top of her left shoulder in her thickly knit wrap sweater. She had worn this sweater almost every day, and that evening at dinner, but it was not torn then. He stood and looked more closely at it. He saw the threads were dark, as if burnt, and he knew the bullet that hit Tomo grazed her first. He gently moved the sweater from her shoulder and pushed aside the sweater beneath it to check to see if she was injured. Luckily she was not, and so he moved her sweaters back in place.

Thinking of the consequences, he sighed as he looked at her emotionless expression. He pulled the covers down and moved her backward on the bed where her head touched the pillow. Removing her wet boots, he placed her legs under the blankets, covered her, then sat next to her. Looking down at her, she still stared, giving him no response.

"Sleep now," he whispered, then stroking her cheek, he leaned toward her, and kissed her forehead. Slowly sitting straight, he saw her looking at him, and in her eyes he saw such passion. In her eyes, he thought he saw her love for him, but he was not sure. Perhaps the passion he saw there was hatred of him, not the love he longed for.

At that moment, he yearned to take her in his arms and kiss her. He longed to tell her how wrong he was and beg her to forgive him until she did. But before he could speak, she closed her eyes and turned away from him. With that action, he knew his opportunity had passed, so he stood up and walked to the fireplace. Adding wood to the fire, he then blew out all but the candle on her vanity and the one next to the bed. He walked back to her and pulled the blankets up higher over her shoulder, then he took the burning candle from the other side of the bed and left the room.

Walking through the kitchen, Ivan entered the dining room. There he found his men had returned after pursuing and killing the other soldiers. He sat at the head of the table, and his men were silent as they looked at him, silent as they waited for his next orders. Breaking the silence, Lukáš walked in the front door with Miša right behind him.

"Do we know who hijacked the train?" Ivan asked as he looked past Lukáš and directly at Miša.

"Serbian military, but not by direct order," Miša answered.

"What where they doing that far north and west?" Ivan asked.

Miša shrugged. "No information on that so far, but they must have moved troops nearby," he said.

"Find out where they're stationed and how many," Ivan ordered, then he expelled a heavy sigh.

They had not had trouble like this with Serbian forces in a long time and he imagined they hijacked the train out of desperation, or thinking they were delivering a blow to Bosniak forces in that area. He could not decide if this complicated or simplified the situation and he also wondered who else knew about the train. Shaking off that thought, Ivan then discussed his plan for regaining possession of the train.

This meeting lasted until just before midnight. Then Ivan ordered Dragan and Željko to take the dead soldier's bodies up into the mountain and bury them there, then to go to the Rebel camp, for he would see them there tomorrow. The other men went to bed, and only Sergej and Ivan re-mained seated at the table. Knowing a barrage of questions from Sergej was imminent, Ivan stood and started to walk to the front door.

"What the hell was that?" Sergej asked.

Not answering, Ivan stopped in place.

As Sergej continued, Ivan turned around and saw Sergej's face contort in disbelief. "You could have killed her. For God's sake, I saw her hair move with the second round."

"What was I supposed to do? Let them kill her? Let them shoot straight through her to get to you?"

"But—"

"I did what needed to be done!" Ivan said, then he turned around and continued to the door to secure it for the night.

Sergej shook his head. Expelling a shocked sigh, he rubbed his eyes as if he could clear the vision of that night's happenings from his mind.

"Why? Why did you question her like that? We heard you yelling at her."

Again, Ivan stopped in place. He did not answer, which Sergej expected.

"Will you finally admit that you love her, now that you know she's not on their side?" Sergej asked.

Still, Ivan said nothing. He had tried to hide his feelings for her. How-ever, he could not hide them from Sergej, who wanted nothing more than for him to be happy.

"If you don't love her, get her out of here before she gets killed. Tonight was too close for comfort," Sergej said.

"It could be her ex-husband looking for her," Ivan stated.

"What does he want with her?" Sergej asked.

"I don't know," Ivan answered.

"We should find out, don't you think?" Sergej recommended as he walked toward Ivan.

Ivan did not answer; he was lost in thought about what Tess' ex-husband could want with her. That was, if he were the person searching for her.

"I know you love her," Sergej said.

Ivan's dilemma was obvious. Sergej saw pride and fear standing in the way of Ivan's happiness: pride in his beliefs, and fear from his past actions toward Tess. But mostly, Ivan feared what Tess would do as a direct result of those actions. Sergej also saw fear that Ivan had now lost Tess. This doubt in Ivan's eyes answered Sergej's question as he could see that Ivan did love her.

Along with this fear came the silence Ivan now experienced. The helplessness that finally came to the surface as Ivan, for a moment of being just a man and not a leader, saw his mistakes. He saw how, with both hands, Ivan threw away all that he longed for, and because of this, Ivan felt powerless.

The situation was out of Ivan's hands and, at this point, anything he did would only make matters worse, or so he imagined. It was Tess' decision whether she would forgive him. Even if she did, could she forgive him when she found out that he knew where Mara was? He was the cause of Tess' failure and anguish. Could she forgive him for that? All this Sergej knew, and he saw Ivan's lonely expression, although Ivan tried to hide his disappointment in himself.

"Everyone falls in love. Look at how many people have gotten married during this war. Life goes on. Why should you be any different? Where does it say that you can't love a woman because she's American, or because she was married to a man that did not love her, or for any other reason?" Sergej said, then he walked toward the stairs. Before going up, he looked back at Ivan. "Tell her you love her before you lose her."

Ivan's gaze questioned Sergej's last statement because Ivan felt he had already lost Tess. Then Sergej pointed to Tess' notebook on the small table in front of the sofa. "She loves you. Read what she wrote. She lets us read it. She doesn't know who you are, at least, I don't think she does, but she writes about the Black Rebel with love and respect. Respect for what you stand for, and you have too much pride to tell her that you care for her? What has this war done to you? If you are no longer capable of love, you should be dead. At least admit it to yourself. You always say that it is bad to lie to oneself." With that final comment, Sergej turned and walked up the stairs to his room.

Ivan stood alone in the living room with his stare fixed on Tess' notebook. For a moment, he did nothing. Then he bolted the front door, pushed the drape aside from the front window, and looked outside. Listening carefully, he heard nothing and saw no one. For a moment, he stared at the spot where Tess had stood off the two soldiers, then shaking his head at himself, he closed the drape.

Walking to the sofa, he sat down, and placing his hand on her open notebook, he debated whether to read from it. Pulling the candle near, he stared at it. As he looked at the top page, he saw a ripple on the bottom. The tear he saw her shed earlier that day caused that ripple. Although he had imagined she shed that tear for Mara, as he began to read, her thoughts about the Black Rebel covered the page. Words of love and respect for the Black Rebel displayed her true feelings, and he knew that tear she shed was for him, as she wrote:

They call him the Black Rebel. Some fear him and some love him, but none love him as much as I do. He must be a man of tremendous strength, superior wisdom, and incalculable compassion to lead so many men with risk as his only reward. He cares not for himself, but for the helpless. For his people he sacrifices his life. The needs of his people command him and their cries pierce his heart. His life is theirs as he fights for their fate. A greater type of man does not exist. His actions echo across a nation divided as he spreads his love for his people like seeds thrown to the wind—carried for centuries—then gently falling to the soil that he himself tills. He alone nurtures those seeds, protecting them from disaster at any cost. No price is too high in his love for his people. The love of his people consumes his heart, and with reverence, I declare, he consumes mine...

Then he read the entry just below where she quoted 1 John:

By this we know love, that he laid down his life for us, and we ought to lay down our lives for the brothers. But if anyone has the world's goods and sees his brother in need, yet closes his heart against him, how does God's love abide in him? Little children, let us not love in word or talk, but in deed and in truth.

By this, Ivan felt that Tess possibly understood him, but he knew the quote from 1 John just before this, which read:

Everyone who hates his brother is a murderer, and you know that no murderer has eternal life abiding in him.

Again, he felt he was a devil. Did he hate those who created this pathetic war, or did he pity them? He was uncertain just then, but sitting back against the sofa, he heard her pledge inside his mind. Did she truly give him her heart? He wondered if she knew who he was.

"Very interesting," he thought, though that was overpowered by another feeling. Exhaustion—he was tired of the war. He yearned to go to her and tell her who he was. Reading this, he wanted to collect the dedicated love she promised with her words, but she had written them before he had accused her. When she would find out that he and the Black Rebel were the same man, would she think differently? Would she see him as that murderous, fanatical, tyrant of which they had spoken? In this passage, there was no mention of suspicions or lies, no mention of temper or harsh words. She immortalized his image in a single paragraph. Again, he wondered if her opinion would change if she knew that he and the man she idolized were one and the same. Would he have her heart, as does the image of the Black Rebel? An image he knew he was unworthy of, just as he now felt that he was equally unworthy of her.

He closed the notebook. Lifting the candle, he walked to the kitchen and secured the back door, then he walked to the bedroom. Entering the room, he closed the door without a sound, and secured it as best he could since the lock was damaged from when he had kicked it open. He walked to the tall dresser and set his candle down. Then he added wood to the fire that burned low in the fireplace, and walked back to her bed.

She was unaware of his presence as he stood there watching her sleep. Bending down, he kissed her lips, then paused as he gazed at her. She did not move. Out of the corner of his eye, he saw the envelope on the floor. It still lay where he had thrown it earlier that evening. Walking to it, he picked it up. Standing there holding it, his mind darted in every direction. He then walked to the fireplace and tossed the envelope on top of the flaming wood. He watched it burn and, with it, he put an end to his inquisition, burning its evidence for all time. If there was more to tell, she would have to tell him. She was correct, he had not asked if she had been married. An obvious question if a man were truly interested in a woman, if a man had honorable intentions toward a woman, which he knew he had.

Shaking his head, he then walked to the small bed and sat. With his entire heart, he wanted nothing more than to wake her and tell her the truth; however, he feared what she would say. Still worse, he feared what she would do.

Staring at her, he reflected on his life and his beliefs. He had never imagined he would meet a woman like her; she was different from what he had expected of Americans. But people were just people no matter where they lived. Perhaps she was the only person like herself in her country. Perhaps a Higher Power had sent her to teach him the lessons he needed to learn in order to continue along his path. But if that were true, then she would eventually leave him, and move on to teach her lessons elsewhere.

He glanced at the dresser where her half-packed luggage lay, and wondered if she would finish packing in the morning. Not that she could leave Sarajevo without him, but he wondered, would he awake and find her gone? Had he destroyed his last chance to be with her?

"Why is it that our mistakes always overshadow our successes? Why are mistakes always the ghosts that come back to haunt us? Always questions with no answers," he thought.

Then he lay back on the bed and pulled the blanket over himself. He longed to be next to her, but he dare not offend her with afterthought affection. He lay there looking at her until his eyes could no longer remain open, as sleep commanded his attention. In his dreams, she would be there, so it was not as though they were apart, at least not in his mind. But he was not satisfied with her only being in his dreams; he wanted her permanently in his life. He wanted the freedom to make her his alone, knowing that she would not leave him. In his heart, he felt the pain of her absence. To himself, he did not have to admit anything, he knew from the start that he loved her, and in his heart, her image would always reside.

CHAPTER THIRTY-SEVEN

The next morning Ivan woke up late, and his heart was relieved to see that Tess had not packed and tried to leave. Exhausted, she still slept and was the same beautiful image as the night before. He stood up, shaved, changed his clothes, then walked to the side of her bed. He bent down and kissed her lips, then he quietly left the room so not to wake her.

When the door closed, she slowly opened her eyes and turned her head in that direction. Then turning her head the opposite direction, she looked at the small bed where Ivan usually slept, but he was not there. "Was it Ivan who kissed me just now, or was it a dream?" she wondered. She did not know. Regardless, she was tired from all that had happened the day before. Tragedy always happened so quickly, then, before you knew it, the damage was done. Thinking about it, Ivan was right. Considering the current situation there, she should have told him whom she had been married to before they left Belgrade. Her need for privacy caused the suspicion Ivan felt and the tragedy that occurred the previous evening. Although her ex-husband no longer mattered to her, her having been married to him mattered greatly to Ivan.

However, what she did not know was that even though Tomo had seen the soldiers, and was coming to warn Ivan, if she had not run out of the house, Ivan and his men would not have had the advantage. Her actions, though unintentionally injurious to Tomo, saved everyone else there by way of distraction, including Mrs. Tomić and Stefan, who were unaware of all that had happened, two houses away.

Thinking about the previous evening's events only confused the situation and, since she was still tired, she fell back to sleep. She wanted to dream what she dreamt when she imagined Ivan had kissed her, that split second of beauty before she awoke. But that dream did not come and, after a little while, she awoke to learn that Ivan had left the house and was not to return until later that evening. He left to go to the Rebel camp to meet with his men. He also left to give her peace and quiet to rest, but mostly, to give her time before seeing him again.

After attending to Tomo, Tess went back to writing. She needed to write about the Black Rebel, so she remained in the bedroom after retrieving her notebook from the living room. Mrs. Tomić tried to get her to eat, but she insisted she was not hungry and diligently worked. Tess did not know if she could face Ivan when he came home that evening. Still, even if he never spoke to her again, she would leave him her writing about him. She hoped that he would read it and understand. Even if he did not care for her, she had something to say about what she knew of him. That was what writing was all about; people saying what they thought and felt. Her ability to describe what she saw in his eyes, all that was Ivan Đurić, all that was the Black Rebel, surprised even her.

This day, Ivan and his men commenced with the first steps to retrieve the supplies from the hijacked train. Their original plan was to drive it further south to a safer location; however, he learned that the train was inoperable because, in order to take possession of it, the Serbians blew up the tracks on both sides of it, so it was stuck right where it was—a stupid move on their part. Now his plan was just to retrieve the food and provisions as quickly and uneventfully as possible. He did not plan to retaliate against the Serbian forces involved, although some sort of skirmish was imminent. It was an absolute risk with the possible outcome being Ivan's and his men's deaths.

One of his informants would leak a false time that the attack would occur on the train. At that time, Ivan's men would attack the outposts that would most likely respond to an attack on the train. Once notified of these successful attacks, Ivan and his remaining men would reclaim the train. Those attacks would force the military detachments at the train back to their outposts, leaving the train loosely guarded. From there, Ivan and his men would remove the food and provisions. Using a convoy of trucks, they would drive the contents through the mountain passes and back to the Rebel camp south of Sarajevo. From that point, the contents would be distributed to the surrounding shelters of Sarajevo; however, this was a two-day process.

On this day, Ivan and his men observed the targeted Serbian camps. They had to know approximately how many men they would confront. He, and a small group of men, drove northwest of Sarajevo, where he had learned that a large number of Serbian troops were currently deployed.

After having spent the majority of the day surveying the Serbian camps from the surrounding forest, Ivan and his men headed back to the Rebel camp where they conferred with the other group of men that investigated Serbian troops due west of Sarajevo. After hearing what his men had to report, they finalized their plans, then Ivan headed back to Sarajevo.

That evening, Tess did not join Ivan and the men for dinner. She remained in the bedroom. Regardless that Mrs. Tomić brought her another plate of food, she refused to eat. Still stunned from all that had happened, she had no appetite. She repeatedly played the previous evening's moments in her mind, as if thinking about it would help her rationalize it.

With her absence from the dinner table, Ivan and his men were abnormally quiet. The entire house was hushed, which before then they had not noticed. This hush forever imprinted Ivan's tirade in the memories of his men, and in his own heart. It was as though her presence was their reward for all their risk. However, when they did speak, it was to tell Ivan how Mrs. Tomić said that Tess took care of Tomo throughout the day.

Ivan only looked at Tomo, shook his head, and stifled a laugh at Tomo having let Tess take care of him. Tomo was well enough to go with Ivan on his surveillance mission; however, he left Tomo at the house to protect Tess, Mrs. Tomić, and Stefan in the event anything happened in his absence.

Since most of their families were sent away to safe areas of Europe for their protection, the men substituted Tess as a family member. They looked forward to seeing her, and talking with her at mealtime. And though the men missed her presence, no one felt her absence as much as Ivan did. Without Tess at his side, there was a massive void that he could not imagine anyone else filling.

Pushing his untouched plate of food away, Ivan stood and left the room. Sergej and the men watched him, but made no comment as he passed through the kitchen door. He stopped and stood in the entrance to the hall leading to the bedroom. Soft light flowed from the slightly opened door, and he debated going to Tess. He had not seen or spoken to her since he arrived home that evening.

Anguished over his own actions, he sighed. Then he walked soundlessly down the hall and stopped short of the bedroom door. Looking inside, he saw her sitting quietly in the middle of the bed. She was writing; working on a book, he imagined. He remembered the tender words she had written about him as the Black Rebel and he wondered if she still wrote of his goodness. Stepping closer to the door, he knocked softly.

She looked toward the door and, in a hushed tone, she acknowledged whoever knocked as she said, "Yes."

"Tess? It's Ivan. May I come in?" he asked, then listened eagerly for her reply.

"Of course," she answered timidly, then looked back to her notebook.

He pushed the door open, stepped inside, and smiled at her as she continued writing. He noticed her dinner still sitting on the vanity where Mrs. Tomić had left it. He worried about her because he noticed she looked thinner than when he had first met her in Belgrade. Seeing the effect of the war on her, he truly felt he should get her out of Sarajevo. But taking her back to Belgrade would make leaving him easier for her, and he was not prepared for that.

Closing the door, he walked to her and sat at the bottom of the bed. She was quiet and, if he did not know better, looking at her now, he would think she was content. Except he now knew her, and he recognized her remote expression. This look told him that she was deep in distressed thoughts, which he surmised were of Mara, or his unmerited conduct, or both.

He moved closer. He desperately wanted her to notice him, but she only continued with her work. The moment was awkward and he imagined she wished she were anywhere except there with him. From her disposition, he wondered if she felt foolish in her efforts to find Mara. If she did, he had caused her to feel that way. As she quietly wrote, he sensed she attempted to be as inconspicuous as possible. Looking at her now, he believed she wished she could disappear. If so, did she want to disappear because she was afraid of him after his outburst the previous evening? Perhaps she was tired of existing in this war or worse, perhaps she was tired of him?

Feeling she would not be willing to talk with him, he had to be the first to talk. So he tried to draw her from her saddened introspection by lightly placing his hand on her outstretched legs, as he asked, "What are you writing?"

She did not look at him. She only looked at his hand that delicately stroked her shins as he sought her attention. "I'm just writing about things—that's all," she answered as she looked back at her notebook and continued writing.

"What are you listening to?" he asked as he touched the headphones plugged into her compact disc player.

"I don't think you'd like it very much. It's American," she said; however, not sarcastically, but quite innocently.

His gaze darted toward her. Her comment told him that she was not only consumed by the events from the previous evening, she was equally consumed by his past comments about Americans.

Still, he moved closer to her. Trying to gain her attention, he spoke softly as his hand gently grasped her wrist. "How do you know? I enjoy American music," he said, then he waited for her next comment and hoped it would be gentle. While he waited, his feelings for her continually plagued him: the touch, the embrace, the longed for kiss, and the desire to possess her. He felt that by her gentleness, she would consent to his acting on his feelings. However, to his disappointment, she did not respond. After all that had happened between them, she no longer knew how to respond.

He picked up the disc player. "May I?" he asked, indicating that he wanted to listen to her music.

"Of course," she said.

As he picked up the headset, she glanced at him briefly, then returned her attention to her writing. He held the headset to his ears and played the first track on the disc. He knew the song; it was about a farmer that lost his land to Capitalistic American banks. The song spoke of lost dignity and the past pride of America. "How similar to the situation here," he thought, and as he continued to listen, he watched her. He wondered why this song appealed to a woman that lived so far away from the troubles of the farmlands of America—what once was the life's blood of her great country, the country he imagined she loved.

She continued writing and ignored him as the song played on. The man singing portrayed the lost causes of the world in his simple story. When the song ended, Ivan put the headset down, then turned the player off. For a moment, he was speechless, and could only look at her as she wrote while lost in thought. He was curious about her interests, but the silence between them was deafening, and it appeared to block all avenues to her. Then again, perhaps he was only desperate for her attention.

"Why do you listen to such a tragic song?" he asked, trying again to get her to look at him, and hopefully to talk to him.

She paused, looked past him, then looked back to her notebook.

He grasped her wrist again. He felt he had to anger her to make her respond. "Don't you have an answer? Don't you know? Or do you enjoy hearing about other people suffering?" he asked, although he hated talking to her that way.

But it worked—sort of. She jerked her hand away from his gentle grasp. Closing her notebook, she set it to the side along with her pen. Then she slid from the bed and walked to the window. Peeking out at the moon, she was silent.

"Why?" he asked in a low voice.

She felt his need to know why she played this particular song. After a short, soft sigh, she satisfied his curiosity, as she asked, "Did you ever hear of a book called *Heaven's Tears Are Black* by T. Ford?"

He thought for a moment. He remembered reading it. It spoke of the same emotion as the song. It emphasized the experiences of the American farmer and their crisis from government boycotting of the country's own resources. Looking at her, he said nothing. Then he stood, walked toward her, and stopped behind her.

"Yes, I read it when it first came out a few years ago. A client sent it to me; he thought I would enjoy reading it because it somewhat paralleled the start of the breakup of Yugoslavia. He was right; it was a slightly political book. Does it have something to do with this song?" he asked.

"Indirectly, it does," she answered.

"Do you know the man who wrote that book? If you do, I'd love to meet him. His views are similar to those of the victims of this war," Ivan said.

"You already know him," she answered as she turned and looked directly into his eyes. Then she walked past him and stopped at the bed.

He shook his head. He did not remember meeting the author. "How do I know him? When did I meet him?" he asked.

"You're in the same room with him. T. Ford...Tess Fordel."

His expression froze. He could not imagine why she had written such an unsettling book about something a woman like her should have no interest in. "What? You wrote that book? Why?"

"Are you really interested?" she asked.

"Yes. Tell me, please. I want to know what made you write it," he answered, then he walked to the bed and sat down facing her. Bending sideways, he tried to enter her line of vision.

Not looking at him, she began to tell him about the man behind the story, a man similar to Ivan, as she said, "It all began when I bought a new car. Strange, a black Porsche. I picked it up in the evening and thought I'd take it for a drive. This was before I lived in New York. At the time, I lived in Chicago. It was Wednesday. I had driven south from Chicago and, I don't know why, but I just kept driving. It got late, and I stopped at a hotel, got myself a room, and went to bed. The next morning, I got back in the car and drove farther south. Searching for a gas station I took a wrong turn from the major interstate and was lost. I drove into a little town just north of the Shawnee National Forest. Shawnee being a Native American tribe. When driving down the main street of the town, which consisted of a small convenience store, a gas station, and a police/fire station, I saw this parade of sorts. It was all farm equipment, one tractor after another. I pulled into the gas station, filled up, and asked the attendant what was the purpose of the parade. Of course, here I am in this fancy car and wearing this shapely black dress and high heels. I guess he thought I was from another planet. He told me, in a very hateful tone, that the farm equipment was being driven to an auction. The surrounding farms had been foreclosed on because the farmers could not pay their loans. And that day, the farms, and everything related to them, were up for auction."

She stopped and shook her head as she remembered the event in vivid detail. When she continued, he felt the sadness of that event from her words as she portrayed the lost emotions she felt that day.

"I paid for the gas and followed the tractors. I still see those children sitting on the back of those gigantic pieces of farm equipment. They stared at me in my expensive car as they appeared to have nothing, and I had everything, at least in their eyes. The farmers parked their equipment in a vacant lot at a closed fair ground, while others stood helplessly watching. Then the crowd saw me and their helpless stares became somewhat threatening. I didn't know why I was there, but I parked and got out of my car. I had on these black sunglasses so no one could see my eyes, and I imagine that was intimidating, though that was not my intention. Then I approached a platform that held the maps to the farms being auctioned, where on another platform, several men in suits spoke loudly to those who listened."

"As I approached, the men on the platform became silent. One of the men, an auctioneer, sort of asked me what I wanted. I remember his words: 'Are you lost, little girl?' I didn't answer, nor did I remove my glasses, but he knew I stared right at him. He went back to talking to the crowd and explained the procedures that the farmers were to go through in surrendering their land and equipment. I started looking around and noticed a group of men surrounded by what I imagined to be local sheriffs. This group of men sat on folding chairs on another low platform. At a safe distance away, the farmers stood in the dirt as their lives were being stolen and probably because of being a few thousand dollars behind on their loans."

"Not wanting to cause any disruption, I reached for an auction program that listed each farm, the amount due, starting bid amounts, late fees, and the auction fees. They also listed each farm's gross revenues, and the appraised value of each farm. I read it and reviewed the terms of the auction just before it all began. The farms were listed from the highest amount owed to the lowest. Most of the farms were deeply in debt. So deep, that they would never be able to produce enough to get out of debt even if someone gave them the back payments. But the very last farm listed had a debt of a little over fifteen thousand dollars. I thought about how lacking such a small amount of money could ruin someone's life. Especially since the auction program stated this amount equaled the owner's final payments—the land would be theirs if they had made those payments." She paused for a moment. "So close, yet so out of reach." She shook her head, and he knew from her expression that she could not comprehend greed.

"First, they reviewed the land up for auction; the entire town was being stolen. After the potential buyers viewed information on the individual farms, the auction then began. The first farm was up for bid. The men behind the sheriffs began calling out dollar amounts: Fifty thousand, seventy-five thousand, one hundred thousand, and so on. The bids went up fairly high, but nowhere near the appraised values of the farms. It was ridiculous, it was sick. Farm after farm was sold for next to nothing. Then the bidding began on the last farm up for auction. This farm belonged to a man who stood quietly next to his parents. He stood as sure of himself as you do. He was handsome and self-assured, just like you. The other farmers made scenes when their property was sold, but not him. He was silent and, in his own right, elegant, and it was obvious that he was educated. I took off my glasses to see him better and he stared at me. I don't know why, perhaps because I was a stranger. But in his eyes, I—" She shook her head. "I saw him crying out to me. He had these beautiful, desperate eyes that begged me for help."

"Then, as the bidding slowed, he returned his attention to the auctioneer and I put my glasses back on. The bidding had stopped at fifty-eight thousand dollars for land that had been appraised at nearly two million dollars. It was not the largest farm up for auction, but it was the farm with the highest revenue on the list, because it was still operational. The auctioneer was waiting for last bids. Just before he was going to slam the gavel, I looked at the man who owned the farm and I saw tears in his eyes. Tears of acceptance for what he did not have the power to change, and his tears broke my heart.

"One of the clauses of the auction was that the owners of the farms had up until the auctioneer said 'sold' to pay what they owed. If they did, the auction would then be cancelled. I knew the amount owed on this man's farm. Still looking at this man, who was just about to lose his farm, and without knowing why, I yelled out, 'Fifteen thousand, seven hundred and eighty-nine dollars and sixty-three cents, plus auction costs, and late payment fees on behalf of the owners.' The entire crowd stopped everything, even breathing, as you could hear the crowd's collective gasp. Everyone stared at me, but I kept looking at him. I smiled at him, thinking I could reassure him, although of what I didn't know. Perhaps he thought I mocked him like the others. I had no idea, but now his tears were gone."

"'What?' the auctioneer cried out. 'Those are the rules,' I said. The auctioneer tried to argue with me, but I did not yield. Well, the man who bid the highest amount of fifty-eight thousand protested, but then he hesitated as his partners whispered to him. They had already bought seven farms and probably thought that I was an easy target for a later day. I looked at this greedy bidder, started walking toward him, and he froze. As I walked, my attention did not leave him and that frightened him even more. The auctioneer spoke to me. His words were meant to be demeaning as he said, 'Listen up, little girl. What makes you think you can just walk in here, unqualified as you are, and expect this reputable firm to accept your offer to pay the past due, plus other fees owed, on this farm? We don't know you.' He paused, thinking he had embarrassed me. I did nothing, seeing he wanted to continue with his harassment, and he did. 'Now if we take your offer to be good, what do you have to prove that you have the required funds in the first place? Huh? What do you have to give me as collateral until your,' he cleared his throat, *funds* get here?' he asked sarcastically. He looked around to the men, investors, and farmers, and he then started laughing."

She shook her head and smiled. From her expression, Ivan could tell that what she did next was not only appropriate, but she had enjoyed it immensely.

"At the time, I was standing about, oh, I don't know, say ten feet from him. I had the keys to the Porsche in my right hand. Out of impulse, and not wanting that farmer to lose his land to some greedy, heartless man, I threw the car keys at the auctioneer and hit him in the chest. Then I answered, 'One hundred and twenty-five thousand dollars of German perfection, that's what! According to *your* rules, that will pay the debt, but I'll have cash wire transferred into the account of your choosing in less than twenty minutes. And if you will be so kind as to provide a telephone, I'll even pay for the long distance call.' He squinted at me and asked, 'You got the papers for that thing?' I smiled. 'Sure! They're in the glove box, and they have my name on them too. *Imagine that!*'"

Ivan smiled and tried to imagine her doing all of what she described. How he would have loved to have seen her at that moment in time. She was briefly silent, and he could tell she relived the event in her mind. He could also tell that something about the event touched her deeply.

"There was not a sound to be heard from anyone. The auctioneer looked at the man who had bid fifty-eight thousand, so I looked at him too. Knowing the rules of the auction, the other farmers started yelling, then chanting at the auctioneer, saying 'Close!' meaning to close the auction. With a slam of the gavel, the next thing I knew, the auctioneer said the property was released, and all debts were paid as agreed."

She stopped, took a breath, walked back to the window, and looked outside. Just then, the image of Edmund Blair Leighton's painting, *The Accolade*, came to Ivan's mind. The painting's subject was a beautiful lady, knighting a brave man for his outstanding valor. How she resembled the gentle strength in the image of the lady to him at that moment, and he knew her actions, that long ago day, were equal to that farmer being knighted. Ivan looked at her as though she was the most unusual and just person he knew.

Without seeing this look, only sensing it, she addressed his thoughts. "You still don't know what I planned to do, I can feel it. You definitely understand Capitalism better than I do. Just as I could feel that man's desperation when he looked at me, I knew that he had no idea what I had planned. But when I looked back at him, he was happy. Happy that the man named Durrell, who had bid on his land, did not get it, and when I looked at him this time, the look in his eyes was *very* different.

"You see, Ivan, I've been very fortunate, although not from lack of hard work. But that man worked hard, much harder than I ever had, so I shared part of that fortune with him. What I did was pay off the loan, the late payments, and the auction fees. I then got the farm back to the person it rightfully belonged to. I got it back to that man with the desperate and beautiful eyes. Before the day was over, he signed a new deed to the land with him owing no one other than me. As I mentioned, that fifteen thousand plus dollars amounted to their final payments. With very little effort, he had his farm back. Since I knew Willis long before I moved to Manhattan, I called him for assistance. He thought I was insane, as always, but he wired the funds and set up a very simple personal loan repayment document that laid out twenty-five years, without interest, to pay back the funds to me personally. The loan was paid back in less than two months. The payments were behind because his father had lost an arm in an accident. The farm fell into debt at that time, and the son, who had been studying for a law degree, left school to run the farm because his father no longer could."

"At the end of the day, and after finalizing the transaction, I said thank you and good-bye, and walked toward my car. Seeing me leave, the man ran after me. He stopped behind me and asked me why. I told him I just knew I had to when I saw the desperation in his eyes. He was a man whose dignity was being stolen from him because of being a few dollars short, and it wasn't fair. I couldn't help all the farmers, but I did what I could. Still, he just stared at me. I looked back at him and smiled. Then he stepped closer, and I said, 'Don't wonder why the rest of your life, and don't ask me why all this happened because I don't know why. Just live your life and be happy. It all worked out the way it was supposed to.' He then told me that I had saved his and his parents' lives. Saved his farm from the steady stream of men who sought for years to destroy it, and steal the land for pennies on the dollar—again, land which was now worth close to three million dollars, not the nearly two million as was the appraised value stated on the auction program. Besides thanking me for my business help, he wanted to repay me personally. All I had to do was tell him what I wanted. I knew what he meant, and I didn't want that. I would not want that out of debt, only out of love." She attempted to collect her feelings as tears came to her eyes with this memory.

Ivan felt that somehow, someway, something had directed her to that man. Now Ivan had the opportunity to meet her and to help her, but he had not helped her; he set her back in her quest. As Ivan fell into deep thought about his actions toward Tess, he heard her continue, and his attention immediately returned to her, as he stood and walked to her.

"He didn't want to say good-bye, but I got in the car and drove away. From my rearview mirror, I saw him standing in the middle of the road. I could have stayed. Perhaps another woman would have stayed, perhaps used him up, then thrown him away. Another woman might have made him feel like he owed her something, and been harsh in collecting it. It would have been easy to stay with him, so easy, but not right. Shortly after that, I sold my apartment in Chicago and moved to New York. But before I moved, I drove the car back to the dealership and asked them to sell it for me, which they did."

Standing directly behind her, Ivan did not know what to do to comfort her. In silence, a tear ran down her cheek as she concluded her story with a link to the present situation. "Perhaps God sent me there just for that purpose, as now, I am sent here for another purpose. It's not for me to know, but you asked, and I haven't lied to you, nor will I at any time. That was how I came to write that book. All because of the desperation in one man's eyes."

Ivan placed his hands on her shoulders and started turning her to face him. At that moment, he had the courage to take her in his arms and kiss her. He now had the courage to tell her all that he felt for her, but she walked away from him and back toward the bed. Again, she did not want him to see her cry. She did not want to break her promise and she did not want him to be kind to her only because she had done something good. She wanted him to be kind to her because he loved her and he wanted her, for she needed pity from no one.

As he remained standing at the window, he saw her sadness, her solitude. Once more, he felt as though he stood on the opposite side of the world from her. At times, he found her unreal; doing things no other human would even consider, like helping that farmer. And Ivan wanted to repay her for her kindness, especially her kindness to him. But he sensed that she wanted to be alone, so he changed the subject, as he said, "If you won't eat, then you should sleep."

Not answering, she only looked at her notebook on the bed. He walked toward the door, but stopping before he exited, he turned around to look at her. After he and his men recovered the food and provisions from the train, Ivan had an additional task that would take him far away from Tess for several days. He did not want to think about that just then, but he had no choice—he had an appointment in Rome.

"I will be away for five days, maybe six. I will leave Alek and Lukáš with you. They will guard you at all times. They will sleep right outside of this door. They will protect you. If you need anything, just ask them," he said.

"Will they take me to the shelters?" she asked over her shoulder.

"Yes, they will," he answered. He walked back to her. Standing behind her, he placed his hands on her shoulders. "Would you rather go back to Belgrade until I return? Get away from here for a while?" he asked, as he needed her to turn around and look at him. He needed to look into her eyes. He was curious if he would see what he imagined was her love for him there, but to his disappointment, she only looked over her shoulder at him.

"I'll be fine. You go and take care of your business. I wouldn't want to be in your way. Have a safe journey."

He pulled her back against him and kissed her hair. "Five days," he whispered, and kissed her hair again. Then sighing, he let her go and walked back to the door.

She turned around as she heard him leave. For a moment, her heart skipped a beat. She worried about him because she felt he was most likely going out to take care of whatever brought those soldiers to their area the previous evening. She had no idea that Serbian Military had seized the train with their food and supplies, but she also worried because she felt she may not see him again.

"Ivan, be careful," she said, but what she really wanted to say was, "Please don't leave me alone. I don't want to be without you, ever." Yet, she would not keep him from doing whatever he needed to.

"I will," he answered, and smiled at her. From the concern he heard in her voice, he felt she forgave him and cared about him as a friend. He only hoped she could forgive him and, one day, love him as a man. Then, without another word, he stepped from the room, closed the door, and left the house.

She gave a small, despondent sigh, wishing he would come back and not do whatever he felt obligated to do. She shook her head at the thoughts inside her mind, but there was nothing she could do except pray for his safety.

Changing into her robe, she sat at the small table she used as a vanity and brushed her hair. Then she added wood to the fire, blew out the candles in the room, and went to sleep thinking about Ivan. She worried about him and petitioned God for his safety. He had not been gone a half-hour and already she missed him. The thought of never seeing him again tore at her heart as she knew he was going out to risk his life for others. Her final thoughts, before sleep overtook her mind, were her longing for Ivan to return. To Tess, the next five days could not pass quickly enough.

CHAPTER THIRTY-EIGHT

Ivan spent that evening at the Rebel camp. The first attacks would happen after the Serbian forces had secured their compounds for the night, and would most likely be drinking and less attentive to their surroundings. He and his men worked best at night; the darkness enabled them to get in and out of situations with few casualties.

Shortly after midnight, dressed in full camouflage and face paint, Ivan stood in the center of the camp and directed his men. Once he finished issuing orders, the groups dispersed to commence with their plans. Miloš and six other men left the camp to meet with their informants. It was Miloš' job to learn the current intel being issued from the Serbian commanders. Ivan needed to know if the soldiers that were killed the previous evening were sent to find Tess, were there on another mission, or were deserters.

Two additional groups were deployed: one to the west of where the train was being held and one southeast of it. The men were to cut lines of communication and block all escape routes from these camps, then destroy munitions supplies and any vehicles located at the camps. Once that was accomplished, they were to return to the Rebel camp south of Sarajevo.

Ivan and Sergej, followed by eighteen additional men, left the camp for the hijacked train. At their rendezvous point, they received word that the attack on the Serbian encampment to the west of the train was successful. As expected, the Serbian outposts deployed the troops nearest to the train to aid the wounded and defend the attacked encampment.

Shortly after, the second report came in that the camp to the southeast of the train had been rendered inoperable. The only available personnel to assist were from the seized train, so Ivan patiently waited as the majority of soldiers departed from the train. And though he could not figure out why the hijackers had not already cleared out the train, he was grateful that they had not.

With the train loosely guarded, now was the right time to make their move. While six men stayed with the trucks, Ivan ordered six other men to make their way around to the north side of the train, while Sergej and the remaining six approached from the south. Crouching in the darkness, they quickly crept up on the train.

It was a strangely silent night, and the only sounds heard were the soldiers' voices from inside the train and the wind that blew briskly outside of it. Aided by the clouds covering the moon, Ivan and his men were able to get within twenty feet of the train, which was just at the end of the trees parallel to the tracks. As the wind blew cold against Ivan's back, he signaled his men to stop. He then radioed the men to the north to enter the train, but as they neared it, the skirmish began as the soldiers inside the train fired at them. From the number of discharged rounds, Ivan approximated that five to eight men remained inside.

Ivan waited for the cease-fire and soon all was quiet. The soldiers in the train misjudged that the intruders were either gone or dead. But in the darkness, Ivan watched them through his night-vision goggles, and he saw his men, on foot, approaching the rear of the train. Then one of the soldiers ventured from the train and Ivan raised his rifle into position. Following the soldier in the rifle's scope, he squeezed the trigger, then the shot rang out. The round pierced the soldier's thigh, forcing him to the ground, where he rolled, moaned, and grabbed for his wounded leg.

When the soldiers inside the train figured out it was not over, they fired into the darkness toward Ivan, who positioned himself behind the trunk of a large tree. He fired a few rounds back at them to keep their attention in his direction, while Sergei and his men successfully entered the train from the opposite side.

Within minutes, the train was under Ivan's command as his men took control of the soldiers and led them out onto the snow covered ground. They forced them to kneel five feet apart from each other and to clasp their hands behind their heads. Then they began tying their hands behind their backs. Sergej approached Ivan as the convoy of trucks drove up behind the group. Then the men from the trucks immediately began transferring the food and supplies from the train.

Casually carrying his rifle in his right hand with its barrel pointed toward the ground in a non-aggressive position, Ivan walked past the soldiers, now his prisoners. One by one, he looked at them. The truck's glaring headlamps proved a harsh light against the night as Ivan's shadow overpowered the kneeling men as he passed them. He stopped at one man who tried to hide his face, but something about this man was familiar, so he said, "You! What is your name?"

The man did not answer.

Tipping the end of his rifle up, Ivan rested it on the man's chest. *"What is your name?"* he asked again.

"Burić," the man mumbled.

Ivan could not hear him, nor could he see his face, which annoyed him. Taking a firmer grip on the rifle's stock, it made a snapping sound as Ivan secured his index finger on the trigger. He stuck the end of the barrel under the man's chin to raise his head so that he could see the man's face. "Look at me when I talk to you. When you answer me, speak so that everyone will hear you. What is your na—" Just then, Ivan stopped as he beheld a man he knew well. He gave a small laugh. "Josip Burić. On your knees is a good place for you."

Burić glared at him, but did not recognize him.

Staring at Burić, Ivan's subconscious recalled every memory of Burić that he had, and reliving them further angered him. "Tell me, did you have a brother named Jasa?" Ivan asked, although he already knew the answer was yes.

At once, Burić began cursing him in Serbian as he tried to move from the end of the rifle. Ivan knew Burić had respect for no one, and he stood there as memories of Burić's cruelty haunted him. From Burić's actions, Ivan could tell that nothing had changed, but he could also tell that, still, Burić had no idea as to his true identity.

"Be still!" Ivan ordered.

Burić immediately stopped moving.

Ivan removed the rifle from his throat, but he did not point it toward the ground as he previously had. "You're angry because of your brother's death. Am I cruel? If so, it is because this is a war that greedy men like you have started. But you are the type of man that would always be bad," Ivan said, then he walked on and stood a few feet away.

The other soldiers were quiet as they watched Ivan, and they saw the anger and strength of the Black Rebel; however, Burić was angry and he attempted to upset Ivan's plans. Ivan knew this, and so he ignored his ranting, when he said, "He is the one who killed your brothers!" Burić looked at his comrades, then back at Ivan. "They will find you and they will kill you!"

"Who are *they?* Your dog friends here? The sadistic leaders of your army? Who are these people that have such big plans that they leave a fool like you in charge of nothing?" Ivan said, then he took several steps toward him, although Burić only laughed as Ivan waited for answers. He knew Burić could not tell him what he did not know, and since no one had mentioned Tess, Ivan felt his carefully planned rumor that the American woman had already left Bosnia, and returned to America, had circulated. Ivan had spread this rumor, and his informants confirmed that it had spread, but how far it had reached was unknown until now.

"One good thing will come from this meeting. You will no longer be taking young boys from shelters and making them fight in your army," Ivan said.

When Burić stopped laughing, Ivan smirked at him, lifted his rifle to his shoulder in a ready position, and pointed it at him as the other kneeling men watched. Then Burić started laughing again because he was positive that Ivan would not shoot him. Where he gathered this idea, no one would know. But this moment was serious and, again, Ivan reminisced about Burić's cruel ways. Then, without a second thought, Ivan fired a single round into his chest, although he stayed staring at Ivan for a moment, then he fell forward to the ground.

Out of anger, the man to the left of Burić's body struggled to stand, then he rushed toward Ivan. Turning the butt of the rifle toward the charging man, Ivan struck him once in the chest. The blow took the man off guard and he bent over, gasping for air. With a shove, Ivan pushed the man over and onto the ground, where he remained.

Ivan's display of anger paralyzed the other soldiers and they wondered what would be their fate. Then Ivan pointed his rifle toward the ground as Rurik approached him. Rurik told him that they had emptied the train and were ready to return to the Rebel camp. The sun would rise in several hours and Serbian troops would soon converge on the area. As much as Ivan wanted to, he could not go back to the camp to help; he had to leave, he had to get to Rome, and the sooner he left, the sooner he could return to Tess.

As if conversing with himself, Ivan shook his head and looked at the row of soldiers. Then he looked back at Rurik, who waited for orders. "Load them in the train and lock them inside. Tend to the soldier with the leg wound, then get him inside the train as well," he said, then he turned around and walked away.

"Then what?" Rurik asked.

"Then nothing. Their comrades will find them soon enough," Ivan answered over his shoulder as he continued walking toward his jeep.

The loaded trucks began to leave in two convoys, and Sergej watched them pull away from the train and head back toward the Rebel camp. He then saw Ivan walking away and went after him. "Hey, don't go," Sergej said as he attempted to convince Ivan to not keep his appointment. "Think of Tess. Don't be reckless. Do you really need to check in with them? If they're so interested in Catholics in Sarajevo, let them come here instead of hiding behind their pristine robes."

Ivan did not look at Sergej. "I have to go. Load the soldiers in the train, lock them in, then go home," he said.

"You need protection getting out of Bosnia."

"I'll be fine."

"When they find these soldiers locked up, the authorities will be all over the area trying to find—"

"Protect the camp," Ivan said, interrupting Sergej.

"Protect it? How?"

"Move it, disperse the men, do whatever is needed," Ivan ordered in an annoyed tone.

"Your traveling alone is suicide. There could be ambushes on the roads. You can't do this. You can't drive to Split without protection."

"I have no choice. If I don't go, we become *their* target," Ivan said, referring to the authorities in Rome. Reaching for a towel on the front seat of the jeep, Ivan started to wipe the camouflage paint from his face.

Sergej shook his head. He was unnaturally disturbed with this scenario. "This is a setup. It has to be a setup. Take someone with you."

"No. If it is a setup, you and the others must be safe," Ivan said.

"What do I tell Tess if you don't come back?" Sergej asked.

Ivan looked down at the ground. He did not know what Sergej should tell Tess. He only knew that he needed to go and that the safety of everyone depended upon his keeping this appointment.

"This is insane," Sergej whispered under his breath.

"Take the food and distribute it. Send the best home to Mama and Tess. Leave what is needed at the camp, then feed the children. Feed all of them: Nationalists and non-Nationalists, Serb, Croat, and Bosniak children, and their mothers too. Then if anything is left, give it to whoever remains. Let them know who it is from, and let them know this is the last help we will be able to provide," Ivan ordered, then he sat in his jeep and closed the door.

"What about Tess? What do I tell her?" Sergej asked.

"If something happens to me, make sure she gets back to America safely."

"I can't send her home without telling her the truth!" Sergej said.

"You tell her nothing. Just get her back to New York." Ivan took a deep breath. "If anything happens, Vlaović dies. Find out everyone he has dealings with as well."

Sergej said nothing, he only nodded.

"Don't worry. I'll be back. Just keep the satellite lines open."

"What about Mara? What do I tell her? She'll never be the same if anything happens to you"

"Mama will take care of Mara."

"What about Tess? Shouldn't she ever get to meet Mara? Even if just to know she's okay?" Sergej asked.

"I leave that up to you. If anything happens to me, you choose Mara's fate," Ivan said, then added, "I know you will choose wisely."

Sergej nodded. The thought of Ivan not returning would crush so many lives, but especially Mara's and Tess'. Sergej could not imagine why Ivan's connections in Rome felt a meeting was necessary just then. Nor could he imagine why Ivan agreed to go, except he could only reason that Ivan sensed he had lost Tess. Because of this, he did not care for his own safety.

With a nod, Ivan started the jeep and drove away. Sergej watched it fade into the darkness as he silently prayed, "God Bless the Black Rebel."

CHAPTER THIRTY-NINE

For the five days that Ivan was gone, Tess took charge of Sergej's house. From top to bottom, she cleaned everything in sight: all the linens, the clothes, and even the tattered draperies, which they closed at night to keep out the cold, hide the interior light from leaking to the outside, and to prevent anyone from seeing in. Alek and Lukáš made certain that Tess was safe and always escorted. They took this war seriously. They took Ivan's orders seriously, and his orders were that if anyone touched her, they were to kill them: Serb, Croat, Bosniak, or whoever. Other than his men, Stefan, and Mrs. Tomić, no one was to go near Tess in Ivan's absence. So Alek and Lukáš were happy that she opted against venturing out of the house in search of Mara.

Though sporadic, attacks had resumed. Due to the strikes on the Serbian outposts, and the men that were found on the empty train, the safest place for Tess was out of sight. And though the sounds of the hostilities could be heard inside the house periodically, it did not bother her; she was busy cleaning the house for Ivan's return. She wanted to surprise him, to show him that deep down she was not really a spoiled American. He had protected her during her search for Mara and she wanted to repay him for his kindness.

During the time they spent together, she learned what a great leader he was. She respected him, though he periodically sought to anger her, but possibly he angered her to keep her senses sharp. She sat in the middle of a war, but he made certain that she was untouched by the death and poverty that surrounded them. When she stepped onto the train in Belgrade, she placed her life in Ivan's hands. She knew no amount of money could save her; only Ivan could save her from, and defend her against, the atrocities of the war.

Being the Black Rebel, Ivan had a high price on his head. Though no one knew exactly who he was, they knew of him. All sides in the war wanted to kill him, just so they could say they had. In the beginning, they felt that if they could kill the Black Rebel, they would have slain a major foe, because no one knew what side he was on. Although Ivan barely had that amount of influence, he was the strength behind his men, and the strength that led them in their attacks against all perpetrators' cruelty in this war.

Tess believed that Ivan feared nothing and no one, and he certainly did not fear her. However, she was wrong, he did fear something, although it was not obvious because he hid it from those around him. The one thing that frightened Ivan was losing Tess. Though he sometimes became lost in his righteous intentions, and ignored what she felt, he was a man with extreme compassion. He had an overwhelming quality of devotion that she had not seen in any man, and though at times he appeared superhuman, at others, he was completely human. In her eyes, he was all man and the greatest type of man—one with a heart of an immeasurable capacity for love.

CHAPTER FORTY

Ivan made it safely to Split where he boarded a cargo ship headed for the Port of Ancona, Italy. From Ancona, he would fly to Rome, then make his way to the Vatican for his audience with Cardinal Vlaović—Ivan's liaison to the Roman Catholic Church's highest position, the Pope.

Exiting a taxi near the rear entrance to the Vatican, Ivan waited for the taxi to drive off before he started walking. Briefly scanning the surrounding civilians, he then headed toward a man sitting on a granite bench.

The man was reading a newspaper, but looked up as Ivan neared. "It's good to see you," Vlaović said in Italian, avoiding calling Ivan by name. He then folded his paper, stood, and extended his hand to Ivan.

Ivan smiled, shook his hand, and looked over his shoulder as if he heard someone there.

"Is someone with you?" Vlaović asked.

"No, but it was a long trip and not a good time to be away," Ivan said.

"I understand. I will not detain you longer than required," Vlaović stated, then motioned Ivan to follow him.

They entered the Vatican via a secret entrance used only by the most elite staff. Ivan followed Vlaović in silence, but was ever cautious of his surroundings and of those that he passed. There was to be no conversation until they entered Vlaović's private quarters, but as they walked, Ivan's mind could not concentrate on his reason for being there. He could only think about Tess and wonder if she was alright.

After passing through an extended maze of corridors, Vlaović stopped in front of a set of massive and heavily carved arabesque-arched doors of dark wood where two traditionally dressed guards stood at attention. With a hand signal from Vlaović, they turned the weighty brass knobs on each door, then opened them. Vlaović passed through the threshold as Ivan followed, then the doors closed immediately behind them, sounding a deep clank that echoed throughout the foyer.

Inside was Vlaović's private chamber. And a magnificent chamber it was, with ceiling paintings that Ivan had not seen, not even in photographs. He removed his sunglasses and, for a moment, he stared at the ceiling. He admired the heavenly scenes as valets dressed Vlaović in his red cassock, skullcap, and jewelry. Once they finished, Vlaović dismissed the valets, then he and Ivan were alone.

Ivan looked at Vlaović, smiled, then bent and kissed his ring in respect and proper greeting. When Ivan stood straight, Vlaović noticed his exhausted, red-eyed gaze. "You are tired. After our meeting, you will rest here," he ordered.

Ivan shook his head. "No time. I need to get back."

"Ah, someone waits for you," Vlaović said, as he smiled and sat in his throne-like chair. He hoped the answer was yes and that it was a woman that Ivan needed to get back to, not the war. To Vlaović, all men out of religious order should be married and having children, for that was the Catholic way. He then motioned for Ivan to sit on one of the ornately carved sofas of crimson velvet adjacently positioned to each side of his chair. "Are you hungry? Thirsty?"

Ivan shook his head as he sat. "Your Eminence, why was I called here now? What is so important?"

"We have not heard from you in three months. My superiors have questions," Vlaović said. "What happened with the children?" He meant the children at the three shelters at Kiseljak, Gromiljak, and Fojnica.

"All we know is that they were attacked by troops looking for provisions. The attacks were random. Other shelters were attacked on the same day."

"Did you find the Serbs that did this?"

"Serbians did not attack the shelters," Ivan said sternly.

"Then who? They are the aggressors of this war," Vlaović stated.

"They did not start this war, and they are not the only aggressors. Every side there participates."

"If the Serbs did not attack the shelters, who did?" Vlaović asked.

"The others. They had wrong information and thought they were attacking Serbian refugees," Ivan said, and by this he meant that these attacks were Croatian and Bosniak aggression under the misconception that the shelters housed only Serbians. Yet, those killed were Croatian and Bosniak.

"Our people did this to our children?" Vlaović asked in a slightly accusatory tone as if Ivan would lie.

"You're surprised at how hatred makes people irrational? That it makes people act without reason?" Ivan commented with somewhat disbelief.

Vlaović shook his head and looked away. It was obvious that he felt those he referred to as "our people" were getting out of control. He sighed and looked back at Ivan, donning what Ivan felt was a less accusatory expression. "What about the train with the provisions we sent. That was seized, wasn't it? Did you find who did it? Were you able to salvage anything?" Vlaović asked.

"We have everything," Ivan said, but deep down, he felt that this meeting was useless and only a show of authority.

"Will anyone be able to link the recovery back to you?" Vlaović asked.

Ivan laughed. "Isn't everything my fault?"

"Let's keep it that way for now. This means they all fear you, but they have no idea who you are. Because if they learn who you are, they will learn about me, and that cannot happen," Vlaović said.

"No one will find out. I am a phantom, and it is easiest to blame that which does not exist," Ivan said.

"They worry that you stray from your original purpose," Vlaović said sternly as if preparing to scold a child.

"Stray from my original purpose?" Ivan gave a muted laugh under his breath. "We do not live in the Dark Ages. I'm not a sanctioned knight for the Roman Catholic Church. I am not a sword of God," he said as his temper started to show.

Vlaović's eyebrows jolted up. "You're more a holy knight than any of those soldiers! You're more a sword of God than they could ever wish to be! Your sense of probity is beyond reproach. Your fidelity to God, and to your people, is beyond the call of duty. Your courage to fight to protect the innocent is legendary," he insisted, then added, "Your mercy and charity is displayed as you feed and protect *everyone.*"

Ivan noticed slight condemnation in Vlaović's tone when he said *everyone* and, for a moment, Ivan stared at him, wondering about the meaning behind his words. Then he shook his head, and his gestures displayed his building anger over Vlaović's comment as he said, "I do not discriminate, nor am I the Vatican's Ustaše. We made a deal and I've kept it. I've kept as many Roman Catholics safe and fed throughout this war as you have provided for."

"Some think you overdo," Vlaović commented.

"I live by principle, not by preference. Am I supposed to feed and protect the one on my left and leave the two on my right wanting? These are children! They are innocent! They cannot help what religion or nationality they are. That is their inheritance, and for some, unfortunately, their curse," he said protectively.

He paused and looked away at one of the wall paintings. It was a painting of the Archangel Michael wielding his sword against Satan, depicted as the Dragon. He thought about the responsibility that he felt God had placed on him, and he wondered if his involvement was what God wanted.

Shaking his head, he looked back at Vlaović. "If our deeds are not better than those who oppose us, how will anyone see us as better than the opposition? You want their souls for the Roman Catholic Church? Feed them, keep them safe! The people need kindness while the greedy little boys, who run these countries, play their war games."

Vlaović was silent, but Ivan was annoyed that anyone dared to question him after he risked his life for so many years. Did *they* know the multitude of times that he brushed death's shoulder? Did *they* even care? Did *they* know the multitude of God's children that he had buried and prayed for? *They* were not present at those moments, and his quick analysis deduced that *they* did not know, nor did *they* care.

"I will continue to save all I can. I will not compromise my beliefs. I follow God's law, doesn't the Church?"

"You save many," Vlaović said, and he saw Ivan was deeply upset.

Ivan stared straight at him. "I also take lives, but I am not your executioner." He laughed. "So much for love thy enemy."

"The concern is that the other souls you save will eventually take up arms against us," Vlaović stated.

"That is their liability to God, not mine. The Good Samaritan does not choose who to help, he helps all God puts in his path."

Vlaović leaned toward Ivan. "These are my countrymen as well, and I agree with giving to all. I agree with saving as many of God's children as possible, regardless of their faith," he said, then he sat back in his chair.

Ivan shook his head. He did not believe Vlaović, and from this feeling, he knew his time fighting this war was coming to an end.

"*They* expect something else from you," Vlaović said, and his choice of words suggested that he did not agree with his superiors.

"What do *they* expect now?" Ivan asked.

"They want you to rebuild the Roman Catholic faith in Bosnia."

"I don't think it's fallen."

"It is less than it should be. This war has stripped it from our people."

"It remains."

"Is that a yes?"

"It is a no."

"Are you sure? The rewards will be great."

"Rewards are only rewards if you live long enough to enjoy them. No one knows me. I like it that way and expect it to stay that way. I came into this war like a lion, but I will leave like a lamb. My greatest prayer is to be forgotten," Ivan said, and it was obvious that he was offended by their request.

Vlaović sighed. "This will be difficult to explain. No one knows the situation there better than you do. Are you sure you won't reconsider?"

"Yes, I am sure. That is a position for a church leader. Besides, I will not be a target after the peace accord is finalized."

"You mean it is not finalized?"

"There are disagreements over the new borders."

"And if they don't come to an agreement?"

"The killing continues."

Vlaović nodded and asked, "Are you declining this position because of the American woman?"

Disgusted with his inquiry, Ivan frowned at him, but wondered, "Who told him about Tess?"

"The rumor circulating is that she has left Bosnia, but from your silence, I think she is still with you," Vlaović said, staring into Ivan's eyes as if that would make Ivan tell him the absolute truth.

Staring back at him, Ivan nodded. "The rumor is true. She is gone," he said, fully convinced that it was factual.

"Was the rumor false that she was from America and was Roman Catholic?"

"No," Ivan said, volunteering no additional information.

"Are you certain?"

Ivan said nothing. He only stared at him, indicating that was enough interrogation.

"If for any reason she remains, do not worry, your secret is safe with me."

"Who told you?" Ivan asked.

"If I tell you, would you kill him because he knows?"

"That depends on who he is and who else he plans to tell."

"He will not tell anyone, but if you must know, he was a Sarajevo priest at the church where she attended mass."

Ivan looked at him. He knew the priest had died two days after Tess was at mass there. But more strangely, he was a Serbian Orthodox priest, not Roman Catholic. This told Ivan that Vlaović monitored him from many sources, which was not surprising.

"You shot and killed a man there to protect her. That was risky, but necessary. We understand this. You have helped many and we will not forget that, but even phantoms deserve happiness."

"Who exactly are *we?*"

Vlaović did not answer.

Then Ivan's expression turned cold. "I will not come here again. I do not plan to come to Italy again. Once this war is over, I do not plan to go to Austria, Croatia, or Germany for a very long time. I hope you understand me," he said, waiting for a sign of acknowledgement.

Vlaović nodded slightly. "The account, your account, at the Vatican Bank—the money still waits there."

Ivan purposely did not take any money from them as payment in order to minimize any link between him and the Vatican. Once the war ended, he wanted no connection back to them.

Ivan shook his head. "I do not want their money. I do not risk for money. I risk for love of my country and its people, what's left of both. What the Church preaches, I practice."

"We cannot all be heroes."

Vlaović's comment made Ivan laugh to himself. He shook his head, leaned forward, and rested his elbows on his thighs. "I am no hero. I pray God forgives me someday," he whispered, then he stared at the floor as visions of all he had seen since the beginning of this war passed through his mind.

Seeing Ivan's sudden sadness, Vlaović reached toward him and placed his hand on his shoulder. "You need no forgiveness. The sin is not yours. But," he smiled sadly, "if you have sinned in another way," he said, placing his hand on Ivan's head, "I absolve you of your sins and ask our Heavenly Father to *bless and protect you always.*"

Vlaović then sat back in his chair. When Ivan looked up at him, Vlaović saw the toll the war had taken on him, and he was saddened by the thought that he would not see Ivan in the future. Ivan was one of the few people he trusted, but he knew that Ivan's contribution to the fight was over, and it was right that Ivan had his life back.

They both stood, and Vlaović walked Ivan to the door. "Should you ever need refuge, these doors will always be open to you. You will always be safe here. You, and anyone you bring with you," he said, and smiled at Ivan, who nodded. "You should take a different route back. Choose a way that gives you the most options if you should have to change your mode of transportation suddenly," he said, then he stopped in front of the doors. "Do you understand?"

Ivan nodded again. He understood that Vlaović knew someone watched him. Someone knew he was there. And if that someone knew he was there, what else did they know?

"Please, be safe," Vlaović concluded, then he knocked on the door. Two guards opened the doors and Vlaović turned to look at them. "We are through," he said in Italian. Then turning to Ivan, he extended his hand to him. "May God be with you, my son."

Ivan bowed and kissed his ring. "Thank you for hearing my confession, Your Eminence," he answered in Italian. Standing upright, Ivan smiled, slid his sunglasses onto his face, then left with the two guards by the same route from which he had entered.

Once at the street, he began his journey home. He took Vlaović's recommendation of an alternate route seriously, but he needed to return to Sarajevo immediately. His concern was that if he was being watched, perhaps so was Sergej's house. This put everyone there in danger, especially Tess.

He walked several blocks away before hailing a taxi to the airport. Once there, he exited the taxi at the departures curb, walked into the terminal, and to the ticket counter. Using an alias, Ivan purchased a new ticket to Ancona from a different airline, then he made his way to the gate where he waited for his plane to board. Scanning the passengers in the waiting area, he did not notice anyone suspicious. When they called for his flight to board, he entered the plane and took his seat.

Once at the port of Ancona, he made his way to the docks and inquired about the next cargo ship headed for Split. There would not be one for two days; however, he did learn that a small ship used to transport refugees from Split would leave in two hours, heading back there. Finding the captain, Ivan discussed sailing back with him. The captain was reluctant to allow Ivan on board, but when he revealed his alternate identity as Ivo Zajć, a Croatian citizen and an executive member of the Croatian Delegate's Union, the captain agreed to ferry him across the Adriatic to Split. Unfortunately, nothing was easy during war, and lying became second nature.

Ivan was wary all during the crossing, but once they docked in Split, he disappeared into a crowd of multi-ethnic refugees hurrying to board the ship. From there, he made his way to the warehouse where he had parked his jeep. After checking it for tampering, he then began the long drive back to Sarajevo, the long drive back to Tess.

CHAPTER FORTY-ONE

As promised, Ivan returned to Sarajevo in five days. Once through the mountains of Croatia, and at the Bosnian border, he was met by three of his men: Nikolai, Zoran, and Dragan. As he predicted, there were no ambushes, and no trouble of any kind along the way. He felt whoever Vlaović thought was following him was still in Italy. In Bosnia, all sides were at a standstill after the train incident, and the negotiations of the new peace accord appeared to aid their safe passage on their journey back to Sarajevo.

Driving through the mountains of Bosnia, they did not stop to rest. The weather had been mild, which was to their benefit, and no winter storms impeded their return. Ivan drove the entire way back to Sarajevo with Dragan riding shotgun while Nikolai and Zoran followed in a jeep behind them. Ivan wanted to be back with Tess and, though he was exhausted, her image kept him awake. Mentally, and physically, he felt there was nothing else he could give to his people. Feeling depleted, Ivan's final hope was that Tess would not shun him when he returned, for he needed her more than anyone needed him.

During Ivan's time away, Mrs. Tomić became ill and was unable to cook for the men. In her stead, Tess cared for them. They came straggling back to the house in sets of two and three; none of which came home empty handed—they all presented her with food. They said nothing, only smiled at her as she laughed at them and their edible gifts. Each time the front door opened, she held her breath hoping it was Ivan. She was waiting for Ivan to arrive safely; without him, she felt inappropriate being in Sergej's house.

Yet, Ivan was always the last one to arrive; the strategist who left first and made sure every man returned safely. On those occasions when one of his men suffered mortally, he made sure they were cared for until their passing. He would not let any of his men fall prisoner to the opposition. And if he were in that position, he knew his men would do the same for him. He strove for the safety of his men, and his dedication paid off.

With his eternal gratitude to God, this mission was successful, and his men were unharmed. This mission was not simply to retrieve the hijacked food and supplies. This mission sent his message to the heads of the warring governments to back off. This mission sent the message that said, "I have treated you with mercy, do not interfere again."

And though there was nothing to identify which group confiscated the hijacked train's goods, it had all the earmarks of the Black Rebel. Only he would take risks for his people—take risks and spare the lives of the thieving soldiers left behind to guard the train.

Once the food was back at the Rebel camp, it was distributed as Ivan had ordered—Mrs. Tomić and Tess were first on the list of recipients. Next, they fed the children, then the adults. Since being around Tess, he found it increasingly difficult to be heartless, and as he had previously ordered, he included all the Nationalists' children and their mothers on the distribution routes. Yet, in the past few weeks, Ivan had changed and this reformation was something Tess brought out in him.

Although he had not previously deprived the Nationalists' children, his actions now proved that children should not have to pay for the disagreements of their parents. For Tess, he did this because she showed him the path back to his kindness. And from this, the Black Rebel was becoming known as the Silent Savior of Sarajevo—a term that slipped out, in English, in front of Tess when Stefan was talking to Alek, although Tess pretended not to hear. Because of the Black Rebel's mercy, no direct retaliation from the train incident occurred by any side involved. Nevertheless, all aggressive forces still schemed to kill him, though the mothers, wives, and children that he fed, hoped for his continued safety.

Regardless that the war's end was so near, he was the only man who now saved them from the desolate fate surrounding them. Even though he fought against all aggressors, he was a peace loving man. And though his actions confused many, most revered his ability, as well as his compassion. They now described him as the twin-edged sword of loyalty and justice, with one edge being sharper than the next. However, the meaning was a warning that the Black Rebel's mood could become aggressive just as quickly as it had become generous. And so some of those he helped saw him as the equivalent to the Archangel Michael, taking no side, only obeying God's orders without question.

CHAPTER FORTY-TWO

The sun had set hours before Ivan arrived at the house. Walking through the front door, he smiled, and took a second look around. At first, he thought he had walked through a time warp. Despite the mismatched furniture, the inside of the house looked almost as it did before the fighting had begun, as everything was fresh and clean. The house even smelled different. It smelled like Tess' perfume. Closing and locking the door behind himself, he heard men's voices sounding from the kitchen. He removed his coat, laid it over the back of the sofa, and went to find them.

Walking through the open door to the kitchen, he found Sergej, Alek, and Lukáš, laughing as they stood eating. At once, they greeted him. He asked them what had happened to the house and they told him that, in his absence, Tess had been cleaning. It was then that he noticed their clean clothes.

"Where is Tess?" he asked, smiling, and looking around for her.

Sergej motioned toward Ivan's bedroom. Desperate to see her, Ivan quickly walked down the hall. As he approached the room, he saw the door was open slightly. From his hiding place in the shadows, his eyes followed the long sliver of light that shone through the crack where the door met the frame. As he looked through it, the vanity's candle light illuminated his view. He saw her sitting at the vanity wearing the dress she had on the night he introduced himself to her in Belgrade. Only this time she did not have the front buttoned, and he noticed she wore nothing under the dress. As she raised her hands to brush her hair, the top of the dress opened, revealing what he had only imagined until that moment, and he smiled lovingly at her precious beauty. Standing there in the darkness, he thought that she was a heavenly prize for any soldier to return home to.

It was then that he noticed the scars on her breasts. He frowned and wondered what had happened to her. Who could have done that to her? His fists clenched defensively as his anger built. He wanted to know who was responsible for the offense so that he could seek justice in her honor, but the only person that came to mind was her ex-husband.

Watching Tess, her grace calmed him, and he unclenched his fists. He wanted to go to her, but he stayed there, admiring her in secret. When she finished brushing her hair, she placed the brush on the vanity. She then leaned to her right to retrieve something from a small piece of luggage she kept on the floor. As she did, her clean, soft hair fell gracefully over her shoulder and across her chest. His immediate reaction was to enter and hold her hair out of her way, but he stayed in place.

Sitting up straight, she moved her hair behind her shoulders. In her hand, he saw she held a bottle of perfume. When she removed the cap, a draft quickly carried the scent toward him. It attacked his senses, as his eyes closed, and he wondered what it would be like to be with this mystifying and strong woman. Having no one, she had to be strong—deep down, he knew she was much more than that. But what he needed to know was, if she would be his.

In his mind, he felt as though this scene resembled the fairy tales his mother told him as a child before he went to sleep at night; tales of medieval warrior princes and their fair maidens. As a child, he often dreamt of being a strong warrior prince. As a child, he also dreamt that someday he would fight mighty battles, and find his fair maiden. Looking at her, he now felt that he had accomplished these dreams. He had fought mighty battles, and, when it came down to it, Tess was a fair maiden and more to him.

Opening his eyes, he saw Tess looking down as she stared at the papers about Mara. Placing her head in her hand, she cried, and he heard the helpless words she whispered: "Mara, where are you? Will I ever find you? If only I knew that you're alright."

Seeing this, guilt broke his heart because he had lied to her about Mara. Although she never really cried in front of him, he had never doubted the sincerity of her need to find Mara, he only doubted her purpose. But now that he knew she was not against him, how could he begin to tell her all that he felt for her? How could he make her believe that he had done what he thought was right, though he now knew it was wrong? Dismissing those questions, he knocked softly on the door.

Hearing a knock, she looked over her shoulder and said, "Yes."

"Tess, it's Ivan." He paused. "I'm home," he said, then stepped back from the door.

Wiping her moist cheeks, she then buttoned her dress, and answered, "I'll be in the kitchen in a minute. I'll get your dinner."

"I'll wait for you there," he said, and respecting her implied request for him not to enter, he walked back down the hall and into the kitchen. The men had already moved into the living room, though Ivan waited for Tess at the doorway between the kitchen and the dining room. Leaning against the doorframe, he anticipated seeing her.

Then he heard the sound of her shoes on the wood floor as she approached. Then she appeared in the doorway, and she stood in the shadows of the hall. He saw her smile at him, although he frowned when he noticed her hair tied back. He enjoyed seeing her hair when it hung over her shoulders. He enjoyed watching it—it moved with her, and was alive like animated strands of perfumed silk. Standing there, looking at her, he realized how beautiful she was to him. He wanted to go to her and take her in his arms. He wanted to kiss her to show her how much he had missed her, but he stood still.

Seeing his hesitation, she stepped forward into the dim light of the kitchen. "Welcome home. Was your trip a success?" she asked, then she walked to the cabinet where the mismatched, but clean, dishes were stored. Not looking at him, she reached for a bowl and walked to the large brick stove at the opposite side of the room.

Not saying a word, he stood in place and watched her. The two extreme sides of life he had seen in a single day: from the struggle of fighting a war, to the peace and security of being there with her. Where once he felt peace and security in being alone, since he had met her, being alone caused him immense angst.

"Aren't you hungry?" she asked then waited for him to approach.

He did not answer, only smiled as he stared directly into her eyes from where he stood.

"What's wrong? Cat got your tongue?" she asked, then laughed quietly.

His expression made her look away, then her laugh quickly faded into a sweet smile. She removed the lid from a large pot that hung over a low burning fire in the fireplace, and ladled a freshly made stew into the bowl. Then she covered the pot. Carrying the bowl, she walked toward him. He was at a loss for words. He watched her as she moved closer. Gracefully, in fluid motion, she approached him, and still, he was mute as he recalled his past actions toward her. But in his silence, words of love and devotion passed through his mind, and he stood there admiring her as she awaited his response.

Looking deeply into her eyes, that allowed his entrance into her soul, he pondered many things about her. Like bolts of lightning, questions plagued his mind, but disappeared faster than they had formed. Could she not know the purpose of the men in the house? Why did she come from America to walk into a war for his little Mara? Why was she, out of all the people in the world, so concerned with a seven-year-old child? Was she that lonely? He knew he was, as her arrival forced his loneliness on him like an incurable disease. If she was not lonely, was she so dedicated to goals that, once committed to them, only death could stop her?

Just then, he felt how he was sick and tired of death and destruction. He wanted out, and when he looked into her eyes, he saw his escape—escape in her kindness that waited there for his taking. He remembered the children she had seen on her visits to the shelters. He remembered, and envied, how they laid in her arms as she held them and whispered sweetly to them. He remembered them hugging her as she played with them and held them to her. That was what he wanted. He wanted her love and devotion. He wanted her affection, the tenderness of her embrace, and the fidelity and passion of her love. He wanted her for his own, and he did not want to share her with anyone, not even with Mara, at this point.

Still silent and looking at her, there it was, her affection for him radiating in her gaze. Or was it only his imagination playing tricks on him? Was he so in love with her now that he imagined she loved him equally? Could she ever care for him as a man who loved her for so many reasons? As a man who felt that, without her, the remainder of his life would not happen. If she knew the truth of his life, the twin-edged sword he carefully balanced in hiding behind his back, would she love him? Her world was so different from his, yet so alike. Despite the fact that past difficulties plagued him, his life right then with her was filled with elegance, and the simplicity of living every day without fear. That was a fundamental part of her, not the circumstances around her, and it was all these thoughts that made him helpless in her presence.

Tess stood in front of Ivan and smiled at him as her gaze did not waver from his; however, her smile lessened as she briefly witnessed the helplessness in his expression. She felt he wanted to speak, but was without words to convey his thoughts. She could only imagine his trip had tired him. He looked tired and, little did she know, he had traveled all night and most of the day to get back to her. After all that, as he stood right in front of her, he could not tell her that was what he had done, or why he had done it.

She smiled again, hoping to relieve him of his stress. "Alright. Be silent, but eat, then you can rest," she said.

When she started to walk into the dining room, he touched her arm as she tried to pass. Her demeanor confused him. There was no sign of that sad woman he left five days past. And though he had just witnessed her crying, if he had not seen it for himself, he would have never believed she was sad only moments before entering the room. Ignoring those thoughts, he asked, "Are you not joining me?"

"I'm not hungry. Come, sit down, and relax. You should rest," she said, then she walked into the dining room.

He followed with his hand tenderly holding her arm while his fingers moved delicately on the material of her dress as if to prove to himself that she was real. She sat him down at the head of the table and returned to the kitchen. He watched her rushing to and from the kitchen, bringing him bread and even the wine that he had sent home with one of his men. When it appeared he had everything possible for his dinner, she smiled, then turned to leave the room.

Seeing her leaving, he panicked. "Where are you going?"

"I'm going to clean up the mess I've made of Mrs. Tomić's kitchen."

"What do you mean?" he asked, shaking his head and frowning.

"You don't know? She's been ill, just a cold. I gave her some medicine two days ago. She's feeling much better now, but she couldn't be coming over here to cook. She needed to rest. So, you'll just have to suffer with my cooking. I don't cook often for others in New York, but I do know how. I don't think you'll die from my cooking, but I'm sure it's not what you're used to. So, please, don't be too angry with me," she said, then turned around again to enter the kitchen.

"Tess, wait! Sit with me. Please, I…I haven't seen you in a week. Tell me about all that you've been doing," he said as he looked around the room, referring to her cleaning.

Obeying his request for her company, she returned to the table.

He stood and pulled out the chair next to him. Sliding it up close to his, he waited for her to sit, then he sat down again. "What's all this cleaning about?" he asked.

"I thought it would be a nice surprise for you when you came home. I thought perhaps you might enjoy having things a little more civilized and orderly is all. I know we're in the middle of a war, but—" She did not continue because she considered her intentions useless.

Ivan placed his hand on her arm, then leaned toward her, and asked, "But what?"

She shook her head and shrugged slightly. "I don't know, maybe just to keep spirits high. No matter how bad the situation, there's always something that can be done to make it better, even if it's only a smile and a kind word that greets you."

Seeing Ivan, the men from the living room walked into the dining room and began sitting around the table. Ivan looked at them with a slightly irritated expression. He did not ask them to come and sit with him. He wanted to sit and talk with Tess, not be with the same men he had been looking at since the start of the war.

Tess noticed they were short a chair and she stood up. Slipping her arm from under his hand, she leaned toward him. As her soft voice sounded in his ear, he momentarily did not breathe, as he felt her warm breath on his skin. "If you need me, just call." Then she turned and rushed into the kitchen before he could stop her.

He automatically reached toward her as his lips whispered her name, but he could only watch as she entered the kitchen and closed the door. Without a second thought that Ivan would want time alone with Tess, the men pulled him into their conversation. They commented on how kind she was. How unlike an American she was, though few of them had any long-term dealings with Americans lately, and their judgment came mainly from rumors. They emphasized how much her being there improved things. She always tried to make them laugh, telling them little stories from her life in New York, and answering questions about America.

She did not have anything bad to say about anyone, nor did she complain, and there was no mention of Ivan's past behavior. The men told him that Tess could not wait for him to return. They said that she missed him. That thought made Ivan smile uncontrollably. They said that she would always say the same thing to them when they would try to stop her from cleaning. At first her tone would be strict, but it always reverted to affection when she spoke of Ivan, as she would say, "Go on! Get away from me! I want things to be nice for Ivan when he returns. I don't want him to think he's not welcomed home. He's done so much to make my stay here pleasant and I want to return his kindness. It's the least I can do."

Ivan sat quietly, not saying a word, as the men quoted her. They told him, in detail, all she had done while he was gone, though they mentioned nothing of the surprise she had for him. They spoke about her cleaning and cooking and taking care of Mrs. Tomić, who had improved greatly. Tess insisted she rest more so when Tess left she would not think that she had left anyone in need.

Ivan frowned when he heard them mention Tess leaving. When was she leaving? He had not thought of that lately. He imagined she would stay until she found Mara. If he kept up the pretense of the search, he felt she would not leave at all. Perhaps that hidden truth was why he did not tell her where to find Mara. From the moment he sat down to dinner with her in Belgrade, the thought of them not being together was unbearable to him. And though he did not understand that feeling at first, and passed it off as basic attraction to her, he now knew that he had fallen in love with her then.

After Ivan finished his dinner, he stood up from the table and left the room in silence. He did not excuse himself; he only walked out to find Tess. When he entered the kitchen he expected to see her there, but the room was empty. Continuing down the hall to their bedroom, he found her dressing the large bed, for she had already made the small bed. He smiled upon seeing this. Knocking on the door, he waited for her permission to enter.

She turned around and saw him standing there. "Are you finished already? You barely gave me enough time," she said.

"Time for what?" he asked as he stepped into the room.

"I have a surprise for you. Nothing excessive, but something I hope you'll enjoy," she answered, then stepping away from the bed, she reached for his hand, which he willingly surrendered. Taking him to the small room she had previously surmised was a closet, she pulled back a clean drape. Inside this room she had made a bathing room. It had originally been a bathing room before they had installed modern plumbing. Sergej's house was old and filled with many old things that the men thought were unusable, but Tess saw differently.

She had found an old footed bathtub in one of the rooms on the top floor. The men carried it downstairs and placed it in that room for her. She had figured it all out in no time. When you wanted to empty the bathtub, you opened a trap in the floor and pulled the bathtub's plug. Then the water flowed out the trap, then down a small gutter, and off to the side of the house. With a well on the property, she had the men fill large containers with water, then carry the water into the house where she would boil it prior to use. Looking under the tub, he saw that she had several fat, short candles burning to help keep the water already in the tub as warm as possible for him.

"This room is for you," she said, then added, "The men have their own bathroom upstairs."

To Ivan, this room was for both of them. Amazed at her resourcefulness, he smiled at her, but then frowned when he saw she was carrying heavy pots of boiled water from the kitchen into that room.

"If you've had enough to eat, now you can take a bath. If you want to, that is. I just need time to heat more water," she said.

Smiling at him, she tried to pass him, though he stood in her path and looked at her curiously. She glanced up at him. "What? Is this not alright? Did I do something wrong?" she asked.

Smiling at her, he kissed her on the forehead as a thank you, then he let her pass.

Walking through the bedroom, she pointed to the dresser. "You have clean clothes in there, and a robe is hanging on the hook on the wall in the bathroom. So, give me another five to ten minutes, then you may have your bath," she said, and without another word, she left.

Walking back into the middle of the bedroom, he observed all she had done. How different she made things. How beautiful for being in the middle of a war. "Something from nothing," he whispered, then he left the room and went after her. Again, he thought he would find her in the kitchen, but instead, she was serving coffee to the men in the dining room. She had cleared away his dish, and a hot cup of coffee remained at his place at the head of the table. And though he sat down at the table, he was unable to stop staring at her. He watched her walk through the door to the kitchen, then she was gone, and he waited for her to return, but she did not.

Once more, his men pulled him into the conversation, but he paid scant attention as he listened to the sounds from the kitchen; the delicate sounds she made as she worked to take care of him and his men. The men discussed the success of their mission on the previous days; however, they could not understand why Ivan decided to give food to all the children.

In his defense, he stated his decision firmly, saying, "It is the right thing to do. We can't blame the children for their parents' mistakes. How are they going to learn not to be violent against us if we don't show them sympathy? If we consider ourselves better, we must be better, not just say we are."

He was beginning to sound like Tess, and he paused after he heard what he had said. He had said it with such conviction because he knew it was true. All this time she was right, but still, he could not forget the actions of those children's parents; the aggressors that sought to divide and conquer the land, and that was an unforgivable sin. But now, he was displeased sitting with so many men and arguing over things that became less and less important as the war expired. Who gave what to whom, and who paid whom for what? Who cared anymore? It was all a sick blur to him now. The only clear thought he had was that he longed to be with Tess.

The kitchen was silent and Ivan wondered what she was doing. Quickly finishing his cup of coffee, he stood up from the table, and again, he left without speaking to his men. They noticed his departure and knew he sought Tess. They could only surmise from her hurried actions that she prepared a bath for him, as she had for them when they straggled home in sets of two and three.

"You look like little dirty children. What have you been doing? Playing in the mud?" she had asked them. Little did she know how accurate her guess was.

So, when Ivan left the table, the men thought nothing more than the fact that he was going to bathe. But Sergej, Ivan's closest friend—the one whose life Tess had saved by standing between him and the possibility of death—saw differently. Sergej saw Ivan desperately in love. Though that thought made Sergej happy, he felt that Ivan should tell Tess the truth about Mara; he needed to tell her the truth before the truth no longer made sense.

Ivan walked to the bedroom and saw Tess pouring the last pot of boiled water into his bath as an inviting steam cloud rose from the tub. Standing at the door, he saw she was exhausted. She straightened up, wiped her forehead, and stretched her back. Clearing his throat, so not to frighten her, he then walked into the room.

She turned to see him. "It's all ready and waiting for you." She then walked from the small room and toward him, carrying the large pot in both hands.

He reached for the pot, took it from her, and set it on the floor. Looking down at her, he placed his hands on her shoulders. "Why don't you take a bath? I'm fine," he said.

"I already took one before you came home. You go ahead, but if you don't mind me being in the bedroom, I'd like to lie down."

Ivan could see her weariness. He could feel it as he held her shoulders; it crept through the fabric of her dress, and into his palms, causing them to ache. It was as though she found it difficult to support her weight as she stood there smiling at him, masking what she truly felt. And from this, he knew she would not burden him with complaints.

He smiled at her. "I don't mind. You rest." Taking her hand and leading her to the bed, he then picked up the pot from the floor and returned it to the kitchen, which was clean and ready for breakfast. Taking an armload of wood, he returned to the bedroom and found her finishing making the bed. He placed the wood next to the fireplace and put a few pieces on top of the flames, but when he turned around, she began to walk out, and so he stopped her. "Where are you going? I thought you wanted to rest."

"I just wanted to give you privacy to change," she answered, and tried again to leave.

He shook his head. "Stay, lie down, and rest. You're tired. You've done too much. I want you in here with me, not around the men with all their demands. You treat them better than their own families have, and now they don't want to leave the house," he said, and again, he led her to the bed and sat her down. Then he closed and locked the bedroom door, which one of the men had fixed after his tantrum the previous week. Walking to their new bathing room, he turned around. "Thank you," he said, then he smiled at her, stepped inside the room, and pulled the drape closed.

Rubbing her eyes, she was tired. She walked to the vanity, sat down, pulled off the band holding back her hair, then brushed it. Instead of going to the large bed, she walked to the smaller bed. After his journey, he would have his own bed to sleep in.

Slipping off her dress, she laid down and pulled up the covers. Laying her head back against the pillow, she closed her eyes. However, even when she closed them, she could still see Ivan's face, and she smiled at the sight. And though she wanted to stay awake until he was through, in case he needed anything else, she immediately fell asleep.

He enjoyed the bath. Again, she was right; it was civilized for where they were. She had left her shampoo and soap inside the room for his use. He smiled seeing this, and he appreciated her thoughtfulness as he washed the dirt of his trip from his weary body. He remained in the water until it cooled down, then opening the trap, he pulled the tub's plug, and the water drained silently from the bathtub and out and away from the house. He reached for a towel she had left for him, then blew out the remaining lit candles under the tub.

As he dried himself, he thought, "Clean everything." He smiled brightly as he reflected on her efforts to make things pleasing for him. Putting on his robe, he listened for sounds from the other room, but there was only silence, and he surmised she had lain down and fallen asleep. Carrying the tall candle she left for him, he pulled back the drape, but he did not see her in bed.

Stepping into the room, he walked toward the tall dresser where his clothes were, and there he saw her, asleep in the smaller of the two beds. He released a sigh as he placed the candle on top of the dresser. Shaking his head, he debated lifting her and putting her back into the larger bed, but looking at her, so soundly asleep, he did not want to wake her. He knew if he put her in the larger bed, he would lay there with her, holding her until the morning, but really wanting to make love to her.

In silence she lay there with her long brown hair flowing over the pillow—her face was peaceful, and her lips formed a subtle smile. As he looked at her, he noticed her dress lay across the bottom of the bed, and she wore no gown, or robe, as was usual for her. He surmised she was too tired to put one on.

Looking around the room, he noticed she had turned down the sheets on the larger bed in preparation for him. All she had done, and all he felt for her, overwhelmed him. Like the soldier who comes home to his heavenly prize, her love waited for him and showed in everything she did to welcome him home. She had placed her life in his hands, and he had mistrusted her. Now he knew how wrong his actions were toward her. How he despised himself just then. After all they had been through together, he could not sleep in the bed she had prepared for him. All he could do was wait until the morning to talk with her and to thank her for all she had done.

He opened the top dresser drawer and found his clean clothes that she had left for him. Quickly getting dressed, he walked back to the bed. Pulling the covers up higher over her shoulders, he bent down and kissed her lips. As he admired her in the candlelight, he wondered what it would be like to be with her. If nothing else, just to lie next to her, and to hold her as she slept. What would it be like to be that close and feel her warmth and her trust in him? What an extreme amount of love waited there for him. If only she would awaken then, he would tell everything to her.

With those thoughts, he shook his head at himself and left the room. With no other choice, he left her alone and joined the remaining men that soon would go upstairs and sleep. When they did, he secured the house, then he lay on the sofa in the dark and thought about Tess. Then he thought about his wish that she would not shun him when he returned, and now that his wish had been granted, he was unable to appreciate the simplicity of the situation. Disgusted by his lack of courage, Ivan no longer fought his fatigue, and finally he slept.

CHAPTER FORTY-THREE

The next morning, Ivan awoke later than usual. It was normally cold in the living room, and when he wished to rise early, he occasionally slept there; the cold prevented him from resting for long periods of time. Yet this morning it was strangely warm. As he opened his eyes, he felt as though the sun was shining on him, although he knew the drapes were closed. Sitting up, he saw Tess' sheepskin coat covering him. How warm it was. She had kept it in her luggage as he had requested and, though he saw her cold many times, she did not use it for herself, she only used it now to cover him so that he would be warm.

She had woken up shortly after he had fallen asleep. Not finding him with her, she searched for him and found him sleeping in the living room. Even though he had not slept in the larger bed that previous evening, she still showed him the same tender care. She did not stop to think that switching beds may have angered him, and she should have considered that aspect. Now, she felt she had made a grievous mistake by throwing his hospitality back in his face.

He stood and carried her coat to the bedroom. Knocking on the door, no one answered. Hoping to find her still asleep, he now had the courage to confess everything to her—all that he had hidden from her, then face any consequences that may come from his confession.

He slowly opened the door. "Tess? It's Ivan, may I come in?" he asked, poking his head into the room. His eyes searched for her, however, she had neatly made both beds and the room was empty. He entered and placed her coat on the bed. Worried as to her whereabouts, he returned to the kitchen and finding Alek there, he asked, "Where's Tess?"

"She was up very early. She said she couldn't sleep. Sergej was awake and she asked him if he would take her to one of the shelters. She didn't go anywhere while you were gone, she didn't want to go without you, but this morning she said you were so tired that she didn't want to wake you. It's strange, for an American, being here with this war, all she did was clean and take care of us. Are you sure she's American?"

Ivan gave a brief smile, though deep down he felt lost now that she had sought Sergej's assistance. He felt that his refusal to accept her generosity of the larger bed had widened the chasm between them. Again hurt by his own actions, he turned and walked slowly from the kitchen and into the dining room.

"Tess left breakfast for you, if you want it," Alek said.

Not responding to him, Ivan kept walking to the living room. Grabbing his coat from the back of the sofa, he left the house, got into one of the cars, and made his way to Saint Michael's. This was the orphanage that the authorities took him to after his parents had died. He knew Sergej would not take Tess there. He had saved that as the last searching place, and he had planned to take her there the next day. That was what he had debated before he finally fell asleep the previous evening. He was going to introduce her to Mara, but before that, he had planned to spend this day alone with her, talking with her, and trying to make her understand what he thought. He needed her to understand the depth of his love for her, and that he needed her, but now she was gone, and he would have to devise another plan.

In Tess' absence, Ivan wanted to speak to the Mother Superior at Saint Michael's. She was the first person that cared about him after his parents were killed, and he never forgot her. When he was at the lowest points of his life, he always returned to Saint Michael's, and she always took him in. This sacred place was his secret hideaway in Bosnia. If by chance Tess showed up without him, he did not want the Mother Superior to say anything about Mara; he had to explain first. He had to make Tess understand why he hid Mara, and he had to find a way to make Tess forgive him.

Making his way from the car, he reached the entrance to Saint Michael's. Once inside, he walked down a long stone corridor toward the children's quarters. He did not want to see Mara this day. He had promised her that the next time he saw her he would take her home. Since that day, a month had passed and he was not prepared to tell her that she had to stay there a little longer.

Asking one of the sisters to find the Mother Superior, Ivan waited at the end of the long corridor. As he waited, he remembered one night during the first week that Tess was in Sarajevo. While Tess was asleep at the house, Ivan drove to Saint Michael's to see the Mother Superior. It was then that he told her about Tess' search for Mara, and about all that Tess was supposedly involved in back in America. Because of that visit, he knew the Mother Superior would not tell Tess anything about Mara.

Ivan waited patiently and, after a short while, the Mother Superior appeared at the end of the hall. He walked to meet her, and after kissing her hand, he looked at her, and his smile was melancholy.

She smiled at him and noticed his down-hearted expression. "Ivan, where have you been? Mara wants to see you. She misses you. She doesn't play, and all day she sits by herself," she said.

Ivan said nothing, he only expelled a deep breath. As she began to walk with him, she looked at him and knew he was troubled. As a boy, he always kept his troubles to himself, and now, as a man, he was no different. The loss of his family had a devastating effect on him. An effect he had not overcome completely, except when he was with Tess. He felt he could tell Tess anything.

They walked in silence as Ivan thought that, when he would return home that evening, he would send the men from the house. He needed time alone with Tess without the men's constant interruptions. The men were always seeking Tess' attention, always asking her questions, and making requests of her. By her accommodating their needs, he was jealous, although she never neglected him. Even when he had been hurtful toward her, she still cared for him. Shaking off his private thoughts, Ivan was unprepared to talk about Tess to the Mother Superior.

"What about this woman from America? Who is she? Is she a good woman? From the look in your eyes, I see she's not what you expected, is she?" she asked, but from Ivan's first words about Tess, the Mother Superior saw that he was in love with her, although she said nothing. She knew in time he would realize it, if he had not already.

"If she comes here, please don't tell her anything about Mara. I have many things to explain to her," Ivan said.

"What is it she wants? If it's only to give Mara an award, what is wrong with that?"

"She's out with Sergej today. He has a sympathetic side for Tess, but I don't think he'll bring her here. He knows not to, but if for any reason he does, don't tell Tess anything, and please, don't let Mara see Sergej."

When he looked at her, she saw his confusion. Trusting he knew what was best, she smiled and agreed to do as he requested.

"Don't tell Mara that I was here either. Please, I can't take her away to-day. I know I promised, but I can't take her now. I'll come for her, and I'll bring Tess to meet her. I don't know when, but very soon. I first have to make Tess understand that—" He did not finish his sentence. His eyes searched the air for the right words, though he did not know what he wanted to say because he felt he had much to explain to Tess.

"I will do as you ask. If Miss Fordel comes before you bring her, for you, I will say nothing. But come back soon and see Mara. You are the only true family she has. She prays every night for you." She paused, then her look became serious, and as she continued, her voice matched the strength in her aged appearance. "She prays for the Black Rebel also, Ivan."

Ivan looked at her, then looked away.

She knew about his secret life and the sacrifices he made. "I will not ask what you do for the lives of others. I only ask you to remember that you are a man, not a sacrificial lamb to be slain for the people of this country," she said.

Ivan said nothing; he only kissed her hand in gratitude. With a lone-some smile of understanding, he turned and walked away as he contem-plated her words, and he knew she was right. Yet, walking away was diffi-cult for Ivan because he wanted to take Mara home. He knew Mara be-longed with him. He also knew that he and Mara belonged with Tess. Thinking about this, he got into his car and drove to the Rebel camp to meet with his men.

CHAPTER FORTY-FOUR

Tess and Sergej returned home in the early afternoon. Tess thanked him for taking her to the shelters, but said nothing else before retiring to the bedroom. It had been another disappointing day. Sergej could only watch her walk away as he felt her sadness, and he knew she was giving up. Her search had produced nothing, and he could tell that she felt stupid for even having tried. What Sergej did not know was that her despondent mood was not only because of not finding Mara. It was also because Ivan had not slept in the bedroom the previous evening. This made her feel she had imposed herself upon him. And as much as she was in love with him, she was vexed by the conclusion that he was not interested in an American. He needed someone like himself—someone with whom he could relate, someone that understood him and his culture—not someone that threw his hospitality back at him.

She sat on the bed and opened her briefcase. Pulling out the loose papers, she began reorganizing them. Carefully placing a copy of Mara's letter from Idy to one side, she continued her sorting. Finding the piece of paper on which Ivan had written Sergej's address, without thinking, she placed it on top of the letter; for some reason, in her mind, they belonged together. Once she had her papers organized, she sat back and reread the documentation on Mara. She searched for any clues that could lead to the child's location, but found none, so she placed those papers in the back pocket of the briefcase's lid.

Then reaching for the letter, she saw something she had not previously noticed. Looking closer, she stared at the small piece of paper with Sergej's address. Holding the two pieces of paper side-by-side, she thought she was seeing things. She gasped slightly, as a confused frown overwhelmed her expression. The handwriting of the letter was identical to that of the address Ivan had written. "Ivan," she whispered in disbelief as tears welled in her eyes.

Grabbing the phrase book she brought with her from Belgrade, she

315

looked in the back at the page that displayed the Serbo-Croatian alphabet. Not having seen his last name in writing, only having heard him say it, she presumed that it was spelled with a J. Skimming down the list of letters and finding the letter J, she saw that it was written and pronounced as Y, but he did not pronounce his name with a Y sound, he pronounced it with a G sound.

Going over the list again, she found the letter Ð, and saw that it was pronounced as G as in the word genuine. She now knew that not only was Ivan the Black Rebel, but also, he and Iđy were one and the same. That made absolute sense as to why Mara wrote about the Black Rebel. However, Mara had no idea that Ivan was the Black Rebel. It also explained why Ivan became so upset when she had mentioned taking Mara back to America—she would be taking Mara away from Ivan.

"Ivan Ðurić, IĐY." She released a small breath. "Not with a J," she whispered, as she felt her heart plummet in unison with her rapidly flowing tears. Ivan clearly had no intention of letting her find Mara. He had accused her of involvement with Nationalists, and to learn the truth of her loyalty, he brought her to Sarajevo. He never intended to help her. "He must see me as some careless imbecile," she thought.

What a fool she felt like—how inappropriate, and plagued with guilt. How he must have thought her insane trying to take care of him and his men. How he must have thought her stupid when she slept in his smaller bed instead of the bed he gave her to use while there. How he must laugh at her feeble attempt to find Mara. All the men in the house must have laughed at her as well. She felt that if they knew who Ivan was, they must know where Mara was.

Quite suddenly, it was all a sad game. She closed her eyes and shook her head at her stupidity. She knew that Ivan did not trust her, and that meant he could not love her as she loved him. In her desperation, she buried her face in the pillow and cried. She had failed again, and the only thing left to do now was to leave.

Sergej walked down the hall toward the bedroom. He intended to ask Tess to sit in the dining room with him and talk. He wanted to try to brighten her mood, but when he neared the half-open door, he heard her crying. Though he knew that, being her friend, he should go to her, he also knew that she needed time alone. So, he walked back to the dining room, hoping that Ivan would soon return.

CHAPTER FORTY-FIVE

When Ivan arrived at the house that evening, he requested the men leave, except for Alek, whom he requested stand guard on the upper floor, and Sergej, whom Ivan asked to remain for dinner. He felt that Tess would be more comfortable with Sergej there. This way, she would not be alone with Ivan. He felt that after he did not accept her offer of the larger bed the previous evening, being alone with him now would make her feel awkward. He hoped that she would understand his motives, and realize his refusal was a sign of his respect for her as the woman he loved. But more importantly than what happened the previous evening, if they were to be together, he needed to reveal all of his secrets, and give her time to decide if he was what she wanted in her life.

Ivan, Sergej, and Tess sat down at the table for dinner. Where usually Tess sat near to Ivan, smiling often at him, this evening she was distant. Positioning herself away from Ivan, she avoided eye contact with him, and she did not openly talk with either of them. From this, Ivan could feel her vacant emotions and, again, he watched her not eat. In the back of his mind, he wondered what had happened that day while she was out with Sergej. He knew something had happened, but he dared not ask her what troubled her, lest he distance her further.

When Ivan looked at Sergej, Sergej only shrugged and, in few words in Serbian, told Ivan that she appeared upset after not finding what she searched for—by that he meant Mara.

After examining the similarities between the two handwriting samples, Tess now felt like an outsider in Sergej's house. She no longer wanted to be there, but the choice to leave was not hers. She was not in America; she was in the middle of a war in a foreign country. She could not go to the local airport, get on a plane, and fly away; however, she would have loved to do just that. All things considered, she could not blame Ivan. He was right when he said it would be wrong to take Mara from the people that she loved and that loved her. He was right not to tell her that he was Idy, or the

Black Rebel, for he did not truly know her, and so he should not trust her.

Tess' mood softened as she remembered Ivan's story about the death of his little sister. She imagined that he saw Mara as the little sister he had lost and, as a good brother should, he protected her from harm. She now knew that her time was up in Sarajevo. Time had run out, and her only accomplishment was falling in love with a man that wanted nothing to do with her. At this point, she could not imagine anything happening to change the situation, so she resigned herself to failure.

Despite what she felt, while she remained under Ivan's protection, she intended to be her usual self as much as possible. Ivan and his men would not become the target of her sadness. They lived a real and difficult life, not the contrived fantasy of a novelist. She knew everything Ivan had told her since they first met was right. She also knew that she had been blind to the consequences of the war, and she had burdened him with her enchanted ideals. Nothing she could do would make things better. She knew that Ivan and his men did what they had to do to survive a situation they did not create. With that thought, she forgave Ivan, but still, her heart was broken.

The limited discussions at dinner were in Serbian, to which she was not privy. Just one more thing that told her, Ivan did not want her there. But she was wrong. Ivan wanted to fill Sergej in on a few simple facts from his days away without annoying her with talk of war. As Ivan discussed issues with Sergej, he sensed Tess' sadness and, when he looked at her, she looked away, trying not to bother him further. So he decided to wait until Sergej left after dinner to talk with her. Therefore, as the two men conversed, Tess sat quietly and enjoyed the sounds of his language, because she felt one day soon, she would not be privileged to hear him speak it again.

From their stressed tone, Tess imagined his Cause was suffering major setbacks. Contrary to what she thought, Ivan and Sergej discussed the coming peace accord that would end the war, at least on paper. Not knowing this, and still wishing she could help, but not knowing how, she sat quietly, observing Ivan. She felt he was a man that was tired of the endless struggle in which he was entwined, but she was wrong. The end of the war *was* near, and after they discussed the peace accord, they discussed plans for rebuilding the city. As they spoke, she wondered if the hidden purpose for her trip was to help Ivan and not to find Mara.

When they had finished eating, Tess gathered their plates and carried them into the kitchen. After a few minutes, she returned to the dining room and offered them coffee. Ivan observed her, and her distant manner-ism gnawed at him. She tried to smile at Sergej, though failed. Then glanc-ing at Ivan, again, she quickly looked away when he smiled at her. She could not look at him. If she did, she was certain her eyes would divulge that she knew exactly who he was. If there was a right time to reveal this knowledge, right then was not it.

From her avoidance of eye contact, Ivan knew something deeply both-ered her. She appeared sheepish since he had come back to the house that evening. She was intensely silent and it was obvious that she was lost in private thoughts, but about what, he longed to know as he watched her. He imagined after all that had happened she was finally tired of the war and Sarajevo, but mostly tired of him. His singular wish was to go back to the previous evening when she laid sleeping in his small bed. He wanted to go back and choose differently. He wanted to wake her up and bring her to the larger bed. He wanted to lay there with her, and make love to her, but he could not, and he knew that he would regret his gentlemanly decision for the rest of his life. When she returned to the kitchen, they expected her to rejoin them, but she did not. Now Ivan was convinced that his refusal to sleep in the larger bed the night before was the chasm between them. What he felt was respect for her as a woman, he imagined she accepted as rejec-tion from him as a man.

As Sergej looked at Ivan, his expression reflected his concern. Without touching his coffee, Sergej stood up and stepped away from the table. As he shook his head, his voice was filled with upset and anger. "You should have seen her today. She was crying this afternoon. How can you be so cruel? What you're doing isn't fair. This—" He hesitated as he shook his head at Ivan. "This lying! You didn't like it when you felt she lied to you, and you punished her for a crime that she didn't commit," he said sternly.

Ivan remained silent and allowed his friend to say what he had to say. As Ivan listened, he knew Sergej was right. Ivan had been wrong all along, but he was not certain how to correct the situation without losing her. Alt-hough it appeared he had already lost her from his indisputable respect. He understood that sometimes a woman needs a man's acceptance more than other things, and certainly much more than excessive gentlemanliness.

Ivan knew Sergej felt that he was confused over what he felt for Tess, but he was wrong. Ivan knew exactly what he felt for Tess. But not having been that persistent man from Belgrade, he knew he never took the time to show her what he felt for her. He gave into her every time she backed away from him. And every time she backed away from him, she sat waiting for his pursuit. She waited for him to show her what he truly felt for her, but, out of his respect for her, he refrained. Out of respect for her, and in fear of losing her from what he thought were his war-roughened ways, he offered nothing, and he knew that she could not refuse something that he had not offered.

Sergej slamming his hand down on the table brought Ivan from these private thoughts. "You should tell her where Mara is! She should know. Mara's family would want her to know. She came all this way for what? To become a slave to the men? To be made a fool of by you? She's a woman! Treat her like one! No one understands your intentions. Everyone wants to tell her where Mara is, but they don't dare. And so what if she wants to take Mara to America? What one of us, *except you,* wouldn't go with her if she asked? Who wouldn't gladly leave everything here to get out of this hell! For her to have come all this way she must have a great deal of love to give." He gave a small laugh. "She must, if she tolerates you!"

Ivan looked at him, but did not comment.

Then remembering his place, Sergej looked away. "I'll go and join the men at the other house. We'll be there waiting for you," he said, then he walked toward the front door. Grabbing his coat from the back of the sofa, he left Ivan alone in the dining room, he left Ivan alone with Tess.

Ivan sat there staring at the front door. Then he panicked, not knowing where Tess was. "Tess?" he called out.

She did not respond, although he could hear the clanking of plates coming from the kitchen. He stood up, pushed open the kitchen door, and found her washing the dinner dishes. Looking at her, she seemed out of place, but at the same time, strangely appropriate in her kind behavior, and for a moment, he admired her from the doorway.

"If you keep cleaning in your pretty dresses you'll ruin them," he said.

She stopped for a moment, looked halfway over her shoulder, and said, "It's only a dress."

He walked to her, and pulling her hands from the water, he dried them with a towel. Placing the towel to the side, he continued to hold her right hand in his as he looked down at her. She did not speak, she only looked away from his curious stare.

"Why are you so quiet? You didn't touch your food. What are you thinking about?" he asked as he gently stroked the side of her face.

She did not look up to him as she quietly answered, "Nothing important."

Her response was genteel, but he frowned at her rejection of his concern. It was moments like these that he wanted to take her in his arms. Moments like these when he saw her lost and alone. Even though she had put up with all of his ideas, he did not know if she would accept his future affection once he told her of all he felt for her. And suddenly he wondered if she would *ever* accept him as a man she could love. Though he felt he should do exactly what his heart told him to, his mind interfered. Perhaps he was not a man she could love. Perhaps she only wanted to repay him for his kindness and for taking care of her, as that was what she had told his men while he was away.

As quietly as possible, he sighed. "Why don't you talk to me like you used to? Where did your opinions go?"

"All I thought—" She shook her head. "It doesn't matter anymore."

"Do you still think about Mara? Is that what troubles you? Is that why you're sad? Or is it something else?" he asked, hinting to the previous evening, but she did not answer. Then lifting her face, he looked into her eyes. "Tell me, please?" he whispered.

She looked at him. He now appeared so loving and gentle, but love and gentility would not help his Cause. She understood that, so she asked him a question that she knew would harden the softness she witnessed. "When were you planning on telling me that you're the Black Rebel?"

His expression changed immediately and she felt him getting angry. Letting her hand go, he walked to the door to the dining room, but turned to face her. "Who told you I was?"

"No one. Do you think I'm so stupid that I couldn't tell? You walk around Belgrade as if you just stepped out of a fashion magazine. There, you're an impeccably dressed man. Then you come here and, well, look at you. You look like some wild man. You look the way a good soldier would. Then with all the men that come in and out of this house. Amazing how like Christ and his disciples you are. Twelve men live in this house with you, and they look up to you. They don't breathe without your permission. The night you locked me in the bedroom, I saw you and your men with rifles. How about the night Tomo was shot? One gesture from you and they appeared from nowhere—every one of them was well armed and pursued those soldiers. You command an army, but you waste your time trying to help me find a child." She paused. Trying to catch her breath, she then added, "Why?"

She stood waiting for his response, but he had none. When he did not say anything, she slowly walked toward him, but stopped halfway, because his silence tormented her. "You know who Iđy is, don't you? You know everything. You know he doesn't want me to find Mara," she said, and again, she hesitated, hoping that he would interrupt and tell her that he was Iđy, but he was silent and only waited for her to continue. "Is he like you? Does he see me as just another meddlesome American? Does he see me the way you do: cruel, selfish, and unfeeling? Does he?" She paused briefly, then asked as she looked into his eyes, "Do you, Ivan?"

To his relief, his first secret was revealed, although he could not detect her real feelings about it. Did she despise him for being the Black Rebel? But she had written in her notebook that the Black Rebel had her heart. She wrote that passage after that night he locked her in the bedroom, so she wrote that passage, knowing exactly who he was. Remembering that statement, he wondered what she truly felt. Yet, why did she mention Iđy? Why would she think that he knew who Iđy was? However, that thought vanished as he continued looking at her.

Then, out of nowhere, she said, "I know you don't trust me, and by not trusting me, you couldn't ever lov—" She stopped abruptly, and looked away. She was embarrassed for being so bold.

Now Ivan had his answer. He knew what she thought; by not trusting her, he could never love her. And her thinking that he still did not trust her made him speechless.

She shook her head and took a step back from him. "You must have some sort of meeting to go to, so don't let me hold you up. I'm sure your men are waiting for you somewhere safe, why else would they not be here. But don't worry, you can reprimand me when you return. I'll clean up my mess here and, once I'm finished, I'll be down there," she said as she motioned down the hall to the bedroom. Without saying another word, she walked to the kitchen door, opened it, and stepped out into the frozen moonlit night.

For a split second, he stood there helpless as he watched the kitchen door close. Her words told Ivan that she still felt he wanted her to stay in the bedroom to be out of his way—for him to be safe. He knew she tried hard not to take sides in this war. He knew she was not the spy he sought because of her loyalty, not because there was no spy. Though he was too infatuated with her to admit it at the time, he knew she was innocent when he first saw her at the train depot in Belgrade. Suspecting her of disloyalty was easier than admitting that he was in love with her. If he were in love, then, in his eyes, he was no longer immortal to his people. However, he never imagined she felt he did not trust her to be in his life. He trusted her more than he trusted his men, and in the back of his mind, he thought, "When did I ever prove to her that I trusted her?" And now it appeared too late to salvage what he felt he had destroyed.

All this time she knew who he was. When she wrote about the Black Rebel, she wrote about him, knowing and respecting him. Her writing showed how she loved that image. But now that she told him that she knew who he was, he wondered if she would stop loving him because he had not trusted her enough to tell her. Did not telling her make him a brilliant strategist, or did it simply make him a coward? As he now saw himself, he paled in comparison to the man she described with her beautiful and bold affirmations.

And though she had an opportunity to betray him, she did not. She held his secret close to her heart. She protected his life as though it were hers, and surrendered her life to protect his life and the lives of his men. Because of that, he loved her, but not only because of that. He loved her because all that she was, was all he ever wanted.

Ivan went to the living room and grabbed his coat from the back of the sofa. Putting it on, he walked to the bedroom where he pulled her coat from the hook near to the door, then he went back to find her. Opening the door, he stood behind her and held her coat up for her to slip into. "Here, Tess, put this on."

Hearing his voice, she turned to look over her shoulder, but seeing the coat, she looked away.

"Put this on. You're coming with me," he said, as he reached for her right arm and pulled it back to the sleeve of the coat. She tried to move away from him, though he quickly slipped the coat onto her body, then he turned her around to face him. His expression was gentle, but determined, as he whispered, "Come with me."

"Don't worry, I'd rather die than ever tell anyone what I just said," she answered, and again she looked away from him.

He turned her head back toward him. Placing his hands on the sides of her face, he looked into her eyes and tried to reassure her, as he said, "I want you to be with me. Come with me tonight," he requested, then added, "Please."

She looked at him and, as with that farmer she had helped, she began to see the same desperation in his beautiful eyes. Because of that, and because of her love for him, she could not refuse him. "Alright," she said quietly.

Looking down at her, he wanted to kiss her, but she looked away, and he lost his courage. He saw then was not the time, not when she doubted him as she did, so he closed and locked the kitchen door, then walked down the steps. Turning around, he held his hand out to her though she did not take it. On her own, she moved down the steps and stood next to him. She did not want his help because she remembered Sergej's words, "Many people depend on Ivan," and she did not want to be one more person depending on him; though she was the only one, besides Mara, that he wanted to care for.

He was hurt when she did not take his hand, but ignoring that, he placed his arm around her shoulder. Making their way down the drive, they walked in the eerie streets that the war had created.

CHAPTER FORTY-SIX

From Sergej's house, Ivan and Tess walked through an area destroyed by bombs, plundering, and fires—their destination was a dilapidated house just southeast of where they were. He held meetings at this location so not to attract attention to Sergej's house. Men could come and go from there and no one would notice. Anyone who saw them would think they were looking for usable rubbish left behind after the bombings.

Ivan was meeting with eleven of the men who lived at Sergej's house and several others from the Rebel camp. With the end of the war in sight, Ivan had devised new plans. Small, but sporadic raids from Nationalist offenders on all sides and civilians alike were increasing. It was obvious that Nationalists were still desperate to destroy what was left of the city despite the recent casualties all sides suffered. And the civilians were only attempting to retaliate, but they had no real clue how to.

They entered the front of the house and walked toward what once was a kitchen. Ivan asked Tess to wait in the dining room. Seating her on a crate away from the window, he smiled at her affectionately. "Wait here. I won't be long. Stay away from the windows, please," he whispered.

She attempted a smile, although she felt his desperation, which she imagined was for his cause. However, it was not for his cause; it was because he was unsure of what she currently felt for him. He paused before leaving her there as he admired her in the soft moonlight filtering through the dirty and shattered windows.

"Ivan? Is there anything I can do to help? Anything at all?" she whispered.

He stroked her cheek. He wanted to believe that she was real, but he denied her the right to be real just then. He felt as though he was dreaming. As if at any moment he would awaken, and she would be gone. Shaking his head, he turned and walked into the kitchen and at once began conversing with his men.

She sat there patiently as she heard the uneasiness in the voices of the debating men sounding from the next room. Throughout the discussion, she imagined that they spoke about money. Shaken over the situation, she stood up and walked to the kitchen door. Standing in the shadows, she saw the men questioning Ivan, and she saw he was upset. Just then, she felt she was there to help him more than to find Mara. Taking a step into the kitchen, the dim light from the hanging oil lamp illuminated her face and her expression displayed a dedicated compassion for Ivan's dilemma.

The men turned to see her. Those from the house knew her and where somewhat surprised to see her there. The others from the camp whispered amongst themselves, not knowing who she was or where she came from. However, they had heard rumors of Ivan's girlfriend, and seeing her attentiveness to Ivan, they surmised she belonged with him.

All but Ivan smiled at her. He approached her with an annoyed look on his face. Grasping her arm tightly, he pulled her back into the dining room. He did not plan for anyone to see her. Regardless that they were undoubtedly dedicated to Ivan, the fewer people that knew she was there the safer she would be.

Sergej stepped in front of the doorway to the dining room after Ivan pulled Tess out of view. He had seen the look in Ivan's eyes, and, better than anyone, he knew whatever Ivan would say to Tess was private—none of the men should hear. So he continued talking to them until Ivan would return.

"I told you to stay put! Why do you disobey me? Why don't you do what you're told?" he whispered, then waited for her answer as he stared down at her. Yet, he found it difficult to be angry with her when seeing her concern for him, and his words did not intimidate her as he had hoped. They spoke of his frustration over whatever the current circumstance was.

Looking up at him, she ignored his comments as she stepped closer to him. Reaching up to his face, she placed her hand on his cheek and delicately stroked it and, in her gaze, he could see her concern for him. "Ivan," she whispered.

That was it. The tenderness in her voice was finally too much for him to ignore. Without a second thought, he wrapped his arms around her. Pulling her up and close to him, he kissed her. Not caring about anything else, just then, he had to feel her against him. He had to hold her and feel her in his arms. He needed to possess her as a man would, even if it was for only once in his lifetime, and now that he had, he did not want to let go. He would have preferred they fade away into that kiss, although they paused and looked at each other. He was about to speak. He was about to say he loved her when her gaze moved toward the kitchen.

Thinking she rejected him, he looked away. "Forgive me. I understand you don't want that from a man like me," he whispered, referring to himself as the Black Rebel.

He began to let her go, but she shook her head and touched his cheek again, stopping him in place. "I didn't say that. I've waited since the beginning for you, but even if I can't understand your language, I understand you. I see you get upset when you talk to these men. How can I help you?"

He let her go and walked to the opposite side of the room. He stood with his back to her for a moment as he tried to calm himself, but it was not working. Under no circumstances did he want her involved in this war. He turned around and stared at her. "What do you understand? You're American. You're a woman."

"Who cares whether I'm American, a woman, or what? What is it you need? Money? I can help you raise funds for your Cause. I have many connections in New York." She paused, wanting him to look at her and wanting to kiss him again.

He shook his head, wondering why he had brought her there. Why had he given into his impulse? But her words kept repeating inside his head that she had waited since the beginning for him.

Then he heard her sigh, and when he did not respond, she answered for him. "But you knew that all along. That's probably why you stayed with me all this time. Well, that is, after you decided I wasn't siding with Serbian Nationalists. Isn't that right? Isn't that what you were so concerned with?"

He expelled a deep breath. He was embarrassed that she knew him so well. And though he had tried to hide his suspicion of her allegiance, she saw right through him. However, he did not stay with her because she had money or resources. He stayed with her because he loved her with a passion he had not known for any woman. Even so, right then, he did not need her questioning him. It was neither the time nor the place to discuss *them*.

Angry at her assumptions, he would try again to make her stay silent, at least until they were alone together later. Nevertheless, the words he spoke did not come from his love for her, but from his pride. "Why can't you be what you are? A woman! I don't need your help. You're just like your country, getting involved in everyone else's business. It's not your fight. It never was and it never will be. Go back to America."

He looked her up and down and his impatience showed. Then his next proclamation came out faster than he had time to analyze it, and he meant nothing of what he would say. "You've been here long enough, and your search has yielded nothing. You don't belong here. It's time for you to leave!" he said in a cold tone.

Turning around, he walked toward the entrance to the kitchen, but stopped and looked back at her through the darkness. He saw her standing alone where he had left her. Looking at her, he saw her tears. He saw he had finally conquered her, and her silence was deafening. Again, he managed to hurt her. He wanted to take her back into his arms and comfort her. He wanted to kiss her and tell her how much he loved her, but his pride momentarily forbade it.

From her silence and motionless expression, he surmised his words had finally inflicted permanent wounds, and he stood speechless at the result of his own actions. Now he knew what her defeat looked like. And though defeat was something he himself would not accept, he had forced it upon her. Having witnessed it in her eyes, he saw she had now given up. She tried to be the strong woman that he insisted she be. At his request she had not become that *crying woman* that he said he would not tolerate, but now he saw she had lost all confidence, or rather, he had amputated it.

Knowing his men waited for him, Ivan walked into the kitchen and left her in the darkness to cry alone—he would deal with her when he was finished. He pushed through his men standing behind Sergej, who kept them from crowding the doorway. Because the men did not hear what Ivan and Tess had said to each other, they were slightly distracted when Ivan continued the previous discussion without any explanation as to who she was or why she was there.

Still stunned from her silence, and with distracted concentration, Ivan started talking. He had expected an argument, but she surrendered to his prideful, heartless demand for her to be silent. With her submittal, he knew that in order to avoid a confrontation, she allowed him to strip away her dignity, just as her ex-husband had. All the time she waited, he refused to show her what he felt for her. And though he had just asked her why she would not be just a woman, he did not allow her to be what she was—a woman who loved him. She was unlike others from the war; she wanted nothing more than to help him, where the others took for themselves or ran away. He knew she tried many ways to reach him, and he now imagined she felt lost in her efforts.

The men that knew her, saw there was more going on than the story of her searching for Mara. They saw her as a woman who was not afraid to fail or to admit failure openly. She was surprisingly not afraid to stand up to Ivan, whom they mostly feared. Those that did not know her saw she was important to Ivan, and though none other than Sergej heard their conversation, they all wondered why Ivan was angry with her. The men from the house witnessed the humiliation of a friend, which they saw her as, but her humiliation was not only caused by Ivan, they were also at fault.

When Ivan stopped talking, the room was filled with an awkward silence; however, it was broken by the unexpected sound of the front door opening, then closing. Ivan froze in place and hoped that he would hear her in the next room, but he heard nothing. The men looked in the direction of the front door, as they too heard her leave; they stood dumbfounded and wondering what Ivan would do next.

Coming to his senses, Ivan looked at his men, though he could not look at Sergej. He knew what he would see in his expression. Ivan walked toward the dining room and stopped. Not seeing her there, he then turned around and gave his orders. "Spread out, find her, and get her back safely," he said to the men from the house. "The rest of you, go back to the camp."

As he started to leave the room, Sergej caught him by the arm. Before Sergej could speak, Ivan addressed his question, knowing it without Sergej having asked it. "No, money is not what I had her come here for." He then dashed out the front door.

Looking in every direction, he searched the darkness for her, but she was not there. As he had demanded, she was gone. He looked at the sky and listened for the slightest sound. In the torment of his mind and heart, he prayed. If God was listening, he hoped that He would hear his desperate plea and protect her. He did not know what to do or where to look for her. He could only hope that she would find her way safely back to the house and stay there. That was if he or one of his men did not find her first, or worse, one of the opposition.

In the back of his mind he questioned himself. If she now planned to leave, would he let her leave only to never see her again? Or would he go to her before she left and tell her all that he felt for her? Tell her how much he loved and needed her. Even if he did, would she believe him when he would apologize for his hasty words?

With those questions heavy on his mind, he began to walk the streets searching for her and, instinctively, taking the same path they had walked there, he walked back to Sergej's house.

CHAPTER FORTY-SEVEN

Tess did exactly as Ivan had hoped and returned to the house, even though she would have preferred to have gotten on a train and left, never to be seen from again. On her walk back, all she could think about was that she had inconvenienced Ivan by overstaying her welcome.

Standing in the shadows across the street, Ivan saw her walk to the front door. She tried to get in, but found it locked, so she stepped back down the stairs to walk around to the kitchen door. Having heard someone walking on the porch, Alek looked out the front window. Seeing her outside the house, he hurried to open the door. He quickly called to her. As she neared the door, he pulled her inside, then looked out to see if anyone had followed her. Spotting Ivan across the street, he looked at him, although Ivan motioned him back into the house.

At once Alek closed the door and pretended that he had not seen Ivan. "Tess, where is everyone? Where's Ivan? And why are you out walking by yourself?" he asked.

She did not want to talk to anyone just then. She walked to the dining room, ignoring his questions, but she stopped at the dining room table when he asked again, "Tess? Where is Ivan?"

Looking slightly over her shoulder she answered, "He's out with Sergej and a few of the others." She paused. "Alek? When's the next train back to Belgrade?" she asked as she turned around, looked at him briefly, then looked away.

From her question, he knew she was leaving. His voice was almost lost to him as he tried to answer. "Tomorrow afternoon, I think. If it's running." He was silent for a moment, then asked, "Are you leaving?"

"I have to get back. There are books to finish writing and my publisher and agent to meet with. Do you think you could take me to the train tomorrow? Please? I'd be more than willing to pay you for your trouble. I wouldn't want to inconvenience you without some sort of compensation," she said, but she frowned, and felt insulting for phrasing it that way.

He could not understand why she offered him money for something he would be happy to do, if Ivan approved it. Her words confused him and he could only surmise that something had happened between Ivan and her to make her want to leave. Then he thought about the situation with Mara and suddenly he felt guilty.

"You don't have to pay me. I'll be happy to take you, that is, if Ivan says it's okay." He paused, then added, "If it's safe."

She nodded. Since she had arrived, she had wanted to go to Dovlići, but Ivan told her that there was excessive fighting in the surrounding area and it was not safe. Even though all hope was lost, she wanted to see this last location. Then she could say that she tried everything to find Mara, then her failure would be complete.

Thinking of this, she looked back at him. "Alek? If the train is running tomorrow, could you take me to Dovlići before the train leaves? There's one last shelter I would like to see," she said.

Hearing her request, he did not know what to say. Ivan's orders were that no one was to take Tess to Dovlići.

When he did not answer, she felt that she had asked too much from him. Looking at him, she saw his confusion, and she smiled, then said, "It's alright. You don't have to take me to the train either. I'll figure it out. Good night, Alek."

Before he had time to answer, she hurried from the dining room and headed to the bedroom. Once inside, she began to pack. When she was finished, she sat on the bed with her notebook and finalized her writing about her experiences in Sarajevo. Though she felt discarded by Ivan, she continued to write about him with sincere love and respect for all that he was and all that he did. Even if he did not care about her, she still loved him.

Not knowing what to do, Alek sat alone in the dining room. Sometime after ten o'clock, Sergej entered the house from the back door, and immediately he called to Tess. Alek walked into the kitchen after hearing his voice, and the look on Alek's face told Sergej that Tess had returned safely, but Sergej already knew that from speaking with Ivan.

"She's leaving tomorrow. Why is she going? What happened?" Alek asked.

Sergej only shook his head. He removed his coat as he walked from the kitchen to the living room. Alek followed him as he waited for an answer.

Exhausted, Sergej laid his coat over the back of the sofa and sat down.

"Ivan wants you to go to the camp. Everyone else is there, except Lukáš. I'll stay here," Sergej said, and added, "When you get there, tell Ivan what Tess wants to do."

Alek grabbed his coat from the back of one of the dining room chairs and put it on as he walked into the kitchen. Without another word, he left the house, got into a car out back, and proceeded to the camp.

Sergej got up and walked to the bedroom to find Tess. This time he would not leave her alone in her sorrow. This time he would be the friend he felt she needed. He thought that if his wife were still alive, he would want someone to care for her with kindness and not to leave her alone when she was sad.

Seeing a light coming from under the door, he knocked lightly. "Tess, it's Sergej. Are you alright? Do you want me to make a fire for you?" he asked, then paused. "Do you need anything?" He paused again. "Do you want to sit with me and talk for a while?"

She did not answer.

"Tess?" he said, and waited.

From under the door, he saw the light go out and he knew she had nothing left to say. Her humiliation was too great, and he knew she not only doubted Ivan, but she doubted him as well. Now he knew he had lost another friend to the heartless side effects of the war.

Shaking his head, he returned to the dining room and sat alone at the table, waiting for Ivan to return. After a little while, Lukáš walked through the door, he informed Sergej that Ivan had decided to stay at the camp that night and not to come home as he had previously said he would; he would return in the morning. Then Lukáš went upstairs to sleep.

After securing the house, Sergej put on his coat and fell asleep on the sofa; someone had to stay downstairs to be close by if Tess needed anything. He had hoped that Ivan would come home that night, but he knew Ivan had many things to deal with. As his friend, Sergej did all he could to help, but now only Ivan could help himself.

CHAPTER FORTY-EIGHT

When Alek arrived at the camp, he went immediately to Ivan's tent. Ivan was discussing issues with a small group of his men, although he quickly concluded the conversation, requesting they leave, as Alek waited to talk with him. Looking at Alek, Ivan waited for him to tell him what happened when Tess went home, but before Ivan looked away, Alek saw a new kind of sadness in his eyes.

"Why didn't you come in the house?" Alek asked.

Not answering, Ivan only shook his head. He was not about to give explanations for his actions.

"Do you know she's leaving tomorrow? Well, she wants to leave tomorrow. She asked me to take her to the train. She also asked me to take her to Dovlići," Alek said.

Ivan's eyes slowly moved back to Alek, who still looked at him with the same confused expression. Ivan said nothing; he wanted to hear the rest of the story.

"I didn't answer her when she asked. Then she told me that I didn't have to take her to the train, that she would figure it out. Why is she leaving? She says she has to go back to write books, but she writes here. She writes about you. Does she know who you are?"

Again, Ivan said nothing. He looked away from Alek as he walked toward the opening of the tent.

"Let her see Mara and make her stay." He paused briefly. "You know, Mara could use a mother, and you could use a wife," Alek boldly suggested.

Ivan nodded. As Alek walked to the tent's opening, he saw Ivan's somber expression. Reaching for the tent flap, Ivan held it open for Alek to pass through. "Thank you for telling me. Go get some sleep," Ivan said, and his gaze was sad when Alek exited. He knew he had caused Tess' humiliation, and now he knew, if given the chance, she would leave. However, the decision he had to make was if he would allow her to go.

From Alek's forward comment about Tess being a mother and wife, Ivan saw how Tess' presence had changed everyone, not only him. She had endured everything Ivan had put her through, while he suffered nothing. At least not until now that he thought he had lost her. Before now, he had everything he could ask for, and it all waited for him in her. Because of his continual disbelief that any one person could care as much as she did, he threw happiness away with both hands—so much sorrow and all because of his pride.

He decided that he would go to her in the morning and take her to see Mara. It was up to him to take her, no one else. At this point, all he could hope for was that she would agree to go with him and not run away without finding what she came so far for. Perhaps with all that she was, she could forgive him, even if she no longer loved him. Because now he was certain, for a brief moment in their time together, she *had* loved him. Now he understood what her actions and words were trying to tell him. In their simplicity, her message was that she believed in him. She knew that he was the Black Rebel and it had no influence on her feelings for him. On what she felt for him, her decision was firm.

He also knew that when others hurried through life trying to achieve greatness, she lived what they sought—the greatness of being. She lived it and accepted all that came along with it: all the sorrow and pain, all the strife and struggle. Yet, somewhere she should have had happiness; however, he saw little of it in her life. She accepted that, just as she had accepted him as another unattainable dream.

It would have been easy to tell him that she loved him, but she would not burden him with her feelings for him. Because of her concern for him, he knew she would leave him to continue his life regardless of what made her happy. Because of that, he could not let her go without showing her that he loved and trusted her, and the only way he knew to do that was to bring her to Mara.

Ivan clearly felt that Tess helped people because it made them happy, and that happiness was where she found her place in life. He knew that for all she gave, she deserved more than others' happiness. He hoped that taking her to Mara would make her happy and make up for the pain he had caused her. In this act of complete trust, Ivan prayed Tess would know that he truly loved her.

Yet, Ivan also needed for her to know that she helped in unimaginable ways. She renewed his faith in his fight to survive this war. He felt she imagined her leaving would give him and his men their freedom. If she were gone, they would not have to protect her anymore. Though she saw herself as a burden to Ivan and his men, in actuality, she was the best part of the entire situation. She reminded them that life continues during bad times, and to allow any part of life to pass because you give in to circumstance is wrong.

She reminded Ivan that happiness can be found in the smallest of things. All you have to do is look for it. It waits for you to find it. Whether it resides in the smiles of children, or in the arms of the person you love, it waits for those who seek it. Because truly, as Tess had said to him one morning in Belgrade: "True love is the only prize worth pursuing—it's the only thing worth fighting for, the only thing worth dying for." Words of truth that were now seared into his very soul.

CHAPTER FORTY-NINE

The next morning, Tess awoke shortly after six o'clock. Placing the last of her belongings into her suitcases, she carried them to the back door. She walked back to the bedroom carrying her notebook and compact disc player. Looking at his bed, she thought about having shared this bedroom with the man she loved. Standing in the same spot she did when Ivan first showed her the room, she took one last look around. It had only been one month, but she had felt more at home there than anywhere she had lived; however, "All of those feelings were false," she told herself.

She walked to the bed and placed her notebook on the pillow. Inside the notebook, she left the letter that she had prepared prior to leaving for Sarajevo—it stuck out slightly from the top so Ivan would see it. This letter congratulated Mara for winning the competition and it had instructions for claiming the award from the foundation. She then placed her compact disc player with the disc containing the song about the American farmer on top of the notebook.

Toward the bottom of the bed, she left the coat that Ivan had bought for her in Belgrade. Glancing out the window, she saw it was a rather nice day; the sun was out and the wind was low. Having dressed warmly, she would manage until she was back in Belgrade where she could put on her own coat. Wrapping herself in a large, woolen shawl, she left the room, and closed the door quietly behind her. Without a sound, she exited the house through the kitchen door. She walked along a snow trodden path to the house where Mrs. Tomić now lived.

Tess knocked on the back door and Mrs. Tomić answered. Curious and happy to see Tess, she hurried Tess inside seeing that she wore no coat. Leading her to the table in the kitchen, she tried to give her breakfast. She spoke half in Serbian and half in English, but was not truly paying attention; however, the only word Tess understood was *Ivan*.

Tess shook her head and said, "No, Mrs. Tomić, I'm not hungry. I need Stefan. Is he here?"

Ivan did not officially permit Stefan to join the Black Rebels. Being that Stefan was only seventeen, Ivan felt he was too young. Even though it was not much of a life in Sarajevo during the war, Ivan wanted Stefan to live it as best he could without fighting.

"Yes, I get him," Mrs. Tomić answered in English, then she walked into the next room.

Stefan was there, and hearing Tess was in the kitchen, he followed his mother. Smiling as he saw Tess, he said, "Tess, what are you doing here so early?" He then sat down next to her. Mrs. Tomić walked to Tess, and standing behind her, she placed her hands on Tess' shoulders as she waited for Stefan to translate.

"Stefan, can you take me to Dovlići, please?" she asked, fully expecting he would say no.

Her request confused him, because he knew Ivan was the one escorting her. Still, Stefan had no idea that Mara was in Dovlići, nor did Mrs. Tomić know this. When they had asked Ivan where Mara was going, he did not say, and they understood it was for Mara's safety.

"Yeah, of course I can, but, where's Ivan?" he asked as he looked around the room.

Not knowing what to do, she lied. "He's still asleep. He's very tired. Will you take me now?" she asked.

Stefan translated what Tess had said to Mrs. Tomić. At once, Mrs. Tomić got upset and began to speak in Serbian. She was panicking and wanted Stefan to ask Tess questions.

"Mama wants to know, where's your coat? And why Ivan lets you walk around the streets by yourself?"

"My coat is at the other house. I just came from there. Can we leave now?"

"What's the hurry, Tess? Eat something first."

"I'm sorry. Stefan, please eat."

"No. I've already eaten. It's just, why leave now?"

She sighed. "I'm sorry, Stefan, I don't mean to be demanding. It's just that I wanted to get to Dovlići early, so I can catch the train to Belgrade this afternoon."

He frowned. "Are you leaving?"

Mrs. Tomić heard Tess say Belgrade and knew something was wrong. Stepping to Tess' side, Mrs. Tomić reached for her hand and looked questioningly at her.

Tess held Mrs. Tomić's hand and tried to smile. "I have to go back. I have obligations. It's almost Christmas and, well, there are things to do," she answered. She felt horrible for lying to people that she cared so deeply for, but she did not know what else to do. All she could think about was Ivan telling her, "You don't belong here. It's time for you to leave!"

Mrs. Tomić heard Tess say Christmas and while Tess had still been talking, she had started talking rapidly, again in Serbian, as she looked at Stefan.

He shook his head. "Mama, *please,*" he said. Then he translated what Mrs. Tomić had been saying. "Mama says you can't go. She wants you to be with us for Christmas."

"That's not possible," Tess said.

"No, you cannot go!" Mrs. Tomić interrupted.

"You can't leave now," Stefan said.

"Don't go!" Mrs. Tomić insisted.

Stefan frowned at his mother. "It's too early. It's too dangerous."

"Don't go!" Mrs. Tomić said once again.

"Mama, *stop!*" Stefan said and frowned again at his mother. Once she was quiet, he continued, "Mama needs," he said, stopped, and changed his words, *"We all need* you to stay here with us!"

"I can't. It's not possible. Please tell your mother that I thank her for her kindness and that I will always be grateful to her. Please tell her that, Stefan," Tess said as she shook her head, but she could not look at Mrs. Tomić.

He told his mother what Tess asked him to say, but still, Mrs. Tomić continued to talk. Tess could tell she protested her leaving, and was flustered, Tess stood up, kissed her on the cheek, and walked toward the door. "Stefan, I'll wait at the back door of the other house. I know it's a long drive and if you don't want to take me, I'll understand."

"Wait, Tess! I will take you. Wait for me," he said, then he returned his attention to his mother as she asked where Ivan was and how he could allow this to happen.

Tess stood at the door not looking at Mrs. Tomić. When Stefan left the room to get his coat, Mrs. Tomić walked to her. Hugging Tess, she spoke in Serbian.

Stefan walked back into the room and heard his mother and, again, he translated as she returned Tess' kiss. "Mama says that she loves you, and she will miss you, as we all do and will. She wants you to come back home to us soon. She says this is your home for always."

Then Mrs. Tomić pushed him on the arm because, even though her English was rusty, she knew he had not said all she wanted him to. She could tell from the look on Tess' face, so she told him to say the rest of what she had said.

He shook his head and expelled a sigh. "Mama says that no matter what stupid thing Ivan has done, this is *your* home. You are part of our family, you are her daughter now."

Hearing those words, Tess smiled as tears filled her eyes. Turning around, she opened the door and hurried from the house.

"Mama, whatever happened is not between you, Ivan, and Tess, it's between Ivan and Tess," Stefan said.

"Men are silly," Mrs. Tomić commented.

Stefan rolled his eyes and told his mother that he was taking Tess to Dovlići, then to the train. Then he said good-bye to her and chased after Tess. He told Tess to wait at the back door and he would bring the car to her. She waited, and in a few minutes, as he had said, he pulled the car to the back door. He quickly put her luggage inside the trunk, then he held the door open for her. Once she was securely inside, he darted around to the driver's side and got in.

As they drove away from the house, she asked him to stop for a moment while she took a final look back. How she wished Ivan would come running from the front door, demanding she get back inside, but she knew that would not happen. With great sadness in her heart, she told him to go as she stared out the back window until the house was no longer visible, except in her mind.

CHAPTER FIFTY

Once they had left, Mrs. Tomić walked to the other house. Entering from the back door, she went straight away to the bedroom down the hall as she frantically called to Ivan. She was suspicious because she knew nothing got past Ivan, and certainly not the woman he loved leaving Sarajevo without him. And if Tess was leaving, it was because Ivan had done something to chase her away. As she had said, *men are silly.*

As suspected, when she knocked on the bedroom door, no one answered. She opened the door, thinking that perhaps she was wrong, and that she would find Ivan asleep as Tess had said, but looking inside, the room was empty. Now she was certain something had gone wrong between them.

Hurrying from the room, she passed through the kitchen, then through the dining room. Seeing Sergej sleeping on the sofa, she shook him. "Sergej! Sergej, wake up!" she said loudly.

Sergej opened his eyes and sat up, thinking something terrible had happened. For a moment, he just looked at his mother.

Seeing him awake, she began ranting through her tears. "Where is Ivan? I thought he was sleeping. He's not home and Tess is gone! *Where* is Ivan?"

"Mama, you wake me up to ask me about Ivan? He's out," Sergej answered, still half asleep.

"Tess left! Why is Ivan not here to take her to Dovlići? She came and asked Stefan to take her. They left a few minutes ago. She's gone, luggage, everything gone! She's going back to Belgrade this afternoon."

"What? Ivan is the only one taking Tess anywhere," Sergej said. Standing up, he started walking toward the dining room.

Just then, Ivan opened the front door. Seeing Mrs. Tomić and Sergej's stares, he wondered what had upset them. "What is it? Why do you look at me like that?" he asked as he closed the door. When Mrs. Tomić began to cry, for a moment, Ivan thought someone was ill or had died.

"Tess is gone," Sergej said.

Ivan's gaze raced back and forth between Sergej and Mrs. Tomić. "Gone? Gone how? Gone where? Who took her? Where did they take her?" he asked, but not waiting for answers, he rushed past them toward the dining room, then through the kitchen. Hurrying to the bedroom, he pushed open the door. Seeing the empty room, his heart skipped a beat in disbelief, then he slowly stepped inside.

Sergej appeared in the doorway behind him and asked, "Are you happy now? Are you happy that you finally hurt her so badly that you chased her away?"

"It's not that simple," Ivan said. Looking at the bed, he saw the coat he had bought for her neatly placed there. Then he noticed her notebook and compact disc player on the pillow. Walking to the bed, he sat down and picked up her coat. Holding it to his face, he closed his eyes and inhaled deeply. It smelled of her perfume, and the sensation of kissing her the previous evening momentarily numbed him.

Opening his eyes, he placed the coat aside and reached for her compact disc player. Looking inside it, he saw the disc with the song about the American farmer's tragedy. He set that to the side and picked up the notebook. Opening it, he read the letter. He imagined that she felt with him being the Black Rebel, he would be able to find Mara and help her get the grant from the foundation. Seeing she had typed it on her foundation's letterhead, which included the telephone number and address, he hoped she had left it in case he wanted to find her; however, he did not need that to find her.

Ivan's eyes filled with tears as he looked toward the window. Then Sergej stepped into the room, but Ivan did not want to look at him—he knew what he would say.

"Mama said that Stefan is taking her to Dovlići, then he will bring her to the train. Now she's out in a car with Stefan, who isn't armed. He can't protect her if something happens. Not that he would know how even if he had a weapon."

Ivan was not listening completely. He was distracted by the over-confident attitude he had possessed, and his feeling that Tess would be there waiting for him. He never thought she would ask Stefan to take her to Dovlići.

Taking a deep breath, he prayed that there was still hope. "Delay the train until I arrive at the station. I'm going to Dovlići, then I'll go to the train. The men will be here any minute. You take them to Dovlići, but *you* come back here once Tess and Stefan leave Saint Michael's. Then have the men follow Tess and Stefan all the way to the train and provide for their safety. Have Stefan come back to the house with a couple of the men after Tess is safely on the train. When you next see Stefan, you had better talk with him," Ivan said.

"Are you getting Mara?" Sergej asked.

"I don't know," Ivan answered, and without another word, he gathered Tess' things, stood up, and walked past Sergej, who only stared at him.

Leaving the bedroom, Ivan walked back to the kitchen where Mrs. Tomić waited to find out what he would do. He approached her and kissed her cheek. "Don't worry, Mama. It will be okay," he said and kissed her cheek again. Smiling at her, he walked to the front door, and left the house carrying Tess' things. From there, he drove to Dovlići.

CHAPTER FIFTY-ONE

In one final attempt, Tess set out to search the last shelter where Mara may possibly be. The one shelter that was accepting children at the time Mara went missing. It was Tess' final hope to find the child she journeyed from America for. And though she wanted to hope that this would be the lucky place where she would succeed in her effort, her heart was already heavy with the sadness of failure. However, not with sadness for Mara's future because she now knew Idy was there to care for Mara.

Stefan took her directly to Saint Michael's. As he drove, they were silent, and he knew private thoughts consumed her attention. Regardless that he had many questions for her, especially why she was leaving, he did not want to disturb her. Once they arrived, Stefan talked to the Mother Superior and explained Tess' purpose. He then waited for Tess in the car, thinking she would prefer to see the children alone.

Tess followed the Mother Superior as they walked to the shelter's play yard. The grounds were not much, considering substantial fighting had occurred in this area. As Tess looked around, she remembered Ivan saying that Dovlići was an especially dangerous location, and that she should not go there, but nonetheless, there she was.

Sergej and seven of the men had driven to Saint Michael's as Ivan had requested. Shortly after Tess had gone inside to see the children, Stefan saw a three-car convoy rapidly approaching and he did not know what to do. Sitting forward in the front seat, he watched the cars as they surrounded his. To his relief, Sergej was the first out. Approaching the driver's side of Stefan's car, Sergej opened the door and immediately questioned him about what he was doing. Once having heard what Stefan had to say about how Tess needed to get back home, Sergej calmed down.

Sergej explained the situation to Stefan, who was shocked to find out that Mara was there at Saint Michael's, and that Tess' purpose for being in Sarajevo was to find Mara. Sergej told Stefan to stay out of the building so Mara would not see him. He then explained that he wanted Stefan to continue on to Užice and get Tess safely on the train. From there he was to return to Sarajevo with two of the men, and he would stay put until told otherwise. Stefan agreed, and once he got back into his car, four of the men went on ahead to Užice, and once there, they would take care of security on the train. Then Sergej and the remaining men drove around the back of the building to keep out of sight until after Tess and Stefan left.

Near to the play yard, the Mother Superior stopped at the gate and turned to Tess. Looking at her, she saw exactly what Ivan found so fascinating about her; she noticed Tess' deep concern as she watched the children playing in the snow. The Mother Superior smiled. "I am sorry, Miss Fordel, we have no little girls here by that name, but you are free to see the children," she said, then she opened the gate, allowing Tess to enter where the children played. After watching Tess for a moment, the Mother Superior left her at the entrance and went back inside the building.

Tess closed the gate and turned to look at the children. "Where to start?" she whispered, then she sighed and watched the children running, climbing, and laughing while they played. She did not know what Mara looked like. She could be any female child playing there. Mara could have been any child she had seen throughout her month of searching.

She looked at the children through tearing eyes. "If only Mara had sent a photograph of herself," she thought, as her gaze examined every child. Just then she noticed one child, a little girl, sitting on a bench by herself while the other children joked with each other as they scampered about in the snow. For some unknown reason, Tess was drawn to this little girl. She walked across the play yard and sat beside her: a beautiful, rosy cheeked child with creamy skin, and dark brown hair that hung to the middle of her back. She wore a slightly tattered coat of dusty brown wool, a pair of mittens, and a woolen cap. She had on trousers of dark gray, a lighter gray sweater, and a pair of brown boots, and all Tess could think about was Mara, and she hoped that Mara was not as desolate as this tender child appeared to be.

"Hi," Tess said and smiled at her. "What is your name?"

The child did not answer.

Tess reached into her purse and pulled out her phrase book. She then went page by page and looked for the translation of what she wanted to say. After a few pages, she found the entry, and placing the book in front of the little girl, she pointed to the phrase that asked her name. However, the little girl looked up at her with sadness in the depths of her large amber-brown eyes.

"What is your name?" Tess asked as she pointed to the phrase again.

The child only looked back at the book.

Reading further down the page, Tess found the translation that inquired whether the child spoke English and she pointed to it.

The girl looked at the book, shook her head, and turned the book back toward Tess, pointing to the next line down, which read: *I do not speak English.*

Tess smiled and felt she had reached this girl even if they did not speak the same language. She pointed again to the phrase: *What is your name?*

Again, the girl did not answer, she just looked down at her lap.

Tess hoped she would keep the child's interest as she pointed to the phrase, "I am from the United States." Then she pointed to: *Are you from,* then said aloud, "Sarajevo?"

As expected, the child did not answer.

Tess was silent as she looked back and forth from the phrase book to the child, but as they sat together, Tess was unaware that someone watched her. From a distance, Ivan observed her with the little girl. He stood on a hill, hidden by a cluster of trees, too far away for Tess to recognize him. Although, through binoculars, he saw her with complete accuracy and extreme love.

Tess leaned sideways toward the child and pointed to the phrase: *Where are your parents?*

Still, the girl was silent, though she gave signs of understanding as her eyes moved in Tess' direction.

Tess found the page with family names and pointed to the words, *mother* and *father,* and she hoped for an answer.

The child immediately began to cry.

"Oh no," Tess said. Then letting the book drop into the snow, she lifted the child into her arms. Quietly, the child cried as Tess held her tightly to her chest and pulled her shawl around her. It was as though the little girl had waited for someone to care about her, waited for someone to comfort her in her loss.

Ivan had tears in his eyes as he saw Tess holding the child. What Tess did not know was that the little girl she held was the same child she had come to Sarajevo to find. The child she tried to speak with, and now attempted to comfort, was Mara Jovanović. After lying to Tess for so long, Ivan could not have thought of a better way for them to meet. And though Ivan had only done what he thought was right, what he thought Mara's family would have wanted, Tess' love drew her to Mara as though they belonged together.

As Ivan saw the instantaneous affection between the two people he loved most in the world, he now thought differently and he was sorry for not taking Tess first thing to Mara. He should have let her take Mara back to America. Mara's parents were dead. Her entire family was murdered in this civil war. The devastation Mara had suffered being without him, and all that he had made Tess endure, was now more than he himself could bear.

Watching Tess, he knew all she had said was right. From the first words she spoke to him, to the last, all she said was the truth, but he had not been prepared to face the truth. He was prepared to kill, and do whatever else it took to survive this war, but he was not prepared to listen to the only person he knew that really cared about the important things in life: God, humanity, and love.

Unselfishly, and with great love for Ivan, Tess accepted his beliefs and goals. She showed him more love and understanding than any woman he had ever cared for. She also showed him more loyalty than any man that fought by his side. His men's families all had a great deal to lose if his men did not survive this war, but Tess would go back to America. She did not need him. She could have any man she chose, and he imagined that any good man would be overwhelmed with the quality and quantity of love she could give him; a love he felt it was too late to beg for, though beg he would, if he had the chance.

Ivan stood in the snow and watched them. Then he saw the Mother Superior approach Tess after the other children had gone inside.

Tess saw the Mother Superior nearing, and she stood up with Mara asleep in her arms. "Where are this child's parents? Is she an orphan?" she asked.

Seeing Mara sleeping contentedly in Tess' arms, the Mother Superior smiled. Against the vows she took to the church, she answered as Ivan had requested, saying, "She was brought to us several months ago. We don't know where this child's parents are. We don't even know her name."

"If she has no parents, can she be adopted? That is, if she would want that. She needs someone to love her. I could do that. Not all Americans are—" Tess stopped momentarily, but then continued, "I could give her everything she needs. I couldn't replace her parents, but she would be loved. I'd always care for her. Is there any chance of adopting her?"

Tess' pleas for Mara affected the Mother Superior. Wanting to say "yes" over the love Tess displayed, her promise disallowed it. She shook her head. "Every child here is on an unknown status list. Their parents may still be alive. Until we know that they are not, and that no other family is available to care for them, they must stay here. I am sorry, Miss Fordel. If anything happens, and we release her for adoption, I will let the authorities know you wish to adopt her. If you leave contact information, they will let you know, and if at that time you still want her, they will work it out," she answered, as she reached for Mara.

Tess did not want to let her go. She could not understand why she was so attached to this child in particular. Softly kissing the child's cheek and forehead, Tess placed her in the Mother Superior's arms.

Pulling a foundation business card from her purse, she handed it to the Mother Superior. "You can reach me at the number on this card, and thank you for letting me see the children," Tess said, and as she stroked the child's head, she smiled, then she watched the Mother Superior carry the child back into the building.

Shaking her head, Tess stood alone in the empty play yard. Looking at the ground, she rubbed her forehead and sighed. She had failed in her quest to find Mara and as she walked away, she felt numb. In silence, she then left the play yard and returned to the car where she asked Stefan to take her to the train depot. It was a long ride ahead to Užice. She turned around and looked at the church as they drove away, and she could not help thinking about that child and Mara. Strangely, somehow, she related the two, but did not know why.

As the car moved further away, the church only a speck out the rear window now, her heart broke for the third time during her stay in Sarajevo. The first time was when she learned Ivan was Iđy. The second time was after Ivan kissed her, then told her that it was time she returned home. Now, not finding Mara was the third.

Her experiences were too much to fully comprehend right then. She decided not to write more about her trip as she had originally planned, and she would try not to think about all that had happened. She would try very hard to forget, though in the back of her mind she knew she could not forget the love she lost there.

As Tess and Stefan made their way to Užice, Ivan saw Sergej head back to Sarajevo, while the other men followed Tess and Stefan from a safe distance. Once Tess would arrive safely at the train station, Ivan would breathe a sigh of relief.

CHAPTER FIFTY-TWO

After Ivan watched Tess leave Saint Michael's, he walked down the hill to the play yard. Standing where Tess and Mara had sat, he looked at the snow and noticed something there. Bending down, he picked up Tess' phrase book, and brushing the snow from the cover, he placed it in his pocket.

He entered the building to find the Mother Superior, and walking down a dark, damp passage, he saw her ahead of him. It was difficult for him to smile, though he tried, as he called after her, saying, "Mother Superior."

Hearing his voice, she turned around. "Ivan, it is good you've returned. Mara needs to see you, and Miss Fordel was here. Just as you said, she came. Miss Fordel picked Mara out from all the children. She asked if she could adopt her. I think that would be a good match. They belong together," she said as they walked down the stone corridor.

"I know. I saw them."

"And you belong with them."

Walking into her makeshift office, they sat together for a while. He told her of Tess' offer to solicit funds for the Cause, which would mean that she would help the homeless children the war had left behind. He sighed and he appeared desperate as he told her of Tess' many kind gestures to him and his men. And to her surprise, he spoke openly about what he felt for Tess.

"I don't know what to do. The only woman I have ever truly loved, I've lost, and that makes me lost: lost without a country, and lost without the one thing I need. The war will be over soon and what have we gained? All this fighting, and for what reward?" He shook his head and took a deep breath. "Everyone looks to me for answers and I have none. I don't know what to do." Again, he shook his head. "But I guess there really is nothing left to do except wait and rebuild."

She smiled and patted his hand. "Ivan, you know exactly what you must do."

He looked up at her and, seeing her smile, he knew she was right. He did know what to do. He would walk away from the war for a while, and risk his pride for the woman he loved. He would find Tess and tell her the truth about what he felt for her. If she rejected him, he would try to accept her decision; however, he knew he would fight to win her back. But no matter what Tess' answer was, he would bring Mara to Tess; Mara would be Tess' daughter, of that he was confident.

"Where's Mara? I'll take her home today," he said.

The Mother Superior smiled and led him to where she had left Mara to sleep. Entering a small room with several beds, he walked to her where she laid crying and facing the wall.

Sitting down next to Mara, he stroked her hair, then whispered, "Mara, don't cry."

She recognized his voice and, sitting up, she put her arms around his neck. Through her tears, he hears her say, "Idy, I want to go home." Her voice was weak from crying, but she sat on his lap, and he held her as he waited for her to calm down. Once she did, she smiled and expelled a heavy sigh.

"Mara, did you like the lady that was here before? Was she nice to you?" he asked.

Sitting with her back toward his chest, she pressed against him and nodded. She pulled his gloves from his hands and played with them as she tried to fit her little hands inside them. Seeing this, he smiled. He loved her as though she was his daughter and in many ways she was. Though he had lost his little sister, he felt Mara was his from the time she was born. She always loved him best and always cried when he left her. When he was in Sarajevo, he took her everywhere with him, but that was before the war, and now he had to provide for her safety and her future.

"Would you like to go to America and live with her?" he asked.

When Mara stopped moving, he knew she thought about it, and he knew her response would be appropriate.

"Will you come with me?" she asked, and as she waited for his answer, she stuffed her hands back inside his gloves, then rested them in his palms.

He looked at the Mother Superior, who stood in the doorway. She, too, waited for his answer.

"I don't know, Mara." He shook his head. "It depends."

"Depends on what?" she asked.

Mara was an intelligent seven-year-old. He had taught her many things and, through his caring for her, he passed onto her his analytical abilities. Even though she asked the right question, he did not know how to explain the circumstances. In the past, he would talk to her as he would any adult and she always understood, but this time was different.

"Mara, do you remember when we mailed your book to America?"

Again, she pulled off his gloves and began playing with them. By this, he could tell she was seriously thinking; yet, not about her book, but about what the purpose of this conversation was. Sliding her hands back into his gloves, she moved her fingers about inside them as though they were hand puppets playing with each other.

When she did not answer immediately, he repeated his question. "Do you remember that?"

She nodded.

"The lady that was here before is the person who controls that writing competition. You have won the competition. She came from America to find you. She wants to take you back to America to live with her. Would you like that?" he asked.

She ignored his question and instead she asked him, "What is her name?"

He smiled at her cleverness in answering a question with another question, then he said, "Tess Fordel."

"Tessy!" she said, smiling at Ivan, as she turned around to see him. Her expression told him that she understood the effort Tess made in coming to Sarajevo to find her. From the way that Mara said Tess' name, adding the endearing y ending, Ivan knew that Mara liked Tess very much. Mara then turned back around and faced the Mother Superior.

"She is a very good person and cares a lot about you. She loves you, and has come a very long way to find you," he said.

Turning toward him again, for a moment, she squinted slightly at him. Then from the bluntness of a child's unique wisdom, she asked him exactly what she wanted to know. "Idy, do you love Tessy?"

Ivan's expression softened as his eyes lowered to her hands that were still stuffed inside his gloves. "Yes, I love Tessy, and I love you, Mara, and I want you to be happy and safe."

"Then we both go to America!" she answered and placed her arms around his neck; however, he could not tell Mara that Tess may not want to be with him, and, in time, he felt that Mara would forget him and be happy with Tess.

His arms moved tighter around her little form, and he lifted her up as he stood. Walking to the Mother Superior, who kissed Mara on the cheek, he told her that he was taking Mara to Tess and that he would return to Sarajevo in time.

"Go to America with Miss Fordel and Mara. *Do not* come back to Sarajevo, Ivan. Your time here is over. Stay in America and be happy. Think of yourself and do this for yourself. Stop sacrificing your life for a war that will only repeat itself. God has given you a great gift. *Do not* throw it away. He *will not* offer it a second time," she advised.

Ivan smiled at her, then he left Saint Michael's with Mara in his arms. He drove back to Sarajevo and dropped Mara off with Mrs. Tomić. Although happy to be home again, Mara still began to cry when Ivan tried to leave.

"I will see you tomorrow in Belgrade. We will stay there awhile, then we will go to America. So, don't cry. Sergej will take you on the train this afternoon, and I promise that I will come and get you in Belgrade tomorrow. How does that sound?" Ivan asked.

Mara stopped crying as she kissed Ivan good-bye. He then asked Mrs. Tomić to pack Mara's things for the trip, and she agreed. After kissing Mrs. Tomić on both cheeks and kissing Mara good-bye again, Ivan then left the house. Looking over his shoulder, he saw Mara waving to him from the back door. He smiled, waved back to her, blew her a kiss, then continued onto the other house.

Finding Sergej in the dining room, Ivan explained that he wanted him to get Mara to the train at Užice that afternoon. Ivan would be on the train as well, but he did not want Mara to see him. Once Sergej and Mara were in Belgrade, Sergej was to keep Mara at his apartment until Ivan came for her. Sergej agreed, then he left for the long drive to the train station.

Ivan was grateful that the weather was mild that day, so he would make good time. As he had requested, Sergej had already sent a message to delay the train to wait for Ivan's arrival. As he drove, he wondered how he would tell Tess the truth when he introduced Mara to her. Just then he did not know, but he would find the right words when the time came. Just then, his mind was on what he needed to do before he went to the train station—he had one stop to make on his way. He needed to meet with one of his informants and pick up two of his men who waited for him in

Višegrad, and so he made haste in order to get to the station as quickly as possible.

CHAPTER FIFTY-THREE

Once in Višegrad, Ivan met with the informant, who confirmed that the Serbian military had removed soldiers from the trains running to and from Belgrade. After that, he and his two men made their way to Užice. He drove as one of his men sat in the front seat and one in the back, and, without interruption, they made it to the train station in record time.

Stopping in front of the depot, Ivan took Tess' notebook, compact disc player, and coat from the trunk. He ordered his men to return to the Rebel camp and to wait there for further orders. Then he walked into the depot. Finding Sergej inside, Ivan and Sergej then walked into an empty compartment toward the rear of the train.

"Who's with Mara?" Ivan asked.

"Alek has her inside the train near the front," Sergej answered.

"Have Alek go back and stay with Mama. Don't take Mara off the train until you see Tess go through the train station. I don't want any chance of Tess seeing either of you in Belgrade."

Sergei nodded.

"Tomorrow morning, I will call you at home. I will let you know what will happen then. If Tess agrees to stay in Belgrade with me, I will pick Mara up from your apartment and take her to meet Tess. If for any reason I can't pick her up, I'll have you bring her to the hotel," Ivan said.

"Why tomorrow morning? Why not tonight? Don't you think bringing Mara would be the best way to explain?" Sergej asked.

Ivan shook his head. "It's more complicated than that."

"Why?" Sergej shrugged

"I need time with Tess, time alone. I want her to stay with me in Belgrade awhile, but not out of obligation because Mara's there. I want her to make the decision before she knows about Mara. She might change her mind after she finds out, but it all depends on Tess. Whatever happens, I will let you know tomorrow morning," he said.

"So if she says she doesn't want to stay in Belgrade, then you won't let her meet Mara?" Sergej asked. He did not really understand Ivan's plan, but he knew in this instance it was difficult to have a plan.

"No. I will have them meet anyway. If Mara wants to go to America to live with Tess, and Tess still wants her, I will allow it. It's just that I'd like the three of us to spend time together in Belgrade. I'd like Tess to see that things here are not so uncivilized and not so different than in Manhattan."

Sergej laughed, shook his head, and said, "I think you underestimate Tess. She'd live in a cardboard box with you."

"I know you and Tess have formed a friendship, but you don't know everything," he said and, pausing, he looked out the window as his gaze searched the few people on the platform. "Where is Tess? Is she secured on the train?"

"She's fine. She's in the middle of the train. Stefan got her on, then he left with Dragan and Željko. He said that she's very quiet and very upset. Mama is very upset. Everyone's sad that Tess left. I guess we all thought she would stay," Sergej said, but then he changed the subject. "There are six men on the train from front to back. There is one man in each car on each side of the car Tess is in. They are all armed and the train is secured."

Again, Ivan looked through the window toward the depot. He sighed deeply as he recalled the events that had occurred since he had met Tess. For a moment, he wondered what their future would be, or if they would even have a future together.

"If all goes as I want it to, let's get Mama to Belgrade to take care of Mara for a while. Even if Tess agrees to stay in Belgrade, I still want time alone with her. I need that. Mama will miss Mara if we go to Manhattan, so this will give her time to visit with Mara before we go," he said, then added, "I'll see you tomorrow in Belgrade."

Sergej smiled, stepped from the compartment, and closed the door. But he quickly opened the door again, handed Ivan an envelope, and said, "I almost forgot. This came for you. It's additional information on Tess."

Ivan looked at Sergej, then at the envelope. He hesitated, because he had closed that investigation. However, wondering what else was discovered about Tess, he took it from Sergej and thanked him.

Sergej nodded, stepped out again, and closed the door. He walked toward the front of the train and entered the compartment where Mara and Alek waited for him. Seeing him, Mara stood on the seat and reached up to Sergej so he would pick her up. He asked her to sit back down for a minute and motioned Alek to step outside with him. Sergej told Alek what Ivan wanted him to do. Alek agreed and left the train. When Sergej went back inside the compartment, again, Mara stood for him to pick her up, which he did. He then sat near the window with her on his lap so she could look outside.

As Sergej had told Ivan, Tess was sitting in a compartment in the middle of the train. And though Ivan longed to go to her and talk with her on their way back to Belgrade, he stayed where he was. Not wanting to be bothered, Ivan locked the compartment door and pulled down the shades on the windows leading to the passageway outside, then he sat next to the window.

As the train pulled away from the station, he stared at the envelope Sergej had handed him and debated opening it. He had burned all the rest of the documentation he had received about Tess, and he wondered why this last bit of information only got to him now.

He turned the envelope over and started to open it, but stopped himself. He looked out the window at the desolate landscape as if he would find answers there. Then he looked at the envelope again. Tapping his finger on the envelope's flap, he shook his head, and opened it. Pulling out several pieces of paper, he unfolded them, and started to read them.

It was a medical report on Tess, and he frowned as he read the document. The report said that she previously had breast cancer. All of a sudden, the scars he saw on her breast made sense. From the report, he now knew both breasts were affected. Looking at the date of the report, he saw it was dated three years before Tess moved to New York.

Turning the page, he read about the procedures she had endured from this illness and the surgery that took part of her body. He then read about the numerous surgeries that she went through to reconstruct what was taken. Thinking of the small part of her that he had seen, to him, she looked perfect, with only faint scars as proof. He shook his head and wondered what effect this event had on her as a woman.

Folding the papers, he slid them back into the envelope. As he wondered what this ordeal caused her to feel, he slid the envelope into his inside jacket breast pocket. He thought about the time frame and knew that she had no family other than her husband, who had abandoned her just after the first medical report date. He then wondered how she managed on her own.

His mind spun so rapidly that, for a moment, he could not form a cohesive thought. All he could hear were his last words to her, "You don't belong here. It's time for you to leave!"

How that must have reminded her of her ex-husband. How that must have demeaned her as a woman. He hoped she did not think that he knew about her illness then. Still, even if she knew that he did not know about it, nothing could lessen the hurt his hasty words had caused her. No matter how strong a woman she was, no matter how well she could go on by herself, he knew she needed him, and he knew he needed her as well.

For a moment he thought about her ex-husband. The thought of anyone causing her harm made him want to protect her more—protect her, even if from himself. Disgusted with himself, Ivan sighed. His gaze locked on the passing landscape out the window and, without knowing it, he became lost in private thoughts.

CHAPTER FIFTY-FOUR

Ivan was unaware how long he had been daydreaming, but as he came back to the present, his gaze moved to her notebook. Opening it, he began to read what she had written about her time in Sarajevo. She spoke plainly and, in her writing, she did what she had said she wanted to do; she expressed Ivan's ideas regarding the disintegration of his country.

As he read, he saw their views were identical. Just as the book she wrote about the farmer she encountered, she wrote with complete conviction about what she had experienced while in Sarajevo. Tess believed that what she had learned while she was there was the only way to see the situation, and that was Ivan's way.

Yet, Tess did not only leave her writing so that Ivan could read it. She left it because, in a sense, she felt that he had sent Mara's writing to her for safe keeping. So in return, she placed her writing in his hands for safe keeping, or for whatever he felt was just to do with it. In her heart, they were even; this was a sign of her complete trust in him.

As Ivan continued reading, he knew that they had both changed in that month. Their views, though possibly opposed in the beginning, had now come to a point of compromise and understanding. From her words, he knew that she not only accepted and respected him and his ideals, but also loved him completely. From the tone of her writing, if she had stayed, she had planned to do whatever it took to help him and his people. As he saw it, she believed in the Cause he fought for almost more than he did.

As he read on, his heart was heavy and he wondered what could have happened to change her so drastically in one month's time. Though he had not initially agreed with her opinions, he never wanted to steal her freedom of thought; however, he had not. He only showed her that there were many ways of seeing the same situation, and all were proper for the viewer; it all teetered on the individual's viewpoint. And now her opinions were very definite—definite, and exact to his.

She concluded her writing with a folk song from his country. It was called *Heaven Above*. Reading the words, it was as though he heard her voice speaking them inside his head:

Heaven, heaven above, oh my dearest love! With your hands so tender, with your fingers slender, you have torn away my heart! Yes, with hands so tender, and with fingers slender, you have torn away my heart.

In honor of the two people she loved, Tess titled this book *The Yugoslavian: In Search of Mara Jovanović.*

CHAPTER FIFTY-FIVE

Issues with the tracks delayed the train several times; nothing serious, but the train arrived late in Belgrade. Ivan watched carefully as Tess exited the train with a station attendant carrying her luggage behind her. Shortly after, Ivan saw Sergej carrying Mara into the station. Mara was asleep by then, and Sergej pulled up her hood so the bustle of the station would not wake her. Once they had gone, Ivan's men gathered near the station's entrance and waited for him. When he joined them, they spoke briefly, then he left the station and went to his apartment, and the men went to theirs.

After stopping at the front desk of the hotel to retrieve her key, Tess had the bellman take her luggage to her room. She handed him a tip and, after he left, she closed the door and walked to the dresser. She planned to leave on the next Red Cross flight to Budapešt, which she hoped would depart the next afternoon—their flights always arrived and departed on Wednesdays, and this day was Tuesday.

Too weary to worry about it just then, she quickly undressed, took a hot shower, and went to bed. From all she had experienced, she lay there unable to sleep. Her mind was troubled over Ivan and Mara. She could not imagine how she failed so tragically to help the two people she loved. Yet, she had a fondness for that mysterious child at Saint Michael's, so that made three people that touched her heart.

At half past one the following morning, she still lay there staring at the ceiling. Exhausted from her trip, but mostly from her heartbreak and failures, her mind found no answers. To her, the entire situation was a fiasco. She always found a way to help those in need, and, now, continuing her position in her own foundation appeared unnatural. She would resign the position and elect a new chairperson. She would continue to fund it and make her public appearances, but reading another child's story was impossible. The pain was too much and, in the end, she could not face her failure. With that tormented thought, she finally slept.

It was five o'clock when the door to her room slowly opened. She was exhausted in sleep and did not hear the intruder as he closed and locked the door behind himself. As he stood in the doorway watching her, his breaths came silent, long, and deep. In the darkness he moved toward the bed and looked down at her. He could tell she lay naked beneath the covers, just as she did that night in Sarajevo when she gave up the comfort of the larger bed to him.

How beautiful she was to him. Even with the scant light filtering through the drapes, she was the most beautiful woman he had ever seen. For a moment he lost his courage and wanted to leave. He felt he should let her get on with her life, but looking at her, he had to have her—he needed her in *his* life.

With the slightest movement, he sat on the bed and leaned over her. His lips touched hers and, as he kissed her, she stirred. Slipping his arms around her back, he lifted her to his chest. As he continued to kiss her, she awoke. Seeing him, and feeling the familiarity of his touch, her arms moved around his neck as she whispered, "Ivan."

"I love you," he said. "From the first moment I saw you, I loved you. If only I—"

She pulled him closer and kissed him desperately. "I was so worried about you. I embarrassed you in front of your men. I talked to you in a way that I had no right to. I'm sorry. That was wrong. I presumed so much and I was so wrong. I wanted so much to help…I thought—"

Stroking her hair, he kissed her again. Pushing her back toward the pillows, he slipped the covers from her and glanced down at her body.

Sitting up, she pulled the sheet to her chest as she shook her head, saying, "Ivan," but she did not really know how to tell him what she needed to.

Seeing her hesitation, he reached for her hand, lifted it to his lips, and kissed it.

Again, she shook her head. "I don't know how much you know about my past other than who I was married to, and my foundation, but what I told you about my time with," she hesitated, "him." She said *him*, not wanting to speak her ex-husband's name. "And the real reason I filed for divorce," she said, but hesitated again.

"It doesn't matter. I'm happy you did."

"No. I have to tell you. It wasn't just his running around with other women and his abusive nature. He left me when I told him that I had—"

Ivan put his fingers to her lips, stopping her from continuing. "I know. He left you when he found out that you had breast cancer," he said.

She expelled a deep sigh, looked down, then back at him

He shook his head in disbelief. "I am sorry you had to go through all that by yourself. I want you to know that I just found out before I got here. I didn't know before."

"It's my past, but that's not why I'm telling you. You need to know that my body isn't what you might expect."

"To me, you are perfect," he answered, and not saying another word, he looked into her eyes as he quickly undressed, then he lay next to her. Smiling at her, he kissed her again as his hands moved down her body. With tenderness he made love to her, and every moment of pleasure balanced the pain and loneliness they both had endured until that moment.

When he awoke awhile later, she was asleep in his arms. He took a smooth, deep breath as though seeing her there with him, belonging to him, lifted a tremendous weight from him. He had not worked out the details of their life, but those were no longer decisions he would make alone. Those were decisions they would make together. Looking at her, he kissed her gently not wanting to wake her, but she moaned softly, waking anyway. Opening her eyes, she saw him and smiled.

His life had changed drastically since they had met. Changes he now appreciated as he held her. How he ever survived without her, he could not remember. In one month, she had become an integral part of his existence. Looking at her now, what he saw in her eyes displayed her immense love for him. Smiling, he kissed her again, and, again, he made love to her, trying to realize she was his.

CHAPTER FIFTY-SIX

This was a different type of morning for them. Lounging about in bed, nude, no hurry to go anywhere, or do anything, and no pressing thoughts about the war. Their empty breakfast plates were neatly placed on the room service cart near the door, and the aura around them was contentment.

In the back of Ivan's mind, he was deciphering the facts of their past month together. Holding her close to him, he sighed. "Were you really leaving me?" he asked.

She thought for a moment, then began to turn away from him.

He held her in place as she lay next to him with her head resting on his shoulder. Then he lifted her face to see her. "Were you?" he asked again.

"I didn't know what else to do. I felt—" She paused, thinking she should tell him that she knew he was Idy, but she then thought he should have the opportunity to tell her.

Wondering what she was thinking, he waited for her to continue.

"I felt I burdened you. I felt I was in your way and you were helping me when you should have been out taking care of—," she said, not exactly knowing how to label what he did as the Black Rebel. "You and your men were in danger because of me. Though I still don't understand why anyone wanted to find me except, perhaps, to find you. You didn't need to waste time with me. I accomplished nothing. All my fairy tale notions of helping were useless."

"You did help. I couldn't admit it at the time, but you kept up the morale of the men when it seemed that nothing else would. When you fight a war, as we do, you never know where you'll find help, or what kind of help you'll receive. One minute people believe in what you're doing, and then, when you're not successful, they lose faith. My men are mercenaries of a different kind. Much of the help we receive is from anonymous sources. Just as they don't know who we are, we don't know them, but they believe in our Cause. We receive aid from many religious avenues and that money helps feed and medicate refugees, mostly children. We have our contacts, they have their contacts, and all involved want to be paid. You have to pay for loyalty in war. Unfortunately, the currency of war is currency, not favors. We pay all our informants well, yet we make no money, but no matter how this war will end, we fought for peace and to save lives."

"It's so complicated. How did you know what to do to survive?" she asked.

"What you don't know, you learn. But there isn't one man in the Rebels that didn't do their required time in the army. They are all trained soldiers," he said.

"How did you know it began?" she asked.

"Tanks surrounded Sarajevo, and that was the day our lives changed forever. That day, I knew we could never go back to what we were before. Our country was shattered and there was no way to fix it. At first we didn't think we'd survive, but we had to try, and so we did survive. And even if this feels like it is the end of this war, even if it ends for fifty or one hundred years, it will start again, but no one really won this time, and many lost so much," he said.

"No one won?" she asked.

"Tomorrow, in Paris, the presidents from Serbia, Croatia, and Bosnia will sign what will be known as the Dayton Agreement. This document officially ends the war in Bosnia," he said.

"So it's over," she said, and expelled a sigh.

"Do you think I would have dared to take you to Sarajevo unless the end was near?" he asked, as he pushed the hair back from her cheek, smiled briefly at her, and kissed her lips. In his eyes she could see he remembered everything he had endured. It was as though he suddenly opened the gates to his soul and the horrors of this war, which he had locked away, were free for a while. When she looked away, she felt him sigh.

"In April of 1992, eighteen thousand Serbian troops surrounded Sarajevo from the mountains around the city. I was not there at the time. I was here in Belgrade. The only reason we remained in possession of the house you lived in was because Sergej's family, and the surrounding families, are predominantly Serbian. Because of that false allegiance, there was little interference with our daily lives, but we saw what the war did to the innocent," he said, trying to explain what, who, and how, though he had been in the game so long that none of what he said made sense any more. It was all faith, lost faith, and regained faith, only to be lost again, and the only thing that mattered was that soon the current conflict would be over.

Then he noticed she had looked back at him. Not belaboring the point, he stroked her face and tried to change the subject. "I did what I had to. I did what I could, but none of that matters any more. What really changed everything for me was seeing your defeat that last night in Sarajevo. When I saw your expression, I knew—" He looked up toward the ceiling. Shaking his head, he then looked back at her. He noticed her attentive stare and he knew she understood what he was trying to say, but he said it anyway. "I knew *I* had defeated you, and I hated myself for it. That was never my intention. I was no better than any Nationalist in their attempt to conquer what didn't belong to them. Though, in my conceit and selfishness, I never imagined you'd leave. Thinking about how I treated you, I don't know why you didn't leave sooner."

"It's over now. My opinions have changed. You were right about everything, Ivan. So don't think about the past, only the future," she said, then she sat up and looked toward the bottom of the bed.

He sat up and positioned himself to face her. She smiled at him when he looked at her, then she leaned toward him and kissed him. Placing his arms around her, he pulled her back down and as close to him as he could.

"What is our future to be? Do you even want to be with me? I can't expect you to go back to Sarajevo, but I don't want to be without you. I need you, I need you with me. Will you stay with me? Stay here in Belgrade with me for a while?" he asked.

"You must have to get back. You can't just walk away," she said.

"You let me worry about that. I don't have to spend all my time in Sarajevo. We will stay here at my apartment in Belgrade. When I travel, you will come with me, except when I go to Sarajevo; then you will stay here. You will be protected at all times. I won't let anything happen to you. I promised that before and I will keep that promise. No one will ever take you from me, and anyone that tries will die."

As he held her, she moved her head from the pillow to his shoulder. Though she did not look at him, she knew he looked at the scars on her breast as his fingers began softly stroking them. For a moment she watched his fingers moving gently along the scar on the left breast, and though she could not feel his touch, his motions told her of his delicacy, and she smiled. When she looked up at him, he smiled at her to hide what he was thinking.

"I see questions in your eyes. Please don't be afraid to ask," she said.

He shook his head.

"It's okay, Ivan, as I said before, it's my past. The fact that you don't mind, and you don't look at me with pity, is why I can talk about it with you."

He shook his head again. "How did you go through it alone?"

"I wasn't alone. I had wonderful doctors, and thoughtful friends, but I had one friend, the best friend, and in times of trials, the only friend. He was there every step of the way. He never left me once. I had God with me. Who could possibly be a better ally? He alone held my fate in his hands, and I trusted Him to do what was best for me."

Ivan smiled and knew she was right, but he still wondered why, and asked, "Why did you have to get this disease?"

"I read a very interesting article that said cancer is not a disease, but a warning mechanism that something is wrong in your body. It said, once cancer is found you need to take immediate action, so I did. I had the tumor removed. Everything had to change, especially the way I thought. I knew that I could no longer be a servant to people that were hurtful. I could no longer feel sadness, anger, and resentment."

"You, resentful? There's not a resentful bone in your body."

"I harbored a lot of resentment, but I changed that."

"Who wouldn't resent him?" Ivan commented, since he imagined she had been resentful of her ex-husband, but he was wrong. Then his arms moved around her to hold her closer to him as if to protect her from her ex-husband's memory.

"No, not toward him, toward me," she answered.

Ivan frowned, not understanding why she would feel resentment toward herself.

"I gave into everyone and tried so hard to fulfill others' needs and ignored my own needs. My entire life, I took what others gave, I was everyone's helper. You'd be surprised how when you don't do for some people, they disappear very quickly. I don't mean friends living their lives and you don't talk to them for a while, even years. I mean people that don't have time for you when you aren't doing favors for them; once they get what they want from you, they're on their way, and don't give you a second thought until they need something else from you. Because I was always doing favors for unappreciative people, I resented myself. I could only blame myself for the way that I was, so only I could change me."

"All you do is help others," he said.

"It's different now. I don't help others because they demand that I do, or cry to me with their sad stories to try to make me help them. I help others because I want to. I *choose* whom I will help. It's all in how you see others and how you see yourself."

She was quiet for a moment. Now she was the one to remember and he could see it in her eyes.

"If I weren't married to him, and he hadn't been who he was, and how he was, things could be very different for me at this moment. But what worries me now is, when I look into your eyes, I see your hatred for him. You must let it go; I did. Please do that for me. He's insignificant."

Ivan made no comment to her request. He only shook his head, looked at her, kissed her, then changed the subject. "So there are no more signs of this warning in your body?"

"I don't know," she answered.

"What do you mean?" he asked as he frowned, obviously upset with her answer.

"I had the surgery to remove the cancer and remove both breasts so there would be no chance of any reoccurrence within the breasts. Then I had reconstructive surgery, but I didn't follow the doctor's recommendation to undergo chemotherapy."

"I'm happy that you didn't, but, why didn't you? So many people follow their doctor's orders."

"Even though it may help others, I knew pushing such a chemical through my veins would not benefit me. I don't know how I knew it, I just felt it. There was no proof that any cancer cells were floating around in my body, and until they proved there were, I felt no reason to treat what wasn't there. I don't like 'what if' scenarios and, in the end, it ended up that I did not need treatment. One simple test proved I wouldn't have benefited from it," she answered.

"Could you be sick now?"

"Yes, but so could anyone else be sick with another condition and not know it. Just as the victims of this war that have suffered and died, had they known their fate, would they have done something as drastic to escape it? Maybe some of them, but not all of them. If I am to perish from this, I will do so on my own terms. I certainly will not help it along by abusing my body with radioactive chemicals, that in *my individual case,* wouldn't have helped me. I won't kill the healthy cells I need to survive on the random chance of killing what bad cells may exist. No. Instead, I will do the best I can with my health. The rest is in God's hands. Besides, no matter what I want or what I do, when God wants me, I'm His," she said.

Ivan was silent. He looked deeply into her eyes as if he could enter her body, find any stray cancer cells, and kill them in order to protect her. Then the thought of losing her to an invisible foe twisted his insides, but the strength he saw radiating from her gaze calmed him, and from that he knew she was not afraid.

Just then, everything made sense to him: her lack of fear to travel so far to find Mara, how she stood up to him so many times, and how she walked into the middle of a war with complete disregard for her own safety. He knew then, beyond all doubt, how similar they were, how sensible she was, and how very much he loved her.

Pushing all this aside, he wanted to tell her many things, but Sergej was waiting for his call, and he thought about taking Mara shopping for new clothes so she would look pretty for Tess. With those thoughts pestering him, he became more tenacious to make her agree that she would stay.

"Tess, tell me you'll stay. I need to hear you say that you will. I need to hear you say, yes."

Not looking at him, she considered what the right thing to do was, but he grew impatient, and all he could think about was how much he loved her.

"I love you, Tess. I want you with me always. What I may have to do back in Sarajevo doesn't matter, so tell me you'll stay."

She looked at him, smiled, and nodded.

He kissed her, then sat up while she remained back against the pillows. "I want you to rest. I have to go and do something, but I'll be back in less than two hours. I have to get something, but I'll be back quickly. So rest and be ready when I return. We'll go to my apartment then."

She smiled.

Kissing her again, he stood up, and walked into the bathroom. Once he turned on the shower, she put on her robe, and sat quietly at the table near the window. She imagined that he was leaving now for some covert meeting. Staring out the window, she still felt other issues pulled him away. As much as she knew that he loved her, she felt his heart would always belong to his country even if it also belonged to her. As she saw it, her staying in Belgrade would only take him away from finishing what he had started.

After Ivan showered, he exited the bathroom wearing a towel about his waist. He walked to where she sat at the window and kissed her forehead. As he dressed, he watched her looking outside, and she appeared sad and lost in thought. Walking to her again, he stooped down by her side. Looking up at her, he turned her face toward him. For a split second he saw defeat in her eyes, and he panicked. He saw her lost and alone, but then she smiled at him, and her desolation vanished.

Standing up, he pulled her up from the chair and into his arms and kissed her again. Now he felt free to hold her and kiss her whenever he chose, but as he held her, he could feel her uncertainty.

"Tess, everything will be fine, you'll see. If we're together nothing else matters."

He looked at her, and examining her gaze, he saw her hiding her fear from him. She now had the same look as she did that day he left her on the train with Sergej. He saw her doubting that he would return, and he wanted her to be sure.

"I'll be back in less than two hours. I must go and take care of something. It's something for us that I'm doing now, not something for the war. You'll see when I return, so rest now, and before you know it, I'll be back," he said, then he led her to the bed and forced her to lie down. Sitting next to her, he kissed her and, again, he could feel the fear in her reaction. The only thing he could do was leave, get Mara, and come back quickly. He decided to save shopping for Mara until they could all go together. He imagined that Tess would like that.

Ivan knew that once Tess met Mara, and knew that he was Idy, he would ask her to marry him. He would have to wait to ask her, because he wanted no lies or secrets between them—a thought that made him smile. With that, his life would be complete and he would be united with the two people he loved the most: Tess and Mara. He hoped Tess wanted to marry him. He was never married, he never thought that he would be, but now he knew that was what he truly wanted. He imagined that once Tess felt he would not leave her, the loneliness she knew would eventually disappear.

"Two hours," he said, and kissed her again, then he walked to the door. Turning around before he left, he smiled at her. "I love you, Tess," he said, then he left. Waiting at the elevators, he heard her room door open. Looking back, he saw her looking at him.

"Ivan," she said.

He immediately rushed back to her and took her in his arms. Kissing her, he moved her back inside the room and closed the door. Holding her securely against the wall, he felt her desperation to be with him, and he was fearful, but he was not exactly certain as to why.

"Get dressed and come with me," he said.

"I'm alright. You go. I just—" she said, the she shook her head as if dismissing some strange thought.

Seeing she still doubted him, he held her by the chin. "You think I'm not coming back. I can tell. Get dressed. I know you're tired, but come with me now."

"I know you'll be back and, you're right, I am tired. And if I'm going to stay, I have phone calls to make. I have to leave messages at the Foundation at least, and with my agent. They probably think I fell off the end of the earth. So go ahead, I'll be fine."

Even though she smiled at him, he still felt her fear, though he could not pinpoint the source. "Alright. Make your calls and rest. We'll have a busy afternoon," he said, then he kissed her good-bye, again, and left her standing at the door. As he waited for the elevator, he turned and smiled at her. "You will be very happy when I return, I promise. I love you, Tess."

"I love you," she said.

The elevator bell sounded, and the doors opened. For a moment, he remained in place, holding the doors open with his hand. Then he stepped inside and, as the doors closed, he heard her say: "I will always love you, Ivan." Her statement was so final, and it made him feel uneasy as he rode to the lobby. He felt he should return and force her to go with him, but he knew she was right. She had not contacted anyone since she arrived in Belgrade, and surely there were arrangements to make since she was staying longer.

When the elevator doors opened, he walked out into the lobby and hurried to a taxi. Getting inside, he directed the driver to take him to Sergej's apartment building. As he left the hotel his only thought was that he had to get back to her as soon as he could. He knew that she needed him, and he wanted to be there for her.

CHAPTER FIFTY-SEVEN

Tess walked back into the room and closed the door. From her briefcase, she pulled out an envelope and a sheet of stationery. She then pulled out a business card that the Red Cross pilot had given her on her flight to Belgrade. Sitting on the bed, she picked up the telephone and dialed the number on the card. She spoke with the Red Cross office and they told her that there was a flight leaving Belgrade in ninety minutes. She asked if she could take that flight and they said yes. Next, she called the airlines and changed her flight to go from Budapest to Zurich; however, she would have to change planes in Vienna, then go to Zurich. From there she would fly directly to New York.

After her flights were rearranged, she called Willis at home in New York. The first call did not go through, so she tried several times more and eventually the call connected.

"Hello?" Willis answered.

"Willis?"

"Tess? Where have you been? Are you alright? We're all worried about you."

"Look, I don't have a lot of time to talk. My plane leaves in less than an hour. I need you to do something for me, and I need it done as soon as you get into work this morning."

"Okay, what do you need?"

"You know the Swiss bank account I set up prior to leaving New York?"

"Yes. What about it?"

"I need you to transfer one hundred thousand dollars to that account. Can you do that for me? It would be easier if you did it rather than me calling. I'll miss my plane if I do. On the way back, I'll stop in Switzerland to sign the paperwork. So if there are any problems, tell them I'll be there late today, early tomorrow at the latest. Will you do that for me?"

"Of course, but what's all this about? That's a lot of money, and where have you been all this time?"

"Please, don't question me, just take care of this for me."

"Alright, consider it done. Do you want me to pick you up at the airport?"

"No, thank you. I'm not sure what flight I'll be taking from Switzerland. I'll be in touch when I get back to New York."

"Okay. Have a safe flight, and if you need me, call me," he said, but he could tell she was under stress and he hoped she would tell him about it when she returned.

She hung up and went to the small table near the window, where she sat, and began to write a letter to Ivan. She knew she could not stay as she saw how she pulled him away from what he needed to do. Now she knew the only way to prove she loved him was to give him his freedom. Then there was Mara, who had not received her award from the Foundation, and she could not stand the thought of Mara being deprived of anything she needed. What Tess would leave behind would help both Ivan and Mara.

When she was through writing, she quickly showered, dressed, then packed the last of her belongings. She locked her suitcase, then called for the bellman to take it to the lobby. Walking back to the table, she carried the remainder of her local currency, the bankbook from the Swiss account, Willis' business card, and her diamond cross necklace. She carefully placed these inside the envelope with the letter. Once it was sealed, she left it on the table with Ivan's name facing up on the outside of the envelope.

Putting on her coat, she heard a knock at the door. Opening it, she allowed the bellman to take her suitcase to the lobby. And as she stood in the doorway, she took one last look around the room. With tears in her eyes, she spoke into the room as if Ivan would hear. "I love you, Ivan. God bless you, my Black Rebel."

She left, thinking that she was doing the right thing, because in the back of her mind, she thought that if someone was looking for her, her going back to Manhattan was wiser than staying in Belgrade with Ivan. If whoever looked for her found her there with Ivan, they would all be in danger, so her leaving felt to be the safest action she could take in order to protect the man she loved.

At the front desk, she requested they keep the room closed and not allow the maids inside until the next day, in the event she needed to return because of issues with her flight. She then attempted to pay her bill, but the front desk clerk told her that Ivan had paid her bill. She asked him to reverse the charges, so she could pay the bill herself, but he refused. Smiling at him, she nodded, then she left the hotel for the airport.

Once there, she directed the driver to take her to the private jet terminal where the Red Cross plane was located. At the gate, she was met by military personnel, who checked her credentials, rummaged through her luggage, then allowed her to board the plane as her luggage was put into the hold.

Chapter Fifty-eight

When Ivan arrived at Sergej's, he found no one was there. He remembered he said he would call, but he had not done that; instead, he had gone straight there expecting they would be home. He walked back outside to wait for them as he dialed Sergej from his cell phone.

"Zdravo," Sergej answered.

"Where are you? Where's Mara?"

"She's with me. We went out for breakfast. You can't imagine how much—"

"I'm at your place. Come back now," he said, interrupting Sergej.

"Is everything okay?"

"Yes, just get back here, I need to get back to the hotel."

"Are you standing outside the building?"

"Yes." Ivan looked around, then spotted Sergej carrying Mara from a few buildings away. When she saw Ivan, she wiggled to get down and ran to him. He picked her up immediately and kissed her cheek.

"So is she staying?" Sergej asked as he approached.

"Yes, she said she would."

"But?" Sergej said, expecting there was more, and felt something bothered Ivan.

Ivan did not know what to say. He felt something was wrong, but he did not know what. In his mind he still heard her last words to him that she would love him always, and he wondered, "Why did she say it like that?"

"Ivan?" Sergej said.

"It's fine. I'll call you later, once they've met," he said, then he walked across the street to a taxi stand.

Sergej watched him walk away carrying Mara as she waved to him over Ivan's shoulder. He waved back to her, then walked into his apartment building.

Still holding Mara, Ivan slid into a taxi, and directed the driver to take him back to the hotel. Mara sat on Ivan's lap as they rode through the city.

Ivan was anxious to introduce Mara to Tess. Though he knew he had explaining to do, he also knew that Tess would feel happier when she saw Mara. Especially when she saw that Mara and the child from Saint Michael's were one and the same. Ivan hoped that she would know her feelings were right, and that they all belonged together. That thought brought a smile to Ivan's face as he looked to the future with happiness, and with that happiness he knew his life would be complete.

Once at the hotel, he slid from the back seat, carried Mara into the lobby, and walked directly to the elevators. When they were inside he looked at her. "Now you are going to meet Tess, and I want you to be a good girl."

"Will we go to America with Tessy?" Mara asked.

"We'll stay here in Belgrade awhile, then we'll see. Perhaps a short trip to America, then we'll return. Would you like that?"

Mara nodded.

When the elevator doors opened, he stepped out, carrying her toward the room as he removed her hat and smoothed her pretty, clean hair. He pulled her mittens from her hands and slipped them into her coat pocket. Stopping outside the room, he smiled at her. Then he pulled the room key from his pocket and unlocked the door. Excited to see Tess' reaction, he pushed the door open and entered. "Tess? Tess! I have a surprise for you," he said.

With her arms around Ivan's neck, Mara anxiously looked into the room for the woman who had comforted her the day before. However, silence surrounded them, and Ivan saw that the room and the closet were empty, and Tess' luggage was gone. The smile dropped from his lips, and he felt his soul plummet to depths never seen by human eyes.

"Where is she, Idy? Where's Tessy?" Mara asked as she looked at him.

Ivan could not look at Mara. He knew he should have taken Tess with him. He saw the sadness in her eyes when he kissed her good-bye, but he never thought she would leave him again—not after their morning together. Looking to the far corner of the room, he saw a thick envelope lying in the middle of the table. Placing Mara on the bed, he walked to it. Nearing it he saw a name written on the front. It read *Idy*, and he stared at it. Unable to move, he now knew that Tess knew who he really was all along, and he knew that he should have told her the truth in the beginning.

Mara walked to him, and placing her little hand inside his, she stared up at him as she sensed his sorrow. He looked down at her, forcing a smile as he sat at the table. "Sit back on the bed, Mara," he said in a quiet voice, and walking backward, she obeyed, though her gaze did not leave him.

Looking back at the envelope, he swallowed hard, then reached for it. Something inside it moved, making a scratching sound as he lifted it. Turning the envelope over, he opened it and slid the contents out onto the table. Inside was a folded piece of paper, Sergei's address that he had handwritten for her, a copy of Mara's letter that he had translated into English, all the documentation she had brought with her on Mara, and a thin collection of local currency. Underneath this he saw a business card, Tess' diamond and gold cross, and a bankbook.

He opened the folded piece of paper and saw it was a letter from Tess. He looked at Mara, though no smile came to his face, then his eyes moved back to the letter, and he began to read what she wrote to him.

Ivan, My Dearest Love,

Your leaving this morning only reminded me that your destiny is here. Your future is rebuilding your country and helping your people. I recall hearing a priest once say, you cannot lay down your life for something you do not love, and I can only imagine the countless times you laid down your life for your countrymen. Because of this, as much as I want to be with you, is as much as I would be in your way right now.

I know you were right all along, right about fighting for your country and your beliefs. I was wrong to tell you what to do, wrong in my opinions of your opinions. I knew it when I saw you that last night in Sarajevo. The fierce determination in your eyes told me of your dedication to your Cause. And though the war will officially end tomorrow, there is so much to do, so many lives to rebuild.

You were right about Mara. It would be inappropriate for me to take her from her home to a strange country like America. I know Idy will continue to take care of her and love her.

That last day in Sarajevo, by some strange coincidence, Mara's handwritten letter to the foundation and Sergej's address, which you had written for me, lay together. When looking at the handwriting, I knew that you had written Mara's letter for her. You are Idy.

Please don't think I'm angry. I'm just sad for having troubled you, for having delayed you with my foolish and righteous intentions. My help is the last thing you or Mara need.

An unknown person once wrote, "A man stands tallest when he stoops to help a child." In my eyes, you stand taller than the Messenger of Victory. Now I know that both Mara and Iđy are safe.

I am sure you have examined the contents of this envelope, and you have found my cross. I want Mara to have it. I don't know if she was one of the many children I saw at the shelters. I would like to imagine that she was the last child I saw, the one whom I held and tried to comfort. You were not with me to see her, but she had a silent strength to her. I only hope that child's parents are alive, and come to take her home, wherever home may be.

After thinking long and hard this past month, there is nothing I can give Mara that you cannot. Love is all she needs, and you have more than enough love for all the children of this war. If you could love me, you could love anyone.

So, please give her this gift from me, and let her know that I did not forsake her. Let her know that I love her, and I came to answer her call. I came to dry those tears you spoke of when we first met. Maybe someday you can tell her about me and she will know her efforts were not in vain. She should grow up knowing that she is loved more than anyone is, and I know Iđy will make sure of that.

One of the last items in this package is a bankbook for an account in Switzerland. Open it now please.

At once, he took the small black book and opened it. Written inside was the deposit amount of one hundred thousand US dollars, and on the first page, as account owner, she had written, Ivan Đurić. He frowned, then quickly returned his attention to her letter, and as he continued reading, tears filled his eyes.

This is the Foundation's award for Mara. I want you to have it. Use it to take care of her. Use it to take care of yourself, your country, whatever you see fit. You see, I too believe in a Cause, and his name is Ivan Đurić. If you love me, really love me, you'll do the right thing and follow your dreams. If you need more, contact Willis Beechum—his business card is enclosed. He'll help you with whatever your need. No matter what it is, he'll see that you get it. Finally, the paper money is the remainder of what I brought with me. I won't need it.

I hope you don't think that I don't love you, because if you do, you're wrong. I love you so much that your dreams have become my dreams. If I would have stayed, your dreams would fail, and a man with broken dreams is a lost man.

Maybe after you have done all you promised yourself that you would do, and if you have found no one else to love, well, maybe then God will bring us back together. I don't know, but I do know I will always think of you and I will always love you. I can only hope you believe that.

Life is strange, the only thing I have ever really wanted is the only thing I can't have. Please don't think I'm running away because I can't love you, or I fear loving you. I'm stepping out of your way to let you continue where I stopped you. I wish I could help, but I don't see how. As you told me that last night in Sarajevo, this is not my fight. It never was and it never will be. In the vast configuration of existence, my efforts were insignificant; however, to your people, you are a savior—the silent savior of Sarajevo.

I did want to tell you that, before I got onto the train with you in Belgrade, I made you the promise that I wouldn't cry or become hysterical. Yet, I didn't tell you why, or how, I could make that promise without knowing what I would encounter. The only reason I was able to make, and keep, that promise was you. You held out your courage in the palm of your hands to me, and it was up to me to accept it—and I did. You were my bravery, you were my reward for all the bad I had been through in my life; and what a beautiful reward you are.

I will miss you, Ivan. I learned more about life in this past month than in all my time on this earth, and all because of you. What you taught me about love, I will not forget. I thank you for that gift, and I pray that God keeps you safe. God Bless the Black Rebel...

I love you, Tess

Looking toward the ceiling, tears rushed down his cheeks. Her words forced a shiver down his spine, and he lowered his head to his hands as her letter dropped to the floor.

Seeing his sadness, Mara left the bed and moved to his side. Picking up the letter, she forced her arms around his neck. He grabbed her and, in his desperation, he pulled her up on his lap. As he buried his face in her hair, he cried in silence.

Tess had given him what she thought he needed, and that was his freedom. He did not need money for the war, nor did he need money to take care of Mara. He had more than enough for both. Though he fought for those who remained in Sarajevo, he also fought for those who ran away from the war. All those people who would someday return once someone else had restored peace. And though he fought to help the people of Sarajevo, he did not use his own money, but she would, because she believed in him.

Now that she was gone, the war seemed unimportant. She did what those fleeing death dared not do, and in doing so, she showed him the meaning of life and of love. She had said that in the past she tried to fulfill the needs of others. Now he wondered, "Who would fulfill her needs? Who could possibly return her exactness in knowing what others needed and when they needed it?"

As he lifted his head, and stared out the window, Mara looked at him. Seeing his tears, she understood Tess was gone. She wiped his tears with her hands and smiled at him. With a child's innocence, and confident of herself, she commanded his attention. "Iđy, we find her," she said with absolute determination.

He looked at her as her large amber-brown eyes stared into his, and her resolve forced him to smile. She was not ready to give up, and through her determination, he found his strength to continue.

Tess was right; a man with broken dreams was a lost man, and his dream of being with Tess was currently broken. Without her, he felt lost, and now, he had to make it right.

With Mara sitting on his lap, he reached for the necklace. Opening the clasp, he placed it around her neck and told her it was a gift from Tess. She smiled and admired it, then looked back at him.

Sliding the letter back inside the envelope, he gathered the bankbook, the currency, and the business card, and placed them inside the breast pocket of his suit jacket. Lifting Mara, he carried her to the door and opened it. And as Tess had done, he turned around and looked back into the room. His gaze lingered on the bed, then he smiled at Mara, and they left the room, closing the door behind them.

Determined to find Tess, he entered his future, as they left the hotel for Sergej's apartment. Ivan would win Tess back, but before that, the Black Rebel would pay a visit to Jacek Kralj.

CHAPTER FIFTY-NINE

On the plane, Tess sat in a row by herself. The flight was not crowded and, actually, there were only a handful of passengers on the flight—all military personnel. Pondering the past month's events, she sat and looked out the window. She wore her sunglasses to block eye contact with the other passengers, who looked at her, wondering who she was. As the plane taxied down the runway, she felt as if her heart was being torn from her chest. When the plane's wheels left the ground, she felt she had just made the biggest mistake of her life in leaving Ivan, but it was too late.

She looked at her left hand and at her Claddagh, which Ivan had slipped onto her finger. Then, without warning, all the tears she held back while in Sarajevo flooded her gaze, and suddenly she no longer cared about anything, except Ivan. Numb from all they had been through together, she sat motionless. Sadness of unequaled torment filled her heart while scenes from her life played inside her head. What a life she had lived so far; its major events reminding her that she was alive to simply serve others.

Was there no one who had time to see her sorrow? She thought back to the multitude of people who had passed through her life, accepting her love and giving nothing in return. She knew the only person who truly cared was the man she left in Belgrade, but how could she take him away from everything else that he loved?

She always tried not to become too attached to anyone she helped. She knew that life was transitory, passing through one situation to the next, but in her mind was the ever constant and desperately loved image of Ivan. All others dimmed in his presence. His heroic ways overpowered all that came before him and all that would follow. As she closed her eyes, his indelible image resonated and she thought, "God bless the Black Rebel."

Why she had met him, she could only wonder. Was it some warped version of poetic justice divvied out by the hand of God? Was there some deep inner lesson she needed to learn from all that had happened between them? The only clear message was that she had failed another time in her life:

born at the right time, but in the wrong place; however, soon she would learn that she was wrong…absolutely wrong.

CHAPTER SIXTY

It was a busy ride from the hotel to Sergej's apartment. Ivan paid the driver, then exited the taxi with Mara asleep in his arms. He was happy that she was sleeping, for he imagined she had not slept much during her time at Saint Michael's. Once the taxi drove away, he carried Mara inside the building. Walking up the stairs to the third floor, he approached the second door on the left side of the hall. Knocking twice quickly, then three times, he waited for Sergej to answer the door.

A flash of light from the peephole caught Ivan's eye, then Sergej quickly unlocked the door and stood staring at Ivan. "What's going on?" he asked, then he stepped aside as Ivan carried Mara inside. Sergej looked out into the hall for Tess, and not seeing her, he closed the door. "Where's Tess?" he asked.

Ivan did not answer. He walked into Sergej's bedroom, laid Mara on the bed, and covered her so she could continue her nap. As he exited the room, he saw Sergej staring at him. "I put Mara on your bed," he said, then he walked to the windows and looked out at the street below.

Sergej knew something was wrong, and he went to the kitchen for a bottle of Šljivovitz, then he returned with it along with two shot glasses. "Ivan? Where's Tess?" he asked again.

"She's gone," Ivan answered quietly.

Sergej was silent. He did not understand what could have happened. When they parted earlier, Ivan was worried, but happy, and now he looked as though all hope was lost. "Where did she go? New York?" he asked.

"I don't know. She didn't tell me. She was gone by the time I—" He shook his head. "We returned to the hotel. I—" Ivan paused as he shook his head again at his stupidity. "I presume she went home. Where else would she go, except where I told her to go?"

"She didn't say anything? Not even good-bye? That doesn't sound like Tess," Sergej said, then he looked away. Stunned at the situation, he walked to the sofa and sat down. Then he opened the bottle and filled the glasses.

Ivan now sat on the sofa. Seeing a glass of Šljivovitz waiting for him, he stared at it. "She left me a letter. She thinks she's in my way—Isn't this war over yet?" he said, and inhaled in a deep breath. Letting it go, he frowned and passed his fingers through his hair. He quickly glanced at Sergej, then back at the shot glass that waited for him, "She knows I'm Iđy. She knows I'm the Black Rebel. Even Mara doesn't know that—Dear God, please help me, I'm so sick of this war!" Smiling sarcastically, he took the glass and drank a sip of Šljivovitz. He then looked at Sergej and saw his concern. "Don't worry. I'll go to her. I'll work it out," he said.

Sergej sat forward. "She won't tell anyone who you are. You must know that," he said, thinking Ivan was worried about his identity.

Ivan nodded. "I know that. She couldn't be unfaithful to her beliefs. I'll never know why she believes in me, but that's not what I'm thinking about."

"What do you mean? What are you thinking about?"

Ivan downed the remaining liquid in his glass, then set the glass back on the table. How warm it felt going down. How enticing was its delicate plum flavor. He then revealed a thought that had been bothering him for some time. "I'm thinking about Kralj. He had to know what she was doing with her foundation. He had to know that she came to Belgrade; he has to be behind the search for her."

Sergej thought for a moment as he looked around, wondering why Kralj would search for Tess, since they were divorced. Looking back at Ivan, he only came up with more questions. "How would we find that out? Oddelek's dead. Out of all the men we found searching for Tess, no one ever said anything about Kralj."

"Why would they mention him? They wouldn't communicate directly with the son of a powerful Nationalist leader. They would take orders from someone in between."

Sergej took his glass from the table and sat back against the sofa cushions. Rubbing his forehead, he strained to think of who else they had information on that was immediately involved. "It must be someone at the travel agency. They provided her photograph to Oddelek. Perhaps one of the secretaries or someone else? What about Cravst? The prisoners had mentioned him," Sergej suggested, then drank the contents of his shot glass and set the glass back on the table. Then he filled both glasses again.

Ivan's mind spun at light speed as he began to piece this vile puzzle together. "Forget about Cravst for now. Get a location on Kralj. Get dossiers on the employees and owners of the travel agency in Belgrade and in New York. If it's Kralj, someone involved with one of those companies will know something." He then reached into his pocket and pulled out Willis Beechum's business card. Walking to Sergej's desk, he wrote down Willis' name, telephone number, and address of the bank where Willis worked. He then walked back to Sergej and handed him the piece of paper.

"What's this?" Sergej asked as he looked at it.

"That is the name, address, and telephone number of the Secretary of Tess' foundation. He's the Vice President of the bank she uses and her good friend. Call him, posing as the Belgrade travel agency and inform him that Tess is returning to New York, but first, get into the airline ticketing database and confirm that she is on her way back. If he is a good friend, he will be calling her to check on her. This way, if she doesn't show up, someone will be aware. If he's not such a good friend, he will be making other telephone calls to other people. He would need to let people know that she's on the move."

Sergej nodded, then he went to his computer. At once, he began punching the keys of his keyboard and logged onto the Belgrade Airport's mainframe computer. "She must have left about eleven-thirty this morning to catch JAT's twelve-fifteen flight for Budapešt. It is their only departure today. As long as she didn't go back via military flights, she would connect in London, then go on to New York," he said, although Ivan was thinking of other things.

Scrolling through the screens from the airport's database, he searched every airline, but found nothing with Tess' name. He then logged onto the local NATO military travel server. Searching for her name there, he still found nothing.

"I'm not finding her anywhere. Did she say which airline she flew into Belgrade on? With her press pass, did she fly into a military base?" Sergej asked.

"It wasn't military; it was a Red Cross plane. Where are they stationed here?" Ivan asked.

"I think they're based out of the private jet terminal at the airport. They don't release passenger lists for their flights, but I know someone that works at the tower for that terminal. Let me call him." He picked up the phone and dialed the number, as he asked, "So how did she get on a Red Cross flight?"

"I guess she was allowed on because of her documentation from the London Post."

Sergej nodded. After a few minutes, his contact came on the line, and he asked him about a reporter named Fordel that worked for the London Post. At first no one had information, but after checking the flight plan and passenger list for the Red Cross flight, his contact came back on the line and confirmed that a journalist named Tess Fordel was on the flight for Budapešt. When he asked where she was headed after that, his contact said that no information was given prior to takeoff, so he concluded the call and went back to searching flights from Budapešt.

"She was on this morning's flight headed for Budapešt. I'm going to search for her flight from there to London," he said.

Typing away at his computer, Sergej read through screen after screen, but did not find her name on flights to London, so he then left the destination open, and another screen loaded. He searched down the list of names. If he were not experienced in the mistakes airlines make with the spelling of passengers' names, he would have passed it.

Stopping on the line with her name, he called Ivan to see. "Here it is. They spelled her name wrong and didn't give her the right first initial—P. Froder."

"That's all for the better. If anyone is searching for her, they won't stop at P. Froder, they'll keep searching," Ivan said.

The only way Sergej knew it was definitely Tess was by the New York travel agent's identification number attached to her ticket. He had made a note of it the morning he searched her hotel room in Belgrade.

"She's going to Zurich, not London. She will arrive in Zurich approximately four o'clock this afternoon, after a stop in Vienna," Sergej said.

Ivan shook his head as he wondered why she was going to Zurich. Then he remembered the bankbook, and felt the stop had something to do with the money, but he did not mention that to Sergej. "It's good she's going back a different way. Maybe she's worried that someone is looking for her," he said, then added, "Only Kralj could be looking for her."

Sergej watched Ivan's expression harden. He knew Ivan was planning something deadly, something to do with Tess' ex-husband. "Are you going to whack him?" Sergej asked.

"Who else saw Tess' dossier? Does anyone else know who she was married to?" Ivan asked as he walked back to the sofa and sat down.

"None of our men saw it. They knew you were angry with her that one night because of something. Even though they heard you yelling at her, they were not sure why you kept talking about Serbian Nationalists. They really thought—" Sergej stopped, and turned away when Ivan looked at him. He could not say that the men were positive Ivan was going to harm Tess. Then regaining his composure, Sergej looked back at him. "I am the only one that saw the report, and that was only when you showed it to me. It came in sealed just the way I handed it to you. That was the way it was handed to me."

"We have to find who obtained this information. The more I think about it, someone now knows who I am, and that someone should be found." Ivan paused to finish his second shot of Šljivovitz. "I will find them, and I will take care of them, just as I will take care of Kralj."

"You can't just walk up to him and kill him!" Sergej said, worried about the outcome of Ivan's hasty plan.

Ivan stood up and frowned hard at him. "Yes, I can. He's a punk. He fed off Tess for years. Then once his father cut him off, he went running back to daddy with his tail between his legs. That's not a man, that's a scared goat. He's no more than a rodent to the Serbian Nationalist movement. If he were powerful, he would hold a position in their organization. He's nothing except the old man's son. His family will mourn him, but it will soon pass, and people will say he got what he deserved."

Sergej sighed. "Okay, I'll find out everyone that had anything to do with gathering the dossier on Tess, but what are you going to do now? Mara's here."

"Get me a location on Kralj; I'm going to watch him for a day. Then find out the rest of the information. I want to know who has been leaking information about Tess. No one should have known that she was in this country."

Sergej frowned at what he imagined Ivan planned to do. He agreed if Kralj was behind the search for Tess, he was going to be a problem in the future, but he worried for Ivan's involvement. He looked at Ivan and saw him considering all outcomes.

"Get Mama and Stefan up here. Get everyone in that area out to some-place safe; no one must remain. No one should talk about anything they may have seen or done at the houses. This isn't the end of trouble, it's the beginning. The war isn't over yet; I'm sure Kosovo will soon be back on the menu. More than likely, we'll have to clear out of Belgrade as well, at least for a while," Ivan said, then he sighed and thought for a moment. "Have the remaining men break down the camp, then have them wait at their checkpoints for further orders. They aren't safe all waiting in one location. They need to scatter and blend in with the population. Just because this war will be over on paper tomorrow, that doesn't mean it's over."

Sergej nodded. He wondered if Ivan was right about the war continuing. Would it start up again in Kosovo? The more he thought about it, the more he felt Ivan was right. The new peace agreement had split up the land that was once Yugoslavia, and the powers that be in Belgrade were not happy, so trying to seize control of Kosovo would be the most logical next step.

Ivan was now quiet as he thought about all that he had to do before he planned to leave Belgrade. He then changed the subject and asked for a favor. "Sergej, I need some documents."

"Sure. Whatever you need," Sergej answered, but from Ivan's hesitation, he knew Ivan contemplated this favor, and so he said, "Ivan, whatever it is, I'll get it for you."

"I need a marriage document with my and Tess' name on it. Date it as of last Friday. I also need a passport for Mara with her name as Mara Đurić, and I need adoption papers stating that Tess legally adopted Mara the same day we were married."

"What are you planning? Is this marriage just for show?"

"I have to get Mara into the US without complications. When Customs sees that we are from Yugoslavia, they will detain us. But if Mara is legally Tess' daughter, there will be no questions, at least not for her. Your friend at the US Embassy needs to notarize the documents. He will be called to confirm the marriage and adoption. If it comes from the US government, it won't be questioned after the first phone call, at least I don't think it will."

"Okay. How much time do I have?" Sergej asked, then he drank his second shot of Šljivovitz.

"How quickly can you get them?"

"The morning after tomorrow, perhaps tomorrow afternoon? If my friend is in."

"Good, as soon as you can get them. We'll leave this week."

Sergej grabbed his satellite phone and called the remaining men at the Rebel camp. Once he finished issuing Ivan's orders, he began searching for a location on Kralj.

Ivan walked to the bedroom and checked on Mara, who still slept soundly on Sergej's bed. Smiling at her, he closed the door and walked back to the sofa to lie down. Closing his eyes, he thought about Tess and about taking Mara to America.

CHAPTER SIXTY-ONE

It did not take Sergej long to locate Kralj, even though during the war Kralj moved several times after threats on his life. Regardless that his father had warned him to keep a low profile, he ignored that advice and was out every night, until early morning, with his women at his favorite nightclubs. From this habit, Ivan knew Kralj would wake up late in the day and be at home alone and unguarded, for his bodyguards were only with him when he left his apartment. He also knew Kralj's father would be busy with matters of state and would not be bothered with reinforcing guards for a rebellious son.

It was early morning, roughly three o'clock, and Ivan had been watching Kralj from the previous day. Kralj had been at a club from eleven o'clock that evening, and Ivan followed him home from there. Ivan parked a safe distance away from Kralj's apartment building. He saw Kralj get out of a taxi with two women, laughing and acting foolishly as they all appeared intoxicated. They entered Kralj's apartment building, and within a few minutes, the light in Kralj's apartment bedroom went on. Turning the car off, Ivan felt it would be quite a wait until the women left, but he was determined to wait however long it took.

To Ivan's surprise, within an hour and a half, the two women exited the building. They were now quiet, and Ivan thought it strange, considering they appeared frivolous earlier. They were now overtly serious, and unlike their arrival, their departure was subdued. Even if they were professionals, they would be talking to each other, but they said nothing. Ignoring each other, they walked to the next corner and, without stopping, one turned to the right, crossed the street, and continued walking. The other crossed the street straight and disappeared into the darkness as she walked away from the building.

This was very odd, and it made Ivan rethink his plan to question, then kill Kralj that morning. He sat there thinking and watching through the windshield as if one or both of the women would return. Then he noticed a tall and bulky figure approaching from the opposite direction. He could tell it was a man by his weighty gait. When the man neared the lights of the building's entrance, Ivan saw it was Goran, Kralj's older brother. Without stopping, Goran walked straight into the lobby.

This was Ivan's cue to leave. In his mind, he knew what had happened; the task was already complete. Starting the car, he drove from the curb, then headed to Sergej's apartment. All the way to Sergej's neighborhood, Ivan continually checked his rearview mirror to make certain no one followed him. When he felt it was safe, he found a spot two blocks away from Sergej's building, parked, then continued on foot the rest of the way.

Climbing the back stairs, instead of taking the elevator, Ivan walked to Sergej's door and knocked on it. Sergej looked out the peephole, then opened the door. He stepped aside and Ivan quickly entered, then Sergej locked the door and followed Ivan inside.

Ivan tossed his coat on a chair. "Turn on the news," he said as he turned around.

"Why?" Sergej asked as he walked to the television to turn it on as Ivan had requested.

"Just turn it on."

"Any channel in particular?"

"No," Ivan answered as he sat on the sofa.

It was already all over the news, Jacek Kralj was found dead. He had committed suicide in his Belgrade home. The cause of death was a bullet to the head.

Sergej turned and looked at him. "Did you?"

Ivan shook his head.

"Then who?"

"I don't know, Goran perhaps."

"His brother?"

"Either him or the two women that went into the building with him at three and came out around four-thirty. If it was the two, they enjoyed him before they killed him. They went in laughing, and having fun, but they walked out quietly with their coats buttoned up and not looking at each other, then went separate ways. Then Goran arrived," Ivan answered.

"Only his father could have ordered this, but whether he did it by direct order or on his own, I'm just thankful you didn't do it," Sergej said, as he turned the television off.

"It was only a matter of time. I would have only sped up the inevitable," Ivan said, then asked, "Is Mara asleep?"

Sergej nodded.

Ivan stood and walked to Sergej's bedroom to check on her. Opening the door, he saw that Sergej had left the dresser light on low. He walked to the bed, pulled the covers up over her shoulders, and kissed her head. She did not move. He stood there briefly and watched her. She was peaceful and he enjoyed the simplicity of the moment. Smiling, he left her, and returned to the living room.

Sergej handed him the list of names of people that were involved with Tess' trip to Belgrade. The list consisted of two women at the travel agency in Belgrade and Bora Oddelek. Tess had contacted the agency in Belgrade directly without using a liaison agency from New York. Ivan imagined that she did this to minimize anyone knowing what she was doing or where she was going. Then Sergej showed him photographs of the two women from the Belgrade agency.

Ivan suppressed a laugh. "These were the two women with Kralj." He shook his head at the supposed coincidence. "Amazing."

"They won't be alive much longer I'm sure. They have served their purpose. Milan will get rid of them," Sergej said, then he showed Ivan the names of the two men involved in obtaining the dossier on Tess. These men were Swiss and, because of that, Ivan felt no reason to pursue them at this time.

Ivan then put his coat on, and walked to the door. "Have them look into Willis Beechum and a journalist at the New York Times named George Preston," Ivan said, wanting to know more about Tess' friends.

Sergej stood up. "Where are you going?"

"Home."

"Stay here with Mara. Go home in the morning," Sergej suggested as he grabbed a large envelope from the table and walked to Ivan.

"I would like to leave tomorrow for New York. I will pack and be here no later than ten o'clock. We'll be on the morning flight to Budapešt," Ivan said and added, "As long as flights aren't cancelled tomorrow."

"Then you'll need these," Sergej said, as he handed Ivan the envelope.

Ivan looked inside and found the papers he had asked for. First, he opened Mara's passport. As requested, her name read Mara Đurić. He smiled at her passport photo because of her exuberant expression.

Sergej noticed his smile and said, "She was always more of a Đurić than a Jovanović."

Again Ivan smiled, knowing it was true. He then saw the marriage and adoption documentation. Sliding everything back into the envelope, he looked at Sergej, and said, "Thank you."

"So when will the wedding really happen?"

"Whenever she says yes." He thought about it momentarily. *"If* she says yes."

"She'll say yes," Sergej said and grinned, then he patted Ivan on the arm and opened the door. "See you tomorrow morning."

Ivan smiled, walked down the hall, and made his way back to his apartment.

CHAPTER SIXTY-TWO

"It's a man with a child, a little girl, his daughter," the customs officer said in a low voice into the telephone. Then he listened to the party on the other end of the call as he looked cautiously at the man on the other side of the counter, who stood patiently as he held his daughter: a beautiful, rosy cheeked child with creamy skin and dark brown hair that hung to the middle of her back. She looked innocently at the officer with her large amber-brown eyes, and her smile made the officer smile back at her.

Hanging up the telephone, the officer still smiled and spoke sweetly to the child in English, as he asked, "Is this your father?"

"Yes," she answered, in English. She then threw her arms around her father's neck and gave him a little girl's kiss on the lips when he smiled at her.

The officer noticed the obvious affection between the man and his daughter, then he asked her, "How old are you?"

"Seven and a half," she quickly answered, then rested her head on the man's shoulder.

The officer looked to the man, and said, "She's tired."

"It was a long trip from Zurich, and she's very anxious to see her mother," the man said, as his English was impeccable, as was the child's.

Contrary to Ivan's previous instructions for Mara not to speak English to anyone while she was at Saint Michael's, when they departed Zurich, Ivan instructed Mara to speak English only. He felt it would be less conspicuous when passing through customs.

The officer looked back and forth between the man and the girl. "What was your purpose for being in Switzerland? And what is your purpose for coming to America?" the officer asked.

"I had business to take care of in Zurich, and the purpose for coming to America is for my daughter to be with her mother and for me to be with my wife," he said and shrugged as if the answer was obvious.

"Come with me, please," the guard requested as he stepped from behind the counter and toward the man and his daughter. He gestured for them to follow him as he led them down the hall and into a small room where they were to wait until he returned.

CHAPTER SIXTY-THREE

Tess sat at her computer and tried to clear her mind of all that had happened, but it was too soon. She had been back one week already, and she had not even unpacked her luggage. Closing her eyes, her tears fell to her hands as they rested on her lap. The telephone rang and she debated answering it, but let it ring until it stopped. A few minutes later it rang again. Shaking her head, she answered the call in a faint voice. "Hello?"

"Finally! It's about time, Tess. Where have you been? The travel agency called me last week to let me know you'd be arriving. When did you get back?" Willis asked.

"Oh, Willis," she whispered and sighed.

"What's wrong? Wasn't your trip a success? I transferred the funds you asked for. I imagined you found the child. You did, didn't you?"

"Yes, I did, sort of."

"So, what *sort of* happened? Were you hit in the head with a grenade or something? Is that why you're hibernating? You've been back how long? And you haven't called me or anyone. Everyone's worried about you. How many messages have I left on your machine? How many times have I stopped by your apartment building only to have your doorman tell me that you weren't home? I wouldn't have known you were alive if I didn't tip him, *substantially,* for the information. We thought perhaps you were carried off by one of those notoriously handsome Slavic men!"

She knew he was trying to brighten her mood, but what he did not know was that the words he chose tore her heart as memories of Ivan flashed inside her mind as she said, "Don't ask, please, just don't ask."

"You didn't do anything you're going to regret, did you?" Willis asked, half joking.

"No, I have no regrets, but I'd rather not talk about it. Besides, I have something to ask you." She paused, thinking of how to phrase her question. "Willis, I want you to take over as Chairman of the Foundation. Will you do that for me?"

Her request stunned him. She had always wanted control of the foundation, and now she wanted to relinquish that control. From this request, he knew something life changing had happened to her while she was away.

"Tess, I think you'd better think about this awhile. I don't mind taking over as Deputy Chairman if you need some time away. Why don't you go to a spa? Go somewhere and get back into the swing of things. For heaven's sake, it's Christmas; the time for merriment and happiness. Come on! Get into the holiday spirit!"

"I'm going out for a while."

"How about if I take you to lunch? I'll come and get you?" he offered.

"No, thanks, Willis, perhaps another day. I just want to get out and get some fresh air or something. I guess I'm a little jet lagged. You don't mind, do you?"

"No, you go ahead, I'll talk to you later, but don't forget the parties on the twenty-fourth, twenty-fifth, and the thirty-first. Okay? I expect you to snap out of this dismal mood and be the Tess everyone knows and loves by then. Sound good?"

"I'll talk to you later," she said, then hung up.

She stood up and walked to the closet. When she opened the door, her eyes looked at the shearling coat she had brought with her to Belgrade. The same coat she had covered Ivan with the night he slept on the sofa. Her hand stroked its soft fleece as memories of Ivan surrounded her. Then, shaking her head, she reached for a different coat, and putting it on, she closed the closet door. Walking to her desk, she grabbed her purse, then she left the apartment.

Lost in her own world, she rode alone in the elevator to the lobby as her mind still wandered to visions of her time with the man she loved. However, she did not forget Mara, and was also plagued with thoughts of which child she had seen that could have been Mara. Then she wondered, "What if something fatal had happened to Mara, and Ivan didn't know how to tell me?" That thought tore at her heart for both Mara and Ivan.

The elevator bell sounded and she was startled as the doors opened. From where she stood, she could see snow falling slowly to the sidewalk, and it momentarily brought back scenes of the snowfall in Belgrade. She stood there briefly, debating whether to go back upstairs and hide from the world.

Looking at the lobby floor, the thought that she would not see Ivan again overwhelmed her, and that was a fact she had to learn to deal with. No one had forced her to start her foundation. She did that all by herself. No one had forced her to go to Yugoslavia. That was her decision. No one had forced her to leave the hotel before Ivan returned. She did that on her own as well, and now she would overcome the sorrow she felt on her own. Somehow she would get through it all. With that thought, she stepped out of the elevator and walked to the lobby's entrance.

With Central Park across the street, she felt a walk in the park would make her feel better. The door attendant was busy helping other tenants while she silently snuck out, unnoticed by anyone, or so she thought, until she heard a man's voice calling to her from the street. "Miss Fordel?" the man's voice sounded.

Turning around, she saw two men approaching from an unmarked car that was double-parked in front of her building. They were dressed in dark colored suits, white shirts, and dark ties, and their overcoats casually swung open as they walked. As they neared, she imagined they were official government employees of some sort. Then the shorter of the two men spoke to her again. "Miss Fordel?" he said.

She tried to smile. Looking at them, she could not figure out who they were or what they wanted. "Yes?" she answered.

"You are Tess Fordel, the writer?" he asked as if she would say no.

"Yes, I am Tess Fordel, the writer." Her smile dissolved into a sterner expression as she waited to find out what they wanted.

The same man spoke again as they each pulled their identification from their pockets and showed them to her. "Miss Fordel, I am Special Agent Durrington of the Federal Bureau of Investigation, and this is Inspector Popovich of the Immigration and Naturalization Office for New York City. If you have a moment, we need to talk with you."

She looked at their badges. Hearing the name Popovich, she looked at him cautiously. "How may I help you?" she asked.

"Miss Fordel, if you could come with us, we need to ask you a few questions. Will you come with us willingly?" Durrington asked.

She gave a breathy laugh. "Willingly? Am I under arrest?"

"No, Miss Fordel, you haven't done anything wrong. It's just routine questioning, that's all. It won't take more than an hour or two," Popovich answered.

"Just an hour or two? That's all?" she asked slightly sarcastic. However, she did not intend to come across as sarcastic, and her questioning expression did not match her tone. Looking at Popovich, his heritage reminded her of Ivan and, instantly, her attitude changed. "Yes, Inspector Popovich, I have time for you. Shall we go back upstairs to my apartment? I have an office where we can talk."

"No, ma'am. We need to take you to other facilities. We aren't actually doing the questioning. So, if you could come with us, we'd appreciate it," Popovich said, then he stepped sideways and motioned for her to accompany them to their car, which she did.

She sat in the back seat, and the two men entered the front of the car. Durrington immediately spoke on the radio, confirming that they had located Tess and were bringing her in, a thought that made her shake her head and laugh silently.

Popovich turned around to see her. "Are you warm enough back there, Miss Fordel?"

She smiled and nodded.

"Don't worry, we just need help with a situation is all."

"What situation?"

"We can't discuss it now. Wait until we get to the office."

"Can I at least ask where this office is located?"

"Sure. We're going to JFK."

"Immigration has an office there?"

"No, this is a customs issue that could potentially turn into an immigration issue. Please, don't worry," he said with a smile, then he turned back around.

She sat in silence and looked out the window. She could not imagine what had happened now. Her only thought was that her ex-husband was in trouble again and was asking for her help. Not knowing what to expect, she had no choice but to wait to find out.

They made haste getting to the airport and when necessary, they used sirens to clear their path. Once on the grounds of the airport, Durrington drove to the international terminal and pulled to the departures curb. Popovich stepped from the car, opened the door for her, and extended his hand to help her out. She accepted his offer, smiled, and stepped out to the sidewalk.

Durrington stopped to speak with what she surmised was a fellow agent, while Popovich led her inside the building. At the automatic doors, four other men, similarly attired, walked behind them as they continued toward an unknown destination.

Approaching the security checkpoint, Popovich stopped her. Helping her remove her coat and taking her purse, they searched both items for weapons, as a security officer ran a handheld metal detector over her. Then Popovich helped her slip on her coat, and handed her purse back to her, then they continued down the corridor.

They reached the international flight's concourse and customs checkpoints. Entering this concourse, they walked one quarter of the way then stopped at a solid door. Popovich pressed a few numbers into a keypad, and the door unlocked. Then he led her inside an empty room with a long metal table and eight matching metal chairs surrounding it.

"Can I get you anything? A cup of coffee?" he asked.

"No, thank you."

"If you will wait here, officers will be in shortly to speak with you," he said, then he smiled at her, and left the room.

The sound of the door closing echoed slightly off the putty colored walls, and not knowing what else to do, Tess sat at the table, waiting and wondering what this situation was about.

After half an hour had past, the door opened. Two men walked inside, and she turned to look at them from where she had been pacing. The first was dressed similarly to Durrington and Popovich, though he did not smile at her. The second was a law enforcement officer. She could not discern which branch of the law he was with, but she surmised that he was for the express use of the Customs Department.

Returning her attention to the first man, she watched him walk around the table and place a legal size manila file folder on it. He looked at her, and said, in Serbian, "Good morning, Mrs. Đurić."

She looked at the folder, then back at him. He had spoken so rapidly that she did not at first notice that he had called her Mrs. Đurić, but after realizing he had, she made no obvious acknowledgement of it because she felt they were scrutinizing her.

Guessing what he had said, but not knowing how to answer in Serbian, she answered in English. "Good morning. Will someone please tell me what this is about? I have no idea why I'm here."

Then the door to the room opened and another suited man entered. This man looked at the first man who had spoken to her in Serbian. The first man shook his head, and she imagined he indicated that she did not answer as they may have expected. Then man number two stepped toward the table and looked at her. "Miss Fordel, please sit down," he said, then he pointed to a chair across from where he stood.

She shook her head, but sat and waited for the new man to continue.

"My name is Detective Stevenson. I work for the US Customs Office in conjunction with the Department of Immigration," he said.

She frowned. "What does that have to do with me? I'm a United States citizen. I was born here."

Stevenson sat on the opposite side of the table. Opening a file folder, he quickly read the first page, then looked at her, and asked, "How long have you lived in New York City?"

"I've lived here around two years. Why do you ask? Does this have anything to do with my ex-husband?" she asked as she looked directly into his eyes, waiting for an answer.

"No. It doesn't," he said coldly, then he paused for a long time, and she felt he waited for her to say something. When she did not, he flipped through a few pieces of paper in the folder. He appeared to be debating his next question, or perhaps this was his attempt at intimidation. That thought made her mentally laugh at him.

"Did you know your ex-husband, Jacek Kralj, if I'm pronouncing the name properly? I'm always mispronouncing those names," he said slightly arrogantly, then added, "Well, he's dead."

For a moment, she froze in place. She wondered how he died and if he were murdered. "No. I had no idea. When? What happened?"

"Three days ago. He shot himself in the head," Stevenson said.

She shook her head. She never imagined that he would take his own life. It was pitiful. "I can't imagine it. That's not like him. Well, from what he was like when we were together, but maybe he changed," she said, then added, "So, that's not what this is about?"

"No, but since you mentioned him, I thought you would like to know," Stevenson answered.

"Thank you, but what can I help you with?"

"We are investigating all civilians who have traveled to and from Yugoslavia since the start of their war."

He looked back to the file and reread one report. Again, he took his time, and she imagined this should make her nervous, but it did not.

"I see here that you spent one month in Belgrade? Is that correct?" he asked.

"Yes. That is correct," she said. Now Ivan's recommendation that she keep her room at the hotel made absolute sense, and she wondered if he knew this would happen.

Stevenson shook his head and placed the paper back in the folder. Then he folded his hands across the file and his expression turned accusatory. "Are you Serbian?"

"No. Why?"

"Do you have friends in Belgrade? Serbian friends? Or family perhaps?" he asked, attempting to lead her into an answer.

"I have no *blood* relatives in Serbia, but of course, I made friends while I was there," she answered, not knowing exactly what Stevenson was attempting to discover.

"How did you get into Serbia?"

"I flew," she said, then quickly embellished so not to add to his obvious confusion, "On a plane."

Stevenson smirked. "Let me rephrase the question. Who authorized your visa into Serbia?"

"The London Post and the Yugoslav government."

"What were you doing there?"

"I was there researching a novel I plan to write about the Celts' peaceful occupation of Belgrade, and their building the Kalemegdan Fortress," she answered, then added, "I'm sure you know I'm a writer."

"Yes, Miss Fordel, we are aware of *your profession,*" he said, and the tone in his voice, when he said "your profession," made her feel strange, but she passed it off as another flaw in his outwardly demeaning character. It was obvious that he was a narcissist, and she knew that a stupid person with a small amount of power was always a dangerous combination.

"So, did anything special happen while you were there?" he asked, again with a tone that attempted to confuse her, however it was obvious that he was the one to be confused.

"Why, several very special things happened while I was there. Why do you ask?" she answered, then after a brief pause she asked, "What is this all about if it's not about my *late* ex-husband?"

"It has to do with another man, an architect from Belgrade."

"You mean an architectural engineer," she corrected, knowing that he referred to Ivan.

He smiled sarcastically. "Yes, Miss Fordel, an architectural engineer, who is also your current husband, or a man claiming to be your husband. He has with him a little girl, who he claims is your daughter. He has provided a marriage license and adoption papers with your signature on them. We only need to know if this is true, is it?" he asked, and then, if it were possible, his expression became increasingly stringent.

Tess smiled at him. She knew it was Ivan and Mara that the detective referred to. "Where are they? Let me see them. How am I supposed to know whom you're expecting me to identify if I don't see them in person?" she said.

"Tell me your husband and daughter's names, then I'll let you see them."

"My husband is Ivan Đurić and my daughter is Mara." she answered, not providing a last name for Mara, considering she did not know what last name Ivan would have used. Then she smiled. "They weren't supposed to be here for two days," she said, lying in order to add validity to their identification.

"How do you spell that name?"

"Which one, Ivan or Mara?"

"Your new last name," he said.

"D, with a slash through the stem, U, R, I, C with an accent on top," she answered. "It is pronounced Gurich—the D, with the slash through the stem, is pronounced like G as in germ, not D as in dumb," she said, looking at him condescendingly.

He forced a smile, then looked back down at the file. "What was the date you were married?"

She stood up and looked down at him. "This is beginning to sound like an official immigration interview? Is that what this is?"

"No. It is not," he answered.

"Then why are you asking me for personal information? I identified, by name, my husband and daughter, even though you haven't showed them to me, as you said that you would. If you want a complete inquisition, file the papers, and request a meeting. I have every right to have legal representation if your course of questions are due to an *authorized* immigration investigation. You do not want to violate *my rights,* do you, Agent Stevenson?"

"Miss Fordel, please don't be alarmed. We are trying to confirm the identity of your husband and daughter. We only have a few more questions," Stevenson said.

"No more questions. At this time, I state for the record that, by my rights given to me as a United States citizen, I claim Ivan Đurić as my husband and Mara as my daughter. Therefore, I would appreciate your addressing me as *Mrs. Đurić!*" she said, pausing for emphasis. "Since it is obvious that my husband has not violated any laws regarding his, or my daughter's entry into this country, and also since this isn't an immigration interview, you will release them before you violate the law further than you already have. I've been without them too long, and this interrogation is against *our rights.*"

"Why did you return to New York without them?" he asked, ignoring her statement.

She looked at him. "You're not listening, *Detective Stevenson,* are you? If you continue with this unauthorized questioning, I will have no choice but to call my attorney. So, it is in *your* best interest that you stop immediately."

He only looked at her.

"Do you understand?" she said, holding her ground.

Without any options, he smiled vaguely. She knew her rights and was not about to be taken advantage of by skeptics that meant to keep her from the man she loved.

Stevenson nodded. "Alright, *Mrs. Đurić,* Officer Kurts will take you to your family. We will be in touch, but for now, thank you for your cooperation." He stood up and closed the file, then he turned and walked toward the door.

"I will take my husband's and daughter's passports and anything else you've *illegally* confiscated," she said and held out her hand.

He returned to the table. Opening the file, he handed her their passports, and the marriage and adoption documents.

"Thank you. If I find out any other documents are missing, and in your possession, my attorney will be contacting your legal department," she said.

"We have no other documents, or anything else, that belongs to your husband or your daughter," he said, then nodding, he turned around and motioned Kurts to take her to her family. Without another word, he then left the room with the first man following him.

At once, Kurts escorted Tess from the room. He grinned and looked at her as they walked. "You gave him hell. I liked the 'D as in dumb.' That pretty much sums him up," he said.

Tess looked at him, and gave a breathy laugh.

"He's always acting like that, but don't worry, he won't do anything. His power is in his own mind. Besides, if they had found any flaw in your husband's entry visa or other documents, you'd be seeing him behind bars, not at the end of the hall," he said, and motioned to the windowed wall at the end of the concourse.

She smiled and, as she walked, she could see a tall, impeccably dressed man standing at the far end of the corridor. He held a small girl in his arms. They looked out the window and the man pointed to different things as the little girl appeared to ask what they were. As Tess drew nearer, she could hear the little girl calling the man Idy as she laughed and looked at him, then looked back out the window. At once Tess' heart began to race. Because of the way the light entered the window, her view of the man's face was obscured, but she knew he had come for her. "Ivan," she said, and hurried toward them.

There was a security guard standing near them and, when he saw Tess approaching, he touched the man on the arm. "Sir," he said and motioned in Tess' direction.

The man and child turned and looked at Tess. Then the man started walking toward her as he still carried the little girl who smiled happily. As they neared, the little girl reached out her arms to Tess. Once she was close enough, Tess put one arm around the little girl, and kissed her quickly on the cheek. Then her other arm slipped around Ivan as he kissed her. For the first time since Mara was born, Ivan wished he was not holding her so that he could fully embrace Tess.

"Hi," Tess whispered, looking into Ivan's gaze, then she looked at the little girl.

"This is Mara," Ivan whispered, looking from Tess to the child. "You found her in Dovlići. Out of all the children you saw, you found her."

"Hi, Mara," Tess said, and kissed Mara's cheek again. She then looked at Ivan. "I only found her because you risked your life to keep her safe." She stroked Mara's hair and kissed her cheek yet again. She then noticed the cross around Mara's neck. "How pretty that is on you," she said.

Mara smiled as she moved closer to Tess so that Tess would hold her.

Taking Mara from Ivan, she balanced her on her left hip as her left arm wrapped securely around her. Tess looked over her shoulder, then she turned back. Kissing Ivan, she handed him the passports and other documents. "Take these. Is that everything they took from you?" she asked.

Ivan quickly looked at what she handed him. He nodded and slipped the papers into the inside breast pocket of his jacket. He then looked past her and saw Kurts watching them. He smiled and nodded at Kurts, who smiled, nodded back, then approached. "Where is our luggage?" Ivan asked.

"It's in the customs curb office. We can pick it up on the way through arrivals. This way," Kurts said, then he motioned for them to follow him.

Ivan took Mara from Tess. "I'll carry her," he said and kissed Tess' cheek.

Mara rested her chin on Ivan's shoulder and watched everything going on behind Ivan's back. Ivan heard her wee, quiet voice as she said, "There are two men following us." She then closed her eyes and nestled her head close to his neck so she could sleep while he carried her.

Tess immediately looked behind them and noticed Popovich and Durrington trailing a safe distance behind. Ivan stopped and spotted them as well.

"Wait a minute. Let's get this over with now," Tess said and motioned them to approach, but quickly whispered to Ivan, "When and where were we married? I didn't read the documents."

"I married you in my heart the day I put your Claddagh on your left hand, but the papers say December eighth in Belgrade at the US Embassy. You adopted Mara the same day," he whispered, then he kissed the side of her head.

Tess smiled and looked at the two agents. "Agent Popovich, Agent Durrington, I'd like you to meet my husband, Ivan, and my daughter, Mara," she said as she stepped to Ivan's side. "So you couldn't tell me on the ride here that my husband and daughter arrived two days early? Thank you for not spoiling the surprise."

"Well, all that matters is that you and your family are together," Durrington said.

Ivan spoke before Tess could answer. "Yes, that is all that matters. Do you have any questions for me? I would rather answer them now, than spoil my daughter's first Christmas with her mother."

Noticing Ivan's platinum wedding band, Durrington then looked at

Tess. Noticing her ring he asked, "You're Irish. You wear a Claddagh, but your husband doesn't."

"Yes, I am part Irish, and I do wear a Claddagh," she said, then looking at Ivan's hand and seeing his ring, her heard skipped a beat. Then looking back into Ivan's eyes, she smiled. "My husband was free to choose his ring as I chose mine."

Ivan noticed Popovich smiling at Tess and Mara. "You're a lucky man," Popovich said in Croatian.

"I know," Ivan answered in English, and asked again, "Do you have questions for me?"

"No, you're free to go," Durrington answered. He then turned to Tess. "Thank you for your help. Do you need a ride back home?"

Tess smiled and shook her head. "No, thank you."

"Merry Christmas," Popovich said. Then Durrington and Popovich turned and walked in the opposite direction.

Ivan heard Tess sigh, and he looked at her. "Take us home," he whispered.

Together, with Mara, they walked down the concourse toward the arrivals terminal. Stopping only to collect their luggage, they quickly stepped into the first available limousine and headed to Manhattan.

CHAPTER SIXTY-FOUR

After having stopped to shop, then eat an early dinner, Ivan, Mara, and Tess arrived home around seven o'clock. The door attendant was happy to meet Tess' husband and daughter. He welcomed them to the building as he brought their luggage and packages to their apartment.

Once he was gone, Ivan stood in the living room holding Mara, who slept with her head on his shoulder. "Where can she sleep?" he whispered.

Tess smiled, stroked his arm, and motioned for him to follow her. They walked across the living room toward a hall to the guest bedrooms. Entering one, she walked to the bed, pulled back the duvet, then stepped aside. Ivan walked past her and laid Mara on the bed. Pulling off her boots, he then unbuttoned her coat, and slid it off her, then he covered her.

Tess kissed Mara's forehead. Then turning to Ivan, she stroked his arm, and sliding her hand into his, she gently pulled him with her as she whispered, "Come on."

Ivan smiled as they left the room. He imagined she was going back to the living room, but she walked through the foyer to the opposite side of the living room and into another room. Walking inside, he saw it was another bedroom.

"This is our bedroom," she whispered, then added, "We can decorate Mara's room for her however she likes. We can start tomorrow."

He stroked her cheek and asked, "Why are you whispering?"

She smiled. "I don't want to wake her," she answered in a louder tone.

"It's so quiet here, and she's so tired, she'll sleep for a very long time," he said.

When she looked away from him, he knew she felt sorry for those left behind in the war. She now knew what he meant when he had said, "In war, even when there was no sound there was sound. The sound of war, even when silent, had its own deafening ring."

Seeing her distress, he turned her face toward his. "It will be alright," he said.

Looking into his eyes, she whispered, "Idy."

He released a small breath. "I'm sorry. I didn't know what to do when you came looking for her. I didn't want to lose her and, once I loved you, I didn't want to lose you either." He paused again. "Please, Tess, forgive me."

She stared at him. She thought he would know that there was no need to forgive him of anything, but as she looked at him, she could see questions in his gaze. "Ivan," she whispered.

Her tone reminded him of that night when she accompanied him to his meeting with his men. And, like that night, he had to have her. He pulled her to him and kissed her, not allowing her to speak; this moment needed no words. Then he smiled at her.

"I love you, Ivan. You are staying, aren't you? You didn't come all this way just to bring Mara. Please say you're staying. Please don't go back, because if you do, you have to take us with you."

"Back there, there's nothing, no safety," he said. Then, remembering the bankbook, he pulled it from his breast pocket, and his attitude changed as he held it out to her. "What is this? I stopped in Zurich and had the account changed back into your name."

"I don't want it back," she said as she slipped from his grasp.

"Here," he said as he roughly shoved the book in her palm and walked out of the room.

Confused by his actions, she tossed the bankbook on a dresser and walked after him. As she pulled at his arm, he stopped and looked to the ceiling as if he could find his strength there.

"Ivan, you can't go. I don't care about the money. It doesn't matter to me," she said, however, his quick frown and swift tug from her grasp warned her. She said nothing, she only looked at him.

"But it does to me! What made you think I needed money to care for Mara? I take care of Mara, and from now on, I take care of you."

"I didn't mean it like that," she said, taking a couple of steps back from him.

His attitude softened as he saw the sorrow in her stare. Yet, when she looked away from him, he felt her mood change to what it was that last night in Sarajevo when he told her to go home.

"Tess, as much as you want to give it to me, why would I take it? I don't need it. What sort of a man would I be if I took money from you? How could you ever believe that I truly loved you if I did that? I didn't bring you to Sarajevo because of money. Look, now you have Mara. You said you wanted her, and for you to have come all that way, you had to have loved her. She needs you. Besides, your competition was all she talked about for months," he said, then he walked into the living room.

"She needs me? It's always what someone else needs from me," she said as she walked past him and looked out the windows. For a moment, she said nothing. "Yes, I love her, but I love you more. And without you, I don't think I could really love her. So take her back with you. Neither of you deserve the fate of living here, when all you love is back there."

He walked up behind her. She ignored him, but heard him sigh then say, "No, all I love is right here, right now, but I won't take her back. She's yours now. She's your daughter and she loves you."

"What? She loves you. She worships you—*both* of you," she said, referring to Ivan as the Black Rebel. "We both do, so, you can't go back."

Ivan said nothing; he only stared at her. In the back of his mind, he thought of all he had left behind that he needed to take care of. Tess noticed his solemn expression and wondered what he was thinking about, but right now, she had to get him to stay with her.

"Did you think you could drop your daughter off with your new wife like a bag of groceries?" she asked, hoping that her sarcasm would get a response from him.

Snapping from his thoughts, he quickly stepped toward her, and his movement displayed that he was upset. His face exhibited exactly what she had hoped for, and that was his passion over the situation.

"What did you want me to say? How else could I get her here?" he asked as he stood looking down at her, waiting for her answer.

She hesitated for a few seconds as she looked into his eyes. As she observed him, she saw how strong a man he really was. He would push his desires aside to do what he knew was right. Then she thought about the adoption papers and the marriage certificate in his breast pocket.

"When they told me that my husband and daughter were here, I thought—" She shook her head at her ideas. "I thought you really loved me and really wanted me in your life, but I was wrong. Your heart leads you back to your people, not to me. That's why I left Belgrade." She paused. "Well, that and the thought that if I had stayed in Belgrade with you, and someone was looking for me, as someone seemed to be, they would find you by finding me."

"Tess," he said as he reached for her.

She stepped back from him and looked directly into his eyes. "All I know is that I love you more than anything else, and I want to be with you wherever you are. I guess all the beautiful words you said that last day meant nothing. All we shared in that month, and those last moments, was all part of your plan. I guess that shows you how stupid I am. I believed everything you said."

When she started to walk away, he stepped in her path, took her in his arms, and moved to kiss her. She turned her cheek to him. When he turned her face toward his, she closed her eyes.

"Look at me," he said, gently tugging at her chin.

She hesitated.

"Look at me, Tess, please. Don't ignore me. I don't ignore you, do I?"

Those were the same words he said that morning in Belgrade when she left the restaurant after his insinuations offended her. She slowly opened her eyes as she heard his voice softly resonating in her ear.

"You're not stupid and you're not wrong. I *do* love you and I *do* need you in my life. I've had nothing for so long except Mara. It's just that—" He stopped, not knowing what he should say. Stroking her face, he wondered how he would explain.

"Just what? I left to let you get on with your life, but those papers change things. Those papers make me your wife, so we belong to each other. Isn't marriage about two lives becoming one, not being apart. I'm sure you could have gotten Mara into the country another way. You could have sent her with one of your men. You didn't have to go through all the trouble of obtaining marriage and adoption papers, then putting my signature on them. Ivan, if you really love me, then nothing else should matter. If you really need me in your life, money, wars, or whatever shouldn't come between us, should they? You have done so much for your countrymen, when will it be time for you to have a life?"

She waited for his answer, although he only listened. She could see in his expression that his past deceit set him apart from her, but she did not see things that way.

"I don't care that you didn't tell me the truth. I'm happy you didn't. You are such a strong man. You aren't swayed from what you believe because of someone else's goals. So, if you believed in me enough to get these documents, what changed? Did you stop believing in me? Or was it all a means to an end?"

He frowned at her and shook his head. "No. No means to an end. I believe more in you than I do in myself, but we have to do this the right way."

"Anyway you choose to do things is the right way."

"Alright then," he said, as he stepped closer to her. Pulling a platinum and diamond wedding band from his pocket, he took her left hand in his and slid off her Claddagh.

She panicked slightly as she remembered when he had said that only the man who put the Claddagh on a woman's finger could remove it.

Looking at her, he noticed her doubt. "Just wait," he said. He then held the wedding band near to the end of her ring finger of her left hand. She looked at the ring, then to the ring he wore, then to his face as he smiled at her. "Will you marry me?" he asked.

"Yes," she whispered and smiled.

"I will love you and honor you the rest of my life, because you *are* my life," he said, then he slipped the wedding band onto her finger and followed that with her Claddagh.

She smiled at the sensations of the rings sliding onto her finger. Then she repeated his vow to him. "I will love you and honor you the rest of my life, because you *are* my life, Ivan." She paused and stroked his cheek. "I truly love you."

He sighed, then he said, "I have to go back. The men are waiting for me. There are things to be finalized and cities to rebuild. That doesn't mean I won't come back." Then thinking about something he wanted to know from the beginning, he stared at her, and asked, "Tell me something. Did you go to Sarajevo to find Mara? Or did you go to Sarajevo to find Mara and the Black Rebel?"

She shrugged. "Both, I guess."

"Good. I just wanted to know. Now to explain why I need to go back, with this part of the war over, there is significant money to be made reconstructing all that was destroyed and I will be in on it. Remember, I am an architectural engineer, and one of my specialties is disaster recovery. But because I have to go back, that doesn't mean that I don't love you. It only means that I must finish what I've started."

"What do you mean by this part of the war is over? I thought the peace agreement ended it all."

"The siege in Sarajevo is over, but as a whole, it's not over yet."

"Do you have to leave right this second? I mean, Mara's not even settled.

She needs an explanation even if you think I don't."

"She understands. We've already discussed it."

"Oh, I see, it's all so civilized, isn't it?"

"Tess," he said.

She stepped back from him. "No, I understand, just go. Rebuild your cities, and do your deals, and, whatever," she said, waving him off as if she wanted him to go. Then she turned and walked away.

As expected, he walked after her. "You can be very stubborn," he said as he grasped her by the arm, turned her toward him, then asked, "What's wrong?"

Throwing her arms around his neck, she kissed him. "Ivan, don't leave me behind. I have to come with you."

"No. It isn't safe. I still don't know who was looking for you or why."

"Why? I'm sure it was my ex-husband searching for me, but he's dead now. I didn't even think about him when I went to Belgrade. I should have. My not thinking about him put you and your men in so much danger."

Ivan was amazed by her intuitiveness, but when she looked at him, he could see she questioned if he were responsible for Kralj's death. He gave a laugh. "No, I was not responsible for his death. Someone beat me to it. But how did you find out?"

"Agent Stevenson told me. Maybe he thought I was in Belgrade because of him."

"Did he ask why you went there?

"Yes."

"What did you tell him?"

"I told him that I was researching a novel I was writing about the peaceful Celtic occupation of Belgrade and the building of Kalemegdan."

"That was a good answer," he said and smiled. Her ingenuity momentarily shocked him, and he was now grateful that he had taken her to Kalemegdan.

"Well, I am a writer, you know. I can tell a good story. Besides, the London Post had no idea why I was there." Then she changed the subject. "So who do you think killed him? Agent Stevenson told me he took his own life, but I doubt that's true."

"His father, his brother, someone else, who knows? I don't know and I don't care. I'm not positive he was the one searching for you," Ivan said. And though he thought Tess' ex-husband's death would trouble her, he knew when she shook her head that it did not linger with her.

"Too bad for him, but I've been through with him for a very long time. Maybe now I'll actually be free of him."

She took his hand again, and started walking back to the bedroom, but he stopped her and stood in place.

"Let's finish this conversation here. I don't want arguments in the bedroom."

"Finish what conversation?"

"You have to stay here with Mara. Your place is with her."

"No. My place is with you. As much as I love her, I won't spend my life without you. She'll grow up someday and leave. She'll have her own life one day, but until then, why should I miss a minute of being with you? Everything that matters to you now matters to me, but none of those things matter more than you do."

"I understand, but now it will be very dangerous there. All the insurgents will be coming out to play, and most of them will claim to be me, and that will make the authorities in all provinces suspicious of everyone," he said and shook his head. "I have nothing to offer you there. Not yet."

She stroked his lips. "No one else can give me your love, except you. No one else has that, and, right now, I feel it slipping through my fingers."

"Nothing is slipping through your fingers. We belong to each other. We will work it out," he said.

Without thinking anymore about it, he kissed her. He knew she loved him, and being with her was the only thing that mattered anymore. He knew he had made the right decision to go to be with her in Manhattan. It was the only decision he could have made. He now admitted to himself that being a man was to first fight for the things he loved.

Holding her close, he finally was at peace with his life. Then, reaching into his jacket pocket, he pulled out the phrase book she had dropped in the snow and he handed it to her. "I found this at Saint Michael's. Perhaps it will help you understand me." He paused, looked at the book, then back at her. "I saw you with Mara that day. I want you to know that I was taking you to meet her the next day. I needed one more day alone with you before you met her. One day to explain everything to you. One day more before you hated me for all I had done, but then you were gone."

Softly her fingers moved to his cheek. "I'm sorry for leaving you. I thought it was what you wanted," she said.

"It's what I said, but it was not what I wanted. I couldn't say what I wanted without telling you the truth about Mara. How could I say that I wanted the three of us to be together, to be a family, when I thought you had no idea who I really was," he said and shook his head at himself.

"Please, don't feel guilty. It couldn't have happened better than this. Any other way could have risked all of our lives."

"So you'll stay here when I go back?"

Even though she knew he was right, she did not answer.

"Someone has to take care of Mara and get her into school here. But when it's safe, if you want to travel with me, Mama can come and stay with Mara," he said.

She put her arms around him and kissed him again.

He took her hand in his, kissed it, and started walking her back to the bedroom, as he said, "Now that that conversation is over, *Mrs. Đurić.*"

"Wait," she said and stopped walking.

"What?" he asked as he turned and looked at her.

She smiled momentarily. "Do you remember the night you came to my table in Belgrade?"

"Of course. How could I ever forget that fateful night? It was the turning point of my life."

"What did you say to me in Serbian when you first introduced yourself?"

He smiled and looked down to his hand holding hers, and his expression made her evermore curious.

"You had the same smile on your face then as you do now. What did you say?"

Smiling, he repeated, in Serbian, what he had said that night in the restaurant at the Metropol.

"Okay, but what does that mean?"

He grinned at her. "You've been waiting all this time to know what I said?"

"Yes."

"It was a bit forward. I was being a...well—" He grinned. "I was being a man from Belgrade."

"And?"

Stepping toward her, he kissed her lips. "I said, 'I'm Ivan Đurić. Thank you for allowing me to join you for dinner. You are beautiful, and I could not help but notice you. We will spend a wonderful evening, and wake up together tomorrow afternoon, after an unforgettable night.'"

He thought his statement may have offended her, but she smiled, and pressed against him. As she looked up into his eyes, he heard her sigh, then whisper, "Strange. That was exactly what I was thinking that night." Then, as her arms slid around his back, she kissed him.

Smiling contentedly, he knew he was home. As they entered the bedroom and closed the door, their new life together began. With her gentle touch, he knew God had answered his prayer, but…was the Black Rebel finally safe?

With eternal gratitude to:

God, first and foremost
Lord, Thank you for the words.
With you, all things are possible.

* * *

My furry children for their love and patience
My editor for correcting my intolerable English

* * *

Other Novels by The Black Rose

The Killing Game Series

The Killing Game, Book One
The Chase, Book Two
The Lost Days, Book Three

theblackrosenyc.com
andrichpublishing.com

Made in the USA
Lexington, KY
17 February 2018